WHEN HEARTS REMEMBER

VICTORIA LUM

When Hearts Remember

By Victoria Lum

Published by Eternal Hearts Publishing

Editing by Theresa Leigh and Amy Briggs

Proofreading by Virginia Tesi Carey

ISBN (Paperback): 979-8-9900169-7-2

ISBN (E-Book): 979-8-9900169-6-5

Author's Note

There are heavy topics discussed in this book and your mental health is paramount to me. For a list of potential areas of sensitive content, please visit:

https://www.victorialum.com/sensitive-content-information

DEDICATION

To my hopeless romantics who believe in the saying, "if he could, he would," I hope you love Ethan Anderson.

RELATIONSHIP TREE
LA HEARTS SERIES

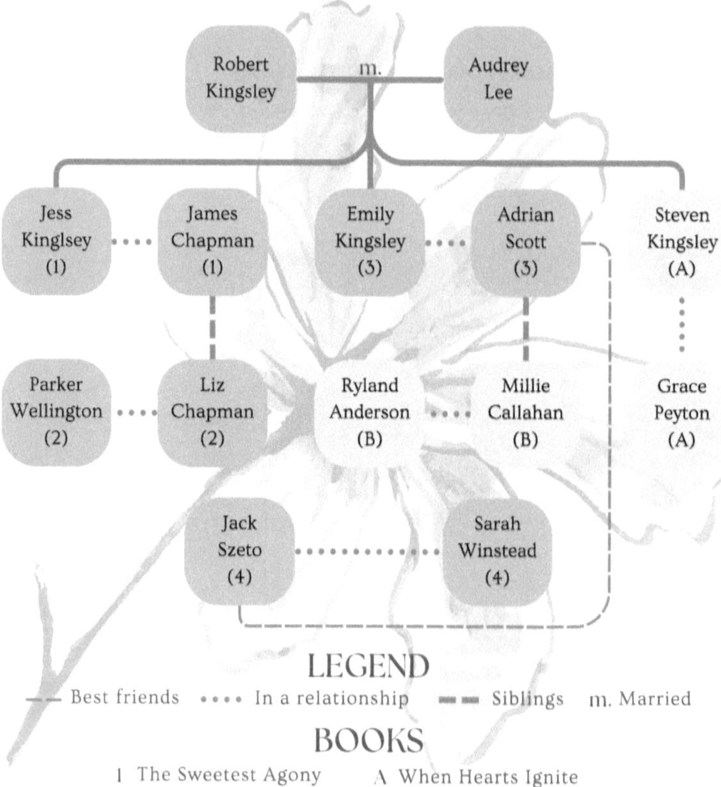

LEGEND

— — Best friends   • • • • In a relationship   ▪ ▪ ▪ Siblings   m. Married

BOOKS

1 The Sweetest Agony
2 The Coldest Passion
3 The Harshest Hope
4 The Brightest Spark

LA Hearts Series

The Orchid Series

A When Hearts Ignite
B When Hearts Collide
C When Hearts Surrender
D When Hearts Awaken
E When Hearts Remember
F When Hearts Unravel

THE ORCHID SERIES

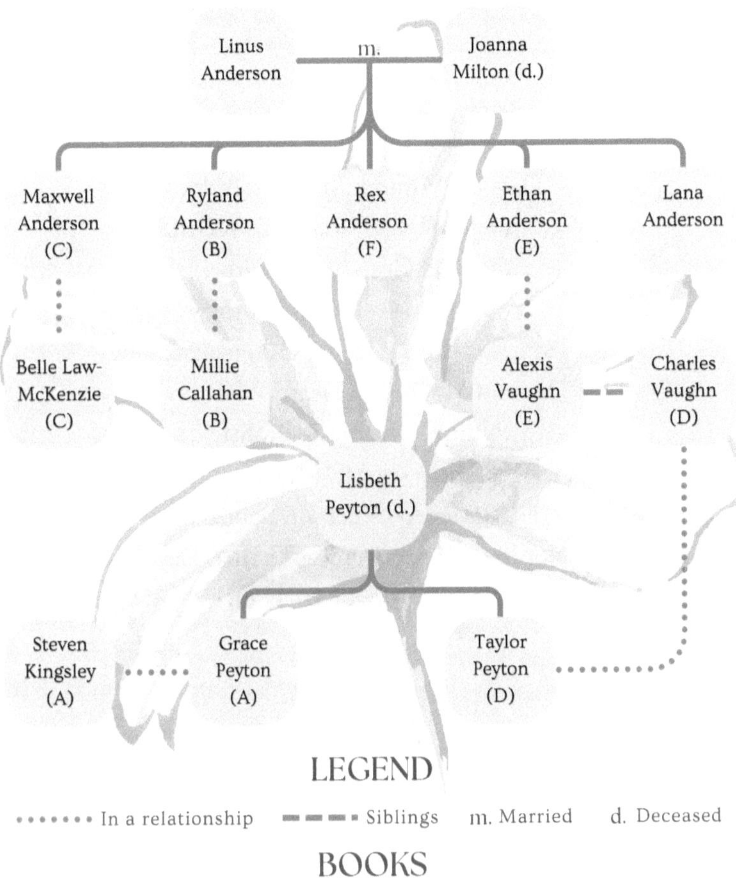

LEGEND

•••••• In a relationship　━ ━ ━ Siblings　m. Married　d. Deceased

BOOKS

1	The Sweetest Agony	A	When Hearts Ignite
2	The Coldest Passion	B	When Hearts Collide
3	The Harshest Hope	C	When Hearts Surrender
4	The Brightest Spark	D	When Hearts Awaken
	The Orchid Series	E	When Hearts Remember
		F	When Hearts Unravel

PLAYLIST

"Dancing Without Music" – Brdgs
"I Was Made For Lovin' You" – YUNGBLUD
"Fire On Fire" – Sam Smith
"Love Is Gone" – Dylan Matthew
"You Are The Reason" – Calum Scott
"Me and My Broken Heart" – Rixton
"Numb" – Tommee Profitt
"You Were There For Me" – Henry Moodie
"Let Me Go" – Benson Boone
"Not My Job Anymore" – Thomas Day
"Broken" – Isak Danielson

CAST OF CHARACTERS

The Andersons are a large family, but their stories are all standalones and can be read in any order. If you're new to their world or diving back in, here's a list of the main characters you'll encounter:

<u>The Anderson Family:</u>

- Linus Anderson – The patriarch of the family and retired from Fleur Entertainment.

- Maxwell Anderson – The eldest son and CEO of Fleur Entertainment; fraternal twin to Ryland. Broody and burdened, he carries the weight of the world on his shoulders.

- Ryland Anderson – The second son and former COO of Fleur Entertainment; fraternal twin to Maxwell. Now a full-time professor.

- Rex Anderson – The third son and CMO of Fleur Entertainment. A self-proclaimed playboy extraordinaire.

- Ethan Anderson – The fourth son and CFO of Fleur Entertainment. Quiet and introspective; an old soul with secrets.

- Lana Anderson – The youngest sister in the main Anderson family line and the Chief of Public Relations at Fleur Entertainment. Sophisticated and fiercely loyal.

- Grace Peyton-Anderson – The Anderson siblings' half-sister, and older sister of Taylor. She's a finance guru.

- Taylor Peyton-Anderson – The Anderson siblings' half-sister, the youngest of the bunch. A gothic, take-no-prisoners ballerina.

<u>Other Important People:</u>
- Alexis Vaughn – Youngest of the Vaughn siblings after Charles and Liam; a former ballerina and now an intern at Fleur Entertainment.

- Liam Vaughn – The middle child of the Vaughn siblings and Ethan's best friend.

- Steven Kingsley – Grace's significant other, the current COO of Fleur Entertainment.

- Charles Vaughn – Best friend of the Anderson brothers and Steven, and oldest of the Vaughn siblings. He's the CEO of the Bank of Columbia and Taylor's significant other.

- Millie Callahan – Ryland's significant other, a PhD student with dreams of changing the world.

- Belle Law-McKenzie – Maxwell's significant other, the belle of the ball who loves rescuing animals and is a fashion designer.

- Olivia Lin – Taylor's friend, a psychiatrist specializing in anxiety and addiction disorders. Observant, smart, and fiercely loyal.

CHAPTER 1

PRESENT: EIGHT YEARS AFTER THE ACCIDENT—THIRTY-TWO YEARS OLD

FOR OVER TWO HUNDRED years, a rumor has loomed over my family—the Anderson men are cursed to be heartbroken and live a lonely life.

I don't believe in curses, but I believe in heartbreak.

Eight years. I've been living with mine for eight years.

I stare outside the window of my private jet, watching workers load luggage into neighboring planes. Memories of better days crush me, making it hard to breathe.

This was supposed to be our trip. Now, it's just mine.

"Mr. Anderson, sorry for the inconvenience. There's a delay by air traffic control, but we'll depart for Beijing soon, where we'll refuel and go through customs before heading to Tibet. In the meantime, may I get you any refreshments?"

The flight attendant's soft voice jolts me out of my thoughts and I swallow, failing to dislodge the lump in my throat. My fingers graze the silver and black cuff link peeking out under my suit jacket.

"No. Please don't disturb me on this flight."

Her eyes widen, and I know she's going to turn around and tell everyone about my pissed-ass mood. She nods and disappears into the back of the jet.

I can't muster a smile. Especially not today. Let them think I'm a cold bastard.

You are a cold bastard, Ethan.

Broken. Hardened. Unrecognizable.

It'd break her heart if she were here and saw you like this.

I stare at the cuff links—the black circular medallion carved in an intricate floral pattern, covering the secret underneath. It's the only pair I own and wear.

The pair Lexy gave me. My Nova. The only woman who has ever made me feel alive. Unbidden, one of my favorite memories of her floats to my consciousness, and I close my eyes, trying to relive it.

Again.

"You're my north star, Ethan. You anchor me. With you, I'm never lost." She had grinned, her sky-blue eyes sparkling with life. She stood on her tiptoes and pressed a soft kiss to my lips.

Warmth rushed through me and I pulled back, just long enough to stare at her beautiful face—her strawberry blonde hair brightening up the gloomy January skies with a flash of copper, her creamy skin pinkened from the blistering cold of the snowstorm.

Just like the day we met.

"And you're ridiculous," I murmured, tightening my arms around her waist. "Who on earth voluntarily goes outside in the middle of a blizzard?"

"It's the first snow of the new year! The sign of new beginnings and fresh starts. Don't be such a grump, you old man. And need I remind you if I didn't go out in a snowstorm, we wouldn't have met?"

I bit back a smile. I'd never forget how we met—two strangers becoming pen pals during a snowstorm much like this one. This was before I learned her real identity.

I was forbidden to love her but did anyway.

"I'm twenty-four and only four years older than you, Nova. If I'm old, then you're getting there too. You know, they say men's shelf life is longer than women's."

She mock scowled and before I knew it, a sharp, icy sting exploded across my face.

"What the—"

"Shelf life, huh? Keep that up and you'll have the shelf life of this snowball!" She cackled and hurled another snowball at me.

Despite it being cold as fuck that day, Lexy only had on PJs and a fluffy pink bathrobe before she dragged me out of the apartment I shared with her older brother and my best friend, Liam.

She grinned, clearly having the time of her life. Abruptly, she ceased fire and spun around in circles, her arms outstretched like she was absorbing the elements.

The gnaw your bones off frigid elements.

She plopped herself on the thick blanket of snow, ignoring how we were in the middle of a New York City sidewalk as people scurried by to seek shelter. *My Nova. Always marching to her own tune and dazzling everyone around her without realizing it.* Then she waved her arms and legs to create a snow angel.

But the blistering winds changed tune, and the flurry of snow became thick clumps of ice and balls of—

Fuck. Hail.

I threw my body on top of hers as the hard clusters pelted my back. She trembled below me.

"Shit. You okay? Are you hurt?"

A few seconds of silence passed by. *Crap. Did I hurt her?* Alarm rang through me and I started pulling away when she suddenly snorted and busted out in laughter. "Look at your face! All worried about me, aren't you? Throwing yourself on top of me like a hero from the movies."

Bracing my arms above her, I mock scowled at the woman who made me feel as though I was enough as I was—just being Ethan—not because I was an Anderson, the illustrious, old-money family who owned half of New York.

Lexy beamed and stuck her tongue out.

I chuckle at the memories. I'm sure I sound ridiculous—laughing by myself in my luxury jet. Grief hits us in the strangest ways. I'd give anything to go back to that day. We were so happy—we had the future in our hands. I continue reminiscing about our day together.

I thought I had time. A lifetime with her. If only I knew.

"I don't know how you do it," I had whispered to her as we laid on the ground, hail still coming down in bullets. I cradled her face with my hands. "You inspire me to be so much more. I...I—"

I couldn't find the words. And I *always* had the words.

Lexy turned her head and pressed a kiss on my fingers. "Be here and be bold. Don't wait to live because..."

I smiled and finished for her. "The clock keeps ticking." Swallowing, I gazed into her eyes and murmured, "Are you going to give me your answer?"

"Do you have a ring on you?"

"You know I don't. You dragged me out here before I even had breakfast. You're lucky Liam isn't coming back until later today. Your brother would skin me alive if he saw you dressed in a bathrobe in the middle of a snowstorm."

"Ha. I think he'd kill *you* because you were with his little sister. Me in a snowstorm would be the least of your concerns."

Damn it. She was right. I'd been avoiding the conversation as long as I could, but I had to tell Liam.

I was desperately in love with his little sister. I had broken the only cardinal rule he had set for me.

I quashed those thoughts into the background. Everything could come after this woman answered my question. "So, my answer?"

She arched her elegant brow, the mischievous glimmer back in her eyes. "No ring, no answer. You'll just have to wait until our curry date next week."

Snorting, I shook my head as my heart skipped a beat. *I'm going to make this woman mine soon. Then we're telling our families, and if Liam, Dad, or my brothers have issues with this, they can go screw themselves.* "You're ridiculous, Nova. And you got it wrong. I'm not your north star. *You* are my supernova, brightening up my dark skies."

"My poet," she had murmured, and I leaned down and captured her lips with mine, tasting her smile and love in our kiss.

The jet engine roars to life, the rumble further splintering the deep frissons inside my heart.

I didn't realize back then we'd never have our curry date. Time giveth and time taketh away.

And so, today, I'll let myself grieve.

My chest tightens. I take out a piece of paper, uncap my fountain pen, and write the last poem I'll ever compose. I haven't been able to write poems ever since what happened to her.

My poetry came to life because of her. Without her, they're meaningless.

Memories dance behind my eyelids as I go to sleep,
Visions of you, soaring high in my dreams.
Ribbons of fire twirling in the wind,
Your lavender scent lingers, a longing I cannot rescind.
Hearts, once on fire, now smolder in smoke,
Our love, bittersweet, broken as fate's cruel stroke.
The world spins on, blissfully unaware,
My life, forever changed, hollow as the air.
My Nova, my star, bright in the sky,
Farewell, my hummingbird, my darling butterfly.

I told myself almost eight years ago, once I completed the last item on her bucket list, to tie a cloth at the Jokhang temple, the most sacred temple in Tibet, I'd stop waiting. I'd move on because she'd want me to.

I'd say goodbye.

My eyes burn, my ragged breath lodging in my throat, and I close my eyes.

How do I say goodbye? How *can* I say goodbye?

I try to imagine her voice, the sweet lilt at the end of her sentences, the raspy undertone of her laughter, the way she drawls her "R's" like she's from Texas instead of being a born and bred New Yorker.

But the memories are fuzzy now. The sounds dulled by the years that have gone by as I waited...and waited.

And waited.

Perhaps I lost her long before today.

How could I have forgotten the exact timbre of her voice? The lump in my throat grows and I feel wetness on my cheek. *Get your shit together, Ethan. You're the impenetrable Anderson.*

You don't feel. Nothing can hurt you anymore.

Staring blankly into the ray of light peeking through the dim clouds, I make a wish. *If there's a higher power, please give us a miracle. I'd give up anything...at any cost. Please—*

What the fuck am I doing?

My cell phone buzzes on the table.

Quickly, I swipe the moisture away from my eyes and answer the call without looking at the caller ID.

"Anderson."

"I worry about you," a gravelly voice rasps on the line, followed by the familiar clicking of an antique lighter the man never uses.

"Elias." I clear my throat. "You're nuts. Don't you have better things to worry about or people to terrorize than being delusional?"

"Hm." The clicking stops.

With Elias Kent, the king of the New York underworld, feared by the elite and the gangs alike, delusional is the least likely option. A long time ago, my eldest brothers, Maxwell and Ryland, saved his life, and since then, he's stuck to our family like duct-tape, solid, reliable, and a close friend.

"I don't think so," he murmurs. "Maxwell told me you took off for Tibet, of all places. He's worried because he's your oldest brother. Liam also sniffed around, saying you were acting strange. I'm concerned because you're my friend—unfortunately for me."

I whistle and force out a chuckle. "Damn. I should go to Vegas instead, huh? Probably will win a jackpot. The great Elias Kent calling me a friend. Aren't you worried your enemies will think that's a weakness?"

He snorts. "Leave the jackpot to people who need it. I know you, Ethan. Don't hide shit from me. You're a man of routine—five a.m. swimming laps, work fourteen hours crunching your fucking numbers at Fleur, eating boring turkey clubs for meals, rinse and repeat."

He sighs and continues, "You have one trip a year and you already went somewhere last month. You don't just up and leave the fucking country for no reason. And somewhere as remote as Tibet. Don't bull-shit me. What's going on?"

"If I didn't know your compulsion to collect the secrets of everyone around you, I'd think you have a crush on me. Fuck off. I'm fine. Can't a man have a break?"

"A *break* in Tibet? You know tourists have altitude sickness there? Not exactly a walk in the park."

My phone pings, and I glance at the screen.

Liam sweeping in to save the day.

Thank God or else Elias will ferret my secrets out of me. The relent-less asshole.

"I have to go. Urgent incoming call."

"Don't you dare—"

Ignoring him, I switch to the other line. "Liam?"

Heavy exhales reach my ear and I sit up, my muscles coiled tightly. "Liam? What's wrong?"

"Fuck, man." More ragged breaths. A thick silence.

Sweat beads on my upper lip, and the beginnings of nausea swirl inside me. Liam is the devil-may-care, nothing can faze me rebel.

Something is wrong. Something—

No. Lexy.

"What happened? Is it Lexy?"

My heart batters against my rib cage. I'm lightheaded, an urge to throw up soon to follow.

"Ethan...she...she's awake."

My phone clatters to the floor.

CHAPTER 2

I REMEMBER LITTLE FROM the next hour. Everything is in fragments. Still frames.

Me telling the crew to cancel the flight. Staff hollering I can't just hop off a jet and sprint across the tarmac because it was dangerous.

The violent wind whipping across my face, followed by my phone buzzing in my pocket as I stood on the ground disoriented, realizing I didn't know where I was going.

And finally now, sitting in a helicopter, my mind in a daze as we head to Manhattan Memorial Hospital. My fingers shake as I scroll through my phone, needing to do something before I spiral into madness.

She's awake. Lexy is awake. It's been eight years.

She's awake.

The refrain repeats in my mind and I don't know whether to cry, to laugh, or to bang my head against the wall to see if I'm dreaming.

I sift through my emails flagging urgent items from Trey Spencer, my mentor, right-hand man, and VP of Finance all rolled into one, who's investigating suspicious cash flow anomalies the auditors found last quarter. There have been strange outflows to familiar-looking vendors, which upon closer examination aren't legitimate.

Something sinister is going on, and my gut is never wrong.

Then there's the email I've deleted every time it pops up in my inbox—once a year, without fail.

An invitation from The Association, the secretive, powerful organization purported to rule governments, control large corporations, and has always wanted my family to join its ranks.

But the price is high—a violent crime of their choice as an initiation.

It's an organization where if you join, doors would open, power unheard of would be yours, but you couldn't walk out alive. And I should know, because of what they did to Taylor, my youngest half sister, all those years ago.

But we Andersons live with honor.

I delete the message without reading it.

A new email pops up. One from Angela, my pen pal from Letters of Hope, a program from Manhattan Memorial I volunteer my time with. I founded it in hopes someday Lexy will be one of those patients, waking up from a coma or recovering from a long-term stay, and in need of an anonymous listening ear as she reintegrates into society.

It's a sign. Good karma or mojo, as Lexy would call it.

She's awake. My flurried heartbeats riot, the roaring pulse almost louder than the whirring of the helicopter propeller.

Chaotic thoughts fling themselves inside my mind as I read Angela's email.

My first day at work was a success. Thanks for your support last year. I couldn't do this without you. Now, instead of feeling sorry for myself, I'm actually moving on with my life.

I wish you well in the future,
Angela

Warmth infuses me, the happy goodbye email made even more beautiful by the news of Lexy waiting for me in the hospital room.

Ten minutes later, I'm darting down the corridors of the long-term care unit at the hospital. The place, usually so quiet you can hear a pin drop, is abuzz with frenetic energy, much like the thrill teeming inside me. Doctors and nurses chatter on, smiles brimming on their faces.

It's unheard of—someone waking up from a coma after almost a decade. The statistics are abysmal. Nonexistent. It's a miracle. I think back to the wish I made in the jet.

A miracle.

All these years of waiting, of closing myself off from the world, burying myself in work and pretending everything is fine, that my heart doesn't have a gaping hole in it.

I don't need to pretend anymore.

She'll be back at my side, and my life can finally restart. The hole inside me will heal. We'll find more things to add to her bucket list. I can learn to open myself to someone else again.

I won't be lonely anymore.

And at last, I'll finally get her answer—the one I've waited to hear for eight long years.

But then, a sudden chill freezes my lungs. I skid to a stop in the middle of the hallway.

What if I can't change back to the man she once knew? What if I'm incapable of loving her the way she deserves because my heart is damaged beyond repair?

What if she can't forgive you? If only you'd taught her to swim back then, maybe we wouldn't have lost eight years.

The floor swirls from the sudden rush of blood curdling fear.

I can't think this way. I'm going out of my mind.

Shoving the illogical thoughts away, I burst into her room. I barely notice the small crowd gathered there. Charles Vaughn, Liam and Lexy's oldest brother, sits by Lexy's bedside. Taylor, who's not only my sister but also Charles's girlfriend, appears shell-shocked. Liam hovers by the bed, his eyes brimming with tears.

I don't acknowledge them.

My attention rivets on the dazzling redhead propped up against the bed board. The beautiful face I'm used to seeing—pale, still, her eyes closed—is now teeming with life.

And her brilliant eyes. That fire. That energy. That spark.

Lexy looks bewildered, her gaze darting around the room, her cupid bow's lips parted.

Until they land on me.

Those sky-blue eyes, the color of a smogless day after dreary rain.

My blue eyes.

My Nova.

Leashing down the emotions threatening to make me keel over, I rush over and pull her frail frame into my arms.

A shuddered breath escapes me. *Home. Finally home.* I bury my head into her fiery strands. She smells like Dawn soap and antiseptic agents, but under it all, I recognize her fragrance.

Her sweet lavender.

"Oh fuck." I close my eyes, clasping her tighter in my hold. "You're awake, my Nova. You're awake." My voice chokes up. "I-I knew you were going to wake up. I've never given up hope."

Liam and Charles murmur in the background, but I can't hear what they're saying, because my pulse thunders in my ears and my heart free falls into oblivion.

But then I feel it.

The *wrongness* of everything.

She's as stiff as a two by four in my arms.

She shoves me away, her eyes wide with shock and...fear? "W-Who are you?"

And my world collapses once more.

"What?" The breath is knocked out of my lungs. "Lexy, you know me. Don't joke right now. I'm going to have a heart attack. Please don't joke with me."

She shakes her head vigorously and scrambles to the edge of her bed toward Liam, who automatically moves closer to his sister and glares at me.

As if he needs to protect her from *me*. As if I'm the villain.

Perhaps I am. If it weren't for me, we wouldn't have lost these years.

If there's a higher power, please give us a miracle. I'd give up any-thing...at any cost, the promise I made earlier whispers in my ear.

Perhaps this is the cost and my punishment.

"*W-Who are you?*" Each syllable hammers into my broken heart.

She doesn't remember me.

CHAPTER 3

PAST: TWO YEARS BEFORE THE ACCIDENT—EIGHTEEN YEARS OLD

I STARE AT THE cursor blinking on my opened document in my laptop.

It's mocking me.

Three paragraphs in two hours. Of course it's mocking you.

Closing my eyes, I try manifesting the answers to everything plaguing me these days. Positive energy and mojo, give and you shall receive.

I know what I'm doing with my life. I have my shit together. I know what I want to study in college. I'm going to ace this project, even though I don't know how to begin this thing.

For now, Lexy. You don't know...for now.

A deep breath later, I open my eyes. I'm supposed to create a project plan to identify and fund scholarships for gifted students from underserved backgrounds. My business class teacher calls the assignment "Growing Future World Leaders."

It's an awful class. A snooze fest. A fancy business class in a fancy prep school where your coolness is measured by the dollar signs attached to your name.

But this project is meaningful. The proposals are submitted to non-profits in the city. And I'm a Vaughn, the family owning the internationally renowned Bank of Columbia. My name will be attached to this submission.

People expect things from a Vaughn. Good, brilliant things.

They always forget the Vaughns have a less than genius youngest daughter.

Me.

I can't make us look bad. But what do I know about gifted students and future world leaders? I'm the literal *opposite* of that statement.

I growl at the screen as my phone pings.

Quickly, I look around the rare text archival floor in my newest favorite place on earth—the Ravenswood Library. It's housed in a five-story gothic building near Riverside Park, tucked among the limestone and brick structures on the Upper West Side.

After a visit to the nearby Columbia University, I stumbled upon this place. The library was built two hundred years ago by Sebastian Ravenswood as a gift to his wife, who loved books. But unfortunately, she passed away before the construction was done.

Love hit me with the precision of a cupid's arrow.

The romance. The darkened stone walls and intricate stained glass windows. The gargoyles perched on the rooftops, guarding the books secured within the building. The beautiful, quiet back gardens with soaring archways which looked like they'd seen plenty of love stories being written over the centuries.

You fall in love far too easily, Firefly. Those daydreams aren't real. Trust me, men are idiots. You don't want any of us.

That's what Liam says, but what does he know? My tattooed, leather jacket wearing older brother gets on my nerves most days. Our love language as siblings is fighting with each other. According to him, he and his best friend from college, Ethan, leave behind a string of broken hearts, melting panties with their charm and good looks.

I'm not looking for a guy like him or his best friend—who I've never met. I don't need heartbreakers. Nor do I need someone like Charles, our oldest brother, who dotes on me and is the paragon of success, but a certified workaholic.

My phone pings again. Seeing no one looking my way, I swipe at the screen.

Summer

> You, me, a night of drinks and hot guys? I've got our brand spankin' new fake IDs!

I grin, imagining my golden-haired friend from Broadbent Academy, dolling it up in a sexy minidress even though there's a blizzard outside. She's a riot, and the two of us are nicknamed The Storm of Broadbent, blowing by and wreaking havoc.

Summer

> Maybe you'll meet someone who deserves to pop your cherry! *wink wink* Make sure to use protection—don't get knocked up! God knows I don't want any kids—they cramp your lifestyle.

The smile slips off my face and my chest pinches.

A guy I want to give my virginity to. Someone special. I used to think it'd be my current boyfriend, Dayton Holden, but it just doesn't feel right.

And I don't want to regret my first time.

Alexis

> You suck. If I'm not doing it with Dayton, I'm not doing it with some rando at a club. You worry about using protection yourself.

The bright laptop screen snags my attention, as if reminding me of my responsibilities. *Focus, Lexy. If there's a time to focus, it's now.*

Alexis

> And I can't go tonight. The project, remember? I'm so screwed, Sum. I'm going to fail this class and be the first Vaughn to get rejected by Columbia.

Chill, girl. You have like ten lives. You'll get it done. All-nighter, last minute, but you always do.

If she only knew I'm currently failing the class.

My phone pings again, and this time, it's Liam.

Firefly, where are you? I swung by the mansion and you weren't there. Grab dinner tonight?

Studying at the library. Not everyone is a tech genius like you.

I can't. I also have ballet practice tonight.

Why are you doing that, anyway? It's not like you're going to be a professional ballerina.

I like ballet. And maybe because Mom did it?

You got to stop doing this to yourself. I'm sorry, I know she's our mom, but what kind of woman leaves her kids alone 360 days of the year?

A familiar heaviness blankets me. I don't want to admit it, but he's right. Peter and Martha Vaughn are the textbook definition of absentee and neglectful parents, completely in love with each other and their partying lifestyle, but forgetting everyone else. We spent our childhoods with nannies and tutors, strangers who were paid to take care of us.

But on the rare days when Mom was around, our large, empty house would sizzle with energy. There'd be dancing, movie marathons, and makeovers. She'd ask me about the guys at school and tell me about her adventures abroad—seeing polar bears in Alaska, lounging on a yacht in the south of France, learning opera from the best soprano in Venice.

She's exciting. You can't help but be drawn to her.

I know that's why Dad is addicted to her.

The highs would be beautiful until it'd inevitably collapse. Slamming doors, screaming matches, hurling curse words at each other, their ugly spats showing up on the front headlines of newspapers and magazines.

But Dad, the man who never cared about anything, not the family business or his responsibilities, would always go back to Mom.

The cycle would repeat itself and they'd jet off on some new exotic adventure, leaving the three of us to our own devices again.

Mom would forget me, just like five years ago, and two years ago, when I asked her to come to my ballet showcases. She'd say yes, but I'd never find her among the crowd.

I stopped asking.

And yet, I'm still that stupid little girl who hopes I can shine brighter, fly higher, so I can finally catch...and hold her attention.

Sure, Grandma and Uncle Ian, Dad's younger brother, tried their best to fill the void—visiting us a few times a month when they were around, but it wasn't the same.

Alexis

She sent me a card and a limited edition Gucci for Christmas. She didn't forget about us.

Liam

I can buy that shit for you. Wake up, Lexy.

My stomach sours. I don't want to chat anymore.

I have to go. Dayton is picking me up in ten minutes and I'm meeting Lil' Tay at the studio. The girl has potential, mark my words. She's going places.

Taylor Peyton, a fourteen-year-old protégé at IBA, our ballet studio, has a sweet soul and is oh, so gifted. While I'm reaching the end of my ballet career, hers has just begun. And she's taken to me like I'm her older sister.

Whatever. Dump the asshole, Lexy. You deserve better. If he makes you cry again, I swear I'll hack his computer and delete his existence from the internet.

I snort. Liam would do it. Both he and Charles are overprotective. It drives me nuts, but I'm grateful I have them in my life.

My phone vibrates. This time, the sound earns a few sharp glares from nearby patrons.

Grimacing, I answer, "Dayton? You here yet?"

"Be there in two. Traffic's insane, Lexy. It's a shit show out here." His voice is clipped.

I glance out the window, seeing nothing but a blanket of white coating the glass panes. A shiver moves through me. It'll be so cold outside.

"Okay. Packing up now."

"Hurry, okay? I can't park long. I passed a cop headed this way. Don't want any trouble."

I frown. "What trouble? You're picking me up, not fleeing a bank robbery."

Silence fills the line.

"Dayton? You there?"

He clears his throat. "Yeah, babe. Trying to merge. Anyway, hurry, hot stuff."

He hangs up before I can respond. I stare at the phone, my stomach knotting.

Something is off. He doesn't talk like he used to—not to me, anyway. He asked me for money a few months ago for an investment and it's been hushed phone calls and all work and no play for him since then.

He wants to prove himself. His family is well-off but they have their sights on becoming a big name in finance.

Maybe things changed because he's in college and I'm a senior in high school.

I sigh and look at my open laptop again. Dammit. I got nothing accomplished today.

Fuck it.

Closing my laptop, I suddenly remember a lesson I'd learned painfully two years ago.

"Back up. Back up. The USB's your friend," I mutter, opening my laptop again and shoving my new USB pen drive into the computer. My old one is full and after one disastrous accident involving my old laptop and a pitcher of iced tea, resulting in me losing an English essay and a science report, I've always backed everything up.

After the flash drive does its thing, I slip the laptop into my bag, my fingers brushing the dark leather volume nestled inside.

The journal!

Grinning, I pull out my most prized possession—a thick, hand-bound leather journal Grandma gave me a month ago. It's special because of what I'm going to do with it.

Lifting it up to my nose, I inhale the rich scent of aged leather, paper, and ink with a hint of lavender from the perfume I spritzed on the pages this morning. I head to the bookshelves housing texts on ancient Greece, one of my favorite time periods to read about. Then, I kiss the cover and slip the journal between two Greek mythology books.

My heart thumps wildly as I take a few steps back.

Go. Find your soulmate. There's a reader for every book, including mine.

After blowing out a deep breath, I traipse down the wrought-iron spiral staircase, past the main floor with soaring vaulted ceilings, old-fashioned three-tiered chandeliers, and rows and rows of dark mahogany shelves.

My phone buzzes in my pocket again as I approach the exit. *Dayton.* I answer the call and push open the heavy metal door at the same time.

A soul sucking gust of frigid air blasts on my face.

"Dayton, coming out right now. I got sidetracked—"

I slam into a brick wall.

That is, if the brick wall is made of a towering hunk of masculine muscle.

A deep, raspy *oomph* reaches my ear.

My things scatter on the ground. My boot-clad foot slips on the icy pavement. I propel backward, swinging my arms out, trying to grab onto anything before I land on my ass and make a fool out of myself.

A powerful arm curls around my back and hoists me up.

The next thing I know, I'm smashed against a hard chest, and the alluring scent of leather and amber reaches my nose.

"Easy there." A gravelly whisper reaches my ears, followed by a chuckle.

I shiver and look up.

The most beautiful pair of slate-gray eyes stare down at me. Eyes belonging to a masculine face—all sharp lines and hard angles—stare down at me just below the dark brown hair effortlessly tousled like he just rolled out of bed. Mystery guy's lips tilt up in one corner, the smirk transforming his face from hot to smoldering with just the right amount of bad boy charm.

Trust me, men are idiots. You don't want any of us. Liam's words barge into my mind.

The mystery guy is who I'd imagine as Ares, the god of war from Greek mythology. Ares, in a dark leather jacket on a break from killing his enemies, transported to the modern world.

I must have slammed my head too hard and am hallucinating. I blink a few times.

Nope, he's still here.

Ares murmurs, "You okay? Cat got your tongue?"

He lets go of me and kneels down, picks up my laptop and papers, his eyebrow arching when he sees my textbooks. He stuffs them into my bag and hands it to me.

"Probably the only useful class I've ever taken." He nods toward the finance book, *Financial Literacy for Future Leaders.* "Good luck."

Mystery guy winks and steps through the library door.

I shake myself. *Manners!*

"Thank you!" I holler after him.

He pauses mid stride and turns around. This time, he unleashes a smile that causes my stomach to flip.

I look away, feeling guilty. I have a boyfriend...probably not for long, but still.

Mystery guy laughs, the husky sound sending another flutter in my gut. "All good...Sunbeam."

Sunbeam. My eyes snap up, but he's already disappeared.

A smile tugs at my lips. People usually call me red because of my hair. But Sunbeam? That's something new. I wonder why he calls me that.

Snap out of it, Lexy. A hot guy is a dime a dozen in New York City. Probably all idiots, as Liam would say.

A car honks and I turn around. Dayton waves, his blond hair a disheveled mess like he's been tugging at it.

"Need to go, babe."

He pokes his head out the window and looks behind him like he's searching for something.

Frowning, I glance around and see nothing out of the ordinary. Just white and gray, the skies hurling down snow like it's taking over for the god of war on vacation.

"Sorry!" I hurry toward him.

But before I get into the car, I turn back and stare at the closed library door, wondering what the god of war is doing in the library in the middle of a snowstorm.

CHAPTER 4

PAST: TWO YEARS BEFORE THE ACCIDENT—TWENTY-TWO YEARS OLD

I WALK PAST THE main floor of the library toward the stairs.

Get in. Do my research. Get out. No time to waste.

A handful of people have their heads down, diligently scribbling on their notepads or reading under the soft glow of the vintage green lamps from the turn of the century. The windows rattle as the storm traps the city in a sea of white and gray.

Except for that flash of red.

Stopping, I glance back at the front door where the girl was, recalling her flawless, creamy skin. Luminous blue eyes. Hair the color of fall leaves. She was a breath of fresh air, momentarily distracting me from my purpose here at Ravenswood.

Sunbeam.

That nickname tumbled out of my mind. She was radiant—the smile, the warmth and vibrant energy rolling off of her in waves.

It suited her—the mysterious girl with the spark in her eyes.

Geez, Ethan. Get a grip. I rake my fingers through my hair and continue walking.

If Liam were here, he'd grumble about how he should be at home gaming or blasting the new Lethal Dead single instead.

Most people assume I'm the same way, wanting to have fun instead of working.

Then again, most people don't have my last name. They don't understand the pressures of being an Anderson.

But here among the books written by the great minds of the past, the smell of aged parchment and worn leather wafting to my nose, I can finally breathe.

There's no judgment or expectation in the library. After all, many authors lining these shelves—like Herman Melville and John Keats—blundered through life before they were considered great. And now, nearly everyone knows the whale in *Moby-Dick*, and poetry lovers still read Keats.

Let's hope you find your place before you die, Ethan.

I shake away my insane thoughts. The stress of what's happening next Monday must be getting to me. After all, that's why I'm here, to read a newly published financial modeling book since my copy was delayed by the blizzard.

My phone buzzes in my pocket, and I fish it out to read the incoming text.

Liam

> Dels the Nerd, you didn't really go to the library, right? We graduated from college already. You don't need to study anymore.

I roll my eyes at his nickname, a play on my middle name, Delaney, and make my way up the stairs.

Ethan

> Just got here. Go play *Final Assault* or something. The rest of us have to adult.

Liam

> What you're doing isn't adulting. It's some sick, twisted, workaholic OCD thing you got going on. Don't think I didn't see you up at the crack of dawn exercising and eating your healthy food like you're still on the swim team.

Liam

And I have a job, fucker.

Ethan

I like my routine. Everyone who's anyone has one. That's how they achieved greatness.

Ethan

And hacking is *not* a job.

Liam

I'm denying your allegations officially. Seriously, why would you text that? To the Feds who are monitoring these messages, Ethan's a jackass, and he's joking.

Liam

And I'm not hacking. I'm exploring vulnerabilities in a corrupted system.

Honestly, I have no idea what Liam does in his "work." He's self-employed and his services are quite in demand, but whenever he talks about firewalls and malware in the apartment we share, my eyes glaze over.

Then, as if his texts aren't enough, he calls me.

"Seriously. I'm at the library. Is it urgent?" I head toward the business section.

"When are you coming back? Firefly's ditching me for dinner and Charles is holed up at work."

"You can't eat alone?" I scan the shelves for the modeling book.

"I can. But then who's going to make sure *you* don't eat alone? You hermit."

"Can't. I have dinner with my fam later. Need to get work done before then." *Aha! Here it is.* I pull out the brand new volume tucked away in the back.

"You're working at Fleur, your family's company. Relax."

I chew my cheek. "They don't know I'm an Anderson. This was the plan all along, remember? Why I stayed away from the press? Why you scrubbed pics of me off the internet? I'm working my way up from the bottom to earn my place there."

And be a worthy Anderson.

Yanking my collar, I rake in a deep breath. My Achilles' heel.

The great Linus Anderson has five kids. The fraternal twins, my eldest brothers, Maxwell and Ryland, are most like Dad. Maxwell, with his quiet shrewdness, the reclusive heir to Fleur Entertainment, and Ryland, the suave, charismatic visionary who wants to improve anything he touches.

There's Rex, the third son, and marketing extraordinaire. The life of the party, womanizer, making people laugh whenever he steps into the room. Sweet Lana, the youngest, who's still in college. She's sharp and can defuse difficult situations the way an explosives expert can disarm a bomb with a few careful snips of wiring.

Then there's me, the fourth son. The quiet one stuck between Rex and Lana, but feels like a pale shade of whatever vibrant color the rest of my siblings are.

Sure, I graduated with honors and received my MBA before I turned twenty-two earlier this year. I have the same dark brown hair and gray eyes as the rest of my family and can crunch numbers to the best of us.

But I'm lost.

Quarter-life crisis, maybe. The swirling in my gut is more apparent these days.

"You know, you're the most stubborn bastard I've ever met." Liam munches on something on his end. "Be like me. I'm a Vaughn. My family owns a bank. But I don't go around trying to prove myself to anyone. I don't need to."

I sigh. He'll never understand.

I recognize I'm the definition of privilege. The CFO position at Fleur is earmarked for me whenever I'm ready. I'm set for life and doors open whenever I throw out my last name.

But it's not enough. I don't want to phone things in. I want to get there because I *deserve* it. I want Ethan Anderson to be synonymous with something.

Is that too much to ask?

"Anyway, I haven't seen Firefly in ages. Thinking I'll drop by her place later and surprise her with some dessert." Liam slurps down some drink. "Want to come with? You haven't met her yet."

I scoff. "You want me to meet your sister? Are you sure? Didn't you always say I'm *not* supposed to meet your sister?"

"Oh fuck, you're right. You and your broody, mysterious vibe with your dark hair and shit. Stay away. Forget I asked. And don't you even think about it—I know you; you can't settle down and commit to any woman. What was I thinking—"

"Chill. I promised you before—you've nothing to worry about from me. I won't do anything to jeopardize our friendship. And I'm not interested in your little sister."

Who probably just grew out of her braces and happily follows her brother around whenever he's home.

"Got to go, Liam. See you later tonight."

I hang up as my phone pings.

Cleo

> Ethan, come on, baby, don't be this way. I didn't mean what I said. I was just hurt. Call me?

I swallow a groan. This is what Liam meant. I broke up with Cleo two weeks ago because our relationship has been circling the drain for a while. She wanted things I couldn't give her—moving in together, meeting the family.

"Why couldn't you have protected me? You shouldn't have made me fall in love with you."

Her tear-streaked face when I left her apartment after our break up haunts me. When we started, I explicitly told her love wasn't in the cards.

Love and Anderson men don't mix. That's been proven time and time again.

Plopping down in a chair, I get to work. Focus. Work is my number one priority. Come Monday, I'll be Delaney Anders, entry-level financial analyst at Fleur, eager to fetch coffee and lunch orders, hungry to climb the corporate ladder as fast as he can.

In order to do that, I need to be current on the markets and financial forecasting models, like the ones described in the book I'm holding in my hand.

The hours fly by as I mull over the text and take notes. It's cutting edge stuff in a nerdy way, but it gets my gears working.

The next time I look up, the floor is mostly vacated, and it's dark outside. Only the howling winds banging against the windows and the glow of the lamps keep me company. I check my watch.

Five p.m. Shit. Almost time for dinner.

I gather my things and put on my jacket, my mind still whirring with graphs, numbers, and worries about work next week.

But as I head toward the lobby, something catches my attention.

A spiral staircase tucked away in a dark corner. The gleaming gold on the banister calls to me, and my pulse quickens.

I stare at the narrow steps which seem to lead up to another world. A minute later, I find myself on the rare text archival floor, a place I've never visited before, since I've only been to this library twice in the past.

My heart pounds as I admire the rows of books—poetry, my secret friend, lining up the walls, leather volumes of science texts and literature in neat stacks, undisturbed and probably gathering dust.

I trail my fingers on the shelves, admiring the beautiful books and the intricate stained glass window with a hummingbird design in the far wall, when suddenly, I see it.

A thick, caramel book that looks newer than its neighbors.

My brows furrow and I read the title on the spine.

Letters to the Universe

I flip it open. The handwriting catches my attention first—elegant, precise...and whimsical? The t's curved at the ends, the y's looping with a flourish. Leaning against the nearest shelf, I read the first page.

To the Keeper of My Secrets,

Yes. That's you, the nosy person reading my journal.
And also yes, I want you to keep reading.
You see? Whoever you are, it's fated we meet like this. Out of the tens of thousands of books in this building, *you* chose to pick this one up. Then you chose to open it, being the nosy person you are.
And you're still reading it even after you know this is someone's journal containing their private thoughts. (See my usage of "their"? I may be an odd duck, but I'm not stupid. You could be a sixty-year-old-creep for all I know. So, there's no way I'm telling you my gender. Or anything identifying, for that matter.)
Anyway, fate.

I snort. This entire passage screams female. Someone younger. Someone who still believes in fate and hasn't had life hammer the magic out of her. I *should* stop reading...it's a private journal after all, but somehow, I can't.

You're probably wondering why my journal is here.
You see, I have a motto. Several, in fact.
First, don't wait to live because the clock keeps ticking.
Second, there's a reader for every book, including mine.
Third, if you believe it, who's to say it isn't true?
I don't know about you, but my life is a giant ball of uncertainty. Like I've reached a fork in the road and instead of the usual two options, I get five, or six, and I can't even ask an eight ball because that thing is broken too. Sometimes, my next steps are

obvious, other times, they're a mess, tangled up in the pressures of real life and the need to know all the answers this instant.

Amid this chaos, I find it hard to be authentic because I'm afraid of disappointing people. My family tells me they expect nothing of me and I should be thankful for that.

But it hurts. It makes me feel replaceable. I think they *do* have expectations—maybe they're not telling me because they don't think I'll amount to anything.

So, the only place I can be me is here within these pages, navigating my colorful stream of consciousness as life hurls at me more questions I have no answers for.

But I believe someone out there understands what I'm feeling. Maybe someone who's completely different from me, someone who probably wouldn't look my way if we saw each other in real life.

Maybe this person is also experiencing the same thing.

And so, I ask fate to find that person. Because if I believe, then he or she must exist. Because the clock keeps ticking and we aren't getting any younger, so we must take action now. Because I believe there's a reader for my book.

So, congratulations. *You* apparently are that person.

If you accept this role, please write back and put the journal in its proper place.

Your greatest secret and newest pen pal,

Alex (and no, this doesn't mean I'm a guy or a girl, for that matter. It's just a name, so you have something to call me.)

I stare at the spot of ink where her pen landed at the ending stroke of her sentence.

Do I want to reply? I don't have time for this crap. I have real world pressures—proving myself, finding my place in the world, moving up the ranks at Fleur, and making it bigger and better than before.

I put the book back on the shelf and walk away. Someone else can be the reader of her book.

But then, her words keep echoing in my mind.

Sometimes, my next steps are obvious, other times, they're a mess, tangled up in the pressures of real life and the need to know all the answers this instant.

Amid this chaos, I find it hard to be authentic.

My breathing quickens. Her scribbles, however whimsical they are, exactly describe the restlessness inside me, like she took a peek inside my mind and tugged out the dark, knotted mess hiding within, ashamed to face the world.

It's a lonely place to be in.

My jaw works, and I make a decision. I spin around and walk back to the bookshelf to grab the journal.

Flexing my fingers, I sit on the ground, flip to the next blank page, and begin writing.

To Alex,

You've made quite the impression...

CHAPTER 5

Saturday. Today is Saturday.

Bubbles gather in my chest and I bite back a grin. I wonder what he wrote in the journal. After checking my reflection one last time, I slam shut my locker at Broadbent. The girls and I had a study session.

"You coming out with us, Lexy?" one girl asks.

Scrunching my nose, I shake my head. "I have plans, sorry. Have fun!"

There's a party today—college acceptances celebrations, apparently. Lot of Ivy League letters being handed out like candy, which isn't a surprise, given Broadbent is a feeder school and everyone here is a legacy and has their family names on school buildings.

I have little to celebrate. I ended up getting acceptances to state schools.

No Columbia. I guess there's a first time for everything.

I hate that the milestone of the first Vaughn not getting into an Ivy League belongs to me. Charles and Liam have been good sports about it, telling me UNYC is a great option.

Grandma looked crestfallen last week when I broke the news to her. "Don't worry about it, sweetheart. You have a place in the Bank of Columbia, no matter where you graduate."

I disappointed her.

Guilt pinches my gut, and I grab my cell and swipe to the photos I took of the journal to reread his last few entries to me.

To Alex,

You've made quite the impression.

I already know you're a girl. If you want to hide your identity, don't spray your journal with lavender. Your handwriting is too neat for a guy. And how do I know you're not a sixty-year-old creep or an undercover cop trying to frame me as a predator?

Your Keeper

My pen pal is a guy. I'd bet the trust fund I don't get until I'm twenty-two on it. I can almost imagine his wry voice as I read his short entry.

P.S. I shouldn't be wasting my time playing pen pal because I have real world responsibilities, but I think you're lonely and that's why you're leaving your journal in random places. So, it's my good deed for the day. I think you need me.

P.P.S. And yes, I understand exactly what you mean. I love how the world—or in your case, perhaps yourself—expects us to "get it" once we graduate. Like a degree or two will magically infuse us with powers to navigate everything and how it's a failure when you aren't sure where you fit in. It's tough. But you aren't alone.

So he's older. My keeper. Fresh out of college, maybe? I smile at his nickname for himself, a play on what I called him in my first entry. There's something refreshing about not caring how you appear to someone else. Strip off the paint until you're left with the nuts and bolts of who you are.

P.P.P.S. I can't promise you how long I can keep this up. But how do we do this? Do we need a schedule? What if I run into you? Can I ask you anything about yourself?

My entry, this time in pink, is right below his. Obviously, I should've done a better job at hiding my gender, but whatever.

Dear You're Not My Keeper,

I regret that nickname. I don't need anyone to "keep me." Ground rules sound smart. How about you leave the book for me before Tuesday, Thursday, and Saturday? And I do the same for you and you can pick up on Monday, Wednesday, and Friday? Or is that too much? And no cheating or else this thing is over.

You can ask me basic questions about myself, but nothing too detailed because you're a stranger. A strange...friend.

But I'll save you the trouble. I'm female, not a cop, legal, and under twenty-five. My favorite food is lasagna—the more cheese, the better, with gorgonzola crumbles sprinkled on top. I tell people I like champagne, but really, my true love is honey lavender iced tea.

That's all you get. I'm assuming you're a guy. Are you a creepy dude? Don't think I didn't notice how you "forgot" to answer that question.

Thank you for your honesty. I knew there were other people out there who felt lost. But we just have to go for it. Try everything and leave no stone unturned.

Eventually, we'll hit jackpot, right?

So, why are you feeling lost? You seem like you have your life together on paper—graduated and everything.

Alex

P.S. I'm going to mix this up. I'm hiding this journal in a different place, but will leave a clue in the original location and also write it in the journal for documentation. Let's test fate again. If you *are* the one, you'll find it again. So, here's the clue. What's the opposite of a public courtyard?

P.P.S. What would be a perfect day for you? And do you have a hunch how you'll die? Toodles!

I snicker at his response on the next page. He obviously found my book.

A fellow reader as a friend. The idea is a warm hug, chasing away my confusing thoughts. I don't have friends who love books as much as I do.

Dear Alex aka Dreamer (I think this fits you. You sound like your head is in the clouds most of the time—not judging),

Frances Hodgson Burnett's *The Secret Garden*. Really? That was your brilliant riddle, a classic that's been made into movies multiple times over the years? I never back down from a challenge.

Fine. Quid pro quo. I'm a guy between the ages of twenty and thirty. Not a creep. Not a predator. Someone who's trying to figure out where I fit in the world post MBA. Drink of choice is craft beer—Pintzer, to be specific. I'm a health nut, but give myself a free day each week to eat whatever I want. Usually, that involves a steak.

And I have a lot of thoughts about gorgonzola and lasagna—mainly in the vein of things I can't say in polite company because moldy cheese does *not* belong on—never mind.

To answer your question, this is going to sound ridiculous, but my path has been paved for me since I was born. I'm from a big family and everyone works in the family business, so I never really got a say in what I should do.

Don't get me wrong. It's safe. I'm set for life, provided I don't screw things up and the plans they have for me sound interesting. But I can't help but wonder if "sounds interesting" will cut it? Or will people just look at me and think I don't deserve to be where I am?

Nepotism, you know?

Some days, I want to say fuck it and branch out on my own. But since I don't know you and I'll never meet you, I'll let you in on a little secret.

I feel like a failure and I haven't even started yet.

And to answer your other strange and random questions:

My perfect day is simple. Sit in a library or a bookstore and read. Maybe even do some writing. Then grab a beer with friends or my siblings and watch a movie or a game. That's it. If I can get a Carlisle's bone-in rib eye, medium rare, my life would be complete.

And death—are you a goth chick? Nothing wrong with that, I'm sure black nail polish works on you. To answer your question, I haven't thought about it. I assume time is on my side, but I guess growing old, falling asleep next to my wife, then never waking up sounds as good as any? Why are you asking?

Happy hunting,

Your Keeper—you don't get to assign me that role and take it away. I'm acing this position.

P.S. You want to play hide and seek? It's a crazy and wild world out there. Same thing, I'll leave this clue behind and hide the journal elsewhere.

P.P.S. The best and worst moment of your week so far. Go.

Oh, please. His challenge wasn't even a challenge. It took me less than five minutes to figure it out.

I snicker as I think about the tiny lollipop I tucked between the pages as a middle finger back to him.

To Keep(er) Being an Idiot,

I think I know why you're feeling lost, even with your fancy degrees, because what kind of idiot leaves a big leather journal in the children's section? Are you trying to get caught? Is this your attempt to ditch me as a pen pal?

Where the Wild Things Are **by Maurice Sendak. You even used a word in the title as your clue. You can do better, Keeper. Is there a meaning behind your book choice? A boy who feels unseen and frustrated goes on an imaginary adventure only to figure out he has what he wants all along and returns home?**

And guess what, being the idiot you are, you've left more clues about yourself. Carlisle's steak? You've had steak in one of the world's best Michelin-rated steakhouses inside The Orchid? I'm wondering about this "family business" of yours. But then you had to throw me off by saying you like beer. I would've expected fancy whiskey or something if you like Carlisle's.

Not that I'd know. I had whiskey and thought it tasted awful. I'd rather have my iced tea. But Charles loves Carlisle's. One time, he brought a steak home for me after he met his friends at The Orchid. The meat was to die for even though it was takeout.

Maybe this is your game. Confusion.

But I agree with your tastes. Bone-in rib eye is the best cut. Tender with the right amount of fat. Yum. And don't yuck my gorgonzola yum.

As for the "strange" questions—I read a psychology study earlier—part of my quest to figure out what I wanted to major in because examining people's minds sounded interesting. Have you heard of Dr. Arthur Aron and his thirty-six questions that'd supposedly lead to love?

Before you freak out, I'm not looking to fall in love with you and I don't want you to fall for me, even though I know the temptation is very real. Heck, in full transparency, I'm seeing someone, even though that relationship will probably end before I can say Happy Valentine's Day. Are you in a relationship?

Anyway, I thought as pen pals, there's some distance to this whole thing, so it'll be nice to get to know you while respecting the rules and what better questions to ask than ones a psychologist came up with? It's also nice to have someone to talk to about the deep stuff. If I tried talking about this with my friends, they'd probably think I'd grown two heads.

My ideal day is strangely similar to yours. I want to have a picnic in the courtyard here at the library. If you look out the hummingbird window, you'll see it far below. The stone archways, cobblestone floors, and the vines along the walls remind me of my favorite book, *The Secret Garden*. I've been saving this day for when I'm certain about my future. Maybe when I work full time? I think I've built it up in my head so much, I don't want to do it now when I'm not in the best mental state and ruin the experience. Anticipation is part of the pleasure. So, I guess this is a future goal.

As for death, I'm really terrified, to be honest. What if there's nothing afterward? What if I have a bajillion regrets? What if I leave the world and people just...forget me? I guess this is why I have my motto—don't wait to live, because the clock keeps ticking. You never know when you'll meet your maker, and I want to make sure I'm leaving an impression.

Can I tell you a secret? I can't swim. At all. I'm sure you think it's ridiculous, but I have this nightmare of me drowning because I can't swim. And this fear keeps me from learning how to swim. It's a stupid cycle. I really should add this to my list of goals—to get over my fear. Can you swim?

The worst part of my week: Getting into a fight with the guy I'm seeing. He's been acting weird these days. Do you believe in love? That you'll recognize it when you see it?

The best part of my week: Doing well in ballet practice. You?

Please try harder with your riddles,
Dream(er)-ing of Kicking Your Ass Again

P.S. Bonus question: What if an asteroid hits the earth? What would you do?
P.P.S. Clue in the old position, clue here as well:
What's fluent in gifts and touches sweet,
In acts and words, or time we keep?
It's the secret code to the beating heart,
But five is really my love's desire.

I grin as I stare at my little poem. Took me ages to come up with it but I'm proud of it.

Hold on, what if he doesn't get it? Did I just end our friendship? Dammit.

The smile slips off my face just as I feel a poke in my back.

"Who's that smile for? Something smells fishy."

CHAPTER 6

I FUMBLE, NEARLY DROPPING my phone, and turn toward the voice. Curly blonde hair and a sly smile appear in my vision.

"Shit, Summer. Stop snooping."

She waggles her brows. "You're hiding something. Don't think I didn't notice all those strange trips to the library."

"Unlike you, I can't work hard *and* play hard. If I play hard, I won't graduate. And look what happened, I'm the only one who didn't get into Columbia. All of you guys did!"

I groan and step out into the night, a sudden brisk wind whipping my hair over my face.

Gee, thanks, universe. Rain while you're at it, won't you?

The failure stings, but I'll survive and find something else to go after because the clock keeps ticking and if I believe it, it'll come true.

I know those mottos will come in handy.

"So, you going to the library again? Why don't you just work from home? You guys have this gorgeous mansion and you're rarely there."

"I focus more when I'm around people."

And it's lonely at home. Eight thousand square feet with more rooms than a family could possibly use, and no one is ever there. Liam lives with his best friend, and Charles is rarely home. Walking around those empty hallways, thinking about better days when Mom visits or when Uncle Ian swings by and whisks us off to Coney Island or somewhere fun, is just plain depressing.

My phone pings, and she leans down to peer at the screen. I angle it away from her.

"You never answered my question. What were you looking at?"

"Just a message from my friend." A tickle niggles my chest. Is that who Keeper is? A friend?

Well, of course he is, Lexy. What else can he be?

And I still have my missing in action "boyfriend," Dayton, to deal with. The last few days I'd barely heard from him other than the occasional generic "I'm busy but miss you, babe," and "my family wants to meet you in person—they're excited about a Vaughn–Holden relationship, but don't worry, babe, I don't care about your last name."

Maybe with graduation around the corner, I should just let our relationship fizzle out. That's what a lot of high school couples do, right?

A headache forms at the base of my neck and I hear the distinct roar of a motorcycle.

"Firefly, over here!" Liam waves from a few feet in front of me, clad head to toe in black leather.

Before I answer, he tosses a helmet at me and he's lucky my reflexes are fast because if they weren't, that thing would've smacked me in the face.

"Warn a girl next time!" I grumble as he ruffles my hair before I put on the helmet and climb on the back of his bike. Summer laughs and throws us a peace sign before getting into her car.

"I knew you'd catch it. But then, if it hits you in the face, that's probably not a bad idea. Get your head out of the clouds."

The clouds. My heart skips a beat when I think of Keeper's words.

"Why are you smiling like an idiot? You're not thinking about the asshole, right?"

I shove him and ignore his questions. "Jerk face. What are you doing here?"

"Prying the answers out of you, Firefly. You're always at the library and I want to know why. Is Dayton giving you shit about college? You know, you don't need to listen to him, right?" Liam growls, and I can feel the vibrations from under his jacket as he whisks us off toward Ravenswood.

"I never asked for your opinion," I yell over the traffic noises.

"Shit! I can hear you just fine without all your screaming."

I wince. I forgot his helmets have a built-in Bluetooth microphone and speaker system. "Sorry. And to answer your question, Dayton just wants me to fulfill my biggest potential."

"He's just cozying up to you because of your last name. The Holdens are social climbers. You can do better, Lexy."

"What do you have against him?" Acid rushes up my throat as indignation chars my insides. The odd thing is, I don't even think I'm mad at Liam for his words about Dayton. It's the comment about people getting close to me because I'm a Vaughn. Like I have nothing else to offer.

Dayton and I have our issues, but he's a nice guy. We made sense when he was at Broadbent. Captain of the football team with the Vaughn princess. He is fun, charming, and the life of the party wherever he shows up. People flock to him, and I wasn't immune when we met.

People can grow apart. Maybe college is really busy for him.

"I don't like him. There's something off about him. I can't place it, but call it intuition."

"Well, lucky for you, you aren't dating him. You're not my keeper, you know."

As soon as the words are out of my mouth, I think of him again. Mystery guy with the beautiful penmanship who seems to understand me even though we've never met.

Liam snorts. "Someone's gotta look out for you. God knows Charles is too busy to do it, so the responsibility falls on me."

"Charles is taking on the family business because you don't want to do it. It's rough being in the spotlight and you know he cares about us."

But my oldest brother spends most of his time in the office or at The Orchid—the famous establishment for the rich and famous I keep hearing about. And of course, both Liam and Charles say I can't visit The Orchid until I'm "older" because there are a few floors for sexy activities.

But Charles carves out time for us. Not a lot of time, but enough for dinners during the holidays, taking me to watch ballet at the Met Opera, and Liam goes to him for advice on women and other man things.

Liam grumbles his agreement, and before long, he stops in front of the library. I get off the bike and hand him the helmet.

He snaps up his visor. "You never answered me, you know. Why you're at the library so much these days? It's not Dayton giving you grief, right? Because I'll find the bastard and—"

"No. It's not him. I have a project to work on." I leave out the entire bare my heart to a stranger in a journal thing because Liam would go all bat shit overprotective older brother if he knew.

He holds my gaze for a second, then his stare softens. "Good. I don't know much about the finance stuff you're working on, but if you need it, I'm sure Charles would help you."

I smile, a warmth filling my insides. I know Charles would.

"And don't sweat college or the future. We'll take care of you. No pressure. There are no expectations of you."

My smile falters, but I keep it in place. "Yeah. I know."

Turning around, I'm careful to keep my posture upright as I walk into the building when I'm all but crumbling inside.

No expectations.

That's precisely the problem. And he doesn't understand how the words hurt me.

But Keeper gets it. My breath hitches when I think about my pen pal and I quicken my strides, wanting—no, needing—to find his journal and read his words because they'll make me feel better.

I head straight to where I hid the journal last time, jittery energy coursing through my veins. Did he figure out my riddle?

Carefully, I push aside the two books in the self-help and psychology section and exhale when I see a small, unassuming scrap of white paper stashed there.

He found it.

Quickly, I open his clue:

Be not just the same,
Learn the names of your feelings,
Share life's meaning.

Grinning, I stare at the masculine writing and pace in front of the shelves. He answered my clue with a poem.

Be not the same...learn your feelings.

I've read this book before and from the journal entries, I can tell Keeper is well read and smart. He wouldn't give me something I can't figure out.

Feelings...share life's meaning.

Pursing my lips, I bang my forehead against the shelf, trying to fit the clue in the puzzle.

I know this. The answer is at the tip of my tongue.

A growl vibrates in my chest and I'm about to throw in the towel and leave a note and a white flag where I last hid the journal, hoping he'd find it when he sees the journal untouched where he left it.

Then it hits me.

I dart to the young adult's section and head straight to the L's section. *Lois Lowry, where are you?*

Bingo!

The familiar leather spine peeks out in between two copies of Lois Lowry's *The Giver*. I loved this book when I first read it a few years ago.

Looking around and finding no one nearby, I plop down on the carpet and open to his latest entry.

Dear Dream(er)-ing of a Payback,

A sucker? Really? You left a lollipop for me like I'm five?

You should be lucky I have a younger sister who read *The Five Love Languages* and relentlessly quizzed me about it, or else there'd be no way I would've gotten your clue.

I don't believe in love and I just broke it off with someone I was seeing. You probably wonder why and I don't mind telling you, since we're sharing things we can't tell the world.

The men in my family have had shitty luck in the love department. Generations of bad luck. Grandma died when she was young. So did granduncle's wife. Then Mom died when I was a toddler. My oldest brother…let's call him M. He had a high school sweetheart he eloped with, and you guessed it, she died too. All random, freak accidents.

My dad never remarried because he loved my mom so much. I'd catch him staring into space whenever a certain song came up, or he'd tell us stories about her during Christmas, because that was her favorite holiday. Then, on the anniversary of her passing, he'd spend the day at the cemetery and his eyes would be red-rimmed when he came back.

So, I don't feel a particular inclination to try this love thing out. Plus, I've never met someone who took over my mind. I never felt the urge to text someone first thing after I wake up, or fall asleep with her face in my mind.

I frown, rereading his words. I've never felt this way with Dayton either. And I wonder if this feeling—the urge he's describing—is what's missing for me.

I'm comfortable with what I have right now—friends, family. I just need a career direction and a sense of purpose, and that's it.

I hope these letters or journal entries have helped you even though I haven't really solved any of your problems. Oddly enough, they're cathartic for me. Perhaps you're right—it's easier

to talk to a kindred spirit than to people who know you. They'd worry about you, try to make you feel better, or try to solve your problems, when sometimes all you want is just a listening ear.

So, thank you.

For your special day in the courtyard—I took a walk down there and you're right. It's peaceful, hidden, and there's a certain magic about the place—you only want a picnic? What are you going to do there? Will you take anyone with you?

And your thing about swimming, I'd offer to teach you—I was on the swim team in high school and college—but since we're never going to meet, the offer would be useless. Go sign up for some classes. Overcome your fear. Something about the clock keeps ticking, right?

Your asteroid question—you need to rethink it because if the asteroid hits the earth, we'd all be dead. I don't think there's much we can do. What's up with the what-if questions?

Your friend,
Keeper of Your Valuable Thoughts

P.S. Not that this helps, but I don't think you're easily forgettable. You know the saying, "A picture speaks a thousand words?" I actually have an opposite belief—words illuminate the soul. I haven't met you in person, but based on your words, your zest for life, I know you're the type of person who leaves an impression. You're unforgettable, remember that. And I'll always remember you. Don't be too hard on yourself.

P.P.S. Good thing about my week: I started a new job and so far it's going fine. Bad thing about my week: My ex is badgering me. She is a good person and I feel like I've led her on, even though I was upfront about my expectations. She deserves someone who can protect her heart.

P.P.P.S. The clue for documentation:

Be not just the same,
Learn the names of your feelings,
Share life's meaning.

Since you figured it out, that was my gift to you. As Lois Lowry depicted in her story, the world would be a dreary place without emotions, ambition, or ups and downs. You may be lost now, but when you've found what you're looking for, satisfaction will taste much sweeter.

P.P.P.P.S. Now that I'm working full time, I can't swing by as often. I want to propose a solution. We can journal once a week, but if you want to chat, we can use Anonytext? My roommate is a tech guru, and he recommends this service for anonymous texts. The service routes messages through a third party number. Here's a QR code. I already set up my account, so if you want to do it, you just need to scan it, set up your account, and we'll be linked.

I close my eyes as I finish his entry. The barbed wire cinching my lungs loosens and the earlier negativity from my conversation with Liam fades. Keeper's words—the way he sees me even though we've never and will never meet—they're comforting.

Somewhere out there, someone believes in me.

I think about the past me, standing on stage watching other parents take pictures with their daughters in their leotards after a successful showcase. How my chest deflated and became numb when I realized they weren't coming. They'd forgotten me.

But to him, my keeper, I'm unforgettable.

Smiling, I close the journal.

A slip of paper falls out from the next page—the QR code.

My hand trembles as I pick it up. It feels momentous. I'm at another fork in the road, and this time there are only two options.

I don't even need an eight ball to make my choice.

Biting my lip, I take my phone out and scan the code.

CHAPTER 7

"THREE HUNDRED GRAND?" I repeat the words—a devastating blow to my ego.

Trey Spencer rubs his temples, his blond hair a victim of his frustration. He looks years older than his early thirties. "It was an honest mistake. That model had flaws in it and I should've caught it. I reviewed your work."

Acid sloshes in my gut. This is a gut punch.

The last three weeks of my undercover mission at Fleur have gone well.

While I've fetched too many caramel macchiatos and Cobb salads to count, my performance evaluations have been glowing. I was put on more complicated tasks—the last being an investment analysis of our current holdings and how to reallocate our portfolio. My coworkers gave me the nickname Deliminator—a nerdy pun on the words denominator and eliminator—because of the shrewdness of my calculations.

It's good to be trusted. The future where Ethan Anderson, the CFO of the largest entertainment and hospitality company in the world, and someone known for his brilliance and precision, seems possible.

But now, because of a mistake I made in the new forecasting model I introduced last week—a model I was so sure of, I even told Dreamer an early promotion is in the bag—I just cost Dad and the budget more than a quarter million. It barely registers in our net worth, but it's the fact I got too confident. Hubris I didn't earn.

Trey must have read my thoughts because he adds, "Look, Delaney, yes, you fucked up. But stuff like this happens. You're early in your career and sharp. Your recommendations were on point. This is a setback, so learn from it and don't let it get to you."

"Fuck. I should've been more careful. Will this impact you?"

A shadow clouds his eyes. He's probably wondering how much shit he's in and whether it'll go up the ladder and make its way to Maxwell, who's the Chief Operating Officer or as we like to call him, CEO in training, or my dad, the CEO.

I need to come clean—it's my shit, and Trey shouldn't take the fall for it.

"You let me worry about it. I share the responsibility of the error."

"Look, I can talk to Mr. Anders—"

"No." Trey forces out a smile. "I like you, kid. I've been here for seven years and have earned enough mileage to cash some out. You just arrived. Don't let this be a CLM."

Career limiting move.

Shame slinks through me. I should tell him nothing will happen to me because I have something more valuable than mileage points—I own the entire airline. But I don't want to debut Ethan Anderson as a failure. How will I ever gain the respect of my colleagues and my family if I out myself now?

"Take the afternoon off. Go to a bar, get a drink, de-stress. Come back tomorrow and we'll strategize." Trey waves me off.

Guilt eats at me, but I nod. "I'm sorry again." Stopping at the door, I turn around. "And Trey?"

My mentor looks up and arches a quizzical brow.

"Thanks. Not everyone has a boss looking out for them."

Trey chuckles. "You're good. Get out of here, Delaney."

Rubbing the back of my neck, I make my way to The Orchid, a few blocks away.

"Mr. Anderson, good afternoon. Your brothers have arrived already." The concierge nods after I step through the double doors of the fifty-plus-stories building. "I'll have them send up your Pintzer."

My preferred drink as soon as I enter the premises. The gold standard, as always—all our members receive the same treatment.

The Orchid is the pinnacle of our company, a place where all dreams can come true—whether it be scrumptious food from world-renowned restaurants to bespoke concierge services, and kink rooms and sex clubs.

After thanking him, I enter the private elevators and press the floor to the gentlemen's club. Rolling out my shoulders, I examine my appearance in the mirrored walls.

Dark brown hair, a little shaggy but presentable. Dark circles around my eyes betray my lack of sleep. A bespoke blue suit—not the highest quality because an entry-level analyst wouldn't be able to afford that.

I force a smile, hoping my brothers won't see through my mask.

The elevator doors glide open.

Adjusting the lapels of my suit, I hold my head high and stride through the spacious lounge toward the private room reserved for our family. The club is half-full, and I recognized a few folks who regularly grace the cover of *Fortune* magazine. Old money is a cesspool of underachievers—half the people in the room didn't earn their place here. They're here because they were born with the right last name.

Without knocking, I enter our room. Maxwell nods at me, his phone against his ear. He looks every inch the future CEO of the company in his wide stance and imposing demeanor. The man reeks of the confidence I hope to have someday.

"Cancel the contract. Fleur doesn't do business with The Association. I don't give a fuck how big this contract is." He turns to face the floor-to-ceiling windows as he continues his conversation.

I cock my brow. *The Association?*

Dad had looped me in once I graduated—several years ago, a few senators attempted to pressure him into letting The Association use The Orchid for their business.

The Rose floors, where sexual appetites were satisfied, could provide a prime venue for laundering money, capturing illegal footage for leverage, and other shady business.

"Never give up your morals for the sake of power. Do the right thing with our privilege. Give back to society instead."

Dad declined and the next thing I knew, Elias Kent was installed to man those floors. Ironically, the crime boss made sure there was no funny business happening within these walls.

I'm damn lucky to be born in this household.

Scanning the room, I see Ryland sitting in his blue armchair, his brows furrowed as he types on his laptop. Rex is nowhere to be seen.

As everyone is working, I park myself at the dining table and tug my tie loose. I can't fucking breathe. An attendant hands me my beer, and I take a sip before pulling out the journal.

A distraction—that's what I need.

A pressed sprig of lavender falls out of the pages, and I smile. She likes to enclose little keepsakes in our journal of things she came across earlier in the week—flowers, photos of sunsets or food, whatever fits her fancy.

Dear Keeper of My Days,

Is it strange to call you my best friend after only two months of letters? I can't explain this, but you understand me. The real me with all the squishiness and dark thoughts, the dreamer and the worrier. You've never seen me before and it doesn't matter how I look or dress, who my family is, so ironically, I can bare my soul with you.

I know I never texted you.

It's a big step to be texting each other, even if the messages will be routed through an anonymous number.

To be honest, it feels like I'll be cheating on D, my boyfriend, even if there's nothing going on between you and me. But that

level of intimacy...I want to have things sorted out with D before deciding if we should text.

Am I overthinking?

My mouth runs dry at her words as the room comes back into focus. For the past few seconds, like all the moments before when I read her letters, I've been transported elsewhere—into an intimate space where I can almost hear her say those words to me. My pulse thumps like a jackrabbit has taken residence in my veins.

I never realized how our connection has grown through these entries until she pointed it out now.

And now, I wonder how I could've been so blind to my evolving emotions to this friend...this confidant.

Gripping the journal tightly, I continue reading.

In all honesty, and I've been the most truthful to you, I scanned the code and almost signed up. But something held me back, and I knew it was D.

The other day, he came to my place to hang out, but I had a headache and took a nap. When I woke up, I overheard him talking on his phone in the living room and he said things like "Leverage," "I'll get an intro soon," and "Money isn't a concern." I asked him about it and he only shrugged and said I must've been dreaming. He kissed me and sat me down to review college acceptances.

My gut clenched when I read the words. He kissed her—it's like her observation about our intimacy has awakened something inside me. I don't like her boyfriend based on what she has told me in the past, but this is the first time I've felt a visceral reaction.

Or perhaps the first time I've noticed. Fuck. What's happening to me?

She's a friend.

Someone you trust with your secret thoughts—things you tell no one else, including your family.

Shit.

He's been sweeter these days. I wonder if the last few months of strangeness have been a fluke.

What would you do, Keeper? We've been dating for a while now and maybe deep down, I'm afraid if I break up with him, I'll be alone again?

You raised a good question a few weeks ago, and I thought about it. For my victory picnic in the courtyard, I want to take the person I love to share the experience with me.

We'd have those fancy little sandwiches—smoked salmon, but no capers because that stuff is gross, fig jam and cheese, cucumber and egg salad. I thought about bringing lasagna—but that'd be too messy. I'd want the lavender scones from Estelle's. And a batch of their honey lavender iced tea—a hug in a drink.

I'd bring my books—romance, Greek mythology (what's your favorite Greek myth, by the way? Eros and Psyche's love story is my fav), gothic mysteries, my scrapbook and journal (yes, I have another one at home), and just doodle my day away with the person I love.

How's that for specific plans? Satisfied?

I hope you find genuine love, even if you don't believe in it. Perhaps I haven't experienced the heart-wrenching twist of loving someone. But I've seen it. My parents, as flighty as they are, truly love each other. But their love is volatile—a tsunami drowning everyone in the vicinity.

I want what they have, minus the wreckage. I hope to find it someday and I wish for the same for you.

And my what-if questions—you called me a dreamer, right? Thinking about what-ifs reminds me of the endless possibilities in life. I should create a list of my dreams—go big or go home.

What if your what-ifs come true? Ha, you didn't expect that, did you?

Here's my random what-if for the week: What if there's no more bacon in the world? What will you eat for breakfast?

Your confidant,
Dreamer and Believer

P.S. Clue: *Another name for this journal.* I know, I'm lazy with this one, but ballet practice and school have been kicking my ass, so I haven't had time to come up with something more clever.

P.P.S. In case you need a reminder, I really admire your drive. You just started a new job and are kicking ass at it, but even if you weren't, you'll be great eventually.

Do you know why?

Have you read Angela Duckworth's *Grit*? She mentions that perseverance and effort are what it takes to succeed in life. And effort counts twice. You have this in spades. So I know, if you trip and fall, you'll just dust your knees off and get back up. Plus, we're often the toughest critics of ourselves. You'll succeed someday. I know it and believe it.

I smile at her words, a soothing balm to the ragged wound in my ego. I was right. Reading her words made me feel better. Her trust and faith is an addictive drug, and I want more of it.

"Ethan? Earth to Ethan, what are you staring at?" Rex snatches the journal from me.

"Fucker. Give that back, C!" I jump out of my seat and throw a right hook at my brother without thinking. Luckily, he dodges out of the way just in time.

The violent impulse shocks me. All I know is when he grabbed the book I had to make sure no one else read it because the words belong only to me and Dreamer.

Rex's eyes widen. I snatch the journal from him, my face aflame. He holds his hands up in mock surrender. "Damn. What do you have there, state secrets?"

"Just notes from work, jackass. You know I hate being disturbed when I'm working." I roll my eyes.

Rex arches his brow before tossing his suit jacket near the coatrack. He plops down on a sofa and stretches his legs. "I don't know how we're related, workaholic."

"I don't know how you're the older one," I mutter under my breath.

"I heard that. And thank you."

"It's on purpose. It's not a compliment."

He smirks and waggles his brows. The Anderson charmer, or Mr. C, because our parents alphabetized our middle names with Maxwell's being Angus, Ryland with Benedict, to Lana with Eloise—the ladies love him and he loves them back.

"I'm not in a rush to carry the weight on my shoulders like the folks over there." Rex juts his thumb toward Maxwell, who just ended his call.

"What are you two fighting over now?" Ryland grumbles and snaps his laptop shut. Maxwell chuckles and takes a seat.

"Rex and his womanizing ways." I stuff the journal back into my bag.

Maxwell eyes the motion and arches his brow. I shake my head. The man misses nothing, but he isn't nosy, unlike Rex. "I heard there was a hiccup with the investments, Ethan."

A muscle tics in my jaw and I fist my hands on my lap. Of course, the loss has made its way to him already. "It's my fault, not Trey's. An oversight with the model."

"Can we course correct?" Ryland steeples his hands. Their attention is heavy—an unwanted spotlight.

"I'm meeting with Trey tomorrow to discuss. We might not make it all back, but hopefully we can break even." I chug down my beer to do something with my hands.

"Don't be too aggressive—learning the ropes takes time, Ethan. There's no rush." Maxwell's eyes soften into something akin to sympathy. "You have time." He smiles encouragingly, the way an older brother dotes on his younger siblings.

I don't want sympathy. Or gentleness. I want pride and recognition from his eyes.

"I'll fix this."

As the words slip out of my mouth, I realize I want to do it not only for my brothers, but also for Dreamer.

Because somewhere out there, she believes in me, not because I'm an Anderson, not because I'm related to her.

She believes in me for me and me alone.

CHAPTER 8

"Babe, so what do you think? Would your brother be interested in investing?" Dayton sprawls on his sofa in his loft in Brooklyn, which unfortunately is littered with his usual man cave mess—half empty bottles of hard liquor and takeout containers.

I pretend I don't hear him as I head into his kitchen to buy myself a few seconds. For the last few weeks, I've done some soul searching. With IBA on spring break and my project for school done—I got a C because I suck at finance—I had time to think about my relationship with him.

Originally, I wanted to avoid hurt feelings and let the relationship end when I graduate from high school. But if it isn't going anywhere and my feelings for him aren't changing, what's the point of wasting more time?

Rip the bandage off, Lexy. Just tell him.

I grab my messenger bag filled with stuff he left at my place, which isn't a lot since I usually meet him here—a Columbia shirt, a sports watch, and a toothbrush—and walk back into the living room, finding him staring expectantly at me.

He gives me the familiar wry grin and tosses me a flash drive. "Found some old pics from Homecoming. Thought you might want copies. It was fun, right? I miss Broadbent."

"Right. Good ol' days. Thanks for this." I strain a smile and stuff the drive into my bag, a small pinch of guilt slicing through me.

"So? The investment? I've burned through the money you loaned me for setup costs. But the fund is an opportunity."

He waves a sheet of paper with graphs and numbers in front of me. "Bank of Columbia would be an excellent fit. I saved a PDF of this on the drive I just gave you—financial stuff for Charles if he wants them. Maybe we can pitch it to him together?"

Dayton takes out his phone, his legs bouncing. He's either excited or nervous, and these days, I can't really tell, but I stop him.

"I don't think this is working."

He freezes, and for a moment, the hardened glint I saw in his eyes awhile back from the guy who was afraid of cops and whispering on the phone is back.

But that expression wipes off his face almost immediately.

"What do you mean, babe? The fund? Come on, we talked about this. We need this fund to work."

No, you need this fund. I don't know the first thing about numbers.

He rambles, "You and I were going to be the Vaughn-Holden all-stars at Columbia. We'd get this fund off the road, grow our own fortune and make a name for ourselves. You'd get to do whatever you want with the profit—go to spas, travel around the world, get some nice handbags."

Spas and handbags. My hand fists the strap of my messenger bag, but he doesn't notice and continues, "But don't worry," he stares at me with that damn pity in his eyes, "I'll carry the weight. We're good together."

"T-That's not what I meant, Dayton. I just don't think you and I are going to work out. I don't—"

He clasps my shoulders and squeezes softly. "Baby, I know I've been too busy. I see you writing to your pen pal all the time and I think you're talking to her because I don't have time for you, right?"

I swallow. I don't correct him that Keeper is a guy, not a girl.

"I'm sorry. But like I said, things are looking up with the fund and I just finished midterms. I have a lot more time now. Do you want to do something fun? I'll take you to that new bookstore you wanted to check out?"

His words are a barrage of bullets, slamming into me at breakneck speed, and my throat closes up.

Dayton clasps my cheek and stares at me reverently. "We don't have to call Charles now. We can talk about this later, okay?"

The vein is still pulsing in his temple.

I stare mutedly at him, my muscles coiled as the air thickens with tension.

"Let's watch a movie? *Gone with the Wind.* You liked that old shit, right? Your favorite?" *No. It isn't my favorite, and you should know that.*

Dayton pats my cheek and walks away, like I didn't just break up with him.

It's wrong. All wrong.

"Dayton, I'm serious. We're done. Things have changed, and I know what I want in a relationship and it's not this. I don't go to bed at night thinking about you or want to text you when I wake up in the morning. I'm sorry!"

"Babe, don't do this. This is about the investment, right? I won't borrow money from you again."

Not wanting to drag this out for longer, I stride to the door. But I pause at the threshold, and turn around. His face is flushed but his eyes are downcast like he's pained. He doesn't follow me.

"Good luck with everything, Dayton."

I close the door and rush out onto the busy streets, barely noticing the crowds of commuters and tourists rushing by.

My heart ricochets against my rib cage and I feel dizzy.

I thought I'd be sad. Crying even. After all, he was my first boyfriend. Dayton was good to me even if it was strange toward the end.

But instead, I feel a million times lighter. Like I can pirouette around the stage effortlessly, with the grace and talent I've seen from Lil' Tay and the other dancers.

My lips split into a grin as I run down the street, not caring about the bystanders pointing at me or the cabs honking their horns when I dash across the crosswalks just as the light turns red.

I don't even know where I'm going until I find myself standing in front of the building with dark columns and intricate carvings of ravens in flight.

Ravenswood Library.

It's Friday and I'm not supposed to be here. Keeper drops off the journal on Fridays. But excitement flutters through me, sending little bursts of electricity through my nerves, all pointing to one impulse.

I want to see him. Keeper.

I want to tell him I broke up with Dayton. It feels important he should be the first person to know. I want to find out if his hair is black or brown, or if he's a redhead like me. Does he have a confident swagger or a shy demeanor? Is his voice raspy or a rich baritone?

Sweat beads the back of my neck as I stare at the familiar wooden door, the *swoosh, swoosh, swoosh* of my pulse obliterating all rational thought.

He's in there. He's got to be.

Swallowing, I push the door and step inside, my heavy breathing sounding loud in the quiet space. I head straight toward the DVD collection in the basement. My riddle for him last week had a twist in it. The answer wasn't a book, but a film, my favorite movie of all time. I wonder if he's figured it out yet.

The fluorescent lights flicker on and off as I tiptoe down the narrow stairs. Soon, the DVD and music rental room comes into view.

People huddle over computers, a few folks with headphones covering their ears. Is he the lanky guy standing by the corner in the black T-shirt, browsing the new releases? Or the balding young man sitting on the floral couch, looking at his laptop? The room spins—or it's the excitement causing the blood to rush to my head.

"Miss, do you know where the romance section is?" a deep, raspy voice sounds from my right and I jolt.

Turning around, my breath stalls as I stare at luminous gray eyes affixed to a handsome face I'd recognize anywhere. The guy I bumped into in front of the building a few months ago.

Ares, the god of war.

He's wearing a gray dress shirt which molds to his muscular chest and showcases his sexy forearms. His eyes rove over my face and I wait for a spark of recognition.

But nothing comes.

Dummy. Just because you remember handsome faces doesn't mean you are unforgettable.

Keeper will recognize me on sight.

I shake myself. "It's down there in the far right corner."

"Right. Picking up something for a friend. Thanks." Ares walks off as I stare at his backside like an idiot.

The encounter is a bucket of ice water doused over my head. I look around, and the room has stopped spinning.

What the hell am I doing here?

Keeper is a trusted friend, and we have set rules. If I break them, I'll lose the friendship.

You are unforgettable, remember that. And I'll always remember you.

His beautiful words from the entry I reread every day on my phone.

He's the only person who thinks I'm unforgettable. I can't lose this connection.

Cold sweat dots my forehead and I quickly rush back up the stairs, hoping Keeper hasn't seen me yet, and we can continue our clandestine relationship longer.

Once I'm in front of the building, I whip out my phone and text the number assigned to me by the Anonytext app.

Alex

> It's me. I did it. Proud of me, Keeper?

A few seconds pass by and he replies.

Delaney

> I figured it's high time you have a name to call me.

Delaney

Does your text mean what I think it means?

CHAPTER 9

PRESENT: EIGHT YEARS AFTER THE ACCIDENT—TWENTY-EIGHT YEARS OLD

THE SPOON CLATTERS TO the ground.

"Shit," I mutter, and begin the tortuous process of moving my legs off the bed.

"I got it, Lexy." Taylor leaps off the leather couch, picks up the utensil, and hands it back to me.

A growl makes its way up my throat and a ball of fire gathers in my chest.

Ten months.

It's been ten months since I woke up to a new world and a new reality and I still can't grip a spoon with my right hand. The same goes for leaning on my right foot, and heck, anything on the right side of my body.

"Dammit, Tay, let me do this or I'll never get better!"

Taylor gasps then her eyes soften.

The outburst shocks me—it's not me. Not the old me, anyway.

I remember when I enjoyed dreaming, laughing, and letting life's hiccups roll off me because I knew the clock was ticking and I shouldn't waste any time focusing on negative events.

But now, these hiccups jolt me.

Not to mention, ever since I woke up, there's a sinister thread of fear and lingering anxiety. I'm always looking behind me, my heart pounding from the slightest surprise.

Like I'm afraid of something.

But what?

Lexy, get a grip on yourself. Now's not the time to indulge in your overactive imagination.

I snort, and Taylor looks bewildered. Heck, I don't blame her. I feel out of control inside too.

"Sorry, Tay. I don't know what's gotten into me. You didn't deserve it."

"You're too hard on yourself, Alexis. Shit, if I were in your shoes, I'd probably be hurling plates and knives against the wall."

A sharp spasm ripples at the base of my skull, and I wince.

Muffled screams. Headlights. Water—so much dark water.

Clutching my chest, I focus on my breathing as my pulse riots inside me.

The same snippets again. I've experienced these episodes a few times since I woke up, but I can't make sense of them. *Nightmare? Memories?*

"You okay?" Taylor pulls up a chair and sits down, her back against the large picture window in the long-term rehabilitation unit in Manhattan Memorial, my new home after I came out of my coma.

"Just the strange flashes again."

"The doctor said don't try too hard. You'll hurt yourself. Let things come back on their own."

"I know. But I don't want to sit there and do nothing. There's got to be something I *can* do."

Taylor laughs. "Man, I never thought I'd be the one lecturing someone on patience."

She grins, her nose piercing, a red heart—something that's definitely the adult Taylor—glints under the lights. The last memory I had of her was when she was twelve and I was sixteen. She just started at IPA and was all arms and legs, skinny as a rail.

It still shocks me every time when she walks through the door—and she visits twice a week, rain or shine.

She's no longer twelve. She's twenty-four and a principal dancer for the top ballet company in the country, ABTC. And I'm not sixteen anymore. I'm twenty-eight—caught in limbo where I don't feel like a teenager, but can't quite accept I'm almost thirty.

Dr. Riordan, my neurologist, told me my body still matured while I slept, my brain too—quietly finishing what time had already started. I may not remember the years I lost, but something in me feels older.

But still, I was robbed.

Taylor ticks off her fingers. "Remember the rules: go to your therapy sessions, don't force yourself to remember or it'll backfire. I want to tell you more but—"

"We have to follow the doctor's orders," I finish for her.

My family and friends were instructed to avoid discussing my missing memories with me, as it may cause additional stress on my brain and also create false memories. So other than basics—my age, my major in college, how I broke up with Dayton—they didn't tell me much.

"My brother always told me we're the hardest critic of ourselves," Taylor says.

Her words. They feel...familiar. I look at her. Thick, raven hair piled up in a high bun. Luminous gray eyes giving me a sense of déjà vu, but not because they're her eyes.

I just can't place it.

"Your brother? Which one?"

She's an Anderson now—another development I've learned recently. Lil' Tay and her older sister, Grace, are Linus's daughters from a passionate love affair long after his wife died. But unfortunately, the Peyton sisters' mom also passed away tragically a few years ago.

She shrugs. "Ethan."

I tense up. Images of the mysterious, brooding man who ran to my bedside after I woke up flash through my mind.

Nope. Not thinking of him.

Taylor narrows her eyes.

"What?" I look away, not wanting her to read me.

"You know I'm going to pry it out of you. You're upset about something."

I sigh. "I should be thankful and happy. It's a miracle. Nothing else can explain it. But I feel so useless."

I punch my right thigh. The sensations are there but muted, like the pins and needles I'd feel if I sat on my leg for too long and suddenly got up.

"My body isn't my own anymore, and I have no memories of the four years before the accident. It's just memories, but I've lost so much already, Tay."

Apparently, I was found submerged in the Hudson when I was twenty after a car accident on a rainy day. I suffered multiple broken ribs, a punctured spleen and liver, a traumatic brain injury, and almost drowned.

Lucky for me, an anonymous Good Samaritan fished me out of the river before my clock ran out and called 911 from a pay phone. They placed me in a medically induced coma after a bunch of surgeries, but I never came out of it.

Persistent vegetative state.

For eight years.

No one expected me to wake up. The odds of anyone waking up after a year were slim to none. I often wondered why Charles and Liam never pulled the plug. God knows my parents couldn't have cared less. They only visited three times since I woke up, and Mom acted like I was hospitalized for a brief stint, not someone who woke up after a life-altering accident.

But the fog has lifted. I'm no longer pursuing their approval. Life is too short to care about people who don't feel the same way.

Tay squeezes my hand. "You were asleep for so long. Look how much you've achieved since you woke up. You can walk now. You're writing with your left hand. You can eat solid foods. And you shit just fine."

She snickers and I chuckle. She's grown up to be snarky with a dry sense of humor.

"I swear, I love this no bullshit side of you, but I still find it hard to imagine you were the sweet Lil' Tay Tay from back then."

Taylor stills, a strange flash of darkness appearing over her features.

The hairs prickle on my forearms.

"Is everything okay? I've asked this before, but did something happen while I was in a coma?"

"You're overthinking." She strains a smile. "No one can stay an innocent little kid forever. We all have to grow up. Shit happens."

"Tay, I—"

"Just drop it, okay? I'm fine. More than fine, I swear. Let's leave the past in the past."

The steely edge in her voice stops me from asking more. She's undergone something painful, and I don't want to push her to tell me until she wants to.

Perhaps I have no right to know about her experiences, but I don't want to leave the past in the past. Almost a decade of my life got stolen from me, and if you include the four years of memories before the accident, that's twelve years.

Almost half of my life.

I want to know what happened to me in those four years—they were *mine*.

"So, your schedule today—physical therapy, then swim lessons?"

"Water therapy, not swim lessons. Even though I'll be signing up for those as soon as I get out of here."

The thought of going back into the water sends my heart racing. The same nightmares I've had since I was a kid fill my nights—me in the water, my lungs burning, but I can't move.

But this time, the dreams are more vivid. Intense. Real.

The pain charring my nose as I gulp down water instead of oxygen.

The darkness surrounding me—so dark I can't tell which way is up or down.

Fear. Bloodcurdling fear. Just like the random visions I have.

I shake myself to dispel the thoughts.

I won't be helpless. Maybe if I knew how to swim all those years ago, I would've gotten out of the car myself.

Taylor gnaws her lip. "Shit, I forgot to tell you. I have practice and can't stay with you today. Charles is swinging by to pick me up."

"I'll be fine. I don't need you to babysit me."

Taylor rolls her eyes. "Who said I was babysitting you? I just missed you and am reclaiming my lost time."

My lips curve into a grin. There's a closeness and comfort I feel with her I can't explain.

"Have you found anything on Summer?" My fingers twiddle with the blanket on my lap.

"No. That girl has vanished. But don't worry, I'm sure we'll find her."

Disappointment crests inside me—I remember Summer well. My high school partner in crime. I'm sure she was worried about me after my accident.

Knock knock.

We swivel our attention to Art, the physical therapist I've been working with for the last six months.

"Hey, Arthur!" Taylor grins.

"Art. Like the subject, Taylor. Arthur makes me feel like I'm a hundred years old." He ruffles his light brown hair and flushes. The man has a little crush on my friend.

Too bad for him, he doesn't know that—

"Minx, you ready?" Charles murmurs from the doorway, his brow arching at the interaction.

A grin curls his lips and he strides in, his blond hair gleaming, and he hauls Taylor up in his arms before delivering a deep kiss like he needs her to live.

Another interesting development that happened while I was in a coma—Charles, my charming, workaholic, older brother, role model all rolled into one, is head over heels in love with a girl I used to see as my little sister. They got engaged a few months after I woke up. It took some time getting used to, but seeing him so besotted and actually taking time to enjoy life makes me grateful for Taylor.

"You know I'm not invisible, right? I'm right here and don't need to see you exchanging saliva with my *best* friend."

Huh? My brows furrow. *Best friend? Where did that come from?*

Taylor breaks the kiss, her eyes bright with excitement. "Did you remember something?"

My mind draws a blank. I rewind my words in my brain to see if I can trigger a memory or unlock a dormant part of my brain.

But nothing comes.

The familiar scorching sensation rises to my chest again.

Useless. So damn useless.

"No. Were we best friends, Tay?"

Her familiar dark eyes glimmer with moisture and she rolls her lips inward. As if sensing her emotions, Charles pulls her to his side and presses a kiss on her hair.

"Yeah, we were close, Lexy." Taylor's voice is raw. "You were the best and loyalist friend. The very damn best." The haunted look is back in her eyes. I want to ask her what she's not telling me, but I know she won't say anything.

Art clears his throat. "Ready for therapy?"

I shove the ever present unease away and nod. "Let's do this. Box jumps, Art. I want to try the jumps again. No half-assing it."

It's a tough challenge to jump up a box a foot tall when you can't really feel half your body.

But I got this. I have to do this...for myself.

I need to get my life back.

"It's so weird how I know how to drive, but can't remember taking the stupid driving test. And now, I'm trying to learn to jump again," I grumble.

Art chuckles. "The brain is interesting. Your episodic memories are stored in a different region than your procedural or semantic memories. But we'll get you there."

I scrunch my nose. *Two out of three's not too bad, I suppose. It could be worse.*

Swinging my legs off the bed with renewed determination, I grit my teeth and take my first steps with a limp. I probably look more like I'm waddling—a toddler learning her first steps, but I find my rhythm.

Taking a deep breath, I force my lips into a wide smile before turning to face Charles and Taylor again.

"Watch me kick some ass next time you guys visit." I wink.

Charles's brows furrow and Taylor is wiping her eyes.

"You got this, Firefly." Charles gives me a hug. "You're a Vaughn. Nothing can beat us."

A lump forms in my throat. I'm getting emotional again. "I miss Grandma and Uncle Ian. It's not fair I didn't get to say goodbye to them."

He stiffens and pulls away. A pulse batters against his temple and his eyes cool to a glacial glint.

The same dread I felt earlier reappears.

"Charles?"

He flinches, the chilly expression on his face disappearing. Squeezing my shoulder, he whispers, "I miss Grandma too."

What about Uncle Ian? Why is no one talking about him other than to tell me he died? Why do I have a feeling something bad happened in those four years?

"My best friend's going to destroy those boxes. They won't know what's coming," Taylor quips and traipses over.

She rests her head on Charles's shoulder, and he relaxes before handing me a small bag I didn't notice he was holding.

"What's this?"

"Ethan told me to give this to you. Thought you might be bored."

I frown. This time, I can't shove the thoughts of *him* away.

The man radiated intensity and coiled tension. I still remember how every muscle inside me seized when he crushed me into his arms after I woke up.

I couldn't breathe. The fear. The panic. The need to scurry away because everything felt too much. Too overpowering. The blistering headache, followed by a sharp throb behind my rib cage when he pulled away.

Then there was the flash of pain in his eyes before a stony mask fell over his face—the same mask I see every time he comes around with my brother.

Nova.

That's what he called me. But I must've misheard.

Because I don't know him.

Later, he apologized for being too forceful. He told me Liam was distraught when I was in a coma and he was happy for his best friend that I woke up.

He's shown up time and time again, usually with Liam, but he's kept his distance, and likewise, I'm wary.

Something about him seems...strange.

"What could he have gotten me? It's not like he knows me."

"Go easy on him, Lexy," Charles murmurs. "He's not an easy person to know, but he's a good guy. He also has a lot on his plate—a financial investigation is taking over his life."

"You have a lot of stuff going on too, Charles, but you aren't an ass."

Charles chuckles and shakes his head as I peel off the wrapping paper.

A gasp tumbles out of me when I see the DVD.

The Notebook. Collector's edition with commentary from the director. A small piece of paper sticks out from the box. I open it to find a Post-it note:

Alexis,

I heard you woke up from a coma and are in recovery. I wish you all the best and hope you recover soon. May this movie give

you some distraction during a challenging time and may you reclaim what you've lost.

Best,
N. S.

The author of the book behind the movie left me a note. A personalized note. My eyes cloud with moisture—a sudden urge to cry.

How does he know my favorite movie? And then, there's the personalized message.

It has to be a lucky guess. He probably sent his assistant to get this. Don't overthink it.

A searing pain hits me behind my rib cage, and suddenly, I'm winded.

Somehow, I feel like I've lost something irreplaceable.

CHAPTER 10

PAST: TWO YEARS BEFORE THE ACCIDENT—TWENTY-TWO YEARS OLD

"DUDE, DID YOU FALL in or something? You're missing your own celebration party!" Rex pounds on the bathroom door. We're at Mystique, a new nightclub that opened inside The Orchid last week.

Deep, rhythmic thumping of the bass reverberates through the walls, followed by the cackling of my brothers and friends on the other side of the door. The atmosphere is electric, the alcohol adding fuel to the fire, but instead of hanging out with everyone in the private room, I'm hiding away here.

I was promoted to senior analyst last week at work.

Trey clapped me on the back as he handed me a glass of whiskey in his office. "What did I tell you, Delaney? You rose from failure and came back stronger. You deserved this."

There was pride in his eyes. After losing the company three hundred grand, I doubled down on my research, testing, and retesting theories with my own money before I suggested investment changes at Fleur.

I checked my work three times—on a computer, by hand, and even reading it aloud—before submitting my official recommendations.

It paid off. The investment changes yielded a two hundred percent return, a nice sum of two million dollars in three weeks. The Deliminator was back in his game again and the office rejoiced.

"Thanks." I raised the glass at him and took a sip.

"I only gave you advice. You did all the work. Don't sell yourself short, D. Keep this up and someday I'll be worried about my job." Trey chuckled.

When I take the helm of this department, Trey would get a promotion—I'd make sure of it.

"Ethan! Dude, seriously. Did our parents swap the numbers in your birth year or something? Why are you hiding in there like an old man?"

Rex the menace. Rex, the nuisance.

"You eat your meals on a set schedule, the same healthy green stuff every day. Shouldn't your bathroom breaks be on a schedule too?"

I roll my eyes and ignore him.

"You're so gross, Rex. And Ethan's been better with his routines now. He's here, isn't he? And at the family dinner last week, I saw him wolfing down lasagna with a goofy smile on his face." Lana's dulcet voice travels through the door.

"Fuck, you're right. But who the hell eats moldy cheese with lasagna?"

I bite back a grin. I had Dreamer to thank for that. I should be upset at her messing with my routines, but oddly, I'm not.

It made me feel closer to her.

"Ignore him, Ethan. I know it's hard to introvert at a party!" Lana giggles.

"Don't make me regret letting you come with us, missy."

"Like you can keep me away, Rex. I'm not one of your women."

"Ew! That's disgusting. Why would you say that?"

The two squabble and I groan. They won't leave me alone until I respond.

"I'll be out in ten. Just need a breather. Chill!" I holler and hear more grumblings from my brother and sister before their voices fade away.

I return my attention back to Dreamer's latest entry in the journal and a rush of warmth infuses my chest.

Dearest Keeper of My Dreams,

My heart stutters at the name she's given me, even though I gave her my middle name in our text messages. But there's something more intimate in the old-school weekly journal habit we've kept up the last two months.

You were tricky with this week's clue.
Dreaming of you,
A day, so special, and true.
The hummingbird's sweet melody.
A future, so momentous, your harmony.
Is this your way of getting back at me with my clue a few months ago when I sent you to the DVD section for *The Notebook*?
Your poetry is beautiful though. Why don't you write more and publish them? When I first read it, I immediately thought of the courtyard outside the hummingbird window. And I hope, someday, when I find my place in the world, I'll be able to have that one special picnic there.
With you.

The thumping inside my chest quickens—every beat eclipsing the ruckus of the nightclub, which seems an entire universe away.

That's her magic, my dreamer. The breathtaking supernova illuminating the inky night skies. Unbidden, a flash of red hair floats to my consciousness—the mystery girl who bumped into me a while back who brightened my dreary day with her presence.

But that was before I met Dreamer—she shines from within, sight unseen. I know she'll eclipse any women I'll ever meet.

My Nova wants to spend her special day with the person she loves.

And she's invited me.

I don't want to overthink this, but I can't help but overthink everything. Her words, the softness in them, the sweetness, they all seem to be meant for me. This connection I feel pulsating through black ink on white paper or digitized in our texts. I can't be imagining this.

I want to meet her.

Desperately.

I've never felt this way about anyone before, especially someone I've never seen. I don't know if she has short hair or long hair. If she wears glasses and has curves, or if she's tall and slim.

I don't care.

I already know she's beautiful.

Congrats on your promotion, Keeper. I hate hearing the words, "I told you so," but I can't help but officially state...

I told you so.

I never doubted you, even as you doubted yourself. Have you found your direction in life now? Are you still as lost as when I first met you?

Good thing this past week: My parents visited from Milan. We all went out for dinner like a normal family. My brothers were angry with them, of course. My grandmother pretended nothing was wrong. And my uncle played the peacemaker. But I was happy. For a moment there, I felt loved.

Bad thing about this week: Ironically, it was the flip side of my happiness at the dinner. Even though everyone was focused on C, my oldest brother's accomplishments at work. Or they were concerned about whether L, my middle brother, would get arrested for whatever punk stuff he was involved in.

Grandma was sad when we talked about me starting my freshman year at UNYC in a month. I'll be the first in my family to go to a state school. Essentially, I'm a failure and a black sheep. But they all quickly told me it didn't matter, that they'd take care of me, and I sat there feeling useless again, like I'd never measure up.

Stupid, huh?

The next day, my parents jetted off to Italy again. Grandmother went back to her place in the Hamptons, and my brothers disappeared off to work or whatever it was they did.

I was alone again. But this time, I remembered I had something special.

I had you.

I was unforgettable.

My heart clenches when I read her words. I feel her loneliness wafting off the pages and I wish I could go to her and pull her into my arms because she *does* have me. Her family doesn't appreciate how beautiful her soul is, but I do.

The sudden thoughts make me lightheaded.

I'm Ethan Anderson, the guy who doesn't believe in love because I don't want the heartbreak. I don't want to tempt luck or fate or whatever you call it. I don't want to be someone who stares at a Christmas tree, grief etched on my face because that was the favorite holiday of the person who still holds my heart, even after death.

But my resolve is weakening.

Maybe Ethan Anderson just needs to meet the right person.

Someone to make me brave enough to do what Dad did with Mom, what Maxwell did with his high school sweetheart. Someone who cares for me sight unseen, not knowing if I was rich or poor, or if my last name would open doors for her.

I let out a ragged breath and keep reading.

And I felt better. Much better.

So thank you again, Keeper. You're my north star.

Your Dreamer

P.S. I hope you have fun at your party. You deserve it.

P.P.S. I've decided to start a bucket list. I'm calling it Twenty by Forty. I'll finish one item per year starting when I turn twenty (ah shit, I just revealed my age, didn't I? But I'm sure you figured it out already, with me talking about college and all). Anyway, the items can include places I want to go, things I want to do, foods I want to try. The skies are the limit. Aside from getting my degree at UNYC and making my way into the world, I'll also do something exciting. Something that's me. Because you know what I'm going to say...the clock keeps ticking...yadda yadda yadda. I haven't decided what to put on that list yet, but I'm open to ideas.

P.P.P.S. This week's clue: Where blades sing in stanzas, and green verses celebrate life and nature.

P.P.P.P.S. Thank you for the art print of Eros and Psyche. But I can't believe you defiled the back of it by scribbling you don't have a favorite Greek myth. What kind of monster are you? Seriously? How can you call yourself a poet?

P.P.P.P.P.S. The what-if question of the week: What if one day a big rock fell on my head and I lost my memories? What would you do? And seriously, I still can't get over how you don't eat bacon. What kind of weirdo are you? If the world had no more bacon, I'll die.

P.P.P.P.P.P.S. I swear, this is the last PS. Why do I always end the letter early? Ugh. What do you want for your promotion? I want to get you a little something. Emphasize little because I can't hide an elephant in a library... Well, I can't hide an elephant, period. See, this is why I should write our letters with pencil, then you won't have to be subjected to this. Here's a four-leaf clover I found in Central Park earlier this week. Sending good vibes your way.

I bust out in laughter, imaging a mischievous voice teasing me, then snickering at her own ridiculousness. Her clue was tailored to me. She knows I love poetry and chose a book that was famous. *Leaves of Grass* by Walt Whitman. A classic.

I don't think she's trying to stump me anymore. The books or films are code—a new love language—perhaps a combination of words of affirmation and gift giving. Lana will be so proud of me for paying attention to her prattling on about the genius of the book.

I reread her ending question. What do I want for my promotion?

I don't need anything—I'm an Anderson; I have the world at my fingertips.

But I do want one thing only she can give.

I want her.

CHAPTER 11

PAST: TWO YEARS BEFORE THE ACCIDENT—EIGHTEEN YEARS OLD

MY PHONE VIBRATES ON the locker room bench inside the IPA. Taylor grabs it before I can stop her and looks at the screen. Her expressive brows arch toward her hairline.

"Who's Delaney? And why is he talking about some gift and—Hey, I was reading!"

I snatch the phone away from her, my blood thrumming. "None of your business, Lil' Tay."

"Dude, I just turned fifteen. Stop calling me little. I'm taller than you." Taylor crosses her arms over her leotard. "What are you hiding there, and why do you look like you've swallowed a whole bucket of red crayons?"

My face flames and I glance away, fighting the urge to look at his text.

We don't text a lot—Keeper and I—we're traipsing on a high wire a hundred stories up from the ground and a slight tilt of our bodies will send us plummeting.

Into something more. Do I want something more?

The warmth spreads to my extremities, and suddenly, the tank top I have on feels too constricting.

Yes, I do.

"Sheesh, you should look at yourself. I've never seen you look this way...not even with Dayton." Taylor prances over and tries to grab my phone again.

"Oh my God, stop it!" I squeal, darting away. "And to answer your question, Delaney is a classmate from Broadbent. He's just helping me move things for college in a few weeks. We're coordinating schedules."

The lies pour out of me. It's silly, falling for your pen pal. If Taylor were the one telling me this, I'd warn her—be careful of strangers. There are a lot of weirdos out there.

"Hm. Not buying it. Unless you want to climb him as payment for his moving services?" A blush creeps up her face. Taylor is a virgin, but she's very curious.

Little does she know, I'm not experienced on that front either.

"You go get some on your own when you're old enough. Stop trying to live vicariously through me."

"I'll wait for my prince before I do it. My very own Prince Siegfried to my Odette." She lets out a dreamy sigh, clearly thinking about the white swan and her prince in the famous ballet, *Swan Lake*.

I look at the clock and tsk. "Don't you have practice now?"

"Ah crap!" She darts toward the door and hollers back, "Don't think you're off the hook, Alexis!" I chuckle as she disappears from view.

Blowing out a breath, I sit down and unlock my phone. Sure enough, a text from him awaits me.

Delaney

> I've decided on a gift. And I have a confession to make.

I frown, my fingers flying over the keypad.

Alex

> You're a sixty-year-old creep and you've been catfishing me all along?

Delaney

> Catfishing usually involves photos. We haven't exchanged any.

A knot appears in my chest. *No way, right?* I shake my head. No way, Delaney is definitely who he is. I know it in my gut.

A few seconds later, he puts me out of my misery.

A pulse batters against my throat and the flush from earlier is definitely back, because the room just got ten degrees hotter.

An array of emotions charges through me, the first and loudest being happiness, the tingling in my chest spreading to my hands and fingertips, and I want to squeal.

He wants to meet me. To date me. He likes me.

It's not only one-sided.

I swallow, my fingers hovering over the keypad, wondering how I should reply. Can't be too desperate, but dammit, I've always been honest with him, so why lie now?

But then, the doubts sweep in. I think about Mom and how she's halfway around the world, not a single call or message to me. Then there's the sad dip of Grandma's head when I mentioned UNYC. Dayton's pitying glance before we broke up when he said he had to carry the weight of being at Columbia by himself. Charles and Liam's sympathetic hugs and pats on the head, telling me everything's all right because they'll always support me. Then they all disappeared back into their lives.

I'm invisible once more.

The more I stare at Delaney's text, the more the uncertainties build—a pressure cooker gathering steam. He just got promoted and is moving up in the world. He has found his footing and direction. He is adulting. What would he want with an average, almost nineteen-year-old who is floundering?

Why would he want you when your family often forgets you?

The thought douses the embers inside me.

Shoulders slumped, I answer him.

Alex

> Why ruin a good thing by meeting? Aren't you worried you'll be disappointed?

Delaney

> How can I be disappointed when you're you? Are you scared? I can share my info with your friends and let them track my phone if you're concerned. We can meet somewhere in public.

He's so damn thoughtful. I find myself wavering.

Alex

> I *am* scared. But not for the reasons you think. We're in different places in life and I want to be more sure of myself before I see you.

I gnaw on my lip and add more. I want him to *stay* in my life.

Alex

> And I *do* want to see you. If I had everything together, I'd say yes, no questions asked. I just don't want to screw it up with you. You mean too much to me.

Delaney

> You won't. Trust me, Alex. You won't disappoint me. Take a leap of faith. Didn't you used to tell me, don't wait to live because the clock keeps

My breath hitches as tears gather in my eyes. My fears. My mottos. He remembers them. I really want to meet him, but I desperately don't want to disappoint him.

An idea occurs to me and my fingers fly across the keys.

A minute passes by. I see three dots appearing, then disappearing. Finally, he replies.

I grin.

I stare at his text and bite my lip. The answer is obvious.

Alex

> Well, if we run into each other, then it's meant to be. And who am I to argue against fate?

CHAPTER 12

PRESENT: EIGHT YEARS AFTER THE ACCIDENT—TWENTY-EIGHT YEARS OLD

SWEAT DRIPS OFF MY forehead, my lungs heaving in loud gasps of air as I stare at my enemy in front of me.

The box. The crate. The one foot tall *monster*.

Art and I just finished our therapy session for today, where I failed at the box jump yet again. I'm supposed to relax and let my muscles rest before the grueling afternoon sessions I'm dreading.

Cognitive games, memory cards and drills, looking at photos and describing the things I see or remember, virtual reality therapy—all exercises for my mind.

It's been months and months of it, but I've made no progress in recovering the memories lost between the ages of sixteen and twenty. Instead, I only have those random flashes of screams and rushing water. Then there's the blistering headaches, gut-wrenching fear, and near panic attacks whenever I try too hard.

It's like my mind is trying to tell me to stay away.

The last two water therapy lessons have also been a disaster. I couldn't get into the pool. I'd throw up before my toes touched the water. Art has canceled those sessions for now. They're doing more harm than good.

But I'm Alexis Vaughn. I may be handicapped, twenty-eight-years-old with no college degree, and no job prospects, but dammit, I'm not a coward.

I won't run away from the past.

My eyes dart to the door and I listen for any footsteps. I'm not supposed to be exercising on my own—someone is always supposed to monitor me.

To catch me if I fall.

It seems like I've been surrounded by people who want to catch me when I ultimately fall my whole life.

Gritting my teeth, I glare at the crate in front of me.

I'm not fucking helpless. Teenage Lexy may have been helpless, but adult Lexy isn't. The familiar lava surges up my chest. The world may have moved on without me, but I'm going to do my damned best to catch up.

Starting with this damn box jump.

The burst of anger propels me to run toward the crate at a breakneck speed, ignoring my uneven gait.

I swing my arms back for leverage and momentum.

My feet lift off the carpet.

Land, Lexy. Land on that damn crate.

My breath freezes mid-inhale as I watch my feet rise and rise, almost clearing the height of the crate.

But I fall short.

My right toe stubs against the edge and I know I'm screwed. My body pitches backward, my arms flailing as a cry rips from my lips.

Squeezing my eyes shut, I brace for the floor.

But it never comes.

Instead, a wall of heat sears me from behind, followed by muscular arms wrapping around my waist.

A burst of leather and amber hits my nose.

"Easy there."

That deep, raspy voice. Two simple words. The masculine scent. They're familiar. A shiver rolls down my spine.

Slowly, he sets me on the ground, the sinuous graze of my backside along his front lighting my nerves on fire.

"You need to take care of yourself better. Think about the people who love you." There's a hard edge to that voice now and I turn around, finding myself staring at the handsome face of Ethan Anderson.

A sharp pain stabs my head and I wince—I don't understand why I react this way to him...this cold, intense...stranger.

His slate-gray eyes flash and his brows pinch into a severe frown. "You hurt yourself, didn't you?"

The molten lava, which has subsided momentarily, comes rushing back—indignation straightening my back.

Narrowing my eyes, I fling him off me and back away. "What's it to you? I don't know you that well, so save me a lecture."

He flinches, a flash of pain appearing in those stormy gray eyes.

But it's gone as quick as it appeared. A mirage.

Ethan stalks toward me, his tall frame poured into an expertly tailored deep navy suit, crisp white shirt, and a burgundy tie. His dark hair is carefully tousled, not a strand out of place, and an enticing five-o'clock shadow peppers his jawline.

My pulse ratchets up as I stumble backward. Involuntarily. A prey in the presence of a predator. He looks every inch the brooding, cold numbers king I've heard so much about.

An Anderson, from one of the richest families in the country.

How is this guy, who looks like he eats interns for breakfast and prides himself with his impeccable control, best friends with my sleeve of tattoos, leather jacket wearing, motorcycle riding rebel of a brother?

The backs of my shoes hit an exercise bench and I waver.

"You need to watch where you're going, Alexis. You're recovering. Can't you take better care of yourself for the sake of everyone around you?"

The anger in his voice is baffling, and a pinch of guilt eats away in my gut. I know he's right. What if I get hurt and undo months of progress?

What if I slip into a coma again?

The familiar tendrils of fear strangle my throat. It keeps me up at night—not knowing what happened in the past and whether I'll slip into a state of nothingness again.

But I don't appreciate his attitude.

"Ethan. Just because you're my brother's best friend, doesn't make you my brother, okay? Your point is noted and I'll be more careful in the future, but don't you dare raise your voice at me like I'm someone you can boss around. And seriously, what happened to you? Can't ask nicely and have to command people all the time?"

He stops in his tracks, his icy eyes flaring with something I don't recognize. "What happened to me?" he rasps. "What happened—" He halts himself, his eyes wild and nostrils flaring.

This man has issues.

I stomp toward him until I'm a foot away.

"I may have gotten nowhere in my life and you may be a hotshot CFO, but that means nothing to me. I *will* get my life back and I won't have you or anyone around me babysitting me because I'm not fucking fragile, okay?"

My chest heaves, my face on fire, and I want to curl into a ball to cry or run my fist through a punching bag.

Ethan is eerily quiet as he stares at me. His intense gaze misses nothing as he scans my face, like he can read every convoluted thought flashing through my mind.

Another urge slams into me—the need to flee, to hide so he can't see how desperate and useless I'm feeling.

Wordlessly, he steps forward, his steps measured. But this time, I don't sense fire and brimstone behind his eyes. They're soft and gentle and my heart flips and a swooping sensation appears in my gut. It has to be guilt. After all, he did nothing to deserve my irrational bursts of anger.

"Look, I...I'm sorry—"

"It's nice to see the color on your face again," he murmurs, stopping a hairsbreadth away.

I crane my neck to look at him, watching as his eyes darken and his lips part for his next words.

"I thought I'd never see it again. The flush." His low voice is gravelly and intimate, each syllable feeling like a caress on my body. My core clenches. "It's beautiful."

His cryptic words barely register. My lips part, my nerves aflame, and I'm hit with an urge to throw myself at him.

What's wrong with me?

"I shouldn't have overstepped. I'm sorry. It's been hard and I don't know how to tell you...I...I...can't..." The muscles in his neck work and I watch, riveted at the flush creeping above the collar of his crisp shirt and knotted tie. "Do you know how much the people who cared about you missed you when you were asleep?"

My eyes bounce back to his, and his ever-changing orbs are now blazing with fire, singeing me with their heat.

"You need to take care of yourself because if anything happens to you again, those people would be heartbroken. I don't think they'd survive it." Ethan's nostrils flares, his low, rumbly words sending a frisson of pain spearing into my heart.

My hand flies to my chest, gripping my T-shirt and his eyes snare on the movement.

His lips part, his attention riveted on my hand, which fails to rub away the soreness behind my rib cage. His pulse batters against his temple.

He lifts his index finger toward the bridge of my nose, and my breath stills. My nerves come to life.

"Liam and Charles. They must've been devastated," I whisper.

His gaze snaps back up, and he drops his hand, fisting it before sliding it in his pants pocket. This strange moment of intensity suddenly disappears, a mask of indifference falling over his face.

He steps back and I drag in a deep breath of oxygen.

His silhouette splits, then merges. My vision slowly clears.

"Of course I'm talking about Liam and Charles. They never gave up on you."

"Right." Except it doesn't feel right. There are holes in the puzzle and I'm missing crucial pieces.

"Alexis, I...I—"

The ache reappears inside my chest as I watch him struggle with his words.

What? Alexis, what?

"Everything okay?" Liam's voice appears from the door. His head cocks to the side as his eyes bounce between the two of us.

Ethan swallows and curves his lips into a half-grin, and my heart flips. The man is too handsome for his own good. He takes a few more steps backward and turns to Liam. "Your sister was trying to do a box jump on her own and nearly broke her neck."

"You fucker!" I hiss, my goodwill vanishing like an apparition.

I'm reminded of why I don't like this man. Something about him unsettles me, and now he's a backstabber on top of everything.

Liam growls and stalks toward me, his leather boots clomping on the floor. The last eight years have been kind to him—he's filled out his black T-shirts and leather jackets, his tattoos on his arms and neck have multiplied but just add an element of danger. But deep down, he's still my doting older brother. More pain in the ass and ridiculously overprotective now, but I can't blame him. It must've been hard for him to see me in a coma.

"Lexy, what did I tell you last time? Don't rush this and don't make me sic a bodyguard on you."

"You wouldn't dare!"

"I definitely would, and Charles would agree with me. If you insist on endangering yourself, I don't give a shit what your opinions are." He swallows, a haunted hollowness appearing in his blue eyes. "We can't lose you again. We've lost too damn much already."

My eyes prickle and I know he's thinking about Grandma and Uncle Ian again. They had to grieve the deaths of Grandma and Uncle Ian alone. I was told Grandma had passed away in her sleep and Uncle Ian had died from a car accident.

I wasn't there for them. I couldn't wrap them in a hug and give them a shoulder to cry on. Taylor also told me Liam and Charles had a rift for most of the eight years and didn't reconnect until this past year.

"Liam." A sob chokes my throat and I throw my arms around Liam. "I'm sorry. I promise you, I'll take care of myself better. I was being stupid and impatient."

Pulling back, I continue, "I just want to live again. Not only recover, but to move forward. And I want to remember what happened before the accident."

"Does it matter, Lexy? What happened? It's all behind us, right? Maybe it's better you don't know." Liam swallows, his eyes shifting away from me and a muscle pulses in his jaw.

My eyes narrow.

"There's something you aren't telling me, isn't there? Tay wouldn't tell me when I asked her about the past either. Charles would always change the subject."

"Of course not, you're overthinking." Liam drags his gaze back to me, his smile as fake as a spray tan in the middle of winter.

I squint, not buying it, but I'll let him off the hook for now. I'm supposed to let the memories come back to me and not ask about my past.

It's so damn tiring.

Yawning, I rub my eyes and grumble, "Fine. Whatever. I should probably rest before the brain doctors pick apart my mind again. A fun few hours of memory games and testing await me. It's exhausting and mentally draining."

A headache forms at the base of my neck and I wince before closing my eyes.

"Maybe Liam's right," Ethan murmurs. "Maybe trying to recover the past is hurting you." He releases a ragged exhale. "Maybe...maybe you need to stop trying."

Something in his voice—an anguished rawness—causes my eyes to snap open. His gaze is shuttered, a muscle twitching at his temple, his jaw clenched. His fingers are gripping, releasing, and tugging at his cuff links—aged silver and black ones which look incongruous with the rest of his expensive outfit.

"See? Ethan agrees with me. He's an outsider, so he can look at this objectively." Liam pats my shoulder. "Anyway, we were headed out to lunch nearby and wanted to drop in to see how you were doing."

A smile twitches on my lips as I see his mischievous grin. "Nice to see you haven't forgotten me. And you suck."

Liam winks before heading back out the door, with Ethan trailing him. "Dels, hurry up. Didn't you used to say time is money?"

Dels. Goosebumps form on my skin. The nickname sounds familiar, even though I could've sworn I've never heard it before.

Ethan turns around at the threshold. "Take care, Alexis." He takes a few steps, then pauses, his back facing me. "Don't worry about us forgetting you."

His hand clenches at his side, and the next words he says are uttered on an exhale so low, I almost don't hear him.

"You're unforgettable."

CHAPTER 13

PAST: ONE YEAR BEFORE THE ACCIDENT—NINETEEN YEARS OLD

THE RAIN CRASHES ONTO the hummingbird window in an apocalyptic deluge. Hurricane Ana, one of the biggest storms in the last ten years, graces us with her presence. The vintage lamps in Ravenswood flicker as the roar of thunder shakes the windows.

Hurried footsteps and sounds of bags zipping shut echo around me. The patrons on the rare books floor rush to pack up and head out before the worst of the storm locks down the city.

I swallow the ball in my throat and look at our texts from three days ago again.

Delaney

> Saturday, four p.m. Ravenswood.

Alex

> ???

Delaney

> You're looking at the newest finance manager of a Fortune 500 company.

Alex

> OMG, really? It's only been ten months! That's got to be a record.

My boss got promoted and his position opened up. He put me up for it. Of course it doesn't hurt I'm doing well.

Does this mean you'll follow through? Meet me in person?

I remember staring at the message for ten minutes before I replied.

A deal's a deal. Yes. I'll be there.

No more secrets. No more fake names. I want to tell you everything.

The last three days, I've been buried by coursework at UNYC. The finance courses are kicking my ass, but I'm loving my marketing classes. Things click when I read about the 4Ps—products, price, place, and promotion.

Unlike ballet—where the gap between my performance and goals keeps widening—I'm acing my marketing courses. My professors have even pulled me aside to ask if I see a future in the field.

For the first time in my life, I see a clear direction of where I'm going.

I was right.

Being in college has given me perspective and the confidence to know I'll be fine after graduating.

And it's time to meet Delaney, the keeper of my dreams, in person.

I'm breathless with excitement.

Our texts and journal entries have grown more intimate. Love poems from him—a card tucked in between the journal pages inscribed with "How Do I Love Thee" by Elizabeth Barret Browning, or "Bright Star" by John Keats, or ones he penned himself.

We write about the future—tackling our bucket list together—because he wants to be there for every milestone. He even has a few things of his own to add to our list.

I send him pressed flowers I've plucked from campus—vibrant pansies, the deep purple, the color of the fading sunset, or fiery mums a shade darker than my hair.

Our first texts in the morning and the last texts before we go to bed will be to each other. We've decided not to video chat or call, wanting to leave the big reveal for when we meet in person. As I used to say, anticipation is part of the pleasure.

But nonetheless, we're in a relationship, there's no doubt about it. Maybe it's not official, but it's more intimate than anything I've ever had.

My phone buzzes.

Taylor

> I really think you're hiding something. It has to be a man, right?

Taylor

> But whoever he is, I'm glad he's putting a smile on your face.

I grin. My pseudo little sister has grown up—a ball of sweet and snarky energy—and becoming a close friend.

Sadly, Summer and I have grown apart. Our calls and texts are becoming fewer and far between. I guess that's what happens when friends move out of state and begin lives of their own.

Out of sight, out of mind.

I blow out a heavy breath, a weight settling on my chest.

But Keeper has never even seen you, and he hasn't forgotten about you.

Butterflies swarm inside my gut, and I get up and walk to the hummingbird window. Peering outside, I see vague shapes of trees whipping against the wind. The rain fogs up the glass and I can barely make out the courtyard far below.

It's a shit show out there.

Will he come? Is he on his way? Or will he decide it's too much effort for a stranger?

Deep down, the little girl who once stood alone at her ballet showcase, used to being forgotten, whispers, *I hope he won't be disappointed when he meets me.*

Silly. You're unforgettable, Lexy.

Squaring my shoulders, I stroll to the back bookshelves where the poetry section is. Lightning splinters through the windows, blinding the room in a flash of violence, the bellow of thunder soon to follow.

Then it's silent. So quiet, I can hear a pin drop.

Goosebumps pebble my skin as I look at the aged leather tomes. Dickenson. Keats. Shakespeare. Love letters and stories from centuries past all shelved in orderly rows. I know why Delaney asked me to meet him here for the first time.

This is where our story began.

Suddenly, a loud crack rattles the space, and the room plunges into darkness. I gasp and a few shrieks echo far away.

We've lost power. Dammit.

Pulling out my phone, I get ready to text him to reschedule because this storm looks like it's about to take a turn for the worse, when I notice no bars on the screen.

Double crap. Cell phone towers must've been impacted too.

Disappointment cresting inside me, I lean against the nearest bookshelf and close my eyes. There's no sense in keeping them open, since I can barely see anything in the darkness.

I believe in fate. Serendipity. If we were meant to meet, then we will. With everything raging on outside, I can't help but think...maybe this is a sign.

But a few minutes later, there's a shift in the air. A presence I can sense without opening my eyes. I feel someone's gaze burning into my skin.

Him.

CHAPTER 14

MY PULSE PUMMELS MY ears, eclipsing the roar of the rain battering the windows with renewed vigor. My breathing grows thready, and every atom inside me vibrates to attention.

Open your eyes, Lexy. Smile. Say hi.

Should I hug him? Should I shake his hand? What's the protocol of meeting your pen pal boyfriend for the first time?

My palms grow sweaty and I rake in a few more unsteady breaths. Quiet but steady footsteps head toward me. They sound strong. Confident.

They sound hot, if footsteps can sound hot.

A whiff of masculine fragrance sifts to my nostrils. I inhale, letting the scent wash through me. I recognize this fragrance from somewhere. Leather. Amber. A tinge of the rain and outdoors.

"Nova?" A low rasp. Seduction in one word. "Dreamer?"

He came. Despite the violent storm, he still came. Warmth spreads from my rib cage to the rest of my body and I smile. I'll remember this moment forever.

My muscles finally obey my mind, and I open my eyes.

The emergency light blinking from far away illuminates him. Just barely. Brief flickers of yellow light. On and off. On and off.

A beacon in the dark.

Shining on him—my north star.

Delaney's face is bathed in shadows, but those piercing eyes, that sharp jawline, that thick, wavy hair.

I gasp. I recognize him.

He's Ares, the god of war, the guy I've bumped into twice here in Ravenswood before. The first time over a year ago, when he picked up my books after I dropped them outside the library, the second time in the basement DVD section when I was tempted to break the rules and search for Keeper.

It's been him all along. The guy who's made me feel *something* in our two fleeting encounters is the man who's stolen my heart with his words and kindness.

"Delaney?" I finally find my voice.

His eyes darken, and a breathtaking smile lights up his face. An enticing dimple winks at me. "It's you. I knew I'd recognize you."

He steps closer, shrinking our distance by the second, and my heart careens, like the slow clanking ascent of a rollercoaster before the free fall.

We stare at each other, our chests heaving—the moment distilling into snapshots, fragments I'm sure I'll never forget. Him standing there, tall, his dark hair slightly damp. His muscles strain against the dark T-shirt and leather jacket he has on.

His glittering eyes hold mine and I'm speechless, but I feel like I can hear his words all the same. After a few seconds of the quiet tension, Delaney finally opens his mouth, his raspy voice holding me captive.

"I knew you'd be beautiful."

With that statement, he wraps his large hand around my wrist, tugs me against him, and crushes his lips to mine.

My world explodes into a kaleidoscope of colors, the pleasure shooting straight from my lips to the rest of my body. It feels right...so right, like I was born to kiss him.

Delaney deepens the kiss. His lips move from gentle caresses into drugging pulls, his hand traveling up to my nape to angle my head so he can delve in harder.

Invading, he conquers my nonexistent defenses.

A groan rumbles from his throat when I melt against him, plastering my curves against his hard muscles. His free hand coils around my waist before he pushes my body flat against the shelves.

"Fuck," he whispers when we part for air, but before I can respond, he dives back in, his arms caging me as he ravages me.

I moan, the sound needy, but I don't care. My head arches back, digging into the tomes of love stories, as he slides his tongue into my mouth and tastes me like I'm his salvation, like he's been waiting for this moment his entire life.

My fingers dig into his muscular back, my nails no doubt causing pain, but that only seems to inflame him more. He slides his thigh between my legs and presses up so his muscles rub against my core.

"Sweet. You taste so sweet, just like I knew you'd be," he rasps, his lips traveling to my cheeks, kissing, sucking, whispering poetry to my skin. "Do you know how long I've waited for this kiss, Nova? How many nights I've lain awake in bed, wanting to hold you in my arms, but I can't?"

"Me too," I whisper, my eyes meeting his in the dark, only seeing the glint in what I know are the most beautiful charcoal eyes.

His breathing is ragged as he pulls back slightly, like he wants to take me in, to memorize every inch of me.

A faint smile curves on his lips and he whispers, "Nova. Because you're a supernova. Rare. Beautiful. Unforgettable."

My breath hitches. *Unforgettable.* I want to bask in his attentions forever.

He drags a fingertip down the bridge of my nose, featherlight, leaving a trail of warmth behind.

It's love and reverence encapsulated in a small caress.

Leaning in, he holds me tightly in his arms. I feel his fluttering heartbeats beating against his thin shirt and the unmistakable hardness resting against my stomach.

Knowing he's turned on has me clenching my legs, the motion he feels because his thigh is still sandwiched between mine.

Delaney's breath quickens, and the tension thickens in the small sliver of space between us. My skin is so sensitive, I can practically feel the individual fibers of the cotton shirt I have on. My breasts are heavy...swollen, and he hasn't even touched me there.

I light up in his presence.

"Before I fall asleep at night, I think of you. I imagine you next to me." He punctuates his words with a soft kiss on my forehead. "But I don't know what you look like." A kiss on my cheek. "I don't know the color of your eyes, the smell of your hair, the softness of your skin. It's been driving me out of my mind." He swipes his tongue on my earlobe. I whimper, and wetness seeps out between my legs.

I'm dying from his gentle touches and words.

"But I knew you'd be beautiful. And I don't just mean physically, though you're the most gorgeous person I've seen. I mean here." He presses his hand over my frantic heart. "Because I'd already fallen for what was inside you."

Delaney cups my face, which I realize is wet with tears. His thumbs gently swipe the moisture away. I've never had anyone treat me this way before—holding me like I'm precious, priceless, like I'm everything he needs in the world.

He rasps, "The last year and a half was torture. And I'd live through it again and again, if it meant I get to be trapped in this storm with you."

My poet. My keeper.

"Delaney."

I touch his face, the dim light guiding me, feeling the fullness of his brows, the crinkle at the edge of his eyes, the tall and straight nose, the perfect full lips, and the small divot on his chin.

"And to finally answer your question," he rasps, "if a rock smacked you on the head and you lost your memories, I'd do everything in my power to make you remember. Even if that meant recreating our love story, reminding you with every touch, every word. Because there'd be no way I'd let you slip away. No way."

When I asked the what-if question back then, it was meant as a joke. To bring a smile to his face when he was stressed at work. But now, it's so much more.

It feels like a vow.

I swallow and whisper, "That answer is definitely worth waiting for."

He grins and cups my cheek.

Before I met him, I thought he'd be disappointed when he saw me. Maybe he'd think the idea of me was unforgettable, but the reality fell short.

I was stupid. Ridiculous.

Nothing had ever felt so right than here in his embrace.

A snap and crackle later, light floods the room as the hum of the generator joins the sounds of our heavy breathing. I wince, adjusting to the sudden brightness as we take in each other clearly for the first time.

I feel shy under his intense perusal. His eyes hungrily rove over my face and he lifts a lock of my hair to his nose and inhales.

"Now I know how your hair smells like. Lavender, just like our journal." He smiles. "I remember you from before... You were breaking the rules that day with *The Notebook*, weren't you?"

I duck my head, my face flaming. But my heart flutters with joy.

He remembers me too.

He tsks under his breath and tilts my chin up so our eyes meet again. "Desperate to meet me, weren't you?" He winks, and my breath stumbles all over itself again.

I find my voice a second later and arch my brow. "You know, that's not the first time we met."

His eyes flare before recognition flickers in them. "Outside the library. You were the girl with the finance textbook. The one I couldn't take my eyes off."

Unable to help myself, I rise to my tiptoes and peck him on his cheek to reward him for his excellent memory.

"Bingo," I whisper.

"I guess it's always been fated—us meeting." Delaney twines his fingers with mine, the gentle touch reawakening my nerves and my skin heats.

Shifting, he pulls out a small box from his pocket and hands it to me.

"I took a risk—I don't know if you even wear earrings, but I saw these the other day and—"

I gasp as I dangle a pair of delicate hummingbird earrings in the air. The artist's light strokes for the wings, the brilliant red chest—they're obviously handcrafted, no brand name to be seen.

They're perfect.

"I love them." I put them on, and my eyes mist with tears. "They're absolutely perfect, Delaney."

"I'm so glad." He presses a kiss on my forehead. Then, I feel a tension stiffening his muscles.

"I want to tell you something," he begins, and a flicker of uncertainty flashes in his eyes. "Delaney is my middle name. My first name is actually—"

His phone rings, the ring tone shrill on the quiet floor.

"Sorry." Quickly, he pulls out his phone, glances at the screen and frowns. His eyes flicker up to mine. "I think it's an emergency. Do you mind?"

I shake my head, my brows furrowing. I hope everything is okay.

Then my phone buzzes. I guess I got cell reception back too.

Delaney steps to the end of the aisle, his low voice in what appears to be an important conversation.

I glance at my phone, finding a dozen unread messages littering the screen.

Liam

> Firefly, I tried calling you. Why haven't you turned on your phone?

Liam

> Are you stuck in the storm? Damn it. I see your location. I'll come get you.

Liam

> Grandma fell down the stairs. She's being air-
> lifted to Manhattan Memorial now. They have
> better facilities than the Hamptons.

Liam

> You know what? You're at Ravenswood, and
> Ethan is heading there to run an errand. I'll just
> have him pick you up. I'll give him your number.

Liam

> Call me when you get this. Stay safe.

A cold front knots my insides. *Is Grandma okay?* A fall at her age can be dangerous.

She's a Vaughn. I breathe in, trying to stem the rising panic. We have money. We have the best resources. She'll be fine. She has to be.

Delaney clears his throat and I see he's done with his call. He rakes his fingers through his hair, frustration rolling from him in waves. "Nova, can we meet again tomorrow? There's an emergency I need to take care of. May I have your phone?"

He walks to me and lays out his palm. I hand my cell to him and he inputs his number and calls himself.

"Let me drop you off and I'll call you tonight and explain everything?"

Wordlessly, I nod. "Is everything okay?"

"I hope so. I'm worried, but my best friend needs me right now. He has a family emergency."

The hairs rise on the back of my neck, and an unsettling weight settles in my gut. Bad news back to back and a crazy storm outside. What on earth is happening?

"I need to make another quick call, okay?"

"Sure. Do what you need to do. We have all the time in the world." I reach out and squeeze his forearm.

He pauses his dialing, the furrow between his brows disappearing as he clasps his larger hand on top of mine. Then, he grazes his finger on my nose again. Those beautiful lips slowly curve up in a grin.

My heart skips several beats.

"Thanks," he whispers. "Despite what just happened, today is the happiest day of my life."

I beam and watch his smile widen, his eyes crinkling at the corners. "Me too. Go. Do your thing."

He nods and dials his number before lifting his phone to his ear. He twines his hand with mine.

A few seconds later, my phone buzzes again.

Frowning, I answer the call. "Hello?"

Delaney freezes, his shoulders rigid. He whips his head toward me, eyes widening in what looks to be alarm.

"May I speak to Alexis Vaughn please?" I hear his voice through my phone.

It doesn't make sense.

He's right in front of me and taking care of an emergency for his best friend.

Emergency for his best friend.

The gears shift into place, and I see the exact moment when he reaches the same conclusion.

Slowly, he ends the call. I hear the click on my end and do the same.

"Liam Vaughn is your brother?" he asks, his face paling.

My pulse riots in my ears. "You're Ethan? His best friend?"

Delaney—no, Ethan—nods.

He swallows, steps back, and lets go of my hand.

CHAPTER 15

PAST: ONE YEAR BEFORE THE ACCIDENT—TWENTY-THREE YEARS OLD

WHEN I FIRST DROVE to Ravenswood Library in the middle of a hurricane, the rain felt like a dawn of a new era, washing away the grime from the past—Anderson men and their bad luck with love, my uncertainties about my place in the family, my fear of commitment. I was going to meet the girl who believed in me, who encouraged me, who made me laugh and liked me as the nobody Delaney, the Keeper.

I wanted to touch her and kiss her and listen to her often random and whimsical thoughts as they popped up in her mind. I was tempted—so very tempted—to dive in headfirst and experience why Dad still has a smile on his face whenever we talk about Mom, even if the smile is tinged with sadness.

My Nova, my dreamer, made me brave.

When my lips touched hers, a shot of adrenaline jabbed straight into my heart. Every inch of me thrummed with awareness.

One taste and I was addicted.

But now, I feel like I've been punched in the gut.

She's *the* Alexis. Liam's sister. The one woman I'm never supposed to look at, not to even mention touch. It's a vow I made—and we Andersons are men of our word. You can blame that on our British aristocratic ancestors for passing the honor gene down to us.

I still remember vividly the day Liam warned me off his sister—a seemingly innocuous car ride toward the lake house our friend owned during our junior year at Columbia.

"You're my best friend, but seriously, you have issues. I'm sorry for any girl who dates you, jackass." Liam had shoved a few Cheetos into his mouth.

I snickered as I maneuvered my car toward the exit on the freeway. "They knew what they signed up for. We can have fun, but I'll never give them my heart."

He whistled. "If I were Cleo's older brother, and I heard you say this, I'd punch you in the face and dismember you a tiny piece at a time. Thank God you're my friend and my sister is out of bounds."

"Who said so?"

"You better not, dipshit. Or else I'd kill you. Lexy is the most important person to me and deserves far better than you. She's better than both of us combined." He glared at me, his jaw tightening.

Liam Vaughn, my evil twin, the guy who said rules were made to be broken, was never serious, but he sure was then. "There's no way on earth I'd introduce you to Firefly."

"Fuck. Chill. You have nothing to worry about from me. I won't do anything to jeopardize our friendship. I owe you one."

"You sure do. You're lucky I got that misdemeanor off on a technicality. Fucking hazing rituals. Imagine the headlines, 'Anderson family's fourth son arrested for theft of the famous school mascot, while running stark naked across campus.' You'd be a pariah."

I rolled my eyes but remained silent. He was right. College fraternity hazing or not, I should've drawn the line at breaking the law, but the lure of having an identity in a family, in a fraternity, was too hard to resist for the eighteen-year-old me.

Liam sighed. "But seriously, you're always keeping everyone at arm's length. Aren't you afraid of growing old and dying alone, dipshit?"

"No. I have you, asshole. Like any girl would want you."

He then chucked a Cheeto at my face. "God, why do I put up with you?"

Another flash of lightning splits across the skies, the thick clouds hanging low, smothering us in its wrath. I yank my collar, struggling to breathe and trying, but failing to ignore the redheaded vixen sitting quietly next to me.

Too quiet. Alex is never quiet. We haven't spoken until today, but her vibrant personality blazes through every letter and text. She's the life of the party, the girl who moves with the wind.

Passionate. Untamed. Impossible to ignore.

The windshield wipers swipe aggressively at the rain, but it's no use—the world is one blurry mess of grayscale, red taillights from other cars winking in front of me, forcing me to drive at the pace of a snail.

"It doesn't matter Liam's my brother, right?" She finally speaks, softly.

I sneak another glance at her, finding her eyes pinned on the road, but her hands are twisting the hem of her blouse. Twisting, releasing, and knotting it again.

My fingertips prickle, the neurons misfiring. I'm floored by my impulse to reach over and hold her hand, knowing how soft and warm she feels against me.

How right it is to have her hand in mine.

"Your brother is the most important person to me outside of my family and—" I stop myself, but I hear her breath hitch and I know she understands what I can't say.

Outside of you.

"You see, Alexis—"

"I liked it better when you called me Nova."

Things were different when she was my Nova.

But she can't be. Not anymore.

I swallow, but the lump in my throat grows. "*Alexis*, I'm an Anderson. Part of a famous family of overachievers. You know how I felt—lost, trying to measure up, to feel like I deserve to be part of that family. I love them, there's no doubt about that. I'd die for them. But I always felt like the odd man out."

Maxwell and Ryland, being twins, were always attached at the hip. Rex and Lana, both extroverted, are the life of the party. They egg each other on and just seem to "get" each other. Then there's me, the quiet one.

After entering the underground parking structure at Manhattan Memorial, I park the car. "Liam and I met at orientation at Columbia. He was the devil-may-care punk who looked like he'd be working at a tattoo parlor than burying his head in books. He befriended the quiet rich kid who sat in the back corner. I'd avoided my classmates—most of them wanted to butter me up because of my family. To them, I was an Anderson. It didn't matter who Ethan was. I could be an asshole and they'd pretend I was their best friend."

Shaking my head, I think back to the forced smiles I gave as people stopped me in the commons, the hushed whispers I'd hear when I went back to my apartment on campus, hoping I'd be able to experience some sort of normal college student life, then, there was the crushing disappointment when yet again, I either felt like a bird on display at the zoo or someone faking it, pretending everything was okay.

"Liam didn't give a shit. He plopped down next to me and said I could use a joint because I looked like I had a stick shoved up my ass." I chuckle, thinking of my best friend's antics. "Then, after insulting me, he asked me to borrow a notepad and a pen because he forgot to bring anything. It was refreshing. He was honest and so damn loyal to me over the years. In some ways, he felt more like a brother to me than my own siblings."

I turn to her, finding her startling blue eyes intent on me. "He saved me on a few occasions, and I owe him one. Maybe you think it's stupid, but I promised him I'd never mess with his sister."

Raking my fingers through my hair, I continue, "My track record with women isn't good. You know that. I've told you in our letters. To be honest, until you, I'd never thought I'd want to commit to someone—not just sex, but emotions and all. I still don't know if I can do it or if I'll screw it up, because shit runs in my family when it comes to love."

My gaze trails down to her fingers, which are tugging at her shirt, plucking at a loose thread, unraveling it, pulling at it some more.

I let myself have this next moment and grab her hand, hearing her soft intake of breath and feeling electricity sizzling through me.

Induction—my Nova and me.

No. Not your Nova.

"I don't want to risk my friendship with him. I don't want to break my vow." I grip her hand tightly. "And...I don't want to ultimately hurt you."

The thickness in the air is stifling.

"Are you breaking up with me before we really start?" My heart clenches at the rawness in her voice. "Just because you're too afraid to tell my brother how you feel and too chicken to give *this*," she shakes our interlinked hands, "a try?"

I drag my gaze up to hers, finding her eyes now blazing with fury, her face flushed, nostrils flaring.

She's a warrior bracing for a battle.

Glorious. She's fucking glorious. She needs someone who can jump in headfirst, someone who knows how to have relationships and be in love. Not someone who still has his training wheels on.

Like me.

"I... Fuck. I can't answer you!"

Lexy pulls the latch and shoves the door open, a burst of cold air infiltrating the car. She gets out and spins around, her eyes fierce. "Well, I won't make the choice for you. I won't beg you either, because I'm *fucking* unforgettable, Ethan Anderson. When you get your head out of your ass, you can come find me!"

She slams the door and stalks away, leaving me sitting in the car in stark silence.

Fuck.

A few hours later, I lay on my bed, staring into the darkness, the cacophony of Hurricane Ana slamming against the windows keeping me company. My mind is a mess.

The shrill ringing of my phone interrupts my thoughts.

"Liam, how's your grandmother?"

"She's stable, thank God. Just a broken leg, but they're going to monitor her a bit. Thanks for bringing Lexy by. How's work? Did you get what you needed done at the library?" Cars honk in the background. He must be on the road.

"It's fine." It was an excuse anyway. There was no way I was going to tell him I was meeting a girl at the library. And thank God for that, because that girl turned out to be his sister.

"Just fine? I thought there was some shit going on at work?"

"Nah. Trey saved my ass again. I thought there was an inconsistency in my financials, but he double-checked and everything balanced." *And this is why I want to start from the bottom. I need the experience before I become a CFO.*

"By the way, I'm spending the night at the mansion to keep Lexy company. Charles had to fly out for a business trip."

"All right." Her wounded eyes appear in my vision again and my chest seizes.

Is she okay? Is she sad? Angry still? Does she miss me?

"Hey, did she tell you anything in the car? Even after we got the good news about Grandma, she still looked really upset. She told me it was because of an upcoming test for her finance class, but I'm not so sure."

I swallow, my mouth running dry. Keeping my voice light, I reply, "No. She didn't say anything. She was pretty quiet."

"Huh. That's not her. Maybe it is the finance class then. She always hated numbers. Never did well in these types of classes at Broadbent either."

"Finance and math are a different language, just like your coding and computer science. But once you figure it out, it's easy."

"Right." Liam mulls over that for a few seconds. "Hey, can you do me a solid?"

I frown, my muscles tensing from the tilt of his voice. I won't like what comes out of his mouth next.

"Tutor her for me. She's asked Charles, but he's slammed at work. I don't know finance or else I'd do it myself. But heck, even if I do, she'll never listen. We'll just fight the entire time. You're the up and coming financial genius. Help her—teach her that 'language,' will you?"

My heart throttles to life and I bolt up on my bed. See her with her brother's blessing? Be close to her? Maybe touch her? My mouth forms the word, "yes," when my conversation with her in the car floods in.

How the hell will I be able to stay away from her? Keep my distance? Keep my promise to Liam?

It'll be impossible.

"I'm not sure—"

"Serious, Dels. I've never seen her this focused before. Ever since she started college, she's got this drive—I can't explain it. But she's happy. She's talking about doing marketing in the future. This class is important to her. Please help me out. There's no one I trust more with my little sister than you. She'll have a bonus brother. She'll love it."

A bonus brother.

Trust.

He used to say I couldn't meet his sister because he didn't trust me enough, but now he does. And it's worse—it's a betrayal.

He'll kill me if he knows what my dreams late at night are. How I can't fall asleep until I've fucked my hand to the thought of his precious little sister.

"Dels?"

I release my breath, my heartbeat now blaring an emergency alarm inside my rib cage.

"Fine. I'll do it."

I'm so fucking screwed.

CHAPTER 16

PRESENT: NINE YEARS AFTER THE ACCIDENT—TWENTY-NINE YEARS OLD

"HAPPY BIRTHDAY, ALEXIS!" TAYLOR crushes me in her embrace as her siblings and my brothers clap after singing "Happy Birthday" in an off-key, chaotic way.

Everyone huddles inside my suite at the rehab center. The room is spacious for a hospital—large enough to fit a full-sized bed with silk sheets, two dressers, and a flatscreen TV with the fancy apps and insane picture quality, which still shocks me every time I turn on the TV. Technology has definitely improved in the last nine years.

Balloons decorate the room, along with bouquets of roses, peonies, daisies—I'm sure I could moonlight as a florist at this point.

I should be excited. Laughing and joking with everyone. I'm grateful for my family and friends. I'm thankful I have a second chance at life when others in my position typically don't.

I've even successfully gotten into the rehab pool the last three times. I still can't swim, but I can float on my stomach. It's a big milestone and I should celebrate it.

But a boulder sits atop my chest, and my lungs can't rake in a full breath. My smile remains plastered on my face, but my mind is chaotic—a compass failing to calibrate, its needle unable to find north.

I've been in the hospital for over a year. I'm almost thirty. I'm so behind in life.

I should be climbing the corporate ladder at Bank of Columbia or some other large corporation, financially independent, dating a wonderful man who's thinking about proposing to me at the end of a romantic candlelit dinner after I've demolished a molten chocolate lava cake for dessert. We should be planning what house to buy, when we're going to have two point five kids, and maybe get a dog or two.

I'm behind. *Behind. Behind. Behind.* My smile twitches and I blink, trying to refocus on the merry group before me.

"Twenty-nine, baby sis. One more year and you'll be ancient!"

Ancient. I'll be ancient.

Liam's smirk is promptly wiped away when Taylor elbows his ribs.

"Shut your trap before I shut it for you, Liam," Taylor growls. "Don't listen to him, Alexis. Thirties are the new twenties, so technically, you're still a teenager. And smokin' hot too."

"Charles, can you leash down your pit bull of a girlfriend?" Liam grumbles.

Rex, the flirt of the Anderson brood, whistles, his eyes widening. "I need a chair, and someone bring me popcorn. A Vaughn showdown. Can't miss this."

"The only thing that'll show down is when I kick your ass, Rex." Liam hurls an accusing glare at him. "Single bros are supposed to stick together!"

Charles grins and curls his arm around Taylor's waist. "Definitely not taming my minx. If she were to chew your head off, it'd be because you deserved it, Liam."

"Whipped. Abso-fuckin-lutely whipped. Charles Vaughn, I never thought I'd see the day." Steven Kingsley, the current chief operating officer of Fleur Entertainment and Taylor's brother-in-law, whacks his friend on the back. "God, how the mighty have fallen."

"What are you talking about? I've always wanted to settle down," Charles mutters.

"Yeah, but you swore to all of us you hated a certain ballerina's guts. What did you say? 'Feral cat?'"

Taylor whips her head toward my oldest brother. "You didn't!"

Charles flushes. "It's completely out of context." He shoots Steven a death glare. "Minx, that was before—"

"I'd quit before you dig yourself into an early grave." Maxwell, the eldest Anderson sibling, says from his spot in the armchair by the windows. His wife, Belle, perches on his lap, cuddling their infant son, Levi. The broodiest Anderson, aside from a certain Anderson who unnerves me, is wearing a smile of contentment as he kisses Belle's forehead.

The room erupts into more chaos when Grace links arms with her sister, Taylor, against Charles, who's trying to defuse the situation, while the rest of the Anderson gang is laughing and fanning the flames in the background.

Their voices merge into a thunderous roar in my ears and the room spins. I grip the bed rail, my arms shaking.

Calm down. This is a panic attack. Your therapist mentioned this might happen. It's normal. You're normal. You're improving at your own pace. Think about the present and not the future.

My breathing quickens and cold sweat beads on the back of my neck. I can't breathe. *Dammit. Breathe.*

I need to breathe—

"Quiet! Can't you tell she's not feeling well?" Ethan's sharp words slice through the excitement, plunging the room into silence. *How did he know I was panicking inside?*

Closing my eyes, I rake in a deep inhale, followed by a long exhale. Acid sloshes in my gut and I fight the urge to dry heave. *I'm fine. I'm okay. I'm tough as nails.*

"Sorry," I whisper. "Can you guys give me a minute?"

I keep my eyes closed, because if I open them, I'll find pity in their gazes, and I don't want anyone feeling sorry for me. *Dammit. Get a grip, Lexy.*

"Sure thing, we'll be back, okay?" Grace whispers.

"I'll go kill the idiots. They were too loud. It's their fault." Taylor squeezes my arm.

I nod, still unable to look at them, and I hear the scraping of chairs against the floor and the scuffling of footsteps followed by the soft click of the door.

My lungs expel a deep breath as my heart rate slows. Without everyone's scrutiny, I can finally breathe.

Opening my eyes, I look around the room, taking in all the beautiful gifts and cards, before opening the drawer on my nightstand. In it are clues to my past, things I've examined multiple times, wishing something would click, that somehow I'd recognize them. They were supposed to be birthday gifts Charles and Liam bought me over the years, and the things I had on me that day of the accident.

My wallet and IDs. A bracelet Taylor told me was a friendship bangle and she had its twin. A beautiful set of gold-tipped hummingbird earrings, so exquisitely made, my breath stalls in my throat whenever I look at it. Then there's a small wooden box with random trinkets inside—an antique Spanish gold coin, a small tin of ghost pepper spices, three pieces of glass shards, each a unique shade of red, blue, and green, a small bottle of what looks to be sand, and an intricately tied tassel with jade beads on it.

Tears prickle my eyes. My chest aches whenever I look at the items—things I swear mean nothing to me, and yet, I can't bring myself to throw them away. I've asked my brothers and Taylor, and they all don't recognize them. They said I was found with a messenger bag strapped across my chest. So they assumed these items were in that bag.

I swallow, and hold up the earrings to the sunlight, watching the golden rays glint off the ruby bellies of the birds. Did I buy them? Why does it feel like I have the answers at the tip of my tongue?

"Do you know that in many cultures, hummingbirds are a symbol of joy, positivity, resilience, and love?"

My heart skips a beat at the gravelly voice, and every inch of me goes on alert. Ethan closes the door quietly behind him, a Styrofoam cup in his hand. My mouth dries. The same coiled tension, searing intensity, and raw masculinity clad in a crisp blue shirt with the collar unbutton, revealing an expanse of tanned skin.

A man. Not like the high school boys in my memories.

"Here. Be careful. It's hot." He hands me a cup of tea, but a unique scent wafts to my nose and I take a sniff.

"It's lavender chamomile tea from the nurses' station. They don't have lavender tea by itself and I thought hot tea would be better than iced when you just had a panic attack," he murmurs, answering my unasked question. "Go on. Drink. You'll feel better."

Bewildered, I take a sip, surprised at the hint of honey he must've added to it. Warmth suffuses me and my tensed muscles slowly relax.

"You're bossy," I mutter. "But thank you."

He smirks, then pulls up a chair and sits down. The familiar scent of amber and leather reaches my nose. "Someone should boss you around and make sure you take care of yourself."

And just like that, all the warmth I've been feeling dissipates in a flash. Biting my tongue, I turn my attention back to the earrings in my free hand and the room falls into silence again.

Ethan Anderson is a quiet man. If he doesn't speak, he'll fade into the background. But his presence is loud.

And oddly reassuring.

"I heard from Charles you're busy at work. An investigation of some sorts?"

He shifts in his seat. "Embezzlement. It's unfortunate."

I snap my head up and take in his appearance again, particularly the dark under-eye circles which are more apparent up close. He does look tired. Maybe Charles was right—I was too harsh on Ethan.

"I'm sorry to hear that. Did you catch the bad guy yet?"

"No. But we'll get him."

Silence falls again.

Glancing away, I fiddle with the earrings. His gaze is on me, and my face heats, but I don't look at him. I'm afraid he'll see through me.

"They're beautiful earrings. Do you know who got them for you?" His voice is soft, barely above a whisper.

I shake my head. "They found them on me during the accident." A thought occurs to me and I face him, finding those intense eyes of his trained on me. Assessing. Calculating. "Why did you think someone gave them to me? Couldn't I have bought them for myself?"

His throat ripples as he swallows and he shrugs. "Just making conversation."

I narrow my eyes and he arches his brow as if daring me. *To do what? Knock. Knock.*

Dr. Riordan enters the room, a clipboard in hand. "Is this a good time, Ms. Vaughn?"

I look at Ethan, finding him already standing. "Is everything okay, Doctor?" He sounds concerned.

Dr. Riordan looks at Ethan, his eyes widening in obvious recognition. "Mr. Anderson." He returns his attention to me. "I'd like to discuss some things with you privately."

Unease churns in my gut. "Sure, Doctor. But my family..." I glance at Ethan again.

"I'll take care of them. They've overstayed their welcome already, and I'm sure there's a limit to Manhattan Memorial's hospitality, even for the Vaughns and the Andersons." A smirk appears on his lips.

Dr. Riordan chuckles. "You'd be right. We rarely allow groups bigger than four in a patient's room."

"I'll be fine, Ethan. Tell everyone thank you for celebrating with me."

He furrows his brows, his eyes roving over my face, like he's searching for tells. I strain another smile. "Really. I'm fine. Thanks for the tea."

Ethan nods, his gaze searing. He leans in before I can react and murmurs, "Happy birthday, Alexis. You might feel overwhelmed with everything, but...I...we're glad you're here with us...because you're unforgettable."

Unforgettable.

A sharp pain pierces my chest and my hand automatically fists my shirt.

Why does it hurt so damn much?

I hear his ragged exhale, his hot breath brushing over my ear, his unique scent wrapping me in an embrace. Awareness seizes me. My body stills, and once again I'm hit with the urge to pull him closer.

The moment splinters and he steps back. My heart thrashes as I take in his strained smile before he turns away and leaves the room.

I stare at the closed door. What the hell just happened? Why does it feel like we just had an entire conversation, even though it was nothing more than a sentence or two?

Dr. Riordan clears his throat, and belatedly, I realize he's still standing there.

"Yes, Doctor?"

He sits down. "So, we've been working on your memory for over a year now and it's not going as well as we've hoped."

The boulder appears back on my chest. At least he's not beating around the bush. "Only random snippets of those four years."

He nods. "Normally, I'd recommend patients move on. After all, you still have a long life ahead of you. You can create many more beautiful memories in the years to come."

"But I—"

He holds up his hand. "Let me finish. I'd like to think I know you by now, Ms. Vaughn. You want your memories back. One could even say you're desperate for them. I've reviewed your charts with your therapist and understand how much they tie into your identity."

Dr. Riordan's eyes sharpen. "This is why I want to discuss something with you. I'm running an experimental drug trial that appears promising for patients who've lost their memories because of traumatic brain injuries. Now, we're only at the trial stage, and there may be side effects—"

"I'll do it. Sign me up." Wings beat inside my chest and suddenly the room appears brighter and sharper. This is what hope does to you.

"Ms. Vaughn. Please think this through. Your body has been through a lot already. Being in an experimental trial means more hospital visits, exams, and tests. Not to mention, some participants have had severe side effects—nausea, insomnia—"

"Please, Dr. Riordan. I want to try everything and have no regrets. I want to do it."

If I believe in it, who's to say it isn't true? And don't I always say don't wait to live life because the clock is always ticking?

Dr. Riordan stares at me for a beat before nodding. "Very well. I'll be back with paperwork and the trial administrator, and we'll go through the details with you. In order to preserve the integrity of the trials, no one in your life may tell you anything additional that transpired in those four years of missing memories. This is critical. So, please think through this. If you change your mind, you can always call my direct line."

He hands me a business card and stands. "Oh, and I wanted to give you this." He hands me a sheet of paper from his clipboard. "I think this might be helpful." He smiles and leaves the room.

I stare at the document. *Letters of Hope.* A program that matches patients recovering from long-term stays to anonymous letter writers.

A pen pal program.

My fingers tingle and a rush of energy flows through me. Words, thoughts, and emotions barrel through my mind. I have so many things I want to say, but can't because I don't want the people I love to worry about me.

But dammit. I'm lonely.

I don't think anyone truly understands what I'm going through. After all, how can they unless they've been in my shoes?

A pen pal may be the perfect answer. Someone to talk to, sight unseen.

Excited, I grab my cell phone from my nightstand and open the email app.

To: <u>Coordinator@LOH.manhattanmemorial.org</u>

From: <u>A.Vaughn@gmail.com</u>
Subject: Pen Pal Assignment

Hello,

I'd like to participate in the Letters of Hope program. Will you assign me a pen pal? My name is Alexis Vaughn, patient ID 35267. Please advise on the next steps. Thank you.

Regards,
Alexis

I press send and release a sigh of relief. Finally, I can have someone to talk to. Someone to be completely honest with.

Smiling at the thought of the future, I grab the cup of tea and take another sip, when suddenly, another thought occurs to me.

How did Ethan Anderson know I like honey lavender iced tea? And why didn't my head hurt this time in his presence?

CHAPTER 17

PAST: ONE YEAR BEFORE THE ACCIDENT—TWENTY-THREE YEARS OLD

"SHE SHOULD BE HERE soon. Thanks for doing this, man." Liam slides his headphones around his neck and walks toward his room from the kitchen.

"No problem. I don't have to work this weekend." I feign nonchalance and tuck my hands into the pockets of my sweatpants, hoping Liam won't notice them shaking.

My Nova is coming to our new apartment. It's her first time, since Liam always visits the mansion and not the other way around, and Alexis spends most of her time on campus these days.

It's a wonder our paths haven't crossed until now.

Fate is a shitty jokester.

"Knew I could count on you. And..." His voice trails off, drawing my attention back to him.

"What? Spit it out."

"I don't need to remind you—no funny shit with my sister, right? I know how women fall at your feet... Your broody persona and all that."

I swallow and fist my hands in my pockets.

"Ethan? I need your word." His voice carries a hard edge now, and he stands taller—the rule-breaking hacker shifting into a protective, older brother. "My sister is off-limits. She deserves a good man with no commitment and trust issues—someone who can give her his whole damn heart and protect hers with his life."

My smile is brittle. *I want to be that man. But can I?* "You don't have to ask."

"Then I need your word. You Andersons take that very seriously."

My word. A promise. Fuck.

A knot tightens in my gut. I feel sick. "You have my word. Alexis is off-limits."

The muscles spasm in my neck and I level my stare at Liam.

He grins, his body relaxing. "I'll be inside working, but if you guys need me, just holler."

As soon as he disappears into his room, I collapse into my chair. Burying my face into my hands, I close my eyes. An image of her appears in my mind. Those silky orange locks. The sweet lavender scent. The smattering of freckles on the bridge of her nose. The way her breath hitched when I invaded her mouth with my tongue. How her soft tits felt on my chest when I pulled her closer. The way she gyrated her hips when she moved unwittingly over my thigh as our kiss spun out of control.

Blood rushes to my groin and my cock flares to half-mast. Fuck. How am I going to do this—

Ding. Dong.

She's here.

Adjusting myself, I stand and head to the door. I grit my teeth and wrench it open.

I promptly lose my breath.

Alexis stands there, her hair piled up in a loose bun, a few tendrils framing her face and grazing her creamy shoulders showcased by the wide neckline of her deep green sweater. A flush blooms on her cheeks when she sees me.

Goddamn, she's beautiful.

I want to pull her into my arms and kiss those pouty, pink lips. That perfect cupid's bow and the full bottom lip. I want to taste them and savor her sweetness. I want to swallow her whimpers and make it my life's purpose to tease more out of her. Find ten ways—no, a hundred new ways—of making her writhe in my arms.

Hell in a handbasket.

The air thickens between us, and her breathing quickens. She bites on that bottom lip now, and I stare at the movement, hypnotized, a fire crawling up my body. Every part of me is burning, my skin hypersensitized. I can practically feel her. Taste her. She's so close to me and I can just reach out and—

"Dude. Are you going to let her in?"

We flinch and footsteps echo behind me. How did I miss Liam stepping out of his room?

I drag my eyes away from my Nova and step aside, sweeping my hand toward the living room. "Hey, Alexis. Come in."

She brushes past me toward Liam, and a cloud of lavender perfume floats to my nose. I breathe it in.

"Don't go all big bro on me, Liam." She pokes his chest as Liam mock growls.

"Too bad. You're the only sister I have. It's my job to boss you around." He unleashes a shit-eating grin.

"You're overbearing, insane, out of your mind—"

I clear my throat. "We going to start? I only have an hour." *Sixty minutes of hell.*

Liam frowns. "I thought you were free—"

"I forgot I have a call with Hong Kong."

"On a Saturday?"

"Our hotels and clubs are open every day, you know."

He harrumphs and Alexis squints at me, her arms crossed over her chest.

Bullshit, she mouths. "Well, let's not waste Ethan's time then. I'm *sure* he's very busy...running an empire and all."

I narrow my eyes at her. She knows I'm undercover at Fleur. What the hell is she playing at?

She ignores me and stalks to the dining table next to the windows overlooking Central Park. "Nice view. Glad to know my brother isn't living in a man cave."

"Oh please, I'm an adult, Firefly. No more college frat boy lifestyle. And this fucker is anal about the apartment." He jabs his thumb in my direction. "Don't leave your shoes on the carpet. Limit the crap you put in your bodies. Don't be a slob even though we have a cleaning service. I can go on."

"How you live reflects on you as a person, dipshit. I swear, why are we sharing a place again? It's not like you don't have money."

"Because you're lonely, dumb fuck. I'm here to save you from becoming one of those reclusive billionaires who rots for two weeks in his fancy penthouse before anyone discovers his corpse. And you like having me around."

"To drive me insane," I mutter under my breath.

Alexis snorts and I snake a glance at her, finding her lips twitching in amusement. A smile curves up my lips and her eyes widen, the enticing flush blooming on her face once more.

God, I want to find a thousand ways to make her blush like that.

Forcing myself to look away, I set up my laptop at the dining table and pull up some notes I took from my Intro to Finance class back when I was a freshman.

"So, which areas have you covered and what parts are you confused about?"

Liam mumbles something about lunch and saunters back into his room as Alexis takes a seat next to me. Every inch of my body tenses when I smell the soft lavender and feel her body heat radiating in the tiny sliver of space between us.

We spend the next hour going over the various financial concepts and some basic terminology she'll need to understand for the rest of the semester. She struggles with the numbers and math but seems to understand concepts as long as I use real world, everyday examples. Alexis is smart, and it pains me to see her doubt herself. I think she just hasn't had the right teachers who'll tailor their teaching approach to her.

"What about formulas? How are you with those?" I cross off a few of the syllabus items on the notepad in front of us.

"We've covered the basics. Some are familiar because of the class I took in senior year. But to be honest, none of this makes sense to me. Numbers and cents. Present value. Future value. Interest rates and cash flows. It might as well be Greek."

"Hm." I see where she's coming from. Numbers have always been easy for me. Like science, they're reassuring. There are rules. There's order. But Alexis is a dreamer. She loves reading, traveling, and experiencing new things. She likes human psychology and feeling the expanse of human emotions.

She doesn't know it, but my Nova thrives on the mess that is the world.

Your Nova? My stomach sours. I shove that thought away.

"So, when I first studied finance, I found mnemonics helpful, especially with formulas. Have you taken any East Asian languages before?"

She shakes her head.

"Well, Chinese characters are a bit like Egyptian hieroglyphs, in a sense they're based on pictures. Each word has its own character and, unlike English, you can't sound it out. So, you have to memorize many words in order to be literate."

"How do you know this stuff?"

"*Wo ke yi jiang zhong wen,*" I reply, enjoying the way her mouth drops open. "I just said I can speak Chinese. The basics. Took seven years of it between high school and college."

She's still staring mutedly at me, and I add, "There's a lot you don't know about me, Nova."

Her breath hitches. "You called me Nova."

My nostrils flare and I ignore her comment. *Damn it, I have to be more careful.* Looking at the textbook in front of us, I continue, "Many teachers recommend spinning up a story about these characters. For example, this is the character for heart." I write it on the paper. "Kind of looks like a human heart, right?"

She nods and leans closer. I rake in a deep inhale of her sweet perfume. So damn sweet. I can get drunk from the scent.

Wetting my lips, I point to the first formula on the opened chapter—how to derive the future value of an investment based on a present value. "So for this formula, FV = PV x (1+r)^n, imagine a garden where the future blooms from my efforts in the present, nurtured by my persistence and care over time. So, the future value is equal to the present value multiplied by one plus the interest rate to the power of n, or the time period. Does that make sense?"

Alexis stays silent for a bit, and slowly a soft smile graces her face. "It's almost like poetry." She turns and stares at me. "You, Ethan Anderson, are a poet hiding behind a fancy last name and a broody personality." The smile turns impish. "Makes sense. All the greats...Byron, Keats...they're all sensitive, grumpy souls."

Her tongue dips out to wet her lips and my eyes snare on the movement. More heated blood rushes south and my cock stiffens.

Her breathing grows heavier. Louder. The swells of her breasts move with each breath, inviting me, beckoning me to lean in and taste them. My nostrils flare and I curl my fingers into a fist on the table.

"Nova," I whisper and lean in.

"Yes, Keeper?" *Keeper. I'm her keeper.*

She's *mine.*

"I..." I swallow. *Take it, Ethan. Take what she's offering. You're her keeper. Screw the promise. Liam can fuck off.* Why is it so hard to breathe in here?

But what if you hurt her? I think back to Cleo, how heartbroken she sounded when I broke it off with her. Or Maxwell, and how much colder and withdrawn he is after his high school sweetheart died.

Who buys their dream car before they even get a learner's permit?

Our faces are now inches apart, and suddenly, I feel her soft hand on top of mine, and electricity courses between us, setting me on fire.

I need to think. I need to distract myself.

"Best thing this week?" I blurt the first thing in my mind. Of course, it has to be what we used to tell each other—the journal entries I treasure.

"Seeing you, Ethan," she murmurs. I watch as her eyes darken, the pupils encroaching on her irises, a siren singing her song, luring me to crash into her rocks.

Swallowing, I close my eyes, feeling her breath graze my face as I dip my nose into the crook of her neck. A sound escapes her lips.

It's needy. Hot. Somewhere between a moan and a whimper.

My Nova needs me. *Only I can give her what she needs.*

The possessive thought crashes in from nowhere, a tsunami obliterating all rationality. I part my lips and kiss the pulse beating at her neck before sucking it.

Hard.

A shriek tumbles out of her mouth, and I slap my hand over her lips. She returns the favor by biting my fingers and grabbing my shoulder, her body melting against me, her tits thrusted against my face.

My brain short circuits. I don't remember why this is a bad idea. All I know is, I need to haul her on my lap, kiss her, shred the damn clothes separating our bodies, make her scream my name in pleasure, and then I'll do it again, and again. Then—

A loud thump sounds from Liam's room and jolts me from my insane thoughts.

I slam back in my chair, getting as far away from her as possible, my lungs short on oxygen, because that's the only rational explanation for why my brain stopped functioning.

Alexis's breaths are heavy, her eyes that were drunk with lust and passion moments ago, now carry a glimmer of pain. She blinks rapidly, and her lips tremble. *I've hurt her. I'm a fucking bastard.* I bite the inside of my cheek, focusing on the pain instead of my impulse to reach out and comfort her.

"You know, I can deal with my brothers. They don't run my life. They're overprotective, but they want what's best for me. But you...I don't get at all."

Her nostrils flare, her lips pressed in a hard line.

"The worst thing about this week," she says thickly as she gathers her papers, "is seeing you pull away."

With that, she shoves her papers and books into the bag and leaves the table.

Fuck.

CHAPTER 18

PAST: ONE YEAR BEFORE THE ACCIDENT—NINETEEN YEARS OLD

THE JOURNAL EXCHANGE AND text messages have stopped.

On top of losing what could've been a promising relationship, what pains me the most is losing what I had with Keeper and Delaney. Over the last year, I've looked forward to our weekly journal entries, to figuring out the next literary riddle, and uncovering the hidden messages behind the book choices.

I've treasured the small mementos he leaves behind—the note cards with poetry, a rare stamp he found because he knew I had dreams of traveling to exotic locales, photos of hummingbirds in flight—a nod to the stain glass window in Ravenswood.

You remind me of them—hummingbirds.
Always in motion, a blur of energy,
Blinding me with your brilliance.
Sunlight dances on your wings,
Golden rays glinting against soft feathers.
Melodies unheard of, yet your lyrics speak to my soul.
With bated breath, I watch you ascend.
Taking flight—effortless, untouchable,
Soaring in the skies.
Leaving me grounded,
How I wish you were mine.

I trace his words with my fingers—feeling the paper dip where his pen stopped.

My feelings are complicated when it comes to him—the initial anger at him pulling away and yet understanding his reasoning. Through his letters, I know he's always felt out of place in his life and Liam accepts and understands him. I have brothers and I've seen the unique bond. I also respect how he wants to stay true to his word—a promise is sacred. That's a rare quality these days.

I'm also frustrated. Liam loves us both—he might be angry when he finds out, but he'll forgive us eventually.

Ultimately, I want a man who'll give up everything for me. I'm worth that. I won't beg him to be with me.

But I miss him.

The longing cinches my chest as I reread the free verse poem. He didn't write the name of the author, but I know it's him.

How can someone capable of writing such heartfelt, romantic poems believe he isn't capable of loving someone? How can he be so blind?

I put the note card away and head to the coffee shop next to Ravenswood Library for our fourth tutoring session. The last two sessions alternated between his apartment—and Liam's always there, dammit—or Central Park. He didn't bring up the neck kiss, and I didn't push him.

But I'd catch the way he stared at me when he thought I wasn't aware. His eyes roved over my face, like he was taking inventory of every freckle on my skin. Sometimes, I'd see him reaching out, like he wanted to touch my nose or my hair, like that day in the library when he kissed me.

While he didn't cross any lines—whatever imaginary boundaries he thought he had because I was Liam's sister—I felt the barriers fading away. It'll be a matter of time before he caved to the chemistry between us.

Smiling at the future where he and I would finally be together, I quicken my pace. The biting wind ruffles my hair and I admire the multicolored leaves twirling in the air as fall bids us farewell in early November.

My phone buzzes in my pocket and I fish it out, finding an incoming text notification.

Dayton

> Hey. How are you doing? I drove by UNYC the other day and thought of you. Miss you. Can we chat?

Dayton

> By the way, this may be an odd ask, but when you mailed back my stuff back then, did you come across the hard drive? I forgot to grab some stuff off it.

My brows pinch at his messages, and I remember the drive he tossed me with the photos that I backed up to my own backup drive. Shit, I think it's still at my place.

While Dayton and I hadn't parted on the best terms, we still shared a lot of good memories together. The last I heard, he took over his family's fledging business after he graduated from Columbia.

The quaint cafe with its redwood exterior and gold lettering on windows, beckons me from the distance as a few raindrops land on my nose. I glance up, noticing the low-hanging clouds and the quickly darkening skies.

I hurry to the door, yank it open, and am met with a gust of warm air and the smell of freshly baked breads and cinnamon buns. Scanning the small space, my feet come to an abrupt halt when I see him.

With a beautiful woman.

Svelte, shiny mahogany hair, leggy, with more curves than I could ever hope for. She looks like she just stepped out of a *Vogue* centerfold. He's smiling at her, a dimple flashing on his cheek.

She giggles the way beautiful models do—womanly, sultry, and sexy all rolled into one and Ethan shakes his head in clear amusement.

An ugly, corrosive sensation moves through me and my jaw tightens.

I march forward and drop my bag into the empty chair next to him as they look at me.

"Ethan, I didn't know you were early. You should've told me." I give him my sweetest smile before leaning in to give him a quick peck.

His breath stalls and I bite back a grin before pulling back. Then I make a show at eyeing the woman who seems like she wants to dig her perfectly manicured nails into my skin and draw blood.

"Hi, I'm Alexis Vaughn, and you are?"

Her eyes widen at the last name and a pinch of guilt slices through me. I don't like name dropping but dammit, I'm petty today.

Ethan slides away from me, that little motion a slap in the face. "Alexis, this is Cleo Marchetti. She's a...friend."

"More than friends, I think?" She smiles adoringly at him and touches his arm. She's his ex. I'm sure of it. The woman he talked about in his letters. The wonderful, beautiful ex-girlfriend who loved him. The woman who'd kissed him, touched him, slept with him before.

She doesn't move her hand, her fingers absentmindedly tracing a vein on his forearm. I want to slap it away, but I hold myself back. *I'm better than this.*

"I ran into Cleo after I sat down." Ethan shifts in his seat and pulls his arm away, clearly uncomfortable with the female version of the dick-measuring contest.

"No need to explain, Dels." His eyes widen at my usage of his middle name. "I love meeting your *friends.*"

"I was thinking how lucky I ran into Ethan here today. My agency is hosting a fundraising ball for the holidays to raise funds for literacy programs. The first person I thought of was him, of course, since he loves books so much. And if he attends as an Anderson, we can shine a lot of attention to the cause."

Ethan flushes and kneads the back of his neck. "You still remembered."

The green monster is pounding its grubby hands on my chest.

She knows he likes books too? Does he write her love poems too?

"So, what do you think? It's in three weeks. Come to the event?" *With me?* The words are unsaid, but I hear them loud and clear. She glances at me and I can see the gears working in her head. Who am I to Ethan Anderson?

Damn good question.

"I'll check my schedule and contact you." Ethan stands, a signal to Cleo, which she smartly accepts. "It's nice seeing you again. You look great." He gives her a hug.

Anger churns through me at his soft voice and how he lets her cling on to him for a few seconds longer than friendly.

But what hold do I have on him? We're nothing. *Stupid Lexy, why would you think a kiss or a few poems and letters would mean as much to him as they did to you?*

A flash of pain tunnels through my chest and I look away, barely mustering a smile when Cleo glides out of the cafe and Ethan sits back down.

"Let's begin." He takes out his notepad.

The anger boils over and I grab his glass of water and chug down a few gulps. "Seriously? You aren't going to address that?" I point toward the door.

"What that? There's nothing to address. Cleo and I are friends, and even if we aren't, it's none of your business. Jealousy doesn't look good on you."

"You asshole!" Stubborn, beautiful, infuriating asshole. I take a deep breath. Blowing up won't help anything.

I turn toward him, finding his face annoyingly calm. "What are we doing, Ethan?"

"I'm helping you with your finance class as a favor to your brother."

"You're using Liam as an excuse now?"

"It's true, isn't it?" He arches his brow, an arrogant glint in his eyes. "Why else would I spend my rare downtime helping a college student?"

A college student. My mouth drops open. *How dare he?*

I've never thought of Ethan as one of those rich guys from my family's circles—cocky, entitled, convinced they own the world simply by existing. But right now, he's certainly acting like one. A fucking Anderson unfurling his wings and looking down on us mere mortals. I never imagined my gentle keeper, my soulful Delaney, would have this side to him.

"You wouldn't have agreed to tutor me unless you wanted to."

"Don't flatter yourself. You're my best friend's sister, and that's why I'm helping you."

My phone buzzes in my bag. I ignore it and instead lean closer to him. "Really? That's all there is to it?"

His nostrils flare as I shorten our distance. He grows rigid but doesn't back up or move away from me. Damn stubborn man.

"So you won't care if I see anyone?"

His eyes darken and a vein in his temple pulses.

"Kiss anyone?" I continue, my thigh pressed against his under the table. His breath hitches.

Then I graze my lips against his ear. "Fuck anyone?"

He growls, the deep rumbly sound making me smile. I pull back, finding his face mottled with anger, his hands clenched on top of his lap. "You wouldn't dare."

My phone buzzes and this time, I pick it up. "Hello?"

"Hey, Lexy. It's Dayton. I sent you a message earlier but thought I should call instead. You free this weekend? Want to grab a coffee?"

"Hey, Dayton!" Keeping my eyes on Ethan, I watch his countenance darkening.

"Don't you dare," he mouths.

I grin broadly. *I win, Ethan Anderson.*

"Sure, Dayton. What time were you thinking? I'll bring the drive you left at my place."

Ethan hisses under his breath, and I bite back a smile.

Sitting back, I twirl a lock of hair, admiring the handiwork I've made of the cocky man from a few moments ago. His tall frame is twitching with fury. He grabs his water and chugs it down before slamming the glass back on the table, drawing attention to us.

He flags down a waiter for another glass. And when he gets it, he downs that one too.

"You have it?" Dayton murmurs. "Awesome. It'll be great to see you..." Dayton chatters on about logistics.

If Ethan can be friends with Cleo, why can't I be friends with Dayton?

"Sure, sounds like a plan. See you Saturday afternoon then."

I hang up and turn my attention to my furious keeper next to me.

"And you were saying?"

He glares at me and I smile.

It takes two to tango and I'm a dancer, Ethan Anderson.

You don't know what hit you.

CHAPTER 19

"YOU'RE SURE ABOUT THIS, Lexy? You know how I feel about him." Summer's voice travels through my laptop speaker as I get ready for my coffee date with Dayton in my UNYC apartment.

"I know. You aren't a fan of Dayton. This is just catching up, nothing more, Sum. He's making a name for himself in finance and didn't you say it's always good to network?"

"If that's what it is. I guess."

They say distance really tests a relationship, and the same goes for friendships as well. Our calls have dwindled from several times a week to monthly, if I'm lucky.

In classic Ivy League fashion, there are mixers and secret handshakes with the movers and shakers in society, and she, being one to never say no to networking, is eating it all up.

Perhaps Keeper inspired something in me, because I want to make it on my own without the Vaughn name as well. Didn't Ethan used to say he wanted his name to mean something?

I want the same thing too.

But at my college, we don't have the same opportunities Summer has, so I'll just have to work harder and hustle. But at least now, I know what I want to do—work in marketing and design groundbreaking campaigns.

"I didn't like how he treated you before."

"I know what I'm doing, Sum. It's different now. I'm no longer the lost girl at Broadbent." I finish my simple makeup look—eyeliner, mascara, tinted moisturizer—with a coat of pink lip gloss.

Squaring my shoulders, I face the camera. "Trust me, Sum. You're looking at the new badass Alexis Vaughn, ready to take on the world."

Keeper always believed me—ah, stop it, Lexy. Keeper is your imagination and Ethan Anderson, an infuriating asshole, is the reality.

"Fine. You win. You do you. Just don't make me say 'I told you so' later on. Well, I think you're—"

The doorbell rings and I frown. "Someone's at the door. Got to go."

We hang up and I walk through my colorful living room filled with *National Geographic* and *Travel Leisure* photo prints of places I want to see and experiences I want to try out—all part of my meticulous Twenty by Forty plan—not every item makes it onto the master list.

The doorbell blares loudly again. *Who the hell is it?* I'm not expecting anyone, and the doorman holds the packages.

Someone pounds on the door now and my hackles rise.

I scurry to the foyer and peek through the peephole, finding Ethan tugging his hair and pacing back and forth in the hallway.

Huh? Quickly, I open the door.

"Ethan? What are you doing here and how do you know where I—"

"You're seeing him, aren't you?" His voice is hushed. Urgent. He looks like he ran all the way from his place in Manhattan to see me.

"What?"

"Dayton. Your ex. You're dressed like *that* to see him, right?" He clenches the doorframe, his biceps bulging inside his dark blue Henley. He throws an accusatory glare at my outfit.

"It's none of your business, right? I'm just a *college student* you're tutoring as a favor, remember?"

"Answer me."

I roll my eyes and close the door—I have no time for this bullshit. He shoves his foot in.

"Go away, Ethan. Come back when you grow a pair." I kick his boot, trying to dislodge it from the threshold.

"He's not good for you. Didn't you used to say he never listened to you? He didn't understand you? He was hiding things from you? Wake up, Lexy. Don't throw yourself at men because you don't want to be alone!"

My mouth drops open as fury shoots up my spine. I fling the door open, and it crashes against the wall in a loud bang. Ethan stands there, his arms crossed over his chest, his lips curving in an annoying smirk.

"That's low, Ethan. I never thought Delaney would have this ugly side to him, but like you're implying, I have horrible taste in men, so what do I know?"

Lips twitching, I can barely see straight. I march up to him and stand on my tiptoes. He arches a damn elegant brow, appearing completely unfazed.

"You know what? I was going to catch up with Dayton because he's a friend. But then, I'm a believer of fate and second chances. He just so happened to call me when you started pissing me off. That's got to be a sign, right? And it's been a while, so maybe he's changed. So fuck off. You're *not* my keeper."

The sneer slips off his face, and a muscle twitches in his jaw. His eyes darken, a blistering fire brewing inside them.

You started it, asshole.

I lean in closer, our faces inches apart. "Don't mind me, I'm only a silly teenager, desperate for love, right? Maybe I'll even let him fuck me tonight."

Ethan's body stills—his fingers dig into the doorframe, a slight tremble in his arms betraying his coiled strength. His chest stops moving, like he's forgotten how to breathe.

It's then I know.

I may have pushed him too far, unleashing the animal caged inside him. A sudden awareness seizes me, and I realize now is the time for me to escape from the beast who may pounce on me at any second.

My heart shoots up to my throat and I step back to shove the door closed.

But before I hear the telltale click of the latch engaging, the door flings back open and I jump back just in time.

Everything is a blur, and before I know it, he's inside the apartment and the door is shut behind him.

I back up, my lungs raking in quick inhales, my legs tripping over the carpet.

My eyes never leaving him.

Ethan's prowling toward me in measured steps, a forceful energy rolling off his towering frame.

Strength. Power. Passion.

The inferno burning inside my sensitive poet.

"What. Did. You. Say?"

CHAPTER 20

THE GRAYS IN HIS eyes appear almost silver under the daylight as he advances toward me. He looks like the god of war, demanding retribution, the anger and lust sizzling off his body.

"Y-You heard me." I'm breathless, my skin is on fire, and he hasn't even touched me yet.

My back hits the windows and I swallow, watching him close in on me. I wet my lips, and his eyes drop to the movement, his pupils flaring.

He braces his arms at the sides of my head, caging me against the windows. A strangled gasp slips out of my lips when he presses his body on mine, letting me feel every hard inch of him.

How large he is. How strong he is. How he can bend and break me oh so easily if he wants to.

Wetness seeps through my panties, and I clench my thighs.

Ethan brushes his lips against the curve of my ear. A barely there caress, but I feel it straight in my clit.

A whimper floats out of me.

"What did you just say?" His breathing is labored. "You're going to fuck him? Give him these rosy lips and needy sounds? Let him touch you? Kiss you? Fuck you because you're practically begging for it?"

My mind swirls and I arch my head back, baring my neck to him. *Kiss me, Ethan. Kiss me. I only want you.*

I feel the last vestiges of restraint, the honorable Ethan Anderson still holding on, trying to keep his vow to my brother ever since he found out who I was at the library. The sensitive Delaney who's afraid of hurting me because he thinks he doesn't know how to love.

Can't he see how much love he has to give? How in trying to keep me safe, honor his promise to my brother, and prove himself to the world—to his family—he's doing it all because he loves *too* hard?

He shakes against me. I should feel suffocated. Panicked. I *should* want to escape.

But I don't.

I want him to burn me alive.

I want him to choose *me*.

"Kiss me, Ethan." I rub my body against his, the friction of our clothes lighting my nipples and pussy on fire.

I came close to having sex a few times before, but it never felt right. But now, at this moment, I *know* I want my first time to be with him.

Bucking underneath him, I whimper, needing more.

Needing everything.

A growl rumbles from his throat, his labored breaths driving me on. My body is on fire and I can't help but gyrate harder, needing more friction, needing the clothes between us to disappear.

"Fuck," he rasps. "Fuck it all."

Ethan bears down, his hard, jean-clad cock burrowing against my panties. Stars appear behind my eyes. He captures my lips with his, and with one hand, he yanks up the hem of my sweater dress to my waist and hoists my legs around him.

He snaps his hips, humping me through our clothes, dragging that cock deliciously up and down my damp underwear.

A tortuous rhythm.

"Ethan," I moan.

My clit is throbbing, pulsing. I'm sure I'm leaking all over his pants, but I don't care. I've never felt like this—so out of control. I meet him thrust for thrust, needing to reach that cliff so I can throw myself off it with him in my arms. I grip the soft strands of his hair before clawing his back. He hisses and his tongue invades my mouth, and the world turns hazy.

Off. I need everything off. I need to feel him pressed up against me with nothing separating us.

He understands what I can't say in words, and with a grunt, he perches me on the windowsill so my chest is at his eye level.

Breaking apart for air, he stares at me, his hair mussed, a deep flush on his face. His eyes are dark—so dark I can barely see the irises. He looks feral, his gaze bouncing between my eyes, my parted lips, then to my chest.

Another growl rips out from him.

I look down, finding my neckline already tugged past my shoulders, baring one lace covered breast. My nipples are as hard as diamonds and poking out of the thin material, saluting him.

My skin heats, and I want to duck away from his intense gaze. I'm overwhelmed with lust, love, anger, anything and everything toward this man.

His breathing falters, his hands trembling as they tug down my dress, then the straps of my bra. He grazes my arms—the light touch sending shivers down my body. Soon, my tits are bared. They're heavy, swollen, the tips sensitive.

Ethan's eyes are glued to my tits—each ragged exhale causing them to jiggle. He dips his tongue out, like he's imagining how they'd taste.

Take me, Ethan. Choose me.

Slowly, with shaking hands, I cup my tits and pinch my hardened nipples. A sultry moan slips out. My thighs clench, unable to relieve the burgeoning ache gathering in my pussy.

"Nova, fuck," he rasps.

He swivels his hips in that tortuous rhythm, each glide more desperate than the one before, like nothing in the world could stop him from reaching me.

With his forehead resting on mine, our breaths mingle with every graze of my nipples against his shirt.

He's not touching me with his hands, but I feel him everywhere.

We're reaching the point of no return. One tiny shove...that's all it'll take.

Choose me.

Ethan lifts his head up, our eyes catching. I see my reflection in those dark, mesmerizing pools.

"Who's your keeper?" he whispers.

"You." There's only one answer. "You, Ethan. Always you. My north star."

An unsteady inhale from me or him, I don't know. My lungs have forgotten how to work.

Then he leaps off the tightrope, tugging me with him.

With one hand, he yanks off his shirt, baring his lean but strong muscles. After hoisting me into his arms, he kisses the ever living daylights out of me.

Our mouths duel—offense, defense, match point, rematch. I bite him; he returns the favor with a soft nip and suckle. He grips my ass, his fingers sliding underneath the thong I have on, and I let out a strangled mewl.

"So wet, Nova. You're so fucking wet."

Whimpering, I take his lips with mine again. Before I know it, he tosses me onto my queen-sized bed, his fingers shaking when he unbuttons his jeans, then kicks off his pants and underwear. My eyes widen when I take in his pulsing shaft curling against his toned stomach. A thick vein curves around the underside and the tip is deep pink, pre-cum glistening on it.

How's that thing going to fit inside me?

My heart ricochets inside my chest as my eyes remain riveted on his hard shaft. *It'll fit. Because we're made for each other.*

With trembling fingers, I slide down my thong and throw it on the floor. Ethan's eyes dart to the trimmed patch of red curls between my legs as he slowly crawls above me on the bed.

"You're beautiful, Lexy. The supernova in my universe." His eyes widen—in shock, awe, a combination—I don't know.

"We are a match made in heaven then." My breath stutters when he settles his hard cock between my parted thighs. "The north star and his supernova."

His lips curve into a wide smile and he slowly links his fingers with mine before placing them next to my head. Every inch of me is plastered against him—my breasts to his hard pecs, my legs curled around his waist. He grips my hands like a lifeline, promising he won't ever let go.

His warm tip notches at my entrance.

"I'm clear, Lexy." His jaw works.

Shit. I didn't even remember about the condom.

Ethan holds my stare, his eyes whispering poetry I can feel. The awe, the passion, the aching want.

"I'm clear too. And I'm on the pill."

His eyes flare and his tip dips inside me. My muscles tense up—nerves and anticipation loading my senses.

My first time—it's significant.

For me and for him.

"Are you sure?" I ask, knowing this is going against his vow to my brother, which he takes seriously.

"I don't think I can ever stay away from you, Lexy. I was a lost cause the moment I read your first entry." He presses a soft kiss on my lips. "Maybe I'll rot in hell for this. Liam will definitely kill me when he finds out, but...I can't deny this anymore. I'm going out of my fucking mind trying to stay away from you."

There's a determined glint in his eyes, a surety in his voice. "It's always been you, Nova. If my world burned around me, the only thing I'd want to save, the only person I'd want by my side...would be you."

Tears spring into my eyes and I return his heartfelt words with a wobbly smile.

He chose me.

His face blurs in my vision as he leans in and kisses my tears away. Then, he trails his lips down my neck, suckling my throat before moving to my collarbone, then to my breast.

"So fucking beautiful," he whispers reverently, then captures a nipple into his mouth.

Fireworks light behind my eyes, each dragging pull from his lips a direct pinch to my clit. His tongue alternates from sensual swipes to teasing flicks, which, combining with his tip inside me, are sending me off into the stratosphere.

He chases away the remaining nervousness inside me, leaving me starving for more.

I gyrate my hips, urging him on.

Wetness seeps out of me as he quickens his shallow thrusts, his cock dragging over my clit, my swollen folds, to my entrance, teasing it, before gliding back up.

Torture. I'm going to die from torture.

He works my other breast while his finger grazes my clit.

"Ethan!" I nearly careen off the bed when he pinches the swollen nub to the rhythm of his thrusting. The opening of my pussy pulses, wetness seeping out. "I need you. P-Please!"

He grunts, his breathing sounding heavier with each passing second. Then, he once again perches his thick tip at my opening.

Holding my hands, he stares into my eyes. "You sure?"

I nod. "Yes. A million times. Yes." *I've never been more sure of anything.*

He thrusts in with one stroke.

I cry out as a sharp pain spears through me, stealing my breath. Ethan freezes, his muscles coiling with tension.

Shocked eyes meet mine as tears roll down my face. "Y-You...You're..."

He's at a loss for words.

Smiling, I lift my head and kiss him softly. "A virgin. Yes."

A strangled growl rumbles in his throat, his cock twitching inside me.

He likes that he's my first. *I like that he's my first.*

"How? Your ex...how?"

"It never seemed right. I never wanted to do it with him. It caused problems."

His lips part, his eyes flaring—wonder, awe, gratefulness.

Slowly, he kisses me—his lips gentle, like he's trying to soothe away the pain with his mouth.

"I'm going to make this good for you. So good for you." He gently withdraws and I hiss, the sensations foreign but not so painful anymore.

Unlinking one of our hands, he dips it back between us, his fingers circling my clit as he gently glides back inside me. Sharp pleasure reignites between my legs, the pain gradually fading away. His hips move faster, his cock sliding almost out before he thrusts back into the hilt.

It hits my clit at the precise angle.

The sparks reignite into a fire and I meet him thrust for thrust, chasing the high, feeling the pressure climb rapidly.

"Fuck. So good. You're so tight, Nova. Are you okay?" His words come out in rough grunts.

"Yes. Oh my God. More. Yes!" He moves harder, one hand squeezing my fingers to the point of pain, the other hand quickening between my legs, his fingers alternating between plucking, flicking, and circling my clit.

Black dots appear behind my vision. Every inch of me is on fire.

The sensations are overwhelming—his fingers on my swollen clit, his cock tunneling in and out of me in quick snaps. Moans and whimpers join the sounds of skin slapping against skin, and I realize those horny sounds are coming from me.

He grunts, his mouth devouring mine, and he drags his thick cock so it hits a spot deep inside that makes me see stars. A cry forms at my chest and moves up my throat. A different burn appears between my legs where we're joined.

"Yes, Nova. You're clenching me so tightly. Shit. I can't hold on." Ethan flicks my clit harder, his movements desperate, like sending me to oblivion is his sole purpose in life. Every atom in my body is focused on the explosion gathering at my core. "Come. Come around my cock, little hummingbird."

"Ethan!" I detonate. My vision blanks and I arch back, my legs shaking, the earth-shattering orgasm blasting through my body, frying my nerves.

Waves of unending pleasure roll through me. I can't think. I can't speak. I can't breathe. All I can do is shudder under him as he plows inside me faster and harder. I open my eyes, my vision partially returning, and take in the sweat dotting his forehead, his wavy hair covering one brow. His eyes are molten silver, and I see the moment he reaches his breaking point.

Ethan throws his head back and bares his teeth, his corded throat rippling. His growl echoes in the room.

His cock thickens and throbs, and a hot gush of cum singes my insides, sending tiny pinpricks of aftershocks through my body.

I moan as he continues his sensuous torture, his hips swiveling, dragging out every ounce of pleasure.

Ethan collapses on top of me, his heavy weight reassuring. Our labored breathing echoes our thundering heartbeats.

"My beautiful, sweet Nova. My hummingbird." He presses a soft kiss on my neck before he lifts his head.

I blink drowsily at him, finding his gaze soft and filled with love. Slowly, he drags his index finger down the bridge of my nose and my heart flutters.

The caress of love and reverence.

"My keeper," I whisper, and he smiles, his dimples showing.

"My unforgettable dreamer."

CHAPTER 21

THE SCREECHING OF THE guitar riffs clashes with the aggressive drumming of Shattered Monarchy's punk rock music blasting from the speakers in the apartment. Liam's twenty-fourth birthday party is chaos.

Literally.

My cheeks hurt from the social smile etched on my face as I do my required mingling with his hacker friends, most of whom I don't recognize. Neon strobe lights ricochet around the room and somewhere near the corner, a machine is churning out a scentless fog, swathing the place in a blanket of white.

The fucker—or one of his buddies—rented a smoke machine.

Soda cans, half eaten snacks, empty shot glasses, and hard liquor bottles litter our normally immaculate living room. Liam currently has a girl with pink hair on his lap as he drinks a Jell-O shot from her mouth.

Fuck. I can barely hear myself think here.

The doorbell sounds. I wonder how many more people we can cram into this place before we get a noise complaint from the neighbors.

Blowing out a breath, I yank open the door without looking into the peephole.

Suddenly, my night turns from dreary to a lot better.

Because my Nova is standing on the other side.

My lips hike up as I take in her appearance—her thick hair tied into a braid, her luscious body poured into a formfitting black tank top and jeans. She's holding two large paper bags.

She beams and pulls out a six-pack of beer—Pintzer, of course—and a bottle of lavender and honey iced tea from Estelle's. I grab the other heavier bag from her.

"What's this?" I peer inside.

"Take a guess." She bites her plump bottom lip, a devious glint in her eyes.

My cock twitches, and I lose my train of thought, immediately reliving the scandalous night we had last week, where I made her come two more times after I took her virginity.

Fuck. I'm the only man who's been with her.

More heated blood rushes to my groin.

Alexis's eyes widen at whatever she sees on my face, and she licks those tempting lips again. The sounds from the party fade away and all I can hear are my rioting heartbeats as I fight the urge to hoist her over my shoulder, caveman style, and have my way with her in the bedroom.

"I swear if you keep looking at me like that, I'll—"

"Firefly! You made it!" Liam claps my shoulder and I jump.

Shit. I really need to be more careful, but I always lose my mind around her.

She grins at her brother. "I didn't think you'd invite me to your 'precious' party."

"Eh. I figured you're in college and all, so you're probably partying it up now."

"I was partying it up in high school."

Liam shakes his head. "I don't want to know about it. So, what have you got there?" He eyes the drinks in her hand.

"They're for me, Liam. Don't even think about it." I close the door behind Alexis.

"Dude, how do you know they're for you? It's *my* birthday." He grabs the six-pack, looks at the label, and blanches. "Ugh. Pintzer. Never liked the taste. You have at it."

He shoves the drinks at me before he slings an arm around Alexis, the way a protective older brother will.

"Seriously, Firefly, don't you know by now your brother likes whiskey and not beer? And if I had to drink beer, it'd be Colgan's? Fail, sis. Complete fail. And where's my birthday present?"

Alexis chuckles. "Charles and I already took you out for your birthday two nights ago. My presence is your present."

"Cheapskate."

"You have your trust fund! I don't get my trust fund yet. Get your own present!"

The two squabble and I laugh under my breath. Liam ruffles Alexis's hair.

My two most favorite people in the world.

A slither of unease curls around my gut. *You can royally fuck this up by sleeping with her. Fuck, you've probably fucked it up already. He'll never forgive you if he ever finds out.*

The what-ifs chase after the unease like a tidal wave. What if this thing between Alexis and I don't work out? What if I can't give her the love she deserves? What if...what if...what if. Cold sweat forms on my back and a wave of nausea stops me in my tracks.

"Hey, Ethan!" Liam calls after me.

A group of friends pulls him somewhere to do God knows what. One punk who looks like an extra for some superhero movie is giving Alexis the elevator glance. I want to punch him in the gut and rip his eyes out.

He grins and extends his hand. "Hey, Gavin here, I work with—"

Liam shoves his face away. "Back off, leech. You touch one hair on her head and you're dead." He pushes Gavin and their friends toward the living room as he hollers at me, "Take care of my little sister, okay? You have my blessing to be her older bro and boss her around for the night."

"Hey! I'm almost twenty!" Alexis yells, and Liam flips her off, leaving us standing in the foyer.

"Honorary brother, my ass," she mutters before sauntering to me, her lips tilting in a teasing smile.

The niggle of guilt makes a reappearance, but it's quickly quashed when she walks her fingers up my chest.

"Feeling brotherly, Ethan?" Her voice is raw sugar, a sultry rasp sending all my blood rushing south.

I swallow and let the fly of my pants brush her belly. "What do you think?"

Her eyes widen when she feels my hard on.

"Maybe I should reevaluate my whole 'sensitive poet' idea of you."

"Oh yeah? I'm definitely sensitive...*so* fucking sensitive for you," I rasp and watch a blush creeping up her face in fascination.

"Who knew my keeper had this side to him?" The blues of her irises are eclipsed by her dilated pupils. "Maybe I should add visiting The Orchid Rose floors to one of my Twenty by Forty lists."

My dick twitches at the mention of the sex club floors of the crown jewel of my family's business. "How do you know about that?"

She doles out a knowing grin. "I have ears and Liam and Charles aren't exactly discreet with their 'activities.' I wanted to visit, but they always shot me down."

"You aren't going to the Rose floors without me." An unfamiliar wave of possession tightens around my lungs. I can't have my Nova on those floors without me protecting her. The sleazebags will eat her alive.

"Bossy. I should've known. You were bossy in your journals. Snarky too. All the red flags."

"And yet, you're here with me. So what does that say about you?"

She winks. "Well, someone once told me I have bad taste in men."

I chuckle. My hummingbird—dazzling, awe-inspiring, the perfect balance of impishness with sweetness.

Dipping my head down, I watch her lashes fan over her cheeks as she closes her eyes. I want to count the freckles on her face, to kiss each of them, to write poetry about how they're constellations in the skies. I rake in a deep inhale of her sweet lavender.

Liam laughs in the background, his voice shocking me back to reality. We spring apart, and I look around, thankful the place is so crowded, no one seems to notice the two of us hovering in a dark corner.

We shouldn't be doing this, I tell her with my eyes.

I don't care, she responds with a defiant glare.

The seconds stretch on and I keep Liam in my peripheral vision to make sure he doesn't see us because that fucker will notice. It's a miracle he hasn't caught on yet. Alexis is guileless, easy to read, and has desire stamped all over her features.

Suddenly, the blond asshole, Gabriel or whatever, props his arm over Alexis's head and leans over her. "Sweetheart, when Liam told me he's finally bringing his precious little sister around, I never expected he'd be bringing a goddess." He unleashes a slimy smile. "How about I show you a good time? A real party, just you and me?"

"Uh, no thanks, Gavin." Alexis tries to wiggle out from under him but the bastard cages her in again.

Flames lick my insides and I'm gripped with a violent need to wrench him by the collar and hurl him against the wall before pummeling the daylights out of him.

Insane. I'm going insane. That's the only thing that can explain any of this.

Calm yourself, Ethan. This is Liam's birthday party.

"Come on, it'll be fun," Gavin murmurs cajolingly, his fingers grazing her face.

I see red.

You fucker. Screw calmness.

"Hands off, asshole." I shove him away from her and insert myself in between them. "Didn't you hear what Liam said? Touch one hair on her head and you're dead. She's a teenager, practically a kid. Back off."

I hear Alexis's shocked gasp and I wince. I've hurt her with the last remark.

Gavin arches his brow and looks me over, clearly seizing me up. "Anderson, right? Does Liam know you have the hots for his sister?"

"Watch what you're saying."

His eyes gleam. "It's obvious. This fake brotherly shit is fooling no one. You want a piece of that ass too. Teenager, *riiight?* See you around the cell block. But I don't blame you. She's fucking hot. Maybe we can share."

Blood. Violence. Murder. Fury unlike anything I've ever felt before thrashes inside me and I grip his collar and snarl, "Shut your mouth before I shut it for you."

Gavin chuckles, his eyes defiant. "I'm—"

"Ethan! Ignore him. He's baiting you." Alexis yanks my arm, drawing my attention to her. Her eyes are frantic. "Let's go."

I twist his collar in my grip, watching in sick fascination his face becoming mottled. God, it'd be so satisfying to smack him across the face and hear the bones crack.

"Come on, Ethan. Please." Then she turns toward Gavin and narrows her eyes. "Yo, asshole! I'm an adult and in case I wasn't clear before, I. Am. Not. Interested. *Capisce?*"

Alexis's sweet voice tethers me to sanity. Shoving Gavin back, I growl, "Don't let me catch you looking at her, or Liam will be the least of your problems."

Spinning around, I place my hand on Alexis's back and usher her through the partygoers overflowing into the living room, the dining room, to the main hallway where a few couples are making out in darkened corners.

After leading her into my bedroom, I close the door. The clicking of the lock is loud as we're finally cordoned off from the riot outside.

I set the drinks and the bags on top of my dresser.

Rage is still burning hot in my veins. Liam and Gavin's words hammer inside my brain—brother, trust, teenager.

She's not even twenty yet.

But I can't imagine her with anyone else. My dreamer, the girl with words that touch my soul, the muse to my poet, the one person who's ever made me feel enough just by being me.

"I got you a steak from Carlisle's. Rib eye. Medium rare. That's your favorite, right?" Alexis says. I can hear the smile in her voice.

Turning around, the oxygen escapes my lungs when I see her staring at me in the dark, the moonlight streaming in from the window behind her, her glorious fiery tresses loosened from her braid. Even in the dimness, I can make out her chest heaving, the fluttering of her pulse on her neck, her lips parting before curving up into a sweet smile.

Mine.

I don't think there'll be anyone else for me.

CHAPTER 22

My heart throws itself against my rib cage, and I'm hit with a desperate urge to touch her, kiss her, to feel her joined against me. I'm dizzy—this must be what it feels like to be high.

Everything is more incandescent with her.

Was this how Dad felt with Mom? How Maxwell felt with Sydney? Is this why generations of Anderson men fall in love even though our love stories end in tragedy?

Reaching her in a few strides, I cup her face and hear her sharp intake of breath before I seal my lips over hers.

It's like coming home.

Our kiss turns harried. Messy. Uncoordinated. She unbuttons my sky-blue shirt while I wrench up and toss away her tank top. I haul her to me and spin around, backing her to the closest wall, needing to feel her softness pressed up against my body.

"Mine," I murmur against her lips as I unhook her bra and drop it on the floor.

She grips my hair and arches her back against the wall, offering me her perfect teardrop tits.

"Fuck me." I close my mouth over her pebbled nipple, laving the hard, distended tip.

A cry reverberates from her mouth, and I slam my hand over her lips. "You want them to hear us, Nova?"

Somehow, the idea of someone barging in and finding my face buried in her tits, her eyes glazed over in passion, has my cock hardening to full mast.

Everyone will know she's mine then.

I'm going insane. The possession. The obsession. All things I never thought I'd feel for anyone.

Perhaps I was saving these emotions for her.

"Ethan." She gasps as I rake my teeth up the slender column of her neck before swiping my tongue around her pulse. "Y-You said I was a teen—"

"I was an idiot. The moment I saw him leering at you, I wanted to kill him on the spot." I nibble her earlobe and she rewards me by curling her legs around my waist and urging me on.

Plucking her nipple, I spend the next few seconds worshipping her other breast—biting it, teasing it, nipping it until the tip is all red and pointy.

All for me.

Alexis's whimpers are muffled against my hand as I work her pants off her legs and throw them behind me.

With a grunt, I hoist her up and place her legs over my shoulders and take in a deep inhale—her heady arousal giving me another shot of the most potent drug.

Looking up, I find her gazing dreamily at me, her lips swollen, tits heaving, those damn fucking nipples still beaded like the tips of erasers, begging me to play with them some more.

But I have more important things to focus on.

"Stay quiet, Nova. Wouldn't want Liam barging in and finding out his best friend is fucking his sister."

Her eyes darken—my little sweetheart has an exhibitionist side to her. When she's older, I *should* take her to the Rose floors inside The Orchid and explore with her. I never wanted to visit before, but with her, the idea suddenly seems appealing.

Adjusting her so she's stable against the wall, I dip my nose against the damp scrap of lace between her legs.

"Baby, you're soaked." I nibble her clit and she whimpers. She quickly clasps her hand over her mouth.

"Good girl. Stay quiet, okay?" With that, I tug the cloth aside and deliver a swipe from the top to the bottom of her swollen lips.

More muffled cries echo in the room as she gyrates her hips against my face.

She needs this. Satisfaction roars through me.

She needs the pleasure only I can give.

"Yes, Nova. Move that pussy over my face. Suffocate me. Drench me with your juices. Make yourself come."

"Ethan!" A strangled whisper slips out of her and she moves harder, faster, her legs locking around my neck almost to the point of cutting off my oxygen supply.

Dots appear in my vision but I eat her out harder, faster, tasting her sweetness, the drug that is her, inhaling her unique scent, surrounding myself with everything that's her.

My lungs are starved of oxygen, and her legs tighten some more. She's trembling all over—her sweet moans and cries urging me on. Using the last of my strength, I slide my hand between us and insert one finger into her sopping entrance.

She explodes. Her mouth parts in a silent scream, her pussy convulsing around my face as her wetness gushes out of her. I lap it up, every single drop, my cock so hard a single stroke can set me off.

Quickly, I unbutton my jeans and tug down my zipper and underwear. My dick, already beaded with pre-cum, flips up and points north, needing to be inside her this very moment.

Before she comes down from her high, I drag her back down and wrap her legs around my waist.

Alexis is still shuddering in my arms when her eyes flutter open. Her pupils swallow the blues of her irises. Fuck. She's orgasm drunk. My cock pulses again, needing to put that look on her face again.

And again. And again.

With a growl, I slam into her, my eyes nearly going blind from the white-hot pleasure traveling up my shaft when her entrance tightens around my cock. I should go slower. I should be more gentle. She was a virgin not long ago. She needs love poems and soft kisses.

But I can't.

My mind is mad for her. My body only answers to her.

My hips move of their own accord. Faster. Harder, I can't think. I can't speak. My mind is in an alternate universe, blank and yet filled with too many colors.

"Yes! Yes! Yes!" she cries, and I deepen my strokes, angling so it hits her G-spot with each glide.

Sounds of our lust and lovemaking fill the room—the clinking of my belt buckle, the slapping of skin against skin, the loud, rhythmic thumping of her back against the wall as we come together repeatedly.

Soon, a scream funnels out of her throat and I swallow the sound with my mouth as she shatters around me, her pussy pulsing and strangling my cock into nirvana.

Breaking our kiss, I throw my head back as ecstasy barrels through me. I bite my tongue to keep from yelling her name when I unload unending streams of cum inside her, emptying myself until there's nothing left to give.

Our ragged breaths fill the dark room, the rhythmic pulse of the bass from the music outside finally registering.

I plaster her against the wall, sweat dripping down our bodies, unable to move an inch. My cock still pulses from aftershocks and her pussy flutters around my semi-hard cock. I feel the wetness of our cum seeping out and it fills me with a satisfaction I've never felt before.

Eventually, my brain starts functioning.

"I should stay away, but it's impossible." Breaking apart, I stare at her beautiful eyes, luminous even in the dark. "I want to be the one to sit next to you in your courtyard picnic outside the hummingbird window. I want to feed you sandwiches and iced tea while you read. I want you to be the first person to read the poems I write…poems I've stopped writing until I met you, because you—"

I rake in a breath and grip her thighs tightly. Her lavender scent surrounds me in the sweetest embrace. "You, Lexy…you make me feel like everything is possible. Words flow out of me when I'm with you. I feel whole—and I've never felt that way before. So fuck, maybe I'm screwed up like Liam said—"

She shushes me, putting a finger over my lips. "My brother doesn't know you. The poet. My dream keeper. And you don't show this side to him. You're not screwed up."

"I've never been in a long-term relationship. I was always too chickenshit to try. But I want to try with you, Lexy. I can't promise I won't do something stupid or hurt your feelings, but I've *never* wanted to fall in love until I met you."

Her lips tremble and she unleashes another devastating smile. "You can never mess up. And even if you do, I'll be there to pick you up. Because my world isn't complete without Ethan Anderson."

She cups my cheek with one hand before dragging her index finger over the bridge of my nose, and I smile.

My gesture. My love for her in one simple stroke.

Leaning in, she whispers, "You always tell me I'm unforgettable, Ethan. But really, you're the unforgettable one. My north star."

CHAPTER 23

PRESENT: NINE YEARS AFTER THE ACCIDENT—TWENTY-NINE YEARS OLD

MY LEGS BOUNCE ON the floor as I review my program readmission letter from UNYC. My brothers pulled some strings for me to get me readmitted because my enrollment lapsed a long time ago. My heart pinches at needing the help of my brothers again. The familiar frustration, anger—everything my therapist keeps telling me is normal—burns inside me.

A lot of "I shouldn't needs" bounce around my mind, which is completely unproductive.

I snap my fingers—a new quirk I've picked up the last few months, the sound and movement reminding me I'm being too tough on myself. A literal "snap out of it."

"I got this. I got this," I chant under my breath and review the student portal—they've recognized most of the general education classes I've taken before, so that's good.

But you don't remember shit. What a clusterfuck. Do the credits count if I remember nothing? *Eh, who cares? People learn on the job, anyway.*

Dr. Riordan told me I most likely kept my accumulated knowledge—as evidenced by how marketing concepts were familiar when I read old textbooks to re-familiarize myself.

I just don't remember learning the concepts.

I snort and shake my head. I'm a hustler. Whichever direction life blows me into, I'll find my way.

If I take a full course load—most of which can be done online—and don't take summers off, I can graduate in two years.

I'll need to bust my ass, but I can do it.

Determined, I click to the next page and review my course selections. BUS 30: Financial Accounting Post Sarbanes Oxley, ATH 301: Beginner's Swimming Elective, because I need to do more than just float. I need to fight my nightmares. If I knew how to swim back then, maybe I wouldn't have lost eight years, and I want to take up a physical activity—something that's easier on my body.

I look at my twitchy right leg. The limp has gotten much better, but it'll always be there—a physical battle scar from my accident.

No more ballet for me.

There's no way I can handle the rigors of dancing.

Another devastating loss. My fingers knead the tense muscles on my thigh, my eyes prickling. I used to live for ballet.

It doesn't matter. One bad chapter doesn't mean the rest of the book is horrible. Snapping my fingers, I refocus on the screen.

There's one tricky class—MKT 462: Corporate Marketing Immersion—which will require me to spend six months interning at a company of my choice. This program is new to UNYC and allows students to get hands on experience in the real world. More importantly, the number of course credits is three times that of a normal class, which means I can graduate sooner.

I'll need to find a company to take me on as an intern, but I'll cross that bridge when I get there.

But before I click submit, my mouse hovers over the last course—a general elective class—ENG 203: Creative Poetry.

My heart races and I'm suddenly winded, even though I haven't so much as moved in my chair.

I've always been a reader—that much, I remember—but I don't recall gravitating toward poetry. Romance novels and historical fiction have been my jam. But somehow, when it comes to selecting a general elective course, my mind won't let me pick anything else.

A sudden wave of sadness sweeps inside me.

A hole in my heart. I'm forgetting something important. Something I'm desperate for, but can't reclaim.

My computer pings. A news update pops up.

I scan the headlines. The stock market rallies over news of a potential merger between Fleur and another entertainment company. I flag it for later.

A businessman was assassinated in prison and something about a shady organization known as The Association. I frown—what in the conspiracy shit is this?

A wave of nausea hits me from nowhere and my head throbs.

Closing my eyes, I breathe through my nose as the worst of the churning passes. Sweat beads on my forehead and I grip the side of my desk for support.

What on earth is wrong with me? Is this one of those side effects Dr. Riordan mentioned?

My laptop pings again and after the weird spell passes, I open my eyes to find a new email on top of my inbox.

I exhale when I see the newest email from my Letters of Hope pen pal, Polaris.

To: <u>A.Vaughn@gmail.com</u>
From: <u>Polaris@LOH.manhattanmemorial.org</u>
Subject: The Perfect Ending

Dear Alexis,

Sorry for the late reply. Life and work have been chaotic, and frankly, your question inspired a lot of thinking. "If you could rewrite the ending of a favorite story, how would it go?"

I must admit, I was taken aback when I saw your question—this wasn't something I'd been asked before. But then I figured it out.

You must be asking because you're feeling uncertain in this new world you woke up to. Perhaps this stems from a desire to rewrite your ending. But you see, there's something fundamentally flawed about that.

While you've lost eight years and that is a very long time—I'm not minimizing that at all—your story has just begun. You've far from reached the end. So, I don't think you need to rewrite anything, because you can create the ending you want.

Per the program requirements, I can't tell you anything about myself, but I'll tell you this. I've been exchanging letters with patients for the last eight years and all of them—I repeat, every one of them—find their footing in the new world again.

New perspective. New hopes. New dreams.

So I can say with certainty, you will too.

Warmth floods my veins as my fingers trace the words on the screen. His email is the perfect balm to the nausea and uneasiness I felt earlier.

I wish I could give the email writer a hug for understanding me so well.

He's right. Per program guidelines, my pen pal's identity has to remain anonymous, but I'm free to disclose my personal details.

And I did.

I'm embracing this new Alexis Vaughn. Flaws and all.

As for the answer to your question, if I could rewrite any story, I'd rewrite the love story of Eros and Psyche.

My heart races—*The Secret Garden* is my favorite book and Eros and Psyche's love story is my favorite Greek myth. The unwavering love between Eros, the son of Aphrodite, and Psyche, the mortal woman he was never supposed to be with.

I remember curling up in bed with a flashlight when I was little, imaging the handsome Greek god watching over the beautiful Psyche while she slept, because she wasn't supposed to find out his identity. I was breathless with anticipation, hoping Psyche would wake up and the lovebirds could finally see each other. Then, I was heartbroken when they were kept apart.

Their beautiful story ultimately had a happily ever after, the lovers reunited after Zeus intervened. But there was too much suffering to get there—Eros needing to hide his identity from the woman he loved, Psyche even coming close to death to prove her love to the other gods.

If I could rewrite the story, I'd wish for one thing only.

That Psyche wouldn't have to endure so much to be reunited with her lover. I'd wish her journey was gentler, because any man who truly loves a woman would rather bear the burden himself. He'd want her to be happy and whole, even if it meant facing the darkness alone.

I hope this helps your journey. As always, I'm here for you.

Yours,
Polaris

An ache pulses inside my rib cage. Unlike minutes ago, I don't feel sick.

Instead, I'm hit with an urge to cry.

The spot above my heart hurts, and I don't know why. There's nothing wrong with me—countless scans, X-rays, MRIs have told me that.

Wetting my lips, I process his words—he's never told me his gender, but I'm sure Polaris is a man and someone who's endured loss. Because that's the only way he can write such insightful and thought-provoking responses.

A sense of déjà vu ripples through me. It's like fate has engineered it all—me in this hospital room, randomly assigned to Polaris.

Perhaps he needs this outlet as much as I do. Maybe I can help him heal.

I click reply and a new window pops up. As I mull over what to write, someone knocks on my door.

The door opens, and in walks someone I definitely don't expect to see.

"Dayton?" I shake my head in disbelief. Then warmth floods my body.

Dayton Holden—my high school boyfriend.

"Lexy." His eyes crinkle at the corners—the wide, charming smile, the half tilt of his head—all familiar.

I know we broke up back then, but I don't remember doing it. And seeing the same smile on his face has me heaving a sigh of relief.

Some things remain the same.

He's wearing business casual—a dark sweater with slacks, his golden hair swept up. The last eight years have treated him well.

"I heard you woke up. Sorry for not visiting sooner. I figured you needed time to process everything." He takes a seat next to me.

"Gosh, I, I mean, I don't even know where—" I'm speechless. *Where do I start? How's life? Thanks for remembering me? Have you seen Summer? I'm so happy to see you?*

He chuckles, his laugh still sounding the same. "I know. It's strange right? To you, probably no time has passed, but to me, high school was a long time ago."

"Tell me about it."

"I wanted to see if you're doing okay."

The Dayton in front of me seems calmer, more mature than the football captain I remember, the one who dragged me to parties, won beer pong contests, and gave me my first kiss.

"Thanks. So, how have you been?"

"Good. I run Holden Investments now. One of the top fifty firms in the country." Pride glimmers in his eyes and I smile. He looks down and smacks his forehead. "Shit. I'm an idiot. These are for you."

Dayton hands me the bouquet of lilies in his hand and a small flush creeps up his face.

"Ha. Thanks." I bury my face in the fragrant flowers, inhaling the sweet scent. "You didn't have to."

When I look back up, I find his eyes intent on me, his gaze piercing. "Do I have something on my face?"

He reaches out and brushes the bridge of my nose with his finger. The spot behind my rib cage pinches again.

An echo—very faint—but before I can dwell on it, the sensations vanish.

"Pollen. There. All gone."

"Uh. Thanks." I grab the glass of water next to me and take a few sips, wondering why it's so hot suddenly.

"So, how are you feeling? Rumor is, you have trouble with your memory?"

My eyes snap to his face, finding his brows pinched with apparent concern.

But there's something...something I can't grasp. I shake myself. This entire day has been insane.

"Yeah, unfortunately, the last memory I have is when I was sixteen. But lucky you, I still remember when you stole my parents' car, and the guys TP'd it to prank you."

He laughs and shakes his head. "Seriously? Out of all the things you can remember, you remember this?"

I grin and waggle my brows. "You were so terrified because you just got your learner's permit. It was hilar—"

Someone clears his throat, and I don't need to look up to know who it is.

The temperature of the room drops ten degrees, but a sharp heat burns my back.

Swallowing, I look up, finding Ethan Anderson with his arms crossed over his chest, a dark storm brewing in those startling eyes.

"Am I interrupting something?" His jaw twitches and my pulse races.

Then he strides toward us.

CHAPTER 24

MY PULSE SCATTERS IN my ears as I watch Ethan prowl toward us, a cool, disinterested expression on his face. But his eyes—an unsettling intensity radiates from them.

It's a front—he's hiding behind his frigid mask. The thought barges into my mind. I can't shake the feeling it's true.

Something is bothering him. But what?

Dayton rises, and the two men stare at each other. They couldn't be more different—one easygoing and charming and the other the definition of leashed power, someone owning a boardroom with his mere presence.

The seconds stretch—I'm watching a showdown between two predators and whoever speaks first loses.

"I'm Dayton Holden and you're Ethan Anderson." The skirmish is over and Ethan clearly wins the round.

"Holden Investments, I presume." Ethan scans Dayton, an assessing gleam in his eyes.

"Yes. My family's firm." Dayton clears his throat. "I'm surprised you've heard of us."

"Knowing the landscape is child's play. And knowing who associates with questionable people is just smart business."

Questionable people?

Dayton stiffens. "I'd think you were smarter than to listen to rumors."

"Rumors usually hold a grain of truth."

The staring game resumes and I roll my eyes. They can talk in code and measure their dicks outside my room.

"Done with the intros? Dayton was my high school boyfriend and Ethan is a family...*friend*." The word tastes funny on my tongue. I'm not sure I can qualify us as friends. "He's visiting and we're catching up on old times."

"You're in a medical trial, remember? No one can tell you what happened in the past. Shouldn't you remember these things yourself?" Ethan's words are sharp, his gaze still trained on Dayton.

"Trial? What trial?" Dayton furrows his brows. "Why?"

"I'm trying to get my memory back. It's a long story," I reply and strain a half-smile. Then I face Ethan. "Have you always been an asshole, or did I do something to piss you off?"

Ethan falters, his glare softening. He opens his mouth, then closes it, before finally murmuring, "Someone needs to take care of you."

"I'm an adult, Ethan. I can damn well take care of myself!"

Snapping my fingers, I focus on my breathing—this temper of mine, I don't know where it came from, but I have to control it better.

Guilt knots my chest. Ethan may be an overbearing block of ice, but he did nothing to me.

Ethan's gaze snags on my fingers and I murmur, "I'm sorry. I shouldn't have yelled. I'm just stressed."

I return my attention to my laptop again. "I'm finalizing course selections and need to apply for marketing internships if I have any hope of graduating in two years. Everything's a mess."

"Marketing internship? You can come work for us," Dayton offers. "I can talk to my marketing director. We'd love to have you."

"Really? You won't mind?" Working for Dayton? Will it be strange since we dated before?

"It's the least I can do. Maybe we can spend some time together and—"

"She's working at Fleur." A command, not even a question.

"What?" His high-handedness has me seething. Why did I feel guilty about my outburst again? "*Excuse* me?"

"You need an internship. Work at Fleur. Marketing, right? Rex won't mind."

"I didn't recall asking *or* applying." I narrow my eyes at the infuriating man, who's staring at me like he wants to cut apart my brain to examine its contents. "And I don't want pity offers from you, my brothers, or from Dayton. I want to do this myself. Unlike some people, I don't want to use my last name to get somewhere!"

Ethan's eyes flare and a muscle tics in his jaw. Dayton clears his throat.

Crap. I just insinuated they both didn't earn their places in life. "Look, I didn't mean—"

"We're top five of the Fortune 500, Alexis." The pulse throbs in Ethan's temple now, and a flush crawls up his neck. But his voice is calm. Unruffled. Everything I'm not feeling.

"Let's be rational here. You aren't family and haven't been...romantically entangled with us before." His throat ripples as he swallows. He glances away. "So you won't get any favoritism from us. If it makes you feel better, I'll have HR review your resume and if you pass, you can go through our regular interview process."

His words make sense. Even the teenage me has heard of Fleur Entertainment before. Their hotels, nightclubs, and restaurants are world famous. I remember trying to sneak into some of their venues with Summer back then, only to be turned away by the bouncers who saw through our fake IDs.

Working at Fleur will open doors for me. They consistently show up on lists of top employers to work for. Their hiring process is stringent and they only take the best and the brightest.

If I can get in on my merit, maybe I can make it on my own.

Maybe Alexis Vaughn really will be fine at twenty-nine years old.

You're far from reaching the end. So, I don't think you need to rewrite anything, because you can create the ending you want.

Polaris's words echo in my ears. I can write my own damn ending. *Yes. I'll write my ending.*

Determined, I sit up taller and face Dayton. If I work with him, he'll take care of me. I'll never know if I can stand on my own two feet. "Thanks for the offer. I'll keep it in mind. But I need to do this on my own."

His cheek twitches. "Of course. Whatever you need. Here's my cell." He hands me a business card. "Keep in touch. And it's good seeing you. I'm glad you're awake." He leans in and brushes his lips on my cheek before turning around, leaving me with the cold financial king who looks like he wants to kill every living thing in the vicinity.

After the door shuts, I mutter, "Ethan Anderson, you may be Liam's best friend and maybe you think you're being an older brother by 'taking care of me,' but make no mistake, you are *not* my brother and I don't need your high-handed attitude."

His eyes flash and lips twitch. Is the damn bastard struggling not to laugh? I ignore the small thrill pulsing inside me and point to the door. "Why are you even here? You can go too. I have tons of work to do."

I swivel my chair to face my laptop again before stopping. Ugh, I have to answer that damn man. "And just give me the email of your HR. I don't want you to pass my resume along. I'll submit it myself. And no interference from you."

His low chuckles reach my ears, followed by a warmth trailing up my spine and the scent of leather and amber wafting to my nose.

Goosebumps pebble on my arms and I dig my nails into my lap, struggling not to drag in a deeper inhale.

"Yes, your highness," he murmurs.

His breath ghosts over my neck and heat shoots straight to my core. My muscles seize, my body attuned to his slow, tortuous movements behind me as he sets a bag on the desk. Dammit, do I have a thing for assholes now?

"Charles asked me to give this to you. New journals—the same brand your grandmother used." He pauses behind me, his soft breaths puffing against my neck, and for a moment, time stands still.

"I've missed this," he whispers, his hand grazing my shoulder, and sparks spread across my skin like wildfire.

"What?" *Missed what? Touching me? Arguing with me?*

His fingers trail lightly to my neck, settling on my rapidly beating pulse.

My breath hitches and my eyes flutter shut—a heavy sense of déjà vu and awareness floats over me. *This is so familiar.* "Ethan, what do you mean?"

He freezes behind me and clears his throat. "Nothing. Ignore me."

Then, the heat of his body is gone.

When I open my eyes, I see a familiar amber drink inside a straw cup bearing Estelle's logo—honey lavender iced tea.

I rub the sore spot on my chest.

"And you're welcome, *Nova*."

My breath catches and I turn around, but he's already disappeared.

He called me that when I woke up. I didn't imagine it.

Nova.

CHAPTER 25

PAST: THE YEAR OF THE ACCIDENT—TWENTY-FOUR YEARS OLD

"YOU LOOK SO CUTE when you're serious, Nova." I grin as we sit cross-legged in front of the roaring fireplace in my apartment, watching my girlfriend glare at the leather journal like it's her worst enemy.

Liam is in Aspen with a few friends for the holidays and is coming back later today. The idiot made fun of me when I told him I didn't want to go. Little did he know, I had plans with his little sister.

I stifle a yawn—it's a little past seven in the morning and the skies are cold and dreary outside. Normally, I'd already be up and taking a shower after swimming ten laps in the pool, but a certain vixen kept me up last night, then dragged me out of bed after a few hours of sleep to brainstorm on her list.

Let's just say my routines are now in the trash can.

"It is serious! I'm setting my goals for the next *twenty* years! Do you know how big of a commitment that is?" She stabs her pen on the paper.

Jab. Jab. Jab.

Chuckling, I reach over and stop her. "Patience is definitely not your strong suit."

"I had a year to finalize this list and I still couldn't! And now, I only have," she scans down the list of scribbles that include crossed out words, hearts and stars doodled around certain items, and phrases circled in red, "two items."

She growls. "Two items, Ethan! I'm supposed to complete the list, prioritize them, and start on my first item next week."

"Because you just turned twenty."

"Exactly. No longer a teenager." She sits up straighter, a proud smile on her face. "I'm doing well in college, know I want to do marketing when I graduate, and have a good boyfriend."

I arch my brow. "Just good?"

"Oh yeah. I'd give him a meets expectations. His taste in food is horrible—all that green stuff all the time is such a bore, but we'll work on that."

"What's that container on the dining room table? Leftover lasagna and cheesy breadsticks. And those chips—who bought them? Me." I groan, slapping a hand on my forehead. "You've turned me into a messy man who eats shit all the time."

"Shit! What do you mean, shit? Okay, I take that back. Below expectations. A D-minus. No, an F, because—"

My lips twitch, but I force a growl out of my throat. "An F? Oh, you started it!"

She squeals when I throw a colorful cushion—one of those jewel-colored, Bohemian patterned, with tassels and everything—at her. She brought them over because she said the apartment looks boring with the white walls, gray couch and furnishings. What can I say? Liam and I aren't complicated guys.

Another cushion hits me in the face and I jump up. "That's it. This is war!"

"Ethan!" She laughs when I pin her to the Persian carpet, her delectable body wriggling below me. My breath stalls as I watch her smile slip away when she realizes I have her wrists locked above her head.

Under the flickering glow from the fireplace, I see her pupils dilating and the smallest flecks of gray in her blue irises, which will forever remind me of a bright sunny day, just like her. A flush blooms on her creamy skin and my lungs seize.

"Have I ever told you blue is my favorite color on you?" she whispers.

I look at the navy sweater I pulled on this morning—my closet is filled with various shades of blue now.

"Do you know why I wear blue a lot?" I kiss the tip of her nose.

She shakes her head.

"It's because the color reminds me of your eyes."

"Ethan," she gasps, her eyes slowly welling with moisture.

It's been over a year of us sneaking around behind Liam's back, and I thought I'd be afraid to be in a relationship or I'd get cold feet. After all, I used to run away from commitments like they were contagious diseases.

But with Alexis, my Nova, I've only become more addicted, falling deeper and deeper in love with her with each passing day.

I can't live without her.

It's not a passing thought or an exaggeration.

I know it in my gut and in each strong heartbeat pounding loudly inside me.

"I love you, Nova." I brush the strands of fiery hair away from her face. "So damn much. You made me brave. You made me comfortable with myself."

My index finger grazes the bridge of her nose and a warm smile curves her lips.

Love in a single gesture.

"My world is filled with more colors and possibilities ever since I met you. You opened my eyes and I'm finally seeing."

"My poet," she murmurs and cups my face. I lean into her touch, our breaths mingling. "I love you too, Ethan. My north star. Because when I look at you, I know that no matter what curveballs life throws at me, I'll be fine. Because you'll be there, protecting me, taking care of me, and guiding me. I'll always gravitate toward you."

A desperate urge floods my veins. I crush my lips against hers. Flames singe every part of me—my body blazing not from the heat of the fireplace, but from the entire being that's her.

The rightness of everything.

My Nova with her north star.

The keeper with his dreamer—I'll always be the keeper of her dreams.

"Marry me." The words come out of my mouth, unbidden. My eyes widen, not in shock, but in how *right* they are.

Yes, I want this woman to be my wife. She's it for me. I know it as well as I know my name.

Alexis's lips part in a silent gasp, her brilliant eyes the size of dinner plates. "W-What?"

Pulling her up, a frenetic energy courses through me. There's a thread of unease, a need to make her mine this very instant. A strange fear that someone or something will take her away from me.

It makes no sense.

It probably stems from the intensity of my love—a sensation I'm unfamiliar with until I met her.

"Marry me, Lexy. I know we're young, so we don't need to do it now. But you're it for me. I love you so damn much. I don't think I can breathe without you. It might be too much, but I—"

Moisture pools in her eyes, and she gives me a wobbly smile. "Ethan. I...I love you so much too. I—"

Then she stills. "But our families still don't know about us."

We plan to date in private until she graduates and if we're still together, then we'll tell our families.

I was still a commitment-phobe back then—still puttering around on my training wheels.

Why risk my friendship with Liam over something that may be temporary?

It drove Lexy crazy, but she relented because we set a deadline and she knew I was a man of my word.

I'm an idiot.

"I don't give a shit if Liam or Charles get pissed at me. I don't want to wait to tell them anymore. They'll just have to suck it up if they want us in their lives. I choose you, Lexy."

Her lips wobble, and a tear rolls down her cheek. It's like no one has ever told her that before. My heart clenches—her tears destroy me—and if I didn't know they were of happiness, I'd want to bash my head against a wall for causing her pain.

I'll choose her every day. I'll whisper it to her again and again until she no longer has that sad look on her face.

"I don't want you to regret this, Ethan."

I shake my head. "I won't."

A loud whipping sound crashes from the outside and she shrieks. Instinct takes over—I pull her against me as we snap toward the windows.

"Looks like you may get your wish after all. The first snowstorm of the new year." My breath is uneven, the earlier unease winding tight around my lungs.

Just a snowstorm. Strong winds. Nothing to worry about.

Alexis squeals in excitement and hurries to the window. She smashes her face against it like a kid hoping to glimpse Santa on Christmas morning. Snorting, I walk over to see what has her so enthralled.

"Yes! I had a good feeling today. This is good mojo—the skies are giving us a sign today's the day we'll get those goals finalized."

She leaps into action and flies into the bedroom, appearing a few seconds later in a thick, fluffy, pink bathrobe.

"Come on!" She doesn't wait for a response and darts toward the door.

What on earth?

CHAPTER 26

"Where are you going?" I grab a coat and hurry after her.

"First snow of the year! We need to embrace the snow!"

"What?" Chuckling, I shake my head as we fly down the stairs, her hair whipping behind her.

"We can use the elevators, you know. State-of-the-art technology, Lexy!" I holler after her.

"Too slow!"

She was like this last year—insistent on running outside during the first snowfall in the new year. I thought that was a one-time thing, but apparently, it isn't.

She stops abruptly before we reach the stairwell door to the lobby. I nearly plow into her.

"I forgot to give you this!" She takes a small box from the pocket of her robe. "I'm an idiot. I was supposed to give this to you on New Year's Day and completely spaced out. See? It's meant to be—me grabbing this robe, this box banging against my leg, reminding me what I forgot—"

"Yeah, yeah." Lifting the small blue box, I give it a shake. "What is it?"

"Open it and you'll see." She rubs her hands together in obvious excitement as she nods toward the box.

I flip open the lid and find a pair of black circular cuff links. Amusement flitters inside me as I trace the delicate floral pattern on the medallion. It's beautiful and simple, something I like, but then I'm not surprised she has my tastes down.

But I still don't know why she's bouncing on her feet, looking like a cat who just ate the canary.

"I love this, Lexy. Thank you." I'm about to snap the lid shut when she stops me.

"There's a surprise! Ugh, you're so slow. Let me show you." She grabs a cuff link from the box and shows me a small latch on the side. Then, she pushes it and the medallion swivels out to reveal a lifelike painting of a hummingbird underneath.

"See?" Alexis looks at me expectantly. "Doesn't it look like the earrings you gave me?"

"Wow. Yeah. It does." I marvel at the bird—the delicate strokes for the feathers, the brilliant ruby chest, reminding me of the stained glass window in Ravenswood, the way the wings appear mid-flight and full of life, just like the woman who gave this to me.

Warmth rushes through me, chasing the earlier unease away.

It's perfect.

"I saw this at a vintage store. Not a brand name or anything fancy, but this is so special, don't you think? Simple and elegant on the outside, hiding a beautiful heart inside. Just like you."

I graze the wings on the hummingbird one last time before sliding the medallion face back into place and carefully put it back into the box.

Glancing up at *my* beautiful hummingbird, I murmur, "It's absolutely perfect."

Because my heart only pounds for her.

She beams, grabs my hand, and rushes through the lobby—past a bewildered doorman—into the sea of white.

The frigid air burns my lungs as snow batters my face. Holy shit, it's cold.

But my Nova isn't fazed. She spins around in circles, her arms outstretched.

Then she grins.

"You're my north star, Ethan."

Without a warning, she flies into my arms and an *oomph* tumbles out of my chest when I catch her. She presses the sweetest kiss on my lips and for a moment, I forget about the brisk air, the fact we're wearing two flimsy layers of clothing in the middle of a snowstorm, or how I can barely feel my fingers.

The fire burning inside me keeps me warm.

"And you're ridiculous. Who on earth voluntarily goes outside in the middle of a blizzard?" I smile at her impish face. There's no way anyone can stay mad at this woman, even if she's bound to catch herself a cold if no one takes care of her.

I slowly tug her loosened robe tighter around her body. "Someone needs to take care of you."

She beams. "That's why I have you."

Letting out a joyful shriek, she pulls away and sticks her tongue out to catch the snow. "It's the first snow of the new year! The sign of new beginnings and fresh starts. Don't be such a grump, you old man! And need I remind you if I didn't go out in a snowstorm, we wouldn't have met?"

I think back to how she barreled into me in front of Ravenswood, and how it seems like a lifetime ago. I remember I couldn't look away. My breath caught in my lungs when I glimpsed her sweet smile and fiery locks. Deep down, I knew my life would change from that moment on.

Now, I don't remember life before Alexis Vaughn. It's like a faded black-and-white photo painstakingly restored, then enhanced in technicolor, the before and after effects mesmerizing.

A snowball fight and a snow angel later, hail hurls from the skies. As I hover over her prone body lying on top of the blanket of white—because someone has to protect and take care of my Nova—I marvel at how much my life has changed since her.

"I don't know how you do it. You inspire me to be so much more. I...I—"

I want to write poems about this moment as we lay suspended in the middle of the busiest city in the country. If I were to create a snow globe to represent our relationship, this would be the scene I'd capture.

The magic. The thrill. The perfect snapshot.

Alexis kisses my fingers and murmurs, "Be here and be bold. Don't wait to live because…"

"The clock keeps ticking," I rasp.

Her whimsical mottos. The way she lives, like the grains of sand in her hourglass are running out. The desperation I felt in my apartment moments ago comes rushing back. It's unsettling; the feeling I always get when the winds are calm and an eerie silence settles before a violent storm wreaks havoc and devastation.

Swallowing the lump suddenly forming in my throat, I clutch her hands in mine. "Are you going to give me the answer?"

Her gaze roves over my face before a devious smile graces her lips. "Do you have a ring on you?"

Urgency burgeons inside me.

She teases me some more, then winks. "No ring, no answer. You'll just have to wait until our curry date next week."

An ache appears inside my chest and I fight the urge to rub it. It's just nerves. After all, I never thought I'd propose to anyone. *I'm going to make this woman mine soon. I'll have a lifetime with her.*

But the soreness intensifies.

I have the strangest urge to whisk her out of the country under the cloak of the night.

I shove the ridiculous thoughts away and watch her dance around in the snow, her nose tipped in red. My snowy ballerina.

Before long, we find ourselves huddled in front of the fireplace again, this time bundled up in a pile of blankets.

Her teeth chatter as she takes a sip of the hot lavender honey tea I made for her—I've stocked my cupboard with fresh sprigs of lavender and packets of local honey ever since we got together.

She sighs happily and stares at the journal in front of us.

We've finalized the first seven items of her Twenty by Forty list, and naturally, we've scribbled our thoughts next to each item as well.

<u>Alexis and Ethan's Twenty by Forty list (Well, Ethan will be 44, but that's beside the point):</u>

<u>Item 1: Eat ghost pepper curry.</u>
Dreamer: If we can eat one of the spiciest peppers out there, we can survive anything.
Keeper: We can survive anything without burning our mouths off.
Dreamer: Don't tell me you're chickening out.
Keeper: Never.

<u>Item 2: Find a red heart-shaped piece of sea glass in Mermaid's Tears Beach in Hawaii.</u>
Dreamer: Do you know red is one of the rarest colors of sea glass? Same with the heart for the shape? But it's out there waiting for me to find it.
Keeper: It's only a piece of glass.
Dreamer: *Pssh*. Polished by the ocean for ages. In the shape of a *heart*, Ethan. Imagine this—you, me, walking on the beach, finding a rare heart-shaped glass. Doesn't get more kismet than that.
Keeper: I'd rather be doing something else on the beach with you.

<u>Item 3: Skydiving over the Namib Desert in Namibia.</u>
Dreamer: It's the oldest desert in the world and I hear the views are spectacular where the sand meets the Atlantic Ocean. Enough said.
Keeper: No arguments from me. This actually sounds pretty cool.

<u>Item 4: Write a love letter in a Paris bookshop.</u>

Dreamer: This may be the easiest goal, but it's so damn romantic. A love letter in the city of love in a place hosting love stories from the ages? It has my name written all over it. I think I even know which bookstore I want to visit.

Keeper: Let me guess, Shakespeare and Company? You've been to Paris before. Why didn't you do this then?

Dreamer: There are some days when I think you're the most romantic man on earth, and then there are days when I wonder if you hired a ghostwriter to pen those poems for me. *Hello?* I haven't been to Paris with *you*, Mr. North Star. And it'll be so meaningful to write a love letter with the love of my life.

Keeper: Because I'm the reader of your book. And you're the reader of mine.

Dreamer: You're forgiven because you remember my motto.

<u>Item 5: Get a piece of treasure from a sunken ship.</u>

Dreamer: You're laughing at me, Ethan, but this stuff is out there, waiting for us to find it. Do I need to remind you of my motto again?

Keeper: Good luck going against *professional* treasure hunters, Nova. Need I say it again? *Professional.* As in, they've spent <u>years</u> looking for sunken treasure, and you want to somehow come across it?

Dreamer: Looks like you need a reminder: If I believe it, who's to say it isn't true?

<u>Item 6: Release a wish at a lantern festival in China.</u>

Dreamer: I may even sing a song from a certain cartoon featuring a long-lost princess and the ruffian who saves her from a tower to take her to see floating lanterns in the sky while I'm at it. And you're making a wish too, Ethan Anderson.

Keeper: I don't need any more wishes. All of them came true when I met you.

Item 7: Tie a prayer cloth in Jokhang Temple in Tibet.

Keeper: I think I'm starting to see a trend—going to far flung locales to make wishes. Why do you need so many wishes, anyway?

Dreamer: Serendipity. Fate. Magic. The next great discovery waiting for us just around the corner. The anticipation. Need I say more?

Bonus Item Not Part of the Official List: Teach me how to swim, dammit!

Dreamer: You promised. Or was this a lure to get me to meet you in person?

Keeper: Don't pin this on me. Every time you ask me to teach you, it's during my month-end close and I'm working overtime. It's like you're using me as an excuse <u>not</u> to learn.

Dreamer: Stop knowing me so well. But I don't care. This year is it. Swimming and curry. I can tackle two goals.

Keeper: You forgot to add getting married by thirty. That was another one of your goals, right?

Dreamer: It is, and stop trying to weasel an answer out of me. Be patient. *winks*

Pulling her to my side, I smile at the list—the positivity in her response, the humor, the banter.

It's quintessentially us.

I'll make every one of those wishes come true for her.

"What about the rest? There's thirteen more to go." The crackle from the fireplace joins the soothing rhythm of her breathing as I kiss her hair and inhale the familiar scent of lavender.

She yawns. "We can decide after our curry date next week." Her eyes flutter shut and her lips curve in a smile. "Our first item. Then take me to your pool. No more excuses. I can't wait."

She snuggles closer, and I chuckle as I lift her and carry her to my bed. We have some time before Liam comes back, and I intend to spend every minute loving the woman in my arms.

A soft snore soon fills the air and I pull the covers over her shoulders, watching my hummingbird sleep.

Safe and sound.

"We have a lifetime to decide," I murmur. "All your wishes, I'll make them come true."

I drift my finger over her slender nose, and she moans before curling into my side.

Smiling, I close my eyes.

"I promise you, Nova. They'll all come true."

CHAPTER 27

"An uncharacteristic warm front surges through New York City, sending torrents of rain instead of snow to the streets of Manhattan. Drivers are warned to be extra careful on the roads as wet and icy conditions may cause hydroplaning—"

I click out of the weather forecast video on my browser and stride to the floor-to-ceiling windows of my office at Fleur.

Lightning splinters the gloomy sky, the bruised clouds sinking low on the horizon. Muted sounds of traffic and screeching tires filter up from the streets, the heavy rain making it difficult to make out the details of the ruckus in the city.

Despite the dreary weather and the somber surroundings, a sharp energy sizzles through me. I'm a live wire, ready to combust.

Because tonight is ghost pepper curry night.

And I'm going to propose to her. For real. With a ring.

Taking out the classic Tiffany's blue box from the inner pocket of my suit, I flip open the lid and marvel at the glittering gems nestled inside a bed of black velvet.

A halo of clear diamonds surrounding a three carat, round-cut, flawless red diamond—one of the rarest diamonds out there—the color of the hummingbird's belly on my cuff links and in the stained glass window at the library.

A shade that'll forever remind me of her fiery tresses and the life and energy that is Alexis Vaughn.

I thought I'd be nauseous. I thought my palms would be clammy.

But I'm not.

I'm beside myself with anticipation. I want to see my ring on her finger. I want to show the world this woman is mine.

Knock. Knock.

"Come in." I close the lid and slide the box back into my pocket.

"Delaney. The auditors are here and they're giving the team a lot of grief over sample selections. I need your help to run this because the fucking lawyers are on my case." Trey saunters in and runs his hand through his hair.

He's been extra stressed lately because he's going through a contentious divorce.

I told him I could take on more work to help him out—budget approvals, cash flow analyses—but he said he got it, that keeping busy was good for him.

"I got this. How many selections did they pull?" I walk back to my seat and pull up the audit portal.

"Five-fucking-hundred, and this is just for the Kensington Hotels division alone."

"What? Who the hell has time to pull all that for them?" Ridiculous. They can pull the shit themselves.

"That's what I said. But we're on a deadline and come hell or high water, we need to file the 10K with the SEC for the sub. Talk some sense into them, will you? Their partner is coming on site in an hour to discuss our concerns."

My earlier good mood instantly evaporates. The looming deadline to file the annual financials to the Securities Exchange Commission for our publicly traded subsidiary. And Chuck Raynes, the audit partner, is an asshole—smug as shit and looks down at anyone who's younger than thirty because he deems us as unworthy of his time. If it weren't for the board liking him so much, I'd ask Dad to fire him.

That motherfucker.

Little does he know, I own this department, and my official coming out as Ethan Anderson is quickly approaching. Dad wants me to announce it after the 10K filing. He thinks I'm ready to take on more responsibilities, work closer with him and Maxwell, and eventually take on the CFO role.

An hour later, I'm knee deep into a stare down with Chuck.

"We're not paying for this. It's overkill. I won't subject my department to this nonsense."

Chuck arches his brow at my emphasis on *my* department. His senior manager, a quiet brunette who looks like she wants to shrivel up in her seat and die, speaks up, "Delaney, the new guidance indicates we need to—"

"Guidance is to be interpreted and executed by you." I hold up my hand. "Surely, this is why you test our controls, right? I'm not an auditor, but if we passed your control testing with flying colors, why the hell are you wasting our time in pulling POs, cash receipts, and God knows what for all these transactions? It's sample testing, not coverage testing. Come on, Martha."

"Delaney, you're smart and Trey favors you," Chuck begins, the condescending tone already grating in my ears, "but like you said, you're not an auditor, so you don't understand how the PCAOB and SEC are cracking down on Fortune 500 audits now."

Martha shifts in her seat, a blatant tell if there ever is one. I tamp down the impulse to roll my eyes. This is getting ridiculous.

"I get it, but I disagree with—"

My phone buzzes on the table.

Nova.

I send it to voicemail. I'll call her later. Maybe she's confirming our plans to meet at Bhut Kitchen in two hours. Or maybe she'll tell me what's been bothering her since she came back from her ballet event last night. I asked her earlier, but she said it wasn't anything I should be worried about.

"I disagree with you," I begin again, "because your approach makes no sense. The guidance—"

My phone buzzes again.

Nova.

My pulse ricochets—the foreboding reminding me of what I felt last week when the winds barreled against the windows at the apartment.

She's not canceling on our dinner, right?

Hairs stand on the back of my neck as my palms grow sweaty. *What the fuck, Ethan. Even if she cancels, you can always reschedule.*

But something doesn't sit right with me.

"Excuse me," I murmur, holding up my phone, "I need to take this."

Chuck swivels in his seat, a smarmy grin on his face. He and Martha whisper as I step outside the room and answer the call.

"Lexy, is everything okay?" I pat my suit, feeling the ring box nestled safely in my pocket. But this time, it doesn't give me the same feeling of security.

Instead, I hold my breath, bracing myself for whatever she's going to say.

"E-Ethan. I n-need y-you." Her voice sounds shaky, but it could be static because the reception isn't good and the roaring winds and rain make it damn impossible to figure out what's what.

"What? Sorry, I'm in a dead zone. Just stepped out of an important meeting." Quickly, I make a right and walk to a quiet corner by the windows. "Is this better? Can you hear me?"

"I c-can hear y-you. Something u-urgent came u-up. Will be driving. Can't find Charles. W-Will come to y-you."

Urgent? Charles? The unease simmering in my gut before is now a category 5 hurricane. I look out the windows but can barely see anything outside. A thick fog has rolled in, twisting with the rain into something otherworldly and sinister.

"Need me to find you? Pick you up? The roads are bad outside."

Alexis doesn't drive a lot, usually opting to walk or take public transportation. She rarely uses her family's drivers or car services. It's something I like about her—she has no airs. If you meet her on the street, you won't know she comes from money.

I hear honking in the background and strain to listen to her response. "B-But you're in an i-important meeting, right?"

"Yeah, but if you need me, I can get out of it." It'll disappoint Trey, and Chuck will make sure Dad and Maxwell know about it. I grimace, thinking about excuses I'll need to make up to get them off my back.

We Andersons don't shirk from our responsibilities.

A frantic gasp comes across the line. "Ethan...I-I'm so—"

The hairs rise on the back of my neck. "Lexy? What's going on? I'm worried. You sure you don't need me to come get you?"

Screw Chuck and my brothers. Alexis needs me. I walk toward the conference room, intending to call the whole meeting off.

"I-I'll tell you about it w-when I see you. Y-You're busy. Don't come. I'll call you when I g-get there."

The line cuts off abruptly and my stomach flips as I stare at the screen—a photo of Lexy with her back turned toward me, her vibrant hair draping over her back as she stares out the hummingbird window.

Acid makes its way up my throat and I have the sudden urge to throw up.

She's fine. It's probably the poor reception making everything sound odd. Alexis can take care of herself. *You don't need to worry about her.*

Closing my eyes, I take a deep breath before expelling the stale air from my lungs. My skin is clammy and I wonder if I'm coming down with a cold.

She's fine. She's fine. She's fine.

The chant reverberates in my mind as I straighten my shoulders and put on my game face. I need to take care of this shit with Chuck.

She's fine.

CHAPTER 28

PAST: THE ACCIDENT—TWENTY YEARS OLD

A CAR SCREECHES TO a stop in front of me and I slam on the brakes.

Fuck. A red light.

The rain is pouring, making it hard to see. Lightning splits across the dark sky and I flinch.

Please pick up. Please pick up.

I press a button to call Charles. He'll know what to do.

The call keeps ringing.

"You're reached Charles Vaughn. I'm unable to pick up your call right now. Please leave a message—"

"No!" I cry.

Cars honk and I notice the light turning green.

Images of what I saw last night haunt me. The screams. The cries. The horror.

It was supposed to be fun. A night in the town with the ballet academy. Mingle with the sponsors, network, but more importantly, having a good time with Tay Tay. She aced her performance—she was getting noticed. She was on the cusp of a breakthrough.

A sob chokes my throat. Tears pool in my eyes.

But then, everything happened.

My fingers tremble and I hit the redial button.

Dammit, Charles. Please. Liam's on a flight. Please, just pick up.

It goes to voicemail after one ring.

Tears slide down my cheeks and I shake my head—betrayal, not at my brothers, but at *him*—stabs my heart.

I can't believe it. It has to be a nightmare, right? Because I still can't believe it and I saw it with my own eyes.

My lungs strain out a ragged exhale. That voice I'd recognize anywhere. The light blond hair. The blue eyes I've known my entire life.

I have video evidence.

How could he? How will I face Taylor again?

Why couldn't I save her in time?

Frantic thoughts barrel through my mind, colliding like wreckage. The storm unleashes its fury on us; the rain hammering my windshield in violent sheets. The wipers aren't fast enough.

I can't see.

Calm down, Lexy. Get to Ethan. Tell him everything. He'll help you. He's your north star, remember?

Thinking of the man I love, his quiet intensity, his secretive grin, I feel my panicked heart rate slowing. I grip the steering wheel tighter, my eyes squinting at the blurry road, trying to stay in my lane.

My phone rings and I jolt.

Charles. It has to be him.

Quickly, I answer.

"Charles?"

"You bitch, why did you stick your nose where it didn't belong? You really thought you wouldn't get caught?"

My stomach drops. Horror curdles in my blood. *No. It can't be. But why—*

"Pull over, Alexis. Now!"

Headlights flicker in the rearview mirror. My breath snags. My pulse pounds—a war siren. *No. I can't pull over. I need to get to Ethan.*

The headlights flare into high beams. Blinding.

I slam the gas, ignoring the screech of my tires on wet pavement.

Ethan, he'll protect me.

Past: The Accident—Twenty-Four Years Old

She never called me.

Life is cruel, a demon stabbing you in the heart when you least expect it.

Obliterating grief strangles me as I bang my head against the bathroom stall at Manhattan Memorial Hospital hours later.

Raw, anguished cries echo against the walls, like someone's being murdered before my eyes.

Then I realize those sounds come from me.

She nearly drowned when her car plummeted into the Hudson. My Nova is in surgery—hanging on by a thread—and things aren't looking good.

I should've listened to the ominous warnings my body gave me. I knew something was wrong. I should've taught her how to swim.

I should've. Should've. Should've.

I could've saved her.

If I went to her, despite her telling me I didn't need to. If I told her to find a place to park until the storm stopped. Things would've been different.

I could've saved her.

Sliding down to the floor, I bury my head between my knees, my heart pulverizing under the weight of regret and devastation.

I wish I could turn back time.

To that moment when I hung up and strode back to the conference room.

How I told myself, she's fine.

No. She's not fine.

And now, I'm afraid. Terrified.

Anderson men aren't lucky in love. The belief, which has faded ever since Alexis came into my life, comes barreling back with the force of a tsunami.

Unbidden, Cleo's parting words—words I dismissed before because I hadn't met Lexy yet—whisper into my mind. *Why couldn't you have protected me?*

I should've known. Should've. Should've.

I have a feeling, the same ominous feeling from earlier, but tenfold stronger.

Things will never be fine again.

CHAPTER 29

PRESENT: NINE YEARS AFTER THE ACCIDENT—TWENTY-NINE YEARS OLD

"YOUR CUBICLE IS ALL set up, and this packet contains your initial login information. Restrooms are down the hallway by the elevators to your right and the kitchen is to your left. Don't heat smelly foods. Please…" Felicity from HR blabs a mile a minute, strutting toward the marketing bullpen, as she calls it.

Quickening my pace, I hurry after her. The woman walks like she's running. What would she look like if she were actually on the run?

I stifle a giggle and rub my damp palms on my black skirt—a simple white blouse with a pencil skirt can't go wrong—when what she says stops me in my tracks.

"Mr. Anderson will meet with you in half an hour."

"What?"

My mind flashes to a certain dark-haired man with banked fire in his eyes who looks like he's one wrong move away from detonating.

The mysterious, self-righteous asshole.

Felicity stops and cocks her brow at me. "Why do you look so surprised? He's your boss—the head of the marketing department? He likes to greet new hires—interns and employees alike. You're lucky. He's the most easygoing Anderson out of the bunch—we all like him. Well, Lana's wonderful too, but the others?" She mimes slitting her throat with a knife.

Oh. Rex. Chief Marketing Officer. Of course.

My chest deflates, crushing relief mixing with...disappointment?

Why the hell would I be disappointed? I should be ecstatic I'm not meeting with the storm cloud of the Anderson family. I don't need to endure another "you should take care of yourself better" cryptic comment from him.

I don't even know why the man shows up all the time like a relentless shadow. Two weeks ago, he appeared when Liam helped me move into a small apartment in the Flatiron District. My brothers weren't happy about me getting my own place. But I need them to treat me like an adult—someone who can handle whatever life throws my way. I'm not a child; not a teenager.

And certainly not a patient.

"Don't push yourself, Alexis. Grabbing life by the balls is great, but you need to let yourself fully recover," Ethan had muttered, his voice low and clipped.

"I'm not a fragile flower. I know my limits, Ethan." My words wobbled as a sharp pain sizzled down my bad leg and I faltered.

He noticed. Of course, he noticed.

The cold in his eyes shifted—ice crackling under pressure—but it hardened again. "Doesn't look like it from where I stand."

Before I could respond, he stepped in and took the box from my hands. Carefully, like he knew how much its contents meant to me—like he had done this before.

"Hey—" I started, a flare of irritation rising. I didn't want the movers to handle this box. These were things I'd never let strangers touch.

Something I'd never let strangers touch.

Ethan paused, those intense eyes of his dimming as he stared at my journals. He swallowed and rasped, "You shouldn't carry things that matter if you're going to risk dropping them."

Something in his tone made my heart twist. Like he wasn't talking about the box at all.

A sharp headache splinters my skull, and I focus on my breathing until the agony passes.

"Hey, Alexis! You listening?" Felicity waves her hand.

I force out a grin as the pain fades and refocus my attention on the present.

Felicity stops and points to an open cubicle a few feet away. "There's your workstation. If you have questions, ask Sandra. She's one of the senior marketing managers here. Mr. Anderson likes open floor plans, so only directors and above have offices." She motions to the cubicle next to mine, where a smidgen of blonde hair peeks out from the top.

"Got it."

"My door's always open. Well, fake 'door,' but you know what I mean." She pivots and speed walks in the direction we came from.

"I wish I had her energy. Maybe if I didn't have three kids sucking the soul out of me, I'd be like her," a wry, sarcastic voice murmurs. "I'm Sandra but call me Sandy. You must be the new intern."

I freeze—the timbre of her voice—the slight rasp, the dry wit. I can imagine the beaming smile on her face and the twinkle in her eye.

It can't be.

Slowly, I turn around and watch her eyes widen, her mouth dropping open as recognition flickers in her gaze. "Lexy? What the fuck?"

"Summer?" I blink a few times, not sure if I'm hallucinating.

Nope, she's still there.

Taylor offered to hire a PI to find my friend for me, but I told her no. I figured I could do it myself once I got my bearings on life.

Summer—no, Sandra—grins before rushing forward and crushing me in her arms. "What the fuck? You dropped off the face of the earth and you're here now?"

"Oh my God." I grin, unable to believe my luck. Summer, my Broadbent bestie, here in front of me.

The past me would say this is good mojo. Serendipity.

The adult me is incredulous.

"So, how have you been? Where did you go? Why are you an intern?"

I pull away and take her in—what used to be wild, curly hair is now tamed in a short ponytail. Dark circles rim her eyes and there are a few wrinkles appearing when she smiles, showing a life well lived.

"I was in the hospital."

"What?"

"You didn't know?" Clumsily, I walk to my desk, hating myself when I stumble on my bad leg. "I got into a car accident and was in a coma for eight years. Lucky to have woken up, to be honest."

"Shit." She follows me. "I'm so sorry, I didn't know. You stopped responding to messages one day, and I thought we just grew apart since we were in different states. I was so mad at you too."

Really, Summer? That's what you thought of me?

The strange anger brewing in my gut ever since I woke up flares and I quickly quash it down. *You probably would've thought the same thing if you were her.*

"Yeah. Didn't ghost you." Booting up my computer, I watch the screen flicker on as she props herself against my desk. "I woke up a year ago, and it has been nonstop rehab, and checkups, but I'm strong enough to resume life now."

"Wow," she murmurs. "That's terrible. Now I feel bad for not trying harder to look you up. So, you're interning? Does that mean you're still in college—do you have to redo everything?"

"Not all the classes, but a good chunk of them. Trying to catch up." A lump forms in my throat when I notice the pity in her eyes.

What is she thinking? And why does our conversation feel so...off now?

You know why. Eight years have passed by while you were asleep. Nothing is the same. You're a stranger to her now.

A fresh wave of sadness hits me. We feel different now.

Snapping my fingers, I bury those useless thoughts. No one tells you about the grief you'll endure when you wake up from a coma—and the guilt you'll feel about the grief.

The world as I knew it is gone.

And I never got to say goodbye.

Shrugging, I put on a brave face. "So, what's been going on with you? You go by Sandra now? And you have *kids*?"

She gives me a tired smile. "Yeah. Two boys and a girl. A whole white picket fence and a dog too. Adam and I met in grad school and I guess...with the right guy, kids made sense, you know? It's chaos, but I wouldn't give it up for anything. As for Sandra...Summer didn't cut it when you run in the rich circles. Sandra is more distinguished. Got to grow up sometime."

My chest pinches. She used to be the one who said kids were not for her and couldn't imagine settling down.

I was the one who dreamed of finding my purpose, my man, getting married by thirty, then two kids by thirty-five.

Sandra must have seen something on my face because she leans in and gently squeezes my arm. "You'll get there too. I'll have to live vicariously through you. You get to be free and enjoy your twenties, right?"

I flinch and she chuckles awkwardly, as if noticing her horrible choice of words.

Straining a grin, I reply, "Damn right. Going to party it up. Second chance at life—who knows where the wind will take me?"

She flushes and eyes her cubicle. "You haven't changed one bit—still the same free-spirited Lexy."

We've both changed. It's so clear but we don't say that to each other.

She winks and smiles, but it doesn't quite reach her eyes. "Come to me for anything. I'll leave you be."

After she disappears back to her side, I release a crestfallen sigh and tuck in a few strands of hair that have fallen out of my low bun. It's still damp from my weekly attempt at swimming in my apartment pool.

No dice this time. I couldn't swim without my floaties.

You know the technique—your instructor said so. You just need to get out of your head, Lexy.

But fear still grips me whenever I try—my mind seizes and suddenly, I'm hit with a barrage of still images—dark waters, loud roars, screams.

Then my head would hurt again.

But I'm not giving up. I'm going to get over this phobia if it's the last thing I do.

My cell phone buzzes and I pick it up.

A text message and a new email.

Taylor

Kick some ass, girlfriend. And tell Rex I'll kill him if he doesn't treat you well.

I smirk and reply.

Alexis

I'll whoop his ass myself. Don't worry…and thanks.

Swiping to my emails, my heart flips at a new message from Polaris.

To: A.Vaughn@gmail.com
From: Polaris@LOH.manhattanmemorial.org
Subject: Good Luck

Alexis,

Good luck on your first day of work, not that you need it. You got this.

Impostor syndrome happens to all of us—there are days when I wonder what the heck I'm doing. But remember—you are your own worst critic. When you're down, think about all the impossible hurdles you've overcome, the astronomical odds you've beaten to even be here.

I have faith in you.

Always in your corner,
Polaris

The pressure in my chest loosens. We've been corresponding a few times a month. I sense he's a busy man—he always seems apologetic whenever he's late in his replies.

I wonder what his story is and why he's taking the time to write to patients.

Whatever the reason, I'm grateful.

His words give me peace. With him, I'm my true self—insecurities, flaws and all—and he doesn't judge me for it.

Sometimes, I wonder if he's lonely and if I'm providing any peace to him.

Quickly, I type back a response.

To: <u>Polaris@LOH.manhattanmemorial.org</u>
From: <u>A.Vaughn@gmail.com</u>
Subject: RE: Good Luck

Oh Polaris,

Are you projecting your insecurities on me? Who said I had impostor syndrome? *wink*

Just kidding. I definitely do. If impostor syndrome is a sport, I'm the quarterback in the major league, playing in the seventh inning. Completely beating the offense with my keen EQ.

Thank you for your email. Honestly, reading it has put a smile on my face.

Always,
Alexis

P.S. What's something you've created you are most proud of? Currently seeking ideas for myself.

His reply comes almost instantly, and I jolt in surprise. A sweet bonus for my first day...good mojo.

To: <ins>A.Vaughn@gmail.com</ins>
From: <ins>Polaris@LOH.manhattanmemorial.org</ins>
Subject: RE: RE: Good Luck

I need to think more about your question before answering you, but I can't, for the life of me, let you walk around being completely clueless about sports.
Innings are baseball. Quarterback is football.
Lord help me. Whatever you do, _don't_ talk about sports with your coworkers.
Please.

Polaris

I snicker at the incredulous and sarcastic tone in his email. I don't get to see this side of him often. Grinning, I pull up a reply, intending to write something more outrageous.

Because I'm sure it'll put a smile on his face.

And something tells me Polaris doesn't smile a lot.

"I didn't know marketing was this much fun."

I freeze, recognizing the deep voice before I feel his heated presence behind me.

Ethan Anderson.

CHAPTER 30

FUMBLING WITH MY PHONE, I quickly click it off before turning around, finding the ice monster standing there, looking like an overlord inspecting his minions in his navy suit and tie.

My favorite color on him.

I snap to attention. Where on earth did that come from?

"Did you get off at the wrong floor? This is marketing." What I really wanted to say was, *are you lost, asshole*? But considering his last name, I figured that probably wasn't wise.

His perfectly styled hair—not a single strand out of place—gleams under the office lights. Ethan's lips twitch in a barely there smirk and the smallest thrill trembles inside me.

Smile, monster. Smile, dammit.

"Interesting."

"That's it? A one word response completely unrelated to my question?"

Ethan plays with his cuff links—the same black circular ones I've seen him wear every single time.

"Some things never change, apparently," he murmurs cryptically.

"What are you talking about?"

"You always spoke your mind. It's nice to see that quality hasn't faded away."

I arch my brow. "I wasn't aware I knew you back then. What makes you the expert on me?"

He falters, and that half twitch-smile promptly disappears from his face. Why do I get a sense he's holding back something...something important?

Straightening up, his eyes burn into me. "I've heard plenty of stories from Liam. You were infamous."

Crossing my arms over my chest, I glare back at him. "Have you read *Pride and Prejudice*? In the story, Elizabeth Bennett is prejudiced toward the cold Mr. Darcy and Darcy, himself, is full of pride. They wasted a lot of time because of these qualities."

Those ever-changing eyes of his sharpen, but this time, I see a spark of amusement in them. "Your point is?"

"To have both qualities in *one* person is unfortunate. And sad. And I'm talking about you, if you haven't figured it out yet."

This time, a faint imprint of a dimple flashes on his face and my heart flips.

What devastation will he unleash if he smiles?

I bite my tongue. The man is too hot for his own good.

"I see you'll do just fine here. Maybe give Rex a run for his money. I was worried for nothing it seems." Ethan huffs out an amused breath before walking away. He suddenly stops and raps his knuckles on the wall of my cubicle.

Clickety clack. It almost sounds villainous.

"I was going to tell you something important...but being so prideful and prejudiced, I forgot to think about anyone other than myself. I think I'll wait for you to find out on your own."

His gaze flashes with victory before he strides away, silent as a phantom, leaving me completely befuddled.

The asshole.

How is he related to Taylor and Grace? And why am I smiling? Dammit. *We don't like assholes, Lexy. Repeat after me. No assholes.*

Groaning, I turn back to my laptop and review the introductory emails. Most of the background info is familiar because I did my research before coming in, wanting to prepare myself as best as I could.

I remember being pleasantly surprised at this drive I had for work. I don't recall having this much direction in high school, but maybe I discovered a passion in the years I've forgotten. Dr. Riordan did say my brain matured while I was asleep.

Either way, it's a win, and I'll take it.

My laptop pings and I look up, surprised to see half an hour has passed by already. It's time for the meeting with my new boss.

Squaring my shoulders, I walk to the corner office and knock on the closed door.

"Come in. Your god awaits you."

I snort, recognizing Rex's carefree voice, and enter the room. The man in question leans back in his leather chair, hands clasped behind his head, wearing the biggest shit-eating grin on his face.

"Welcome, welcome. You may kneel at my feet." He waggles his brows.

Laughing, I roll my eyes. It's easy to see why Felicity and the other folks all love him. "Do you do this with all your employees or just me?"

He tsks. "Equal opportunity lover, but HR tells me I'm not allowed to say that. Although, you may get some special treatment, being Charles's sister and all."

"Hold on—I don't want special treatment. That's why I'm working here—"

"Whoa. Whoa. Whoa. Calm down." He leans forward, the earlier jovial expression wiped off his face. This is the other side of him we don't normally see. "All jokes aside, we wouldn't have hired you if we didn't think you could succeed here. I know life has been stressful—thought I'd break the ice on your first day."

My skin heats and I bite my lip. "Sorry. I'm sensitive to people treating me like I can't make it on my own."

"I can't imagine what you've been through," he murmurs, his dark eyes softening. "For what it's worth, I think you're doing a great job with everything. Many people would've cracked by now."

Knock. Knock.

The door opens a second later.

"I'm late, guys. So sorry." Lana brushes in, her long dark brown tresses flying behind her. She pulls out a chair next to me and sits down, her distinct rose perfume wafting to my nostrils.

She smiles. "So, Lexy, how has your first day been? Settling in all right?"

Lana is only a few years older than me and is beautiful, accomplished, everything I want to become.

"It's been great. Can't complain. Hold on." I eye the siblings and crinkle my forehead. "This can't be normal—*two* C-suite members meeting with me, an intern, on her first day? What's going on?"

Lana grimaces before plastering on what I'm sure is a very practiced smile for her Chief of Public Relations role. "Well, no sense in beating around the bush then. The truth is, we need your help."

What?

"I don't understand. This is my first day. What type of help do you need from me? I'll do it, but I'm just confused."

Rex clears his throat. "You've heard of The Strata, right?"

"The boutique hotel chain catered to the college-aged demographic that Fleur opened fifteen years ago? Three hundred fifty-six locations across the globe on all continents, excluding Antarctica?"

He whistles and claps. "This is what I'm talking about. When we saw you working your ass off in recovery, we knew you'd be up to the task."

"Just some basic research—didn't want to waste any more time." Warmth infuses my insides at his compliment and I curl a lock of hair behind my ear, brushing the mysterious hummingbird earrings I'm wearing in the process—they seemed like a good luck charm when I picked them out this morning.

"So, what the public doesn't know is that division is struggling," Lana murmurs. "Our numbers are declining and the stock market has caught wind of it. The target consumers are choosing Airbnb or other options now. With this trend, we're concerned about the stock price and how this may impact our other portfolios."

I frown—obviously, I haven't done any traveling since I got out of the hospital, so I'm not sure how I can help.

Clearly seeing the questions in my eyes, she answers, "As you know, Ryland is a full-time professor now. He's trying to improve student internship programs so that the interns can actually make a difference instead of running errands or grabbing lunch orders. We want to test drive his new program and give him feedback."

"So I'm your guinea pig? But I'm not part of your target demographic."

I'm almost thirty—not the early twenties population who frequents The Strata.

Lana nods, a glint of excitement sparking in her eyes. "True, on the surface. But you bring something rare to the table."

She leans in, her voice confident and persuasive. "You're older, but you're also in college and immersed in their world. And thanks to your time away," I don't miss how she avoids the word *coma*, "you have a perspective unclouded by the cynicism that comes with working in the grind. You're the perfect bridge between generations—mature, driven, and unbiased."

She pauses just long enough to let her words sink in. "This isn't just about market research; it's about shaping the future of a division. You'll gain real world experience, fulfill your course requirements, and leave your mark—all while doing us a huge favor. A win-win, right?"

Clasping her hands on her lap, she looks expectantly at me. The room falls quiet—I can hear the AC humming in the background. A sizzle of energy prickles of my skin as I mull over her words. It sounds exciting and meaningful—a challenge for sure, but she seems to have faith in me.

I glance at Rex, finding a mysterious smirk on his face, then at Lana, who's still exuding whatever positive, bright, magical energy she apparently has been blessed with.

She's good.

"No wonder you're the head of PR. You could probably sell my old ballet shoes at a premium and no one would complain."

Lana laughs. "It's only the truth. So, what do you think?"

"Well, you don't have to convince me since I'm an intern, but from an 'unbiased' viewpoint, what you're saying makes sense. I'm excited to help."

"Damn right, sis." Rex raises his hand and Lana rolls her eyes before giving him a high five. "I taught her everything she needs to know about human psychology."

"Oh please, Rex. Who comes to me with women problems? Who runs his big marketing designs by *me* before they're released?"

Shaking his head, he appears nonplussed. "Have to give you some opportunities to shine. The solar system can't only rely on the sun. Got to let the moon come out sometime."

"Oh, for Christ's sake."

I giggle, watching the two bicker. They remind me of my relationship with Liam—constantly wanting to kill each other, yet ready to destroy anyone who tries to hurt the other.

After a few minutes, Rex clears his throat. "Sorry. Lana drives me nuts. Anyway, to begin this project, you'll be partnering with the bore of the Anderson family."

"What do you mean?"

"A struggling division means numbers. Revenues, occupancy rates, budgets for revamps. This info will be the basis of a new marketing campaign to turn things around. That means," a sharp glint appears the dark gray eyes that run in his family, "your new best buddy will be my younger and most unfortunate brother, Ethan, because he runs the finance department."

My breath stalls in my throat.

Working with Ethan? I must've misheard. "Sorry, come again?"

I think back to the smug look on Ethan's face before he strode away earlier. The damn bastard must've been talking about this.

Rex glances at Lana—a strange look passing between them. I narrow my eyes. *What's going on?*

He clears his throat.

"For the next two months, you'll be working with Ethan—reviewing and analyzing the numbers, interviewing, and whatnot. We know one thing that the younger generation wants—transparency. We also know one type of person the same generation doesn't trust—CFOs and CEOs. So, you'll start with him, gather enough info, then conduct an interview we'll use in our campaign. Then, you'll move on to Maxwell. Finally, we'll put everything together and create another award-winning marketing makeover under the direction of the god of marketing," he points to himself, "and the brat of PR." He points to Lana.

"Asshole." Lana playfully jabs Rex, who bats her away.

"Toxic work environment. I'm talking to HR and—"

"Ugh, how are you older than me?" She shakes her head and pats my icy hand. "It's a lot, but don't worry, you won't be alone—we have other managers and team members assigned to help you. Take some time to soak it in."

The Andersons direct their two toothpaste-commercial grins at me, and I falter, my heart suddenly sprinting laps around my rib cage.

I don't know if it's because I'm overwhelmed at the scale of the project and the spotlight that'll be shined on it...

Or if it's because I'll be in close proximity with a man who unsettles me.

A man who looks like he holds the secrets to my new world.

CHAPTER 31

Alexis

THE CLUB PULSES TO the sultry beats of a hip-hop mix during my second girls' night out with Taylor and her friends at a nightclub inside The Orchid. Taylor's OG gang—her sister, Grace, and best friends, Millie and Belle—couldn't make it tonight.

Pursing my lips, I reread Polaris's email to me last week, answering the question I posed to him. We write frequently now—once a week, at least. Sometimes, they're short. Other times, they're full-on philosophical discussions about life.

The same familiar tingle appears behind my rib cage whenever his name pops up in my inbox. There's an invisible kinship I feel with him, and also a sense of safety.

Fear doesn't grip me when I read his emails.

It's like magic.

To: A.Vaughn@gmail.com
From: Polaris@LOH.manhattanmemorial.org
Subject: Rebuilding

I never answered your question from before—what's something I've created that I'm most proud of. To be honest, it was hard for me to come up with an answer that didn't sound perfunctory or fake.

I could say I'm most proud of my work achievements—developing and growing a strong team at my company, growing

profits exponentially—all the things you might expect some-one in corporate America to say.

But they ring false.

And since Letters of Hope is a program founded to help patients get back on their feet, honesty is something I should embrace.

I want to be true to you, Alexis, without compromising the rules of this program. While I can't give you specifics, I'll tell you this.

My achievements are born from a path of pain and loss—a devastating loss I wish I could turn back time and erase. There were days when I wondered what the point of it all was—to wake up every morning and keep going, to pretend everything was fine when I was dying inside.

I wanted to fade away.

I wanted to stay asleep and keep dreaming of a past I couldn't reclaim.

My heart twists at the visceral grief in his words. So palpable, I wish I could find him and hug him with all my might.

But I knew I had people who relied on me, people who loved me. I couldn't disappoint them. And so, I'd drag myself out of dreamland each morning into the harsh reality of the day. I'd put one foot in front of the other, to live and build my life because I knew the person who mattered most would want me to be strong and continue on.

Slowly, I built an impenetrable armor for myself, and I created a life after tragedy. A successful one. One I knew she'd be proud of if she were here, even though she wouldn't recognize the person I am now.

I don't recognize the person I've become.

The armor is melded into my skin, and maybe I can't feel the breeze on my face or the warmth of the sun. Maybe I'm afraid of shedding it because I might step too close to the flames and get burned again, but I'm alive and surviving.

And that's enough.

So, I guess, I'm proud of that.

Always,

Polaris

P.S. Don't be sorry for me. I'm very thankful even if life didn't turn out the way I wanted. I'm grateful as well. While I'm standing on the sidelines, I get to watch a second chance blossom in front of my eyes. And that's enough for me.

P.P.S. Describe your perfect night out. Let me live vicariously through you.

The aching grief so perfectly described. My Polaris is a poet—he has magic in his words. *Your Polaris? Come on, get a grip, Lexy.*

I blow out a breath. Nevertheless, I wish I could give him my second chance. Not that it'll make a difference since I'm still figuring out my place in the new world now. Polaris didn't tell me anything specific I could identify him from, but the letter feels like something a lover would whisper in your ear in bed.

I don't remember if I've had sex before. I was still a virgin when I was sixteen. But I'd imagine conversations like this would be something that might happen after you made love.

Sharing secrets, vulnerable confessions.

It's intimate. Raw. Tugging at my heartstrings.

I wonder if someday I could hold him in my arms. Not as a patient to a confidant in a pen pal program, but as...friends.

Or perhaps something more? My heart palpitates as the idea takes root.

"Why are you frowning at your phone? Is everything okay?" Taylor nudges me.

"Huh?" I click reply and start typing my response.

To: Polaris@LOH.manhattanmemorial.org
From: A.Vaughn@gmail.com
Subject: RE: Rebuilding

Thank you for confiding in me and being truthful in your response. Someone once told me my ending wasn't written yet, and I'd like to return that sentiment to that person.
Maybe someday, you'll get everything you desire.
I have a motto—if you believe it, who's to say it isn't true?
And perhaps you don't believe it, but I'll believe it *for* you.

"What are you typing over there?" Taylor leans over and tries to peer at my phone. "Is it Dayton?"

"Tay, privacy please."

"It's him, isn't it? Your ex-boyfriend who's been checking in on you in the hospital? I tell you, the man is interested in you."

"It's not him, Tay." Although she's right, Dayton has been texting me on and off. I chalked it up as him being a good friend, but maybe he does want something more.

Nope. Not thinking about that right now. I refocus on my email.

"Hm. Something fishy is going on. This reminds me of the time when you were texting with your—"

She stops herself mid-sentence, causing me to look up to find her clasping her palm over her mouth.

"What? What did I used to do?" My fingers still on my phone.

Taylor shakes herself and grimaces. "Dude, just pretend you didn't hear that. I'm not supposed to tell you anything about those four years, remember?"

Ah, dammit, the medical trial.

There are days when I want to say screw it all and just tell me everything already, because from the looks of it, this trial is failing and I still don't remember shit.

"To answer your nosy ass questions, I'm in a hospital pen pal program. I'm typing a response to a serious question."

"Hm. Interesting."

I arch my brow at her, finding her gaze pensive, reminding me of another Anderson I don't want to think about.

Waving her off, I murmur, "Give me a minute. I just want to finish this first."

It's funny how you asked me what my perfect night out would look like. The past me would probably say going to a party with my friends. Well, I'm here to report the present me doesn't find that as appealing.

I'm at a nightclub with my friends, and I wish I was back home.

Maybe sitting in front of a fireplace and journaling or reading.

Peace and quiet with someone you love. I think that sounds like a perfect night.

Always,
Alexis

P.S. I'm sorry to hear about your loss. I'm sure if she were here, she wouldn't want to see you in your armor, hiding yourself from the world. Whoever she was, she was a lucky person to have had you love her. One day, I could only hope to find someone who'll feel the same way about me.

My chest pinches, and I hit send, then put my phone away.

"Here's to the future as badass single ladies!" Lana cheers as she walks up to the table with a tray of drinks. She hands out flutes of a mystery cocktail to the girls, her silver sequined mini dress glinting in the dim lighting.

"Hey. I'm here, you know," Taylor grumbles.

"Hopelessly in love with my brother." I mock shudder. "Why anyone would love workaholic Charles is a mystery."

A paper napkin hits me square on my face. "Hey! That's my man you're talking about." Taylor narrows her eyes. The fake anger would be more convincing if her lips weren't twitching. "Charles is misunderstood. He just wants what's best for you and holds his cards to his chest, but he really—"

"Stop right there before I puke. To think of Lil' Tay growing up and—"

"Banging your brother?" Lana grins and wiggles her brows. She might as well be Rex's twin at this point.

I mime throwing up. "Disgusting."

"What is this?" Olivia Lin, one of my new friends, courtesy of Taylor and Lana, holds the drink up in the air, examining the contents. "Do I even want to know? It's got the colors of the rainbow in it."

I take a tentative sip. Sweet, tangy, and citrusy, ending with a berry aftertaste.

Taylor sips her water and shrugs.

"Not drinking, Tay?" I ask.

Her jaw works, her eyes not meeting mine. "I don't drink alcohol. *Ever.*"

I frown at her vehement response, and the girls exchange a look. But it's dark in here, so maybe I'm just seeing things.

Lana claps. "Pretty awesome, right? It's called the Jungle Mirage. It's Mystique's new signature cocktail after their revamp." She motions to the spacious club, which is spectacularly designed to resemble an exotic rainforest.

Acrobats and aerial performers swing from ropes attached to the tall ceilings. Dancers show off their moves in bird cages suspended mid-air. There are plenty of trees, green foliage, and beautiful blooms, giving a sweet fragrance to the air.

"Do you guys do this a lot? Changing up the nightclubs?" I take another sip of the fruity drink.

Lana nods. "Our patrons expect novelty. I don't come to the clubs often. The last time I was here, I think, was…Ethan's promotion? Yeah, it was his promo to a senior analyst when he was undercover at Fleur. It's been years."

"Undercover?" I sit up taller. The mention of his name chases away some of the alcohol fuzziness.

In the last month since I started at Fleur, I've seen him a handful of times—usually from a distance as we crossed paths in the grand lobby or in the corridors when he comes down to talk to Rex.

I'd feel his presence each time before I see him—a searing heat prickling my senses or the goosebumps pebbling on my arms for no reason. When I'd look around, I'd always find him in the vicinity, his gaze trained on me even if he was talking to someone else. Butterflies would swarm in my gut. But when our eyes locked, he'd look away and pretend I wasn't there.

This strange connection between us. It feels deep—bottomless, even. And I don't know how to explain it.

"Yea. My brother doesn't talk a lot, but he thinks a lot. Back then, he got it in mind that he wasn't smart enough to be an Anderson." She sighs and shakes her head. "He thought he needed to prove himself, so he worked from the bottom up. Took on a fake name and everything. Naturally, he kicked ass. The idiot."

"Really? Interesting." The person she painted—a person trying to prove himself to the world—is someone I can empathize with, and yet, it definitely doesn't resemble the ice monster who radiates so much confidence and arrogance, he can bottle them up and add to his billions selling the concoctions.

Then I remember what I insinuated in rehab when he offered me a place at Fleur.

I implied he got his job because of his last name.

Shit. I wince. *No wonder he looked upset that day.*

"It's sad though. He works too much. I'm not sure what happened, but after he revealed his identity to the company, he spent all of his waking hours in the office. Almost like he was possessed. You'd think he'd let go a bit. After all, he was climbing the ranks fine on his own when people didn't know who he was. They called him the Deliminator because he was so good with numbers. He didn't need to prove himself anymore." Lana smiles sadly at her drink.

"He withdrew into this dark hole no one could reach, and he wouldn't talk to anyone. Became a loner. Barely smiled. Turned into a block of ice. I worry about him." She downs the entire drink and when she sets her glass down, her eyes shine with moisture.

"Sometimes, I think he's just going through the motions in life and not really living." Lana sniffles. "Anyway, ignore me. It's the alcohol talking."

My heart spasms like someone punched it, and I rub the area, but the ache doesn't go away. My mind flits back to Ethan's handsome and stern face, the way he looms and lurks in shadows as if he's hiding his presence, which is ridiculous because there's no way the god of war could hide his fury—

A gasp tumbles out of me but is swallowed by the club music.

God of war.

Something about that phrase sent my pulse soaring and my fingers trembling.

Then, the searing headache hits again, and I groan and brace myself for the painful wave to pass.

"You okay?" Olivia takes my glass away. "Not feeling well?"

I hold up my hand and let out a ragged exhale, sweat beading on my forehead as the headache intensifies before slowly receding.

The frequency of these spells seems to be increasing. Originally, the doctors said this could be side effects from the meds for the trial. But it's still odd—these random flashes come from nowhere, usually accompanied by other strange physiological symptoms, like random thoughts literally stopping me in my tracks.

Do these thoughts mean anything? Is my mind trying to tell me something?

"Lexy?" Olivia turns me to face her, her eyes roving over my face.

"I'm fine. Just a sudden headache. Gone now."

"Okay. Well, tell us if this is too much for you." She motions at the flashing strobe lights, the loud music, and crowds. "One step at a time. Pushing yourself to the brink doesn't help anyone, and you know that."

Her voice is soft as she squeezes my hand. She's a psychiatrist who introduced me to my therapist because she thought it'd be better if I talked to someone who wasn't in my social circles.

"Yes, Dr. Lin. Don't worry, I'm a hard nut to crack." I wink and she chuckles.

"Well, there's no shame in seeking help when you need it—it's not a weakness, okay?"

I nod.

"Okay ladies, if we don't want to be single, we have to mingle. Well, except for you, Tay. Because if you mingle, I'll have to call Charles, who made me swear on Mom's grave to make sure no red-blooded male goes within five feet of you." Lana holds up her phone and shows a scowling Taylor what must be a text message from my brother.

"Oh, I'm so having a word with him," Taylor growls, grabs her phone, and stomps off as the rest of us dissolve in laughter.

"Hit up the dance floor, ladies!" Lana waves her hands in the air and practically runs to the crowd with Olivia laughing behind her.

I grin, following them into the throng and close my eyes, letting the music wash over me. My body moves to the beats, my left leg carrying most of the effort, but my right side is cooperating tonight.

I'm in a spaghetti strapped black minidress with two sexy triangle cutouts on the sides, my updo perfect, my makeup on point, and I'm wearing sensible flats so I'm not straining my feet and legs. I feel pretty damn good.

Olivia squeals and I open my eyes, finding her and Lana laughing with a few guys, clearly making friends in the crowd, and I go back to my dancing.

With each passing minute, my muscles slowly relax. I didn't realize how much tension I was carrying. I gyrate my hips harder, glee churning inside me when my muscles didn't protest in pain. I'm enjoying myself.

Yes. This is the old me. I'm older, more mature, but a part of the old me is still alive.

Reaching back, I grab the hair clip pinning up my tresses and shake out my waves, relishing in the freedom—the high of the music, my body in one with the beats again.

I'm thrown back to my ballet recitals when I was younger—the weightlessness of my body as I twirl around the stage.

Determined, I hurl myself into a pirouette, my muscles never forgetting the proper technique.

But dammit, I forgot to use my left leg as anchor instead of my right.

A painful spasm ricochets up my calf, and my knees give out. I claw at the air, struggling to regain my balance when a very familiar pair of arms clasp my waist and complete my rotation before tugging me flush against solid muscle.

"How many times do I need to catch you?"

CHAPTER 32

AWARENESS SIZZLES THROUGH ME at the ghostly rasp next to my ear, followed by his distinctive cologne reaching my nose.

My mouth runs dry.

"Cat got your tongue?" A puff of breath hits the sensitive spot under my ear and I shiver.

Ethan's breath catches, and he tightens his arms around my waist, drawing me closer to him.

So close I can feel his body heat singeing into my bare back.

"Ethan, what are you doing here?" I curse myself for the breathlessness in my voice.

My mind finally registers our positions on the dance floor—him pressing my body in front of his, his head dipped down, nose grazing my neck, his hands a firm brand on my hips, slowly moving us to the beat of the sultry music.

We're dancing together.

But it feels way more than that.

"Lana told me to come and give her a flash drive." He clears his throat.

I narrow my eyes. Something isn't computing. "And you didn't think that was weird."

"I was nearby." He sounds strange. He clears his throat again.

"I don't buy it."

Ethan chuckles. "Well, I'm not selling you anything. And lucky I came because you were about to fall flat on your ass...again."

His fingers trail up the sides of my dress to the triangle cutouts at my waist. A new tension radiates from behind me as he grazes my bare skin.

My nerves light up from the simple touch and my clit pulses. Unbidden, I place my hands over his and he freezes, halting us in place.

Time suspends—we're caught in a heightened dimension where everything sharpens—the sounds, scents, touches, colors.

Multicolored strobe lights wash over us, the roaring crowds fading into the background as my thundering pulse thunders inside my ear.

He's waiting for me. To see what I'd do.

He'll let me go if I pull away, if I give him the slightest denial. I don't know how I'm sure of it, but I am.

His heavy breaths caress my ear, his chest grazing my back with each inhale.

Awareness throbs between us—heady and addictive. It's taut, a rope slowly burning, its strands breaking, thinning, until we hang on by the barest thread.

A fire flickers inside me, my nerves sparking with each passing second.

I want, no need, more.

More.

An impulse—no—a surety reverberates in my body.

In this dark environment, with writhing bodies all around us, I want to turn off my mind and let my body take over.

Closing my eyes, I gyrate my backside, enough so that it grazes the front of his pants.

The rope snaps.

A growl snakes through his teeth, raw and unrestrained, as he tugs me hard against him. He takes over, moving us in tandem, his fingers trailing circles on my bare skin before slipping inside the cutouts...just slightly.

It's torture.

I moan, my head arching back, resting on his muscular chest as he sweeps me up in this sultry dance.

I don't know what we're doing. I don't know why my body moves against him like I was born to do this. I should pull away. I should stop this madness.

I wonder if we've been heading to this breaking point all along. Each glare, each barb, the way my body comes alive in his presence, and how he always seems to thaw and become more human with me.

Maybe it's been foreplay all along.

It feels right. Too right.

Like something I've been craving and wasn't aware of before.

His nose grazes my neck again and I whimper as those talented fingers travel higher until they almost graze the underside of my breasts. Common sense flies out the window as every atom of my body focuses on the sensual touches of the mysterious man behind me.

Wetness seeps out of my thong and I'm so glad I'm wearing a black dress because I can't be sure if I'm making a mess between my legs.

"Fuck," a guttural rasp, so faint I wonder if it was directed at himself. "I've waited…"

My mind is a muddled mess as I gyrate against him, every part of me yearning for more. This has to be lust. I haven't been with anyone since I woke up. Heck, am I still a virgin? I can't remember.

"Ethan, I…I…"

"Yes, hummingbird? What do you need?" There's a softest pressure on my neck, my senses delayed until I feel the possessive suction followed by a lick.

He's kissing me. Tasting my neck like he's famished.

Each drugging pull is a direct caress on my clit as I melt into his embrace. I need him to do more, to relieve this building pressure between my legs. I can't think or question what we're doing, or why I'm responding this way.

All I can do is feel the thousand sensations coursing through me—the way my nipples strain against my dress, the heaviness of my breasts as we bob and move to the music, the goosebumps pebbling over my skin as his fingers rove back down, sliding to my hips before dipping under the cutouts again and this time hooking onto the strings of my thong.

"I can smell you. You make it so hard for me to—"

He thrusts against my ass and lets out a tortured sound—something between a hiss and a groan. I clench my thighs when I feel a hard rod pressing against my curves.

Ethan Anderson, the ice monster, is turned on and burning hot.

For me.

It makes no sense, and yet, somehow, it does. I can't bring myself to analyze this right now.

"What?" I whimper, belatedly realizing he didn't finish his sentence.

"Your arousal. I can smell it."

"Y-You're crazy."

He grunts. "Don't deny it, my little hummingbird."

Hummingbird. Why does this word make my heart flutter?

Unbidden, he tugs on the strings of my thong again and the fabric bunches and digs into my folds, hitting the swollen bundle of nerves.

A scream tears out of me and he quickly clasps his hand over my mouth. "Only I can hear those sounds."

Raw possessiveness. Obsession in a sentence.

My knees give out, but this time it isn't from pain, it's from the sharp pleasure coursing through my veins. He supports me with his muscular body as he swivels us toward the floor before standing back up again.

I might not remember if I've had sex before, but I'd imagine it'd feel something like this.

"You were saying?" He sounds smug.

"You arrogant bastard."

He chuckles, the deep sounds direct caresses to my pussy.

"Won't admit it, huh? I'll need to convince you then."

Without warning, he moves his fingers again, tugging, pulling at my underwear strings like I'm a marionette. The sparks begin anew and I whimper and thrash in his hold, my head dropping back against his chest.

"Shit. Fuck me," he grunts, his fingers moving faster.

My thong saws up and down my pussy, each graze hitting my clit at the precise angle. Blinding sparks appear in my vision as my lips part in an open gasp, the pressure building between my legs at the speed of light.

"Want me to stop?" he rasps, pausing his fiery torture.

Wordlessly, I clutch his wrists, not stopping him, but egging him on. "Please...I need this."

He works a quickening rhythm and I can only imagine how we look on the dance floor in the middle of a crowded room, our bodies plastered together, my legs slightly parted and his hands inside my dress through the side cutouts.

His hard cock digs into my back. *Thrust. Thrust. Thrust.*

"Oh my god, yes," I moan and I swear I can feel him grow harder against my ass.

My pussy pulses as he digs my thong sideways, flicking my clit in an expert rhythm.

Wetness leaks down my legs and I arch my tits out, my body wanting to explode, wanting to fall off this cliff and take this maddening man with me.

"Fuck, yes, Nova. You're close, aren't you? I can feel it. You must be dripping, needing a release. Let me give it to you."

His dirty words fan the flames and another cry perches at the tip of my throat as I widen my stance, giving him more access.

My legs tremble and with a growl, he yanks the strings hard, digging the scrap of material deeper into my core.

The lash of pain sets me off.

I explode into a million pieces, my body twitching as ecstasy courses through my veins. A cry rips out of my throat.

Not wanting to draw attention to us, I follow my basest impulse.

I bite the flesh closest to me.

His neck.

"Shit!" he growls and humps me faster before his body spasms behind me. He clutches me tightly against him, his breathing in stuttered gasps, when I feel a damp heat on my ass.

He came. In his pants. In public. Against me.

The next few seconds are pleasure-filled fragments. His heavy breathing against my ear. His fingers rubbing gentle circles on my waist as I ride out the aftershocks.

"I burn...because of you." The faintest whisper. So faint, I wonder if I'm hearing it right.

"What did you just say?"

He doesn't answer me, but instead, there's a soft pressure on my hair—a kiss?

My mind is in a haze. Nothing makes sense. I'm soaring in the skies like the hummingbird earrings I'm wearing.

"Ethan! Lexy! There you are. Sorry, we got pulled away by a few people."

Lana's voice shocks my senses, and I quickly hurl myself off her brother.

Thank God we're in the dark, because there's no way I can hide the flush I'm sure is on my face, or the way my nipples are still poking out of my dress like headlights.

"You guys good? Didn't kill each other, right?" She grins and walks toward us, Olivia quick behind her.

"We're good." I strain a smile and hope it's convincing.

"Here. Your USB." A suit clad arm appears in my peripheral vision, a black, circular cuff link peeking out, and he hands his sister the drive.

Lana cocks her brow, then shakes her head, looking wholly unimpressed. "Thanks, Ethan."

"What's the urgency? You really asked him to come here to give you a flash drive?" I can't keep the incredulity out of my voice.

She grins. "That's for me to know and you to find out."

Ethan scoffs. "Well. Have fun, ladies. And see you later...Alexis."

At my name, I straighten my shoulders and turn around, bracing myself for the full impact of seeing him for the first time tonight.

Common sense flickers online as the remnants of pleasure slowly fade away.

Ethan Anderson, the ice monster, the man who drives me out of my mind with his overbearing ways, just made me come in public. He rutted his no doubt sizable cock against me until he came in his pants.

And I liked it.

What the fuck—have I lost my mind?

Searing eyes meet mine and while the rest of his frame is relaxed in his usual detached indifference, the blistering expression on his face says otherwise.

His jaw locks and nostrils flare. Under the dim light, I can see his pupils are dilated and his pulse battering against his temple.

Holding my gaze, he murmurs, "See you at work tomorrow, Alexis."

Then he nods at the other girls and strides away, out of view, oblivious to the rioting heartbeats in my chest.

A few seconds later, Olivia pops up by my side. "Don't think I didn't see that."

I force out a few chuckles. "W-What?"

"He looks like he could devour you alive."

Devour me alive.

I should be scared. I should be worried. I should go online and buy the first chastity belt I can find.

So why do I want to offer myself as a sacrifice instead?

CHAPTER 33

PAST: ONE MONTH AFTER THE ACCIDENT—TWENTY-FOUR YEARS OLD

"ARE YOU THERE, LEXY? Do you hear me, my love?" I rasp, my throat hoarse.

I slowly climb onto her bed at Manhattan Memorial, careful not to jostle her, and curl my body next to hers.

A lump forms in my throat.

"Lexy?"

She doesn't answer me.

Of course she can't answer you. She's in a coma.

She was transferred to long-term care yesterday. It's been one month since the horrid accident when they fished her out of the Hudson, her skin already turning blue, her body broken and battered. If it weren't for the anonymous Good Samaritan, she'd be dead.

Gone forever.

The odds aren't optimistic she'd come out of it. Too much time in the water, the brain deprived of oxygen for too long, not to mention the severe injuries she sustained.

"Lexy, I love you so much. Wake up, *please.*"

I lift her bandaged hands and kiss each of her fingertips.

With trembling fingers, I pull the ring out from my pocket and put it on her hand.

"You asked for a ring, Nova. I bought you the prettiest one there is. You'll love it. It's one of a kind, just like you." The jewels glimmer under the dim light, my chest clenching as a fresh torrent of grief rains on me.

"W-Will you marry me, Nova?" My voice is barely a whisper. Raw. Trembling. "Make me the happiest man on earth?"

Nothing.

No twitch. No movement.

Only the steady, merciless *beep...beep...beep...*of the machines.

My heart pulverizes, the pain robbing me of breath. All I can do is hold her tightly in my arms, wishing she could feel my presence. I press kisses on her hair and shoulder.

"D-Do you blame me, Nova?" A choked gasp. "If I taught you how to swim...maybe you could've escaped. I keep replaying that day in my mind." My tears seep into the fabric of her hospital gown. "Every moment, every choice. If I'd done *one* thing differently, maybe you'd be awake now. Maybe I could've saved you."

That's the thing with grief. Oftentimes it's laced with regret. Because we never know when the clock runs out—when that brief kiss, that argument, that phone call, might become your last.

And once you realize...it's too late, and those painful, corrosive thoughts eat you alive.

I swipe away the wetness on my cheeks. "Please don't make me do life without you."

My chest is hollow.

I can't imagine a life without her.

I *don't* want to imagine a life without her.

A ragged exhale escapes me, and I close my eyes and breathe in her scent.

My muscles seize. It's all wrong.

Where's the lavender? Her lavender?

All I can smell are soap and cleaning agents. Hospital smells.

Panic rears its ugly head. My pulse quakes in my ears and my lungs constrict. It's like someone is stabbing me with knives—over and over again.

I can't do this. I can't be here.

I can't see her lying there, hooked up to machines.

Clinging to life by the thinnest thread.

My panting breaths quicken and soon the room spins. *I can't breathe. Why I can't I breathe?*

Mind swirling, I stagger off the bed. I tuck the blankets around her shoulders and kiss her forehead.

Then I flee.

***

Some time later, I find myself inside Bhut Kitchen, where we were supposed to meet that night for our first bucket list item.

"*Namaste.* How many people are in your party?"

I blink at the blurry shape in front of me—waitress, waiter, whoever. It doesn't matter.

"One."

She frowns as she grabs a menu and motions me to follow her.

A pressure cinches my neck—the beginnings of a migraine. I barely notice the lush decorations—bright, jeweled tones and fabrics I'm sure are beautiful if I care to pay attention.

A fork clatters as I brush past a table. An older couple gapes at me. I swipe my face, my week-old beard prickling my hand. I haven't shaved since the hospital visit and other than a quick shower this morning to make sure I don't reek; I know I look like a mess.

The headache intensifies, and I wince.

Any normal person would go home and hide from the world, not trying to brave the ghost pepper curry challenge.

But I *need* to do something. For her. For me.

"This is your table, sir. Would you like anything to drink while you look over the menu?"

I shake my head. "Water's fine. And I don't need the menu. One ghost pepper curry please."

She nods and turns away, but quickly pauses and asks me, "Sir. It's not my place to ask, but...are you okay? Do I need to call someone for you?"

Call someone.

I struggle an inhale.

That person would've been my Nova if she were awake.

I finally look at the waitress, a young woman with straight black hair and large eyes, currently shining with concern.

"No." I swallow. "You don't need to call anyone for me."

She nods and slips away. Closing my eyes, I rest my head against the headrest.

Images of her flash through my mind. Hair the color of the most beautiful sunset. The freckles on her cheeks and nose—constellations of the heavens drawn on her face.

Her crystal clear blue eyes. The life in them. The spark.

Will I ever see them again?

My phone buzzes—text messages from Dad or my siblings, no doubt. They're concerned about me. After the accident, I pushed myself to finish the audit. I buried myself with work—doing everything I could to not feel.

Once we submitted the filing, Dad announced my real identity to the company. Trey gaped at me in shock and I promptly put in two weeks of vacation.

I couldn't do it. Keep pretending my life didn't end when her car plunged into the river.

"Sir, here you go. Our famous ghost pepper curry. Please be careful, the bowl is very hot. The ghost pepper is one of the spiciest peppers out there. If you want to switch to a milder curry, do let us know. Here's a glass of milk as well—it helps with the spiciness."

She places the food in front of me and walks away.

Staring at the steaming contents, the spicy fumes make my eyes water. I think back to what she said before.

The gift of hope. Because, if you believe it, who's to say it isn't true?

Grief grips my chest, excruciating, and I make a vow—send a message to the universe, as she'd say.

You'll wake up, Lexy. Because you're a fighter. The girl who chases whimsical dreams and impossible possibilities. Until you wake up, I'll carry your torch, your dreams, your bucket list. One item a year. For you. Because I know you're fighting hard too.

It's the only thing I can do for her.

Starting with the first item on her list, the ghost pepper curry challenge.

"I-I'll fight for you, Lexy." My eyes burn—but this time, it isn't from the spicy fumes.

I dig into the curry and rice and shove a big spoonful into my mouth.

The searing intensity of the ghost pepper hits me right away. My mouth is on fire and my tongue and lips swell. My immediate instinct is to reach for the glass of milk.

But I stop myself.

Moisture pools in my eyes as I shove another spoonful into my mouth, ignoring the inferno, the sensations of a being burned alive, because *nothing* can compare to the agony of being at Bhut Kitchen, eating ghost pepper curry, without her.

She was supposed to be here.

I was supposed to be laughing and crying at the same time with her, my body cursing me for doing this challenge, which would turn into a competition.

She'd joke and say something outrageous to make me lose my concentration. Then I'd pull out the ring and drop to my knee next to the table.

And ask her to marry me.

While our tongues were burning, tears of pain mixing with joy, our faces a mess.

It'd be perfect.

Tears stream down my face as I swallow the curry, the lava scorching my throat and charring my insides. Pushing my drink away, I focus on the physical pain, a distraction from the agony cleaving my heart in half.

Choked sobs rip from my throat.

I'm making a scene, but I don't care.

"It's spicy, isn't it?" An older gentleman chuckles as he passes by my table. "I think I dried my tear ducts when I tried ghost pepper curry too."

Wiping my tears away, I look at the gentleman, who hands me a napkin, a sympathetic smile on his face.

He murmurs, "Damn ghost peppers."

"Everything burns," I rasp, my vision blurring again. More tears fall and I sob into the napkin, unable to face the stranger anymore.

I can't stop the tears. I can't stop the pain. I can't stop *anything*.

My Nova. My future. My heart. My soul. My everything.

Burns.

Everything burns.

CHAPTER 34

PRESENT: NINE YEARS AFTER THE ACCIDENT—TWENTY-NINE YEARS OLD

"I'M GLAD WE DID this, Lexy." Dayton smiles as he takes out his credit card.

I quickly pull out my wallet, but he stops me.

"Don't worry about it." His familiar easygoing grin makes a reappearance.

We're sitting by the windows in a quaint cafe on the Upper West Side. Pedestrians hurry to their next destinations, all bundled up in wool coats and leather gloves, no doubt bracing themselves against the brisk wind of late fall.

Dayton and I have texted occasionally since he visited me in the hospital. He's a good friend, and he's tried, more than Summer—or Sandra—to my disappointment, to reconnect.

I constantly remind myself while it might feel like I just took a nap, for everyone else, years have gone by. Years where they've lived life, experienced hardships, got married, had kids, and became completely different people.

Just like how I've matured, it's only normal for relationships to change.

Maybe someday, the aching loss I feel would fade away.

"So, how's the medical trial going?"

"I honestly don't know. They don't tell me much because they don't want to influence the results—placebo effects or whatnot. Just a bunch of pills and monthly scans and checkups."

"But do you think it's working?"

Something in his voice makes me look up. Dayton smiles at me in that reassuring way of his. He reaches over and holds my hand.

"My memory? Like, has it come back?"

He nods.

"No, not really. I have snippets of images. But nothing I can make sense of." My chest tightens and I stare at our hands—a sight I remember so well. But I want to pull away. "Just a lot of water. Dark waters. Screams and yelling. I can't tell what's real or not."

I shiver, thinking about the helplessness I'd feel whenever I'm in a spell, trapped in pitch black water rushing into my lungs.

"One day, everything will make sense." I snap my rubber band. "Maybe when I can swim without help, I'll finally figure it out."

I've gotten nowhere with my swimming. Floating in the kiddie pool and even swim laps around it, no problem. But put me somewhere deep where I can't touch the bottom, and I'm screwed.

"It must be hard." Dayton releases my hand. He sits back in his chair, his voice soft. He's matured so much and I like this side of him. "But don't force yourself. It can backfire...or so I've read."

"You've done research?"

"Of course. We're friends, right? I care about my friends."

"Right. Of course we are. I'm grateful you're here." The tension releases from my body. Having a second chance at life puts everything in perspective.

To really treasure the people who stick around.

"You know what sucks? People tip-toeing around me. Thanks for not treating me like an invalid." I sigh and look around. "So much has changed. Remember Uncle Ian, Dayton? You met him when you picked me up for Homecoming back then."

He looks at me strangely. "I think so. What about him?"

"You think so? He showed you our gun safe, and you were sweating bullets afterward. No pun intended."

Dayton chuckles. "Oh right. I remember now. What about him?"

"No one would tell me how he died. I asked and even researched online but came up empty."

He leans forward, his voice urgent. "Lexy, you won't get answers to everything. And that's okay. Enjoy the present."

I cock my head to the side, and he shrugs and smiles.

"You're right. I just need to accept that I might not remember everything about the past. I should focus on the present instead." I groan, thinking about who I'll be seeing when I get back to Fleur.

My meeting with the finance department, which includes Ethan.

"What's going on? You look worried."

"Just work stuff." I ball up the napkin in front of me.

Dayton frowns and leans forward. "Is this about...Ethan Anderson?"

Maybe it's the concern in his voice, the familiarity of his gaze, or the fact he isn't related to the man in question, like Taylor is. But suddenly, I get an urge to confess my complicated feelings toward Ethan.

I stare at the napkin in front of me. "He's a man of a few words—cold, and yet hot at the same time. I can't figure him out." *The understatement of the year.*

"Hm." Dayton taps his fingers on the table. "May I give you some advice?"

I look up and nod.

"Ethan Anderson is known to be calculating and ruthless in the industry. He never reveals his cards until he's setting down his winning hand. And it makes me wonder how a person became that way and what deals he had to make to get to where he's at now." Dayton reaches over and clasps my hand again. His voice becomes urgent. "I don't want you to get hurt, Lexy. I might be overstepping, but if I were you, I'd stay away from him."

A pinch appears behind my rib cage. *What if I don't want to stay away?*

The server returns with the bill and Dayton lets go of my hand and signs it. "Shall we?"

We walk outside, and his driver opens the door of his town car.

"You sure I can't drop you off at your office?"

Glancing at the overcast skies, I shake my head. "Nah. Going to walk off my lunch. Thanks though."

Dayton pulls me in for a hug. "Call me if anything comes up. I'm here for you."

His scent of aftershave and mint wafts to my nose and I inhale, slowly deflating when I realize my heart doesn't palpitate the way it does when I smell leather and amber.

The cologne of a mysterious Anderson with stormy eyes. The so-called bore of the Anderson family, as Rex calls him, the ice monster of numbers. The man Dayton warned me about.

But they don't know how he lights me on fire just with his mere presence. How I don't sense danger or ruthlessness in his presence. Instead, I feel...safe.

Why?

A sharp pain stabs my head, and I wince. Damn headaches.

After Dayton and I part ways, I head toward Fleur Entertainment headquarters. The sharp bite of the wind causes me to pull the lapels of my coat tighter. Quickening my pace, my boots crunch over the dried leaves of brown and gold scattered over the sidewalk.

My mind shifts to my most pressing concern—the meeting waiting for me when I get back.

And the person I'll see there.

Ethan.

I've avoided him like the plague for the past month since Mystique, opting to take the stairwell instead of the elevators or looping around the building instead of cutting through the lobby on the off chance I might bump into him. He's swung by my cubicle a handful of times, but as soon as I saw him coming, I'd duck or pretend to be on the phone to avoid talking to him. But I didn't miss the crestfallen slump of his shoulders or the muscle tic in his jaw as he spun around and walked away.

I don't know what came over me that night at Mystique. Or him, for that matter.

My skin burns from the memories seared into my brain—the way our bodies moved together, the masculine rasp of his voice in my ear.

My first damn orgasm after I woke up from the coma, given to me by a man who's driven me insane, and he did it without touching my pussy.

The way I shamelessly moaned and egged him on, my mind delirious with want. How *right* it felt to be in his arms, how my heart and body clamored to life in his presence. It makes no sense—he's a little more than an acquaintance, right? Why am I responding to him this way?

"Shit. What were you thinking?" I groan, mortified at the wetness gathering between my legs.

I wish I could scrub the memories away. I can't even blame the alcohol because I only had one drink at the club.

Dammit.

But I can't avoid him any longer. I have a job to do.

After reviewing the financial data his team gave us—occupancy rates, revenue per season, customer demographics such as age and gender—the marketing team came up with a preliminary plan to go over with him in the first meeting for the joint project.

Otherwise known as Project Dreamer.

What a strange and whimsical name. When I asked Lana the meaning behind the code name, she gave me a brief, knowing glance, and said it was anonymously submitted by a team member.

I remember the breathlessness in my chest when I heard it for the first time.

But why? My life is full of whys now.

Followed by the damn headache again.

A cab honks in the distance, jolting me back to the present. I look up.

Oxygen flees my lungs, my feet rooting to the ground.

A grand Gothic structure looms to my left—it's beautiful and stately, the dark exteriors standing out among the pale limestone or red bricks of the tree-lined street. The warm glow of lights behind the intricate stained glass windows beckons me closer.

Glancing at my watch, I notice I still have an hour before my dreaded meeting. I walk closer and look at the plaque by the entrance, an intense yearning gripping my chest.

Ravenswood Library.

This must be what sailors feel the first time they step into their homes after months at sea.

I push open the heavy doors and step into old world elegance—the smell of weathered tomes and the hushed whispers immediately welcoming me. I've never been here before—at least, not that I remember—but it feels like home.

Mindlessly, I walk around, admiring the rows of mahogany shelves, until I spot a spiral staircase tucked in the back.

My stomach knots, a flashing jab appears at the base of my neck again, and I climb the steps. A closed door meets me at the top.

The door looks new compared to the weathered beams and decor of the building—it must've been a recent addition.

The glass is etched with a name and a beautiful design of a hummingbird, its wings spread.

My breathing quickens, and I trace the name on the door.

The Wing of Eternal Dreams—The Rare Text Archival Floor.

My heart jolts. An avalanche of emotions flits through me—too quickly for me to name, but I'm able to identify a few.

A flare of joy followed by crushing grief.

The throbbing in my neck becomes a violent stabbing, the headache rearing its ugly side, and I close my eyes and focus on my breathing.

Everything hurts.

Sweat beads on my upper lip and I fight the urge to throw up. Slowly, I slide down to the ground and bury my face between my knees, waiting for the wave of sickness to pass.

Breathe in. Long breaths out. Repeat.

I need to talk to Dr. Riordan about these episodes at my next appointment. This can't just be side effects. I want to know what he's seeing on my brain scans.

Ping.

Exhaling deeply, I take out my cell phone and swipe to the home screen, noting Polaris's email sitting on top of my inbox.

A rush of warmth suffuses me.

To: A.Vaughn@gmail.com
From: Polaris@LOH.manhattanmemorial.org
Subject: Haven

Good luck with your work project. You'll do well, and before you ask me why, I'm going to throw your motto back at you.
If I believe it, who's to say it isn't true?

I grin, imagining a small smile on my mystery man's face.

If it helps, there's a good rule of thumb that works. Fake it until you make it.
No one knows you're worried or scared. Only you do, and we're the harshest critics of ourselves. A person wise beyond her years once told me that.
Have you tried meditation or breathing exercises? It helps with anxiety. I have family members who suffer from it, and I've tried to read up on the condition.
**Personally, I enjoy escaping to my haven when the world is too heavy, and my mind is cluttered with negative thoughts. For me, this place is a small library with a beautiful courtyard. It's

close to my work. I walk there when I need a break from regular life.

It always helps.
I have faith in you.

Here for you always,
Polaris

The door swings open behind me and I quickly get up as a middle-aged man hurries past me down the stairs. Considering it's time to head to Fleur, I move to follow him, but before I take my first step, I'm hit with an urge to turn around.

Time slows when I do.

Right before the glass door shuts, I glimpse a beautiful hummingbird stained glass window on the far wall. The cool daylight filters through the unique red chest of the bird, just like the lucky earrings I'm wearing.

My hands tingle.

I smile, watching as the door closes, the image of the bird branded into my mind.

Reading the whimsical name again—The Wing of Eternal Dreams—I notice my head and chest don't hurt anymore.

Instead, the worries in my mind quiet, like the hummingbird somehow whisked them away.

If I believe it, who's to say it isn't true?

Filled with renewed energy, I trot down the stairs and leave Ravenswood Library, a place I know will become *my* haven.

CHAPTER 35

"And so, our estimated marketing revamp costs, using data from the refurbishment of the Kensington Hotels brand five years ago, will be around $1.5 million dollars." Sweat gathers on my palms as I press on the clicker to advance to the last slide of our presentation.

I'm cloistered in Ethan's large office on the seventieth floor of Fleur Towers two hours later, finishing the initial strategy presentation Sandra and the team put together for Project Dreamer after consulting with other departments.

My eyes rove around the room—three folks from finance, three from marketing, including myself, all gathered around the conference table he has next to his large oak desk.

I studiously avoid looking *him* in the eye.

Rex was adamant I drive most of the presentations and interviews under the guidance of my team—part of the giving the intern meaningful work with exposure to upper management initiative.

Exposure—ha.

More like pushing me off a cliff and hoping I'll somehow grow wings.

Seeing no raised hands, I continue, "The breakdown comprises rebranding, website overhaul, social media and digital advertising, and experiential marketing events such as pop ups or in-hotel experiences."

With the end in sight, I rush through the plan our team laid out, keeping my eyes pinned on Sandra, who's nodding encouragingly at me.

But nausea swirls inside me—the same sensation I felt when I had a milkshake and two hot dogs right before I got on the Cycle of Doom in Coney Island.

I nearly puked my guts out afterward.

He hasn't said anything. No "Hi." No "Keep going."

Nothing.

I only feel his burning stare lasering me to the spot.

"Any questions?" I strain a smile after finishing the presentation.

A few nods from the team, but then everyone turns to look at the boss in the room—the icy king of numbers.

The Deliminator.

Ethan leans back in his chair, his fingers playing with his cuff links—the same pair he always wears. "How long until the project breaks even?"

Sandra opens her mouth, but Ethan raises his hand, his eyes still pinned on me. "And your prelim cost analysis, I see nothing for room or infrastructure updates—I assume our internet modems from ten years ago won't cut it for the younger generation who want fast and free Wi-Fi."

"Um, I uh..." Sweat beads my back. "We can take that back and..." *I should know this. I went through this with the team. Why can't I remember anything?*

Sandra clears her throat. "Sir, based on our initial research, we think—"

"And do we think the Kensington revamp is the proper comp for The Strata? The customer base is very different."

He fires off more questions—questions I have no answers for—and my face grows hot.

Stop fidgeting, Lexy.

The Deliminator is in his full glory, completed with one lonely sunbeam streaming through the floor-to-ceiling windows, bathing him in an otherworldly light.

The god of war.

I wet my lips, and his gaze darts to the movement. I think about the night that shall not be remembered. The rasp of his voice. The gentleness in his touch. The way we moved as one, even with all our clothes on.

I swallow a groan.

Dammit, Lexy. You can't remember four years of your life, but you can describe down to every mortifying detail what happened between you and Ethan Anderson on the dance floor.

My skin flames and his eyes flare, as if he can read my lurid thoughts.

The palpable tension stretches on—a strange, awkward silence I can almost taste—I shift on my feet.

"Meeting adjourned." His gaze is inscrutable and a muscle twitches in his jaw. "Ms. Vaughn, can you stay behind?"

Sandra and the others quickly gather their things, a few of them throwing sympathetic glances my way before scurrying out the door.

"You want me to stay with you?" Sandra mouths, her eyes darting between me and Ethan, who looks like he wants to murder his laptop.

"It's fine. I got this." I shoo her away.

"You sure?"

"Ms. Hale, don't you have better places to be?" Ethan's voice is a whip lashing us. Sandra jolts and hauls ass out of the room.

The door snicks shut.

I gulp, my heart palpitating. I must've fucked up the presentation. Why did I even think I could—

"Alexis, did you understand what you just presented?"

His voice was quiet—almost gentle—and I snap my head up, finding him staring at me in his usual unnerving way.

Like he can see through me.

"Just give me another chance. I promise I'll do more research and be better prepared—"

"That's not what I asked." He beckons me over. "Come, sit down."

I swallow, my breathing thready, and take a seat next to him—well, more like he's sitting at the head of the table and I'm sitting to the right of him…as far away as I can without appearing I'm avoiding the proximity.

He arches his brow, his lips twitching, but he doesn't comment on it. "Ryland wanted to improve our internship programs to give interns a better taste of the real world. Decisions to be made. Costs. Pressures. It wasn't meant to torture you."

Ethan's lips form a ghost of a smile and my heart flips.

He continues, "But our interns can't succeed if they don't know the basics. The entire program will be meaningless then. So let me ask you again, were you comfortable with what you were presenting?"

I blow out a breath. I thought I hid it well. "No. Honestly, I didn't really follow the financial analysis."

"That's what I thought. I ended the meeting early because I want to help you."

"Help me?"

"It's okay to ask for help, you know that, right?"

"Do you always help interns? Aren't you a CFO and busy?" I bite my lip, feeling my face burn again. *I shouldn't have asked that. Are you a fucking idiot, Lexy?*

A choked sound escapes him. I snap my eyes back up again, finding him grinning, the rare sight sending my heartbeats into a fritz.

"Became a loner. Barely smiles. Turning into a block of ice. I worry about him." Lana's words at the club floats to the surface.

I made him smile.

Feminine pride sweeps through me, and my lips twitch.

"You always speak your mind, don't you?" He chuckles, then suddenly freezes, as if he's surprised. "Just like before," he murmurs under his breath.

"What?" I must've misheard because it made no sense to me.

"Nothing." He clears his throat and glances at the clock. "I have the afternoon cleared. Why don't I explain the metrics to you?"

His eyes hold mine captive. There's a wistfulness inside them—a hint of sadness. His chest stills, like he's stopped breathing.

I blink. "What?"

The strange expression vanishes, and a half-grin makes a reappearance. "You're a parrot today. I'm offering my help. Tutor you on the financial metrics. Unless you don't think you need—"

"Oh, I definitely do!" I sit up straight, flummoxed at the recent turn of events. But who am I to look a gift horse in the mouth?

He's uncharacteristically nice today and has made no comments about *the event* at Mystique.

Maybe I can pretend it was just an alcohol induced dream?

Standing up, he shrugs off his navy suit jacket and hangs it on the coatrack. His rippling muscles strain under his sky-blue shirt and navy vest—this is a man who works out. Religiously.

God, blue really looks good on him.

Then he strides to his desk, picks up the phone, and presses a button. I look around his office. I was too nervous during my presentation to admire the modern elegant decor of dark woods and sleek lines.

Books line his shelves along with placards and awards. It's obvious this man is well read and successful, and from what Lana said—he got here by himself. I inwardly wince as I think back to how I accused him of nepotism back when I was in the hospital.

I need to apologize.

There are large, framed photos lining the walls—black and white, artistic of exotic locations.

I eye the two closest to me. One of him in a desert, the sun beating down his face, an orange parachute strapped to his back. Another one of him at a beautiful beach, the waves lapping the shoreline.

He's a traveler. I grin at the tidbits I'm learning about this mysterious man. They make him more human.

Then I notice how in each photo, he's standing to the side, completely off-centered, his smile strained. He's holding something, a book or a—I inch closer to take a better look when he speaks.

"Debbie, hold my calls for the rest of the day."

"Sir, what about your meeting with Mr. Vaughn tonight?"

I frown. *Vaughn? Who? Charles?*

"Tell Liam I'll text him later."

"Okay. What about your weekly swim time? Do you still want me to remind you?"

I arch my brow and glance at him. *Scheduled swim time?*

He looks straight at me, his dark eyes giving nothing away.

"Cancel it."

Chapter 36

Ethan's eyes flare as we stare at each other.

I can't shake the feeling he's trying to tell me something with his gaze. But his message is in a foreign language, one I haven't mastered.

Or have you? my mind whispers.

Debbie's voice comes across the speakers. "Sir, I just checked your calendar. Are you sure? Your guest this week is Michael Phel—"

"Have him come back another week."

He hangs up the phone.

"Why are you meeting with Liam in the office? And did you just cancel a scheduled swim meet with one of the most decorated Olympians in history?" My voice sounds screechy. What in the twilight zone is going on? "But everyone says you're a stickler to your schedules."

Ethan grabs a notepad and a few pens from his desk and strides back to the table. "Liam is taking care of an investigation for me."

Ah. The financial situation he mentioned before.

"And yes, I like my routines. Twenty laps in the pool each morning and ten additional laps with a professional on Wednesday afternoons to give me a boost to get through the rest of the week."

He levels his stormy eyes at me. This time, there's a bit of warmth inside them, like the sun peeking out from behind the clouds. "But I can't have our intern failing, can I? And...I'm rooting for you, Lexy."

My breath stalls at the fervency in his voice.

He swallows and continues, "I know I'm not an easy person to be around. I don't say the right things. But I'm on your side. Always."

His words burrow deep inside of me. It's not a passing comment—he means it. And this knowledge has my pulse scattering wildly in my veins.

"Well...thank you." I curl a lock of hair behind my ear and touch my lucky hummingbird earrings, my fingers trembling.

Why am I so nervous? I'm never nervous with the Andersons, not even with Maxwell, who's the recluse of the family.

Why Ethan?

"You're still wearing them." His eyes darken. "The earrings."

"Y-Yeah. They feel special. I like them. You said they represented joy, positivity, resilience, and love, right?" That's what he told me that day in the hospital.

"You remembered." His fingers fiddle with his cuff link, a pleased smile on his face. "You still don't know how you got them?"

"The earrings?" *Why are we still talking about the earrings?* I shake my head. "No. Still no clue."

"I see."

The warmth vanishes from his eyes. A muscle twitches on his temple and he slides the cuff links from his shirt and places them on the table. Then, he slowly rolls up his sleeves—inch by inch—revealing muscular, corded arms and a map of veins that writhe with each movement.

My mouth dries, my breasts feeling tingly. I never knew I had a thing for arm porn. I'm thrusted back into that night, which is *not* an alcohol induced illusion.

I bite my lip when suddenly he stops his movements.

"What are you staring at?" His voice is deeper. Hoarse.

Is he remembering that night too?

My gaze flickers back to his, finding his eyes pinned on my mouth, and the room becomes ten degrees warmer. My tongue dips out to wet my lips, and he strains a breath.

"N-Nothing." I clear my throat. "Before we start, I want to apologize."

Ethan frowns.

"Back when I was in the hospital, I implied you were successful because of your last name. I was wrong."

A ragged exhale escapes him. "Where's this coming from? Did you remember...something?"

I shake my head. "Lana told me you worked your way up from the bottom. I shouldn't have assumed. I'm sorry."

Ethan rolls his lips inward, his shoulders slumping. He looks crestfallen. "Right, of course. Don't worry about it. I already forgot what you said."

Silence falls, but my pulse ratchets and my muscles tighten, like I want to jump into action. To do what?

"Um. You were going to tutor me?"

"Come closer." He motions to the paper in front of him.

"I can see just fine from over here." In fact, I scoot farther away.

I don't want to know how the proximity will impact me if my body is going haywire over him staring at me and flexing his forearms.

Something suspiciously sounding like a snort tumbles out of him. Without warning, he reaches over and yanks my chair, hauling me within breathing distance of his towering frame.

Like I weigh nothing.

I shriek and cover my mouth, my pulse thundering in my ears when my nose is assaulted with the heady scent of leather and amber again.

Butterflies flutter in my stomach.

My core throbs and my nipples bead.

Traitorous body.

"You can't see from over there." He uncaps his pen and writes out an equation. "Break even point equals fixed costs divided by an amount equal to room rate minus variable cost per guest. This is oversimplifying it, but you can use this formula to calculate the number of guests you'll need to break even for a project. Then, using an average occupancy rate per month, you can project the time it'll take to break even."

His voice is velvet, like he's murmuring sweet nothings into my ear. Goosebumps rise on my arms, and I fight the urge to rub against him like a cat.

Focus, Lexy. Focus.

I think I'm seeing a rare side of him—a side he hides from his family.

"Sounds confusing, huh?" He chuckles. "It's not that hard when you—"

"Hold on." Something tugs at me, a whisper in the back of my mind. I pick up a pen and diagram on the paper. "Wait—this makes sense. I think. If I were building a house, I'd have fixed costs like labor or land, but as I lay bricks, those are variable costs. So, the question is, how many bricks I need for the house to stand on its own? Will that work?"

I don't know what I'm saying, but I actually understand it, like my brain has figured it out before my conscious mind registers it.

"Huh." I smile at the house I drew. "It's like a story. If I imagine the formula as a story, it makes so much sense. How did I come up with that?"

He doesn't respond. Instead, his fingers tighten around the cuff links on the table, his mouth parting, nostrils flaring.

"Right," he rasps. "Good job, Alexis. You're exactly right."

His smile is bittersweet. Pained. Like I tore it from him.

I frown. "Are you okay, Mr. Anderson?" Calling him by his first name feels too...intimate.

"Ethan." He leans forward, raising his index finger toward my face before stopping himself. His finger curls inward, and he drops his fist back on the table.

Leaning back, he exhales. "Call me Ethan. Please. Don't call me Mr. Anderson. I think we're past that, right?"

My breath stalls. Is he talking about the night that shall not be named?

"Ethan," I whisper, spellbound by the passion in his voice. He sounds like he'd die if I call him by his last name.

"Yes?" His gaze darkens, his eyes roving over me hungrily.

I swallow. "That night at the club."

Ethan's gaze shutters and his jaw works. "It shouldn't have happened. I was inappropriate. I'm sorry."

The air swooshes out of my lungs. "Oh. Right. That's what I was going to say." I force out a smile. "Forget it ever happened?" My chest tightens. *I should be happy, not disappointed.*

Knock. Knock.

"Come in."

The door swings open. A tall man with blond hair and a friendly smile strides in. "I heard you were here with the intern."

He extends his hand. "Trey Donovan. VP of Finance. You must be Alexis."

Wiping my hands on my skirt, I stand and shake his hand. "Nice to meet you. Everyone's been very helpful."

"My door is always open, you know. I taught this guy," he jabs his thumb toward a smirking Ethan, "everything he knows. And I'm much nicer."

I grin. Trey seems easygoing. I bet the finance staff goes to him for questions instead of the brooding man sitting next to me.

Trey turns to Ethan. "Anyway, Debbie told me you held your calls and canceled your swim meet. Thought I'd check in to see if I could help and get your dinner order while I'm at it. The usual turkey club? What about you, Alexis?"

"Uh, I just had lunch. I don't think I'll need dinner."

"Because you're normal. Unlike someone who eats dinner at five p.m. *sharp* every day." He rolls his eyes. "Ethan, need me to take over the training?"

"I got it."

Trey cocks his brow. "*Okay.* And you want the turkey club? Why do I even ask?" He sighs and turns around.

"Actually, order a rib eye and a Pintzer from Carlisle's for me," Ethan murmurs. "It's been a long time."

Trey whips his head back, his eyes widening. "A steak and beer? On a Wednesday? Who are you and what did you do with Ethan Anderson?"

Rib eye. Carlisle. Pintzer.

The words jostle inside my brain. Why am I so hung up on them? *Why. Why. Why.* I'm so sick of having more whys and no answers.

Sharp jabs hit the base of my neck. I hiss out a breath, cold sweat beading my forehead soon to follow.

Shit, another one of those headaches. This time, it seems like it'll be much more severe than before.

"Alexis, dinner's on us. Take it home if you need to. The least we can do for you for putting up with this asshole." Trey snickers.

The office lighting behind him flares and brightens. I wince, the halo making me dizzy. The jabbing morphs into brutal sawing and I bite my lip to keep from crying out.

"Alexis?"

"S-Sure. Uh. Anything Italian?"

Ethan murmurs, "Luigi's then. It's inside The Orchid too. Trey, get her a triple cheese lasagna. With gorgonzola crumbles on top."

I freeze, his words temporarily distracting me from my burgeoning headache. Between the honey lavender iced tea and the lasagna, he's either a clairvoyant or he knows my tastes.

Did I know him in those four forgotten years? Even so, it didn't seem like we'd be close friends. Liam and Charles certainly said nothing about that.

Trey repeats the order.

I interject, "No gorgonzola, please. I hate the taste of it now."

They say personalities or tastes sometimes change after a traumatic brain injury. I'm still learning who the new Alexis Vaughn is.

Ethan shifts next to me and I turn to him, finding those gray eyes roving over my face again. This time, instead of tethered fire, I sense sadness again.

"No gorgonzola. Got it," he whispers.

"Sounds good. Don't work too hard." Trey raps his knuckles on the door and the sound reignites my pain.

Bang. Bang. Bang.

The office lights flicker and the room spins.

"Stop it!"

"Give it to me. You know you have it."

"No!"

Bang. Bang. Bang.

A white-hot spike drives into my skull, and this time, I'm unable to stop the cry ripping from my throat.

I clutch my ears, my head splitting apart. A fresh wave of pain buries me, and I brace against the table, dry heaving.

"Please, let me go!"

More lights. Screams. I can't breathe.

Water. So much water.

"Alexis!" My name sounds muffled. Like it's coming from far away. "Lexy!"

Someone shakes me, but I can't respond. My head feels like it has been sawed open and mutilated.

Water. I can't get out. Everything hurts.

I squeeze my eyes shut, willing the images to go away.

"Lexy!"

The smell of leather and amber reaches my nose. I rake in a greedy inhale.

Safety. The smell of safety.

Then I feel a wall of heat. Firm muscles wrapping my trembling body. The loud drumming of heartbeats, a rhythm seeming so reassuring and familiar.

"Lexy, I'm here. Don't scare me. Please don't scare me."

Ethan.

The strange visions slowly fade, and with them, the sharp agony eventually dulls. A tsunami retreating to the sea.

I heave out a deep breath, then another. Gentle hands rub my back. Ethan murmurs soft words under his breath and pulls me tighter against him.

Eventually, my senses recalibrate, my forehead damp with sweat. I open my eyes, realizing Ethan has tucked me against his chest, cradling me like I'm precious, all the while whispering, "Shhhh...I got you. You're safe. I got you."

His hand circles my arm now and for one wild moment, I'm tempted to snuggle deeper into his warm body.

I feel safe. I *am* safe.

"Ethan?" I'm parched, and suddenly, a cup of water appears in front of me.

"Drink this." Ethan tips my head back and our gazes lock as I take a sip.

Those startling gray orbs, the tiny striations reminding me of stars in the nighttime sky.

Stars.

I wince, an aftershock blitzing me. His eyes widen with alarm. He looks like he's one second away from carrying me to the hospital.

"You okay? I can take you to the doctor's."

I shake my head, and the movement makes me seasick. "No. I'm fine. It's not the first time."

"Does this happen a lot?" He eases me up and I wipe my damp forehead, the rest of the room slowly coming into focus.

A small crowd has gathered at the door. Trey's face is ashen, his eyes alarmed as he stares at me. Debbie and a few other girls whisper to each other, their hands covering their mouths in obvious shock.

Shit.

"Sorry, I'm...I've had these weird visions, then there's the headache—"

"Visions?" Ethan grabs my forearms, his voice urgent.

"W-What?" Why does he look like I'm the answer to his problems?

Another flash of pain and I whimper.

"Shit. Ignore me." Ethan turns to the crowd, and barks out a command, "Guys, back to work! Nothing to see here."

The group slowly disperses, except for Trey, who lingers behind.

"Alexis, take care of yourself." Trey's eyes hold mine for a beat before he looks at Ethan and strides away.

"You sure you don't need me to call the doctor for you?"

"It's probably the side effects from the meds, but I'll talk to him tomorrow."

As soon as the words leave my mouth, another headache radiates from my skull. I squeeze my eyes shut and grab Ethan's arm.

"Fuck. Alexis, please let me take you to the doctor." His voice is tense, his fingers gripping mine as I ride through the pain.

I shake my head. "No. I-I'm fine. It's going away."

Sweat beads on my upper lip, but eventually, the sharp pain is nothing more than a dull ache. My mind whirs as the events of the last few minutes come back to me.

Slowly, I open my eyes, finding Ethan's dark gazed pinned on me, a muscle throbbing against his temple.

"Ethan," I whisper, "are these visions memories? Why is the past so painful?"

CHAPTER 37

PRESENT: NINE YEARS AFTER THE ACCIDENT—THIRTY-THREE YEARS OLD

TWENTY-ONE.

I throw myself into another lap, my arms thrusting forward as my body rips through the water at five forty in the morning. I should've stopped at the twentieth lap. That's my routine—a routine that has carried me through eight dark years without her.

I have a shit ton of work waiting for me in the office. Under my direction, Trey has unearthed more suspicious financial transactions and Liam has sent me preliminary findings to review.

I should stop fucking around in the pool and go back to my damn routine and responsibilities.

But I can't.

Because my mind is cluttered with thoughts, worries, and impulses.

All about her.

Twenty-two.

I flip under the water and pummel toward the other side of the pool inside The Orchid, my butterfly strokes strong.

I almost broke down two days ago when she sat next to me in the office. When she gazed at me with those beautiful blue eyes, pride shining in them after she drew the house, and realized she could use a story to remember formulas.

My heart splintered then. I didn't think it could break any more, but apparently, I was wrong.

My Nova carried pieces of me in her broken mind. She remembered what I taught her all those years ago.

But she doesn't remember me.

What am I doing?

I hurl myself into another lap.

Twenty-three.

The words I said to her the first time I kissed her all those years ago echo between my ears.

"If a rock smacked you on the head and you lost your memories, I'd do everything in my power to make you remember. Even if that meant recreating our love story, reminding you with every touch, every word. Because there'd be no way I'd let you slip away. No way."

The what-if questions were our inside jokes—they made me laugh whenever I'd read her wild, outlandish questions.

I never thought there'd be a day when I'd be holding onto those answers like a lifeline.

Like my promise to her, I've tried over the past year to tease out her memory, all without disobeying her doctor's orders.

I've brought Alexis her favorite foods, asked her about her earrings, made sure I drew attention to the cuff links she gave me. I've even asked the Letters of Hope administrator to assign me as her pen pal, hoping trading emails will jog her memory.

Rex thought I was nuts when I insisted Lexy start The Strata revamp project with me, and I've been attending every single meeting when I'd normally ask Trey to sit in on these things in the past.

Lana finally cornered me last week after our family dinner.

"What's going on between you and Lexy? And don't bother denying it because it's obvious. The random meal changes, canceling meetings, asking me where she was at when we were clubbing? And don't get me started with this Project Dreamer naming business."

I grit my teeth and look away. My sister is too damn perceptive.

"You love her, don't you? Were you part of her missing four years, Ethan?"

I don't answer her.

Despite my efforts to recreate our love story, Alexis's beautiful eyes are blank, not a flicker of recognition in them.

If anything, there's wariness.

I don't miss how she's in pain whenever she has those visions, or even when I'm too close to her.

Like *I* am causing her pain.

"Ethan, are these visions memories? Why is the past so painful?"

I want to scream at the top of my lungs. As much as I want my Nova to stare at me like I'm everything again, seeing her in agony *guts* me. I'd much rather flay myself with knives than witness her go through this horrendous journey.

So, I told myself to stay away.

Twenty-four.

The words she wrote to me in her latest email appear behind my eyes. Words I've memorized—down to every comma and period—just like every email she's sent me this year.

For the past decade, I not only grieved the loss of the woman I love, but also my confidant, pen pal, and journal partner.

The woman who inspired me to write poetry again.

To: <u>Polaris@LOH.manhattanmemorial.org</u>
From: <u>A.Vaughn@gmail.com</u>
Subject: Missing Pieces

Dearest Polaris,

I've found my haven thanks to you. It's a library as well—perhaps we are kindred spirits. There's a certain peace in surrounding myself with books and feeling hope in the air. The place is filled with stories—people who've gone through unspeakable tragedies but have found their way to the other side.

When they left this earth, they carved their mark on its history.

It makes me feel my problems are minuscule.

Can I tell you a secret?

Ever since I woke up, there's something missing inside me. Not just my memories, but the physical sensation of a hole in my chest. The spot above my heart aches at random moments. Sometimes, it'll be when I hear a certain phrase or when I'm staring at my lucky hummingbird earrings, other times it'll be from a flashing vision, images I'm not even sure if they're real.

I can't trust my mind.

But I think my heart is trying to tell me something.

Do you think there's someone out there who can tell me what those missing pieces are? Someone who can find them for me? Is it worth looking for this person?

Yours,
Alexis

When I read her email, I had to physically restrain myself from bolting out the door to find her. To tell her those missing pieces were of me. Us.

The best years of my life.

I wanted to tell her I was her Polaris, and I never forgot the girl who was afraid of being forgettable.

But then I'd think about her guardedness whenever I approached her. The fact I couldn't tell her why I wanted to hold her and kiss her without revealing our past, which would disqualify her from the medical trial.

Twenty-five.

Throwing myself into another lap, my lungs burn and eyes water, but I persist.

I should end our pen pal relationship. I should recuse myself. It's a betrayal of her trust in the pen pal program.

But I can't.

Damn it. I'm not strong enough. If this is the only way I can have a small piece of her, then I'm a selfish bastard.

A fire sparks in my chest and desperation grips me. I throw myself harder into my strokes, my form erratic as I attack the water like it's my enemy.

I can't tell her anything. Her medical trial. I can't tell her anything.

Recreating our past isn't working. *Nothing* is working.

I tell myself to stay strong for her. Lexy is trying so hard to reclaim her life.

But deep down, there's a fear that works better than any reminder.

What if, after everything, she still doesn't remember?

Even after I tell her the truth.

What if her love for you is just like her memories, lost and gone forever?

A roar shreds my throat as I come up for air. I slam my hands onto the concrete edge and heave in desperate gulps of air.

"Damn. Someone looks pissed off enough to burn the world."

Leather shoes appear in my vision and I look up, finding Rex frowning, dark circles telling me he slept little last night.

I swipe the water from my face and hoist myself out of the pool. "What are you doing here? It's before six. Shouldn't you be asleep? If it weren't for work, you'd probably roll out of bed at noon."

Grabbing a towel, I walk toward the showers.

"I'm here to give you a heads-up, D. The cavalry is on its way to drag you to the club for breakfast in half an hour."

"What's this, an intervention?"

"It's something all right. Actually, Elias texted me yesterday to gather everyone, and if The Kent says something is wrong with you, then something is wrong."

"The Kent?" I snort. I'm sure the king of the underground appreciates a nickname that sounds like a hotel name.

"What? I wanted to call him Hades, but he shot that down."

Hades. The Greek god of the underworld. Lexy loves Greek myths. Fuck.

"You guys have too much time on your hands." I take a fresh towel from the attendant and head toward a private spa shower in the back.

"Half hour, Ethan. Don't make me come down and find you!" Rex hollers at my back.

A quick shower later, I take the elevator up to the gentlemen's club and fight the need to run away and swim more laps in the pool.

I check the time. Six fifteen. I should be in the office reading my morning debriefs now. My routine is a mess.

A few acquaintances greet me and I force out a fake smile and make small talk—ask about their kids, grandkids, the new sports car they got. Unlike the fresh-faced Delaney, who felt like he had something to prove, I've earned my right to walk these halls.

I'm a worthy Anderson now.

A few minutes later, I enter our private room, finding the gang all gathered by the dining table. Their heads snap up in my direction.

I should thank Rex for warning me. My lips twitch. Damn Rex. He may fool everyone with his devil-may-care attitude, but deep down, he has a sensitive soul.

He knew I'd need the heads-up.

"I'm here. Now what?"

I plop down in an open chair and Rex slides a fresh cup of coffee in front of me.

"Steven got drunk off his ass at a racetrack when he and Grace had the debacle. Maxwell punched Ryland in the face when he was in his shits with Millie," Elias murmurs from the corner, his green eyes sharp as he plays with his damn lighter again.

"Hold on. How did you know about that? You weren't there," Steven mutters, throwing a glare at him.

Elias arches his brow, the movement drawing attention to the long scar marring his face.

"Fuck. Pretend I never asked. I wouldn't be surprised if our phones are all equipped with surveillance cameras or some shit."

Everyone shifts in their seats and eyes their phones.

Elias's lips quirk up. "Surveillance cameras? That'd be too juvenile."

I roll my eyes. "Your point, Elias? Why are we all here?"

"Let me finish. Maxwell got into a car accident when he was racing in the fucking rain while he was going through his issues with Belle."

"Like you never made a poor decision in your life." Maxwell shakes his head, then scrolls through his phone.

"Poor decision, yes. Stupid decision, no." Elias snaps his lighter shut. "And I continue, then there's Charles, well he..."

Elias frowns.

"I what?" Charles lifts his brow, a wide grin on his face. "Wasn't an idiot like the Andersons were with women?"

"Hey! Don't include me in the mix. I'm single," Rex grumbles.

"You're an idiot all the time," Ryland supplies and twirls a fountain pen in his fingers. The fucker is already grading papers. I have him to thank for putting Alexis in my orbit again with his internship improvement ideas.

"My point being," Elias resumes his annoying lighter flicking habit, "you guys are ridiculous when it comes to women."

Charles clears his throat.

"Fine. Vaughn excluded. So, when a little bird told me someone was screwing with his routines, canceling meetings, dancing at a nightclub—"

I frown. Hold on a second. This sounds familiar. Too familiar.

I stare at my friend and he falters, then shrugs.

"Watch where you're going with this." I glare at Elias, then look at Charles, who's cocking his head to the side.

I've never told anyone about what happened at Mystique with Alexis. How all common sense flew out the window when I caught her in my arms—when she pressed herself against me and melted into my embrace.

When she begged for more.

Almost a decade of celibacy caused my mind to snap.

It wasn't right of me and I'm ashamed.

But damn if I'll admit that to her older brother.

"That being said, I thought this was overdue. Since your almost trip to Tibet a year ago, you've been acting strange. I recognize all the signs of an Anderson in trouble. Unfortunately."

Elias clasps his hands in front of his lap and stares expectantly at me.

"Since Elias brought it up, I've always wondered." Charles taps his fingers on the table, his blond hair gleaming like a crown on his head. "Whenever you mentioned Firefly in the past...it's always been in present tense. Even when I've given up hope."

He heaves out a heavy exhale. "Of all people, I should've held out hope for her. I'm her brother." His voice is thick, and he looks at me. "But you never gave up, Ethan. Why?"

The tie cinches my neck and I struggle to breathe. My face heats, and I stride to the towering windows and look at Central Park sprawled far below. "It doesn't matter, does it? She's awake now. I'm sure she doesn't blame you."

"I know she doesn't. Lexy's that type of person, but that isn't my question. If what I suspect is true, why are you standing here looking so miserable? Why aren't you doing something about it? If this is about my blessing, you damn well have it. Is this about Liam?"

I think about my best friend and the oath I swore to him about not touching his sister. Deep down, things have changed. Years have gone by and his concerns about me—breaking women's hearts and whatnot—aren't relevant anymore. I haven't been in the scandal rags with any woman for the past nine years.

I know Liam would be okay if I told him. He'd probably punch me in the face first for sneaking around his back, but he'd come around.

"She doesn't remember anything, Charles."

"And you can't force her to love you." A hand clasps my shoulder. Maxwell.

People often told me I resembled my oldest brother the most, and I didn't notice it until now, when he's staring at me with understanding in his eyes.

His jaw clenches, then releases, his gaze trailing to the gloomy scenery outside.

"It's miserable to hold everything inside yourself, Ethan. I, of all people, know that. Don't do this. You owe it to yourself."

"Her medical trial, Maxwell. I can't jeopardize that. I've tried reminding her of things she liked before, phrases we used to say. But she'd shrivel up in pain. I don't want to cause her pain."

"That's a dilemma, isn't it?"

Suddenly, a shadow appears in the reflection.

Elias murmurs, "Not everyone has a chance to make the woman he loves fall in love with him all over again."

Make her fall for me...again.

"Forget the past and look forward, don't you think?"

What if Nova and her north star belong in the past—a past only I remember?

The crushing loneliness of being the only one who carries this secret. A love story born between towering shelves in a hidden library, sparked by a love of words and poetry.

But...what if *I* forget the past?

What if I make her fall for me again?

CHAPTER 38

I TAP MY FEET on the floor, unable to stop my nervous fidgeting.

Not nervous, Lexy. You're excited. Reframe that shit just like what you did with those painful memories.

In the past few weeks, whenever I had a splitting headache followed by brief flashes of memories, instead of focusing on the pain, I'd tell myself this was good because this was progress. The medical trial must be working.

Blowing out a breath, I eye Ethan's spacious apartment inside the sprawling metropolis that's The Orchid. A few of us are gathered here today for the interview segment of Project Dreamer after Ethan approved the budget three weeks ago. The team thought an informal interview at his place would make the CFO more approachable.

I come from money, but even I can't help but be impressed with the dark marble floors, the high ceilings, the modern crystal chandeliers and sleek leather furnishings.

Ethan has good taste.

Needing to keep myself busy, I pull out my phone and read Polaris's latest message.

To: A.Vaughn@gmail.com
From: Polaris@LOH.manhattanmemorial.org
Subject: RE: Missing Pieces

What does your heart tell you?

I'm sure people in your life have tried to give you advice—*forget your past, focus on your future*. Maybe you have a voice inside, urging you to fill that hole in your heart because you've lost too much already.

I wish I could give you an answer. But in the end, what *I* want doesn't matter.

Only *you* matter.

My breath catches and my heart skips a beat. He means it—only *I* matter. Somewhere along the way, Polaris has become more than a friend. Sometimes, I feel like we share a soul and he pulls my thoughts right out of me.

I'm sure there are beautiful memories in your past—moments you probably want to remember. Maybe you're right, and somewhere in those missing years, there's someone who loves you.

But if that person truly loves you, he'd want you to follow your heart. To do what makes you happy. To chase whatever brings you peace, whether that's the past, the future, or something entirely new.

If he loves you, wherever he is, he'll *wait*.

You shared a secret with me once. I think it's only fair I share a few of my own.

Someone once told me she believed in serendipity, fate, and magic. That no matter where life led her, fate would take her to the right path, the right person, the right treasure. I laughed at her. I was pragmatic. Logical.

But it was beautiful—watching her live as if something wonderful could happen at any moment.

Because of her, I started believing in fate. Making wishes. Dreaming. And against all logic, some of those unrealistic dreams came true.

Whoever this woman was, Polaris must have loved her so much. A knot twists inside me, offset by an inexplicable yearning. Am I jealous of her? Am I also grieving for him?

So here's what I want to tell you.
That empty space in your heart? The right person will fill it. Because fate.
Whatever you choose, I support you. Because more than anything, *I* want you to be happy.

Always,
Polaris

P.S. One last secret—Our pen pal correspondence was supposed to end long ago. You've reintegrated in to society. You're thriving.
But I didn't.
Because I don't want it to end.
And so, my next question is this... Do you?

Is he saying what I think he's saying? A warmth rises inside me, and I open a new email to answer him.

The same unsettling déjà vu cloaks me—maybe I've had a similar moment in those four lost years of memories.

But I know this—I don't want whatever we have to end.

"Miss, would you like any refreshments while you wait?" A middle-aged man in a black suit materializes out of nowhere. John, the butler.

I click shut my phone—I'll have to answer Polaris later. "I'm good, thank you. I'm nervous though."

He chuckles. "You'll do great, Ms. Vaughn. I've heard wonderful things about you from Mr. Ethan."

"He's talked about me?"

John's smile slips from his face. "It's the only time he smiles." He shifts on his feet. "It's not my place to say anything, but I've worked for Mr. Ethan for over ten years in various capacities. He's a man of a few words, but if you stick around, I promise you, his words will be the most meaningful."

With that cryptic message, John tips his head and stalks off.

"We're ready for you, Lexy. You'll do great!" Sandra winks as she points to the interview set up by the two lounge chairs next to the windows, which let in some of the cold November daylight.

Rex beckons me over from the hallway.

"Break a leg. It might seem strange, having you conduct the interview, but the entire point of this revamp is to draw in the younger generation. And what screams younger than the intern, right?" He winks.

Despite how he resembles his brothers, they can't be more different. Rex, with his friendly smiles and casually tousled hair, looks like a man you can joke with. Someone who makes you instantly at ease.

The opposite of the closed book Ethan.

"Right. I got this." I snap the rubber band around my wrist, the flicker of pain grounding me.

"You have my permission to give him hell." At his joking tone, I glance at him, finding his head cocked to the side. "Although I think nothing you do will be hell for him. I've had my suspicions...so did Lana, but damn, was I slow."

"What do you mean?" Why does it feel like I'm the punchline to a joke everyone already knows?

His gaze softens into something akin to sympathy. "It's not my place to tell, Lexy. But...keep your mind and your heart open, okay?"

"I don't—"

"We ready?" The familiar scent of amber and leather reaches my nose before his body heat grazes my back.

Ethan places his hand lightly on my lower back, the gentle touch searing me through my dress. I shiver and glance down, hoping my bra is thick enough to hide the hard nipples, no doubt saluting him.

Calm down, hormones. I thought puberty was over. How is it possible I feel something for both Ethan and Polaris?

Seriously, Lexy.

Ethan frowns at us. "Did I miss anything?"

"No. Just idle chitchat. Let's do this."

I stride over to the windows and take a seat, Ethan following suit. Blowing out a breath, I wipe my palms on my dress. The lighting guy adjusts a spotlight, and the cameraman gets into position.

I got this. It's all about mindset. I'm smart and capable. I'm an asset to any team. If I believe it, I can do it, because—

"Remember, if you believe it, who's to say it isn't true?" Ethan murmurs.

I gasp, swiveling my head toward him, finding his eyes glittering with intensity—like the secrets of the universe are hidden among those light striations and dark depths.

He smiles and places his hand on mine, and I jolt from the explosion of tingles spreading through my body.

When he withdraws his touch, I'm bereft.

I want it back.

"Ready, and action!"

Forcing a smile on my face, I turn to Ethan and begin the questions the team put together.

"Mr. Anderson, can you tell us a little about your role at Fleur?"

Intros. I can do this.

Ethan leans back in his seat and smiles. "Ethan, please. Mr. Anderson is my dad."

My heart skips a beat at the teasing expression on his face. It's like coming across a rainbow during a storm or finding a four-leaf clover in Central Park.

"I'm the chief financial officer, which is a fancy title for the man who heads up the numbers—dollars and cents, approving budgets, reviewing financial results. My team makes sure we're headed in the right direction with revenues and profits for the company and our investors."

We spend the next ten minutes chatting about the usual things one expects to be in a marketing or PR campaign to demystify the C-suite management for the younger generation—his hobbies (reading and swimming), where he likes to stay when he travels (boutique hotels or bed and breakfasts), how he got to his position at a young age (hard work and grit—even though there was a fiasco of him spilling coffee on his shirt during an important presentation).

Ethan is easygoing in our interview, reminding me a bit of Rex, but from where I sit, I can see a muscle twitching on his temple, his smile a little too broad, and his fingers continuously tugging his cuff links.

He's faking it.

I wonder if *Delaney* faked it when he worked his way up.

Something about the thought niggles at me, and my breath stalls, but I don't have time to mull over it, because I have the rest of the interview to finish.

"What do you want The Strata to represent for young people entering the real world after college?"

He wets his lips and my eyes snare at the action. I snap my rubber band again and his brow twitches as if he wants to call me out on being distracted.

"I want them to see it as a place where anything is possible. A place where they can belong, even if they don't know their place in the world yet." There's a wistfulness in his voice that holds my attention.

"What's the feeling you hope people take away from their stay at The Strata?"

"That even in the busiest city in the world, there's a place for them. A home away from home. When they walk through those doors, they don't have to be lost anymore." He leans forward, trapping me in the magnetic draw of his voice.

"If you have to sum up this project in one word, what would it be?"

I hold my breath, every atom inside me clamoring for his answer. I don't know why, but it seems important. I just know the next word out of his mouth will be meaningful.

Ethan holds my gaze, his voice dropping into a quiet rasp, a bittersweet smile on his lips. "Haven."

I gasp. My heart slams itself against my rib cage.

A haven.

The same word Polaris mentioned in his email a while back. The same warmth rushes up my spine—curling around me like the biggest hug.

The same feeling—but ten times stronger.

This is silly, Lexy. It's a common word, everyone uses it.

But the words don't click. I barely notice myself leaning forward and him doing the same, like we're opposite sides of a magnet, finally in proximity to each other.

I whisper the last question, "Any final thoughts on what The Strata means to you?"

Ethan pauses, his hand reaching up toward me—the same halted motion I've seen from him before, and the same withdraw, his fingers curling into his palm before he places his fist back on his lap.

His reply is soft. A gentle caress ladened with heaviness. Whoever thought the icy king of numbers is cold has never been more wrong.

"Some places stay with you. Forever. Even when you forget them."

My eyes burn and a sharp ache spears my chest.

An image of a hummingbird with a red chest floats to my mind. The stained glass window at Ravenswood. My laugh. My lucky earrings.

My vision refocuses, and I find his gray eyes clouded in a sheen of moisture, and the pain sharpens in my heart.

What's going on?

CHAPTER 39

SANDRA CLAPS. "AND THAT'S a wrap. That's great, guys. We have a lot of footage to work with."

The spell breaks and we jolt apart.

Ethan swipes his eyes with his fingers before unleashing one of his strained smiles into the crowd. I clear my throat and heave out a few deep breaths before I stand and do the same.

My pulse gallops in my ears. I can barely hear myself think.

My heart feels like it'll give up on me at any second.

Judging from the flush creeping up his neck and how his fingers fidget with his cuff links, I'd guess he feels the same.

But nothing happened. It was just a basic interview—professional questions.

It felt like much more. Like he flipped open the pages of my book and read the passages aloud. Or perhaps he already had my pages memorized.

I feel naked.

What on earth? Nothing makes sense. I don't know him that well, and yet, the way I feel with him—this searing intensity and palpable connection. I *do* know him. Deeply. Why does it feel like I'm staring at a riddle and the answer is on the tip of my tongue?

I glance up, finding Rex scanning us with sharp eyes, confirming what I thought before. The playboy persona is a front. He gives me a sad smile and claps like everyone else, who obviously hasn't noticed anything amiss.

Ethan strides away, his fingers raking over his perfectly arranged hair, rendering it a disheveled mess.

An image of me scribbling in my journal appears in my mind. But I can't make out the words.

The snippet disappears almost instantly, followed by the same flash of piercing headache.

Closing my eyes, I count to ten until my pulse settles, and when I reopen them, the room is in a flurry of activity with folks packing up their things, straightening the apartment. I see John helping people with their coats and scarves.

Unable to keep still, I walk to the glass wall lined with framed photos. I recognize a few of them from the office, but these photos are in color, not black and white. This time, I can make out the details—the tropical beach, the colorful sunset in the background bouncing rays of light against the jeweled colored pebbled sand, and the desert sand dunes with dark waters on the horizon.

He's in each of them, once again standing off-centered, the same bittersweet smile on his face.

My heart tugs, an inexplicable yearning gripping me.

With my mind still racing from the nonevents a few moments ago, I lean in closer, examining what he's holding in his hand—a leather-bound book, like a journal.

I move on to the other photos.

Him standing in front of a restaurant—Bhut Kitchen—his face haggard with an unkempt beard.

Ethan at what looks like a Sotheby's auction, holding a small golden item and the same journal in his hand.

Him leaning against a wall of books in a vintage bookshop.

Ethan releasing a paper lantern to join the thousands of floating fireballs in the deep navy sky.

There's something inscribed on the lantern—but it's too small. I can only make out one letter. An "N."

Then, heat coils around me, sinking into my skin.

I know it's him without turning around.

"Your routines. Traveling must throw them off." I squint, still trying to make out the words on the lantern.

"One trip a year. It's part of my schedule," he murmurs before stepping next to me. "Have you thought about traveling?"

I smile. This, I have an answer for. "Yes. I'm making a list of places I want to go. A bucket list of some sort. I lost almost a decade of my life and I won't waste a single minute of it. I have a motto. Don't wait to live, because the clock keeps ticking."

He lets out a heavy sigh and doesn't reply. I turn toward him, finding him staring at the lantern photo with the same wistfulness I saw during the interview.

"They say if you write wishes on the lanterns, they'll come true."

"Did yours come true?"

He swallows, his corded throat rippling. "Yes." His voice is hoarse, unused.

"Then why don't you seem happy?"

Ethan stills—I don't think he's even breathing. Then he slowly turns toward me, his bottomless gaze once again speaking to me in that foreign tongue.

"What makes you think I'm not happy?" he whispers.

Unable to help myself, I trail a finger over his cheek. Electricity courses through that tiny point of contact, and he shudders.

Closing his eyes, he leans into my touch.

My heart riots—wanting to escape, to flee from the sudden onslaught of unidentifiable sensations burning through me.

"Your smile. I've never seen a genuine one. Your dimples don't show."

Ethan keeps his eyes closed and swallows, and I swear I see a hint of moisture at the corner of his eyes and my own eyes burn.

Something squeezes my lungs in a vise, so much, I can't breathe. *He's in pain. He's hurting desperately.*

I want to hold him. I can't explain it. But I want to draw him into my arms and tell him everything will be okay because I'm here. He doesn't have to be sad anymore.

Who am I to him?

This question has been in the back of my mind, a whisper that's now a bellow.

We can't be mere acquaintances.

But I'm afraid to ask. Somewhere along the way, whenever I think of him, I've associated it with pain. Like there's something my mind is dreading, and that's why I can't remember.

But the headaches have lessened over time.

It feels like permission.

To do what?

Something clangs in the background, followed by someone murmuring apologies.

I snatch my hand away and return my attention back to the photos.

Clearing my throat, I point to the one of the Sotheby's auction. "Why are you standing to the side in every photo? Don't people usually stand in the middle? And what are you holding?"

His eyes flicker open, but he doesn't answer me.

CHAPTER 40

PAST: FOUR YEARS AFTER THE ACCIDENT—TWENTY-EIGHT YEARS OLD

A HUSHED MURMUR RISES from the crowd as I stride to the front row of Conference Room A inside the Kensington Hotel next to The Orchid.

I know what they're whispering about.

The youngest Anderson son was just promoted to CFO of Fleur Entertainment Holdings. And he's interrupting the Sotheby's auction that has been going on for the past hour and a half.

Ignoring the camera flashes and the subtle pointing of fingers, I unbutton my black suit jacket and smooth my fingers over my tie before taking a seat in the spot saved for me and carefully placing Lexy's journal on my lap.

The auctioneer, a tall man with white hair and horn-rimmed glasses, clears his throat and slams the gavel.

"Quiet, please! For the next item on the list, a rare and exciting find aboard the famous Spanish sunken ship, *La Reina Estrellada*, otherwise known as The Starlit Queen. The ship disappeared into the frigid depths of the Atlantic near the Bermuda Coast in 1770. For over two hundred years, explorers around the world have tried, to no avail, to uncover the resting place of the vessel."

He clicks a button and a spotlight shines on a glass box to the left of the podium, the image of the contents also projecting on the large screen behind him.

I rake in a sharp inhale as the crowd gasps.

This is the moment we've all been waiting for.

A single glittering gold coin is carefully displayed atop black velvet, the spotlight highlighting the weathered edges and Spanish words inscribed on the surface.

"Once considered an impossible treasure—the crème de la crème for all treasure hunters—The Starlit Queen has recently been recovered, and with her are twenty-five cases of Spanish gold, coins, and jewels, all of which have been claimed by the Spanish government. However, the government has graciously allowed for one rare Royal 8 Escudos coin to be sold to the highest bidder—a collector who wants to own a piece of haunting history."

Impossible treasure.

The words ricochet in my mind.

Fragments of the January morning five years ago fill my consciousness. My lips twitch when I remember Lexy's teasing grin as we huddled in front of the crackling fireplace after our impromptu snowball fight outside my apartment.

How she bit her lip when she scribbled the fifth item on her bucket list.

Item 5: Get a piece of treasure from a sunken ship.

Dreamer: You're laughing at me, Ethan, but this stuff is out there, waiting for us to find it. Do I need to remind you of my motto again?

Keeper: Good luck going against *professional* treasure hunters, Nova. Need I say it again? *Professional.* As in, they've spent <u>years</u> looking for sunken treasure, and you want to somehow come across it?

Dreamer: Looks like you need a reminder: If I believe it, who's to say it isn't true?

My heart twists, the sharp pain my constant companion. Five years later, my darling Nova is still in a coma.

The agony has never faded—the gash in my heart only widened.

When my assistant, Debbie, told me the sunken treasure was found a month ago, I called in various favors to have Sotheby's host their auction here at The Kensington. My home turf.

Because this treasure is mine.

It belongs to a kindhearted girl with flaming hair and sky-blue eyes, a girl who lights up every room and my cavernous heart with her mere presence.

"This rare coin is one of a kind because of a misprint in the name. The starting bid is five-hundred thousand. Do I have any bidders?"

"Five-hundred."

"Six-hundred from number fifty-nine."

The numbers rise at a breakneck speed, and the blood boils in my veins.

I tug my cuff link and breathe in deeply, letting the vultures fight each other before I go in for the kill.

This treasure is mine.

Her impossible bucket list item—the one thing I thought was unachievable on that list.

No one stands in my way of making her dream come true.

"One million. Do we have any more bidders?"

"One point five."

The bids slow to a crawl and I flinch when I hear the auctioneer slam the gavel down because this is the moment of the kill.

I raise my hand. "Five million."

A collective gasp echoes in the room and my eyes nearly go blind from the incessant camera flashes on my face.

I ignore them and focus on the auctioneer instead.

He nods. "Five million to Mr. Anderson. Going once?"

I hold my breath.

"Twice."

My fingers curl around Nova's cuff link.

"And sold!"

The air rushes out from my lungs and I look down, sliding open the cuff link, revealing the beautiful hummingbird with the red chest.

My eyes burn and nose prickle. A lump forms rapidly in my throat.

People congratulate me for winning such a rare treasure, but I can barely hear them. I'm underwater. Drowning in front of them.

I'd give away my entire fortune to have her back. Because there's no greater treasure to me than the woman lying in the hospital.

Wordlessly, I stand, holding the journal close to my chest, and a Sotheby's assistant rushes up to greet me. It's something I arranged in advance—not part of their normal process, but then again, the Anderson name lets me get away with many things.

I click a few buttons on my phone, transferring the money into their account, and show him the screen. The assistant murmurs a few words and listens to his earpiece, no doubt confirming the receipt of funds.

"Congratulations, Mr. Anderson."

He unlocks the case and hands me the coin.

I hold it up and he stands in front of me, ready to take the photo I requested.

"Do you want to stand in the middle, sir?"

I shake my head. "No. Leave this space next to me."

Closing my eyes, I imagine her scent of sweet lavender, the softness of her hair. How her head reaches my shoulders. My hands twitch and I stretch out my arm, imagining an alternate reality.

She'd smile at me, triumph glinting in her eyes. She'd whisper, "I told you so, Keeper. Because if you believe it..."

"Who's to say it isn't true?" I whisper to no one.

This. This is how I'd hold her if she were here with me.

But all I can feel is air.

The burn intensifies behind my eyes, and I blink a few times before letting my arm drop to my side.

I strain a smile, and the assistant snaps a picture. He'll have someone deliver it to my office later.

This way, my Nova is always with me. Standing next to me as I complete each bucket list item on her behalf.

A tear escapes my eye and I quickly wipe it away as I make my way out of the hotel.

Twenty minutes later, I'm walking down the halls of Manhattan Memorial. The nurses smile—sympathy in their gazes. They know who I'm here for.

They know the statistics and the odds.

They probably think I'm insane for coming here week after week, wishing for a different outcome.

An impossible outcome.

The same steady beeping of machines greets me when I enter her room. The same sterile smells and unsettling humming of the air conditioning.

There she is, my sleeping beauty.

My lungs constrict as I set the journal on her nightstand and take a seat at her bedside. I smooth out her sunset hair, which used to be thick and luscious, but is now dull—a jewel that has lost its luster.

She's still the most beautiful woman I've ever seen.

I lace my fingers with hers. Lifting them up, I press a kiss on the back of her hand.

"I once told you it was impossible to find sunken treasure, and you told me I had no faith," I murmur, my voice thick.

"But look," I pull out the coin from my pocket and press it into her palm, "you were right. *Nothing* is impossible, Nova."

Tears slide down my face, and this time, I don't stop them. "Didn't you used to tell me, 'if I believe it, who's to say it isn't true?'"

I let out a ragged breath and press my forehead against her chest, listening to the steady beats of her heart.

"The impossible is possible, Nova. We found a piece of sunken treasure. C-Can you please wake up? Please?"

A fresh wave of grief stabs my heart—an organ that has never stopped bleeding ever since that rainy night four years ago.

It's a miracle I'm still alive.

It's not fair.

It's not fair.

It's not fair.

"Life isn't fair," imaginary Lexy whispers. *"But we make the best of it, right? We don't wait to live, because the clock keeps ticking."*

Ba-dum. Ba-dum. Ba-dum.

Her steady heart. She's alive, but she *isn't* alive.

It's not fair.

A surge of anger rushes through me as I fist her blankets.

Helpless. I'm fucking helpless.

"I wish I could move on." The corrosive poison pours out of me in a hushed whisper. *I wish it didn't hurt so much.*

I bite my lip hard and taste metallic. A punishment for the lie.

Opening my eyes, my vision blurry, I press another kiss on her hand. A smidgen of blood stains her fair skin and I quickly wipe it away.

I can't dirty my hummingbird.

"No. That'd be a lie, Nova." I swallow. "I'd give *anything* to continue loving you."

Sliding my hand into my pocket again, I pull out the one thing I bring with me every time I visit her.

Snapping open the box, I show her the sparkling engagement ring.

I take her hand in mine again and whisper, "You never gave me your answer, Lexy. I have the ring now. The only ring I'll ever buy for the only woman I'll ever love. Will you marry me?"

I hold my breath—the way I do every time I ask her when I visit—and wait for the impossible miracle. A twitch of her fingers. A spasm of her eyelids. A faint whisper from her lips.

But only the beeping of the machines echo in the room.

Blowing out a heavy breath, I open her beside drawer and tuck the gold coin away with the rest of the treasures I gathered for her.

Mementos from her bucket list. Symbols of hope, waiting for her when she wakes up.

If she wakes up.

Five items down, two more to go.

I told myself I have to let her go when the list runs out. My Nova would want me to because she's selfless that way. It'd hurt her to see me in pain.

The Anderson men aren't lucky in love.

The words Dad said a long time ago haunt me as I stand and tuck the blankets carefully around her.

The Anderson men aren't lucky in love.

I'd take all the bad luck in the world if it meant she could wake up.

Even if she forgets me.

CHAPTER 41

PRESENT: NINE YEARS AFTER THE ACCIDENT—TWENTY-NINE YEARS OLD

RELEASING A HAPPY SIGH, I sit on a blanket under the barren, drooping branches of the weeping beech tree in the quiet courtyard of Ravenswood Library.

It's the Saturday before Thanksgiving, and things are slowing down at work. Not wanting to be cooped up inside my apartment and needing to finish an assignment from my Creative Poetry class, I decided coming here would be perfect.

Ever since I discovered this beautiful place, I've been drawn to it—whether it be wandering the quiet floor of The Wing of Eternal Dreams or hanging out in this private courtyard I came across recently.

There's a peace here I can't describe.

Birds chirp overhead and I look up, finding ravens soaring high in the cloudy skies. We're lucky this year—the weather isn't too cold yet, and the grounds are still dry enough for me to enjoy my lunch in my special slice of heaven.

My haven.

My mind flashes to the way Ethan looked at me last week during the interview—when he told me he hoped The Strata could be a haven for its visitors.

The depth in his gaze and the thickness in his voice.

My chest niggles, the phantom ache reappearing, and my phone rings. I quickly answer.

"Liam, you're up!"

"Lexy, it's noon. I might work in cybersecurity, but I follow normal hours, you know."

I grin. "Sorry, the twenty-year-old you is still fresh in my mind. Punk hair, wild parties, living like a vampire."

"I'm thirty-three."

"Trust me, I know. What's up?" My stomach grumbles. I rummage through a bag I brought with me—the one with the food. Feed the body, feed the mind.

"Did you get the box? The staff were cleaning your old room at the mansion. Said you forgot some things—might be important. I left the box with your doorman yesterday."

I take a sip of the honey lavender iced tea—because iced tea is better than hot tea, even if it's fifty degrees right now—and reach into my other bag to pull out the small box he's referring to.

"Got it. Thanks for bringing it by." Opening the box, I eye the contents—a few old photos of me in my leotard, some Post-it notes with scribbles on them, several pens and markers, two small notebooks, and a wallet I don't recognize.

"You're coming to Thanksgiving dinner on Thursday, right? Charles and Tay are going to be there."

"Wow, the Andersons let Tay off the hook?"

He chuckles. "Charles might as well be married now. They're doing the alternating holiday thing."

Silence falls and a question perches at the tip of my tongue, but I don't want to ask because I know what the answer will be.

Liam figures out and answers anyway, "And no. Our parents aren't coming back."

A knot lodges in my chest. I've made peace with it, but the old wound still flares up from time to time.

How can someone forget their own kids? I'll never understand that.

"I figured. Liam...I miss Grandma and Uncle Ian. Remember how Grandma would make her turkey just right? Crispy on the outside and tender inside? Then Uncle Ian would eat most of it and complain how his students would make fun of his belly later?" Uncle Ian was a world-renowned ballet choreographer. I fell in love with the dance because of him.

It's one of my biggest regrets to this day—not being able to say goodbye to them.

A ragged exhale comes across the line. "Firefly...a lot of shit happened while you were asleep. Some people weren't who they seemed to be. I want to tell you more, because I know you have questions. But I can't, unless you drop out of your medical trial. I'll tell you this, we have the most important people in the world with us right now, and I miss Grandma too."

He doesn't mention Uncle Ian. It seems significant.

My gut clenches and the hairs rise on the back of my neck. Why do I feel like I know the answer? Why is it—

A piercing pain stabs the base of my skull. I cry out, my phone clattering to the floor.

Dark room. Hip-hop music. Moaning and screaming.

Headlights in front of me. So much rain.

My heart palpitating, my lungs not drawing enough air.

Fear. So much fear.

I need to escape. I need to find—

As abruptly as the visions began, they suddenly stop.

"Lexy? You there? Are you okay? Lexy!"

I clutch my head, the world swirling around me. *Breathe in and out. Again. I can do this. These have to be memories. The meds are working. This is good.*

Panting heavily, I quickly pick up the phone before Liam goes ballistic. "S-Sorry. Dropped my phone. A squirrel darted in front of me."

"Shit! You scared me, Firefly. Fuck."

The aftershocks rock my body, and I close my eyes. "You worry too much, Liam. I'm an adult now and I'm healthy. I got to go. I'll see you on Thursday."

I don't wait for his response before ending the call.

A brisk breeze sweeps across the courtyard, dragging up crusty leaves and ruffling the evergreen foliage of the vines on the walls. I shiver, my forehead damp with perspiration. Slowly, I open my eyes and focus my attention on the intricate hummingbird stained glass window.

Why are my memories so painful?

What is my brain hiding from me?

Is it worth it? I think back to Dr. Riordan's advice and Polaris's words. Should I leave the past in the past? But the heavy sense of loss that suffocates me whenever I want to give up.

I growl and take another sip of tea.

I have two paths forward—to withdraw from the trial or to face my problems head on.

I want to live my life with no regrets, and something in those missing four years tethers me to the past. I don't know if that something is horrific, and that's why my mind is working against me, but I know, deep in my gut, I can't move on until I figure it out.

After swiping to the email app on my phone, I check to see if Polaris has replied to my email. He'll understand me.

Inbox zero.

I gnaw my lip and reread my response to him for the thousandth time, wondering if it scared him away.

To: Polaris@LOH.manhattanmemorial.org
From: A.Vaughn@gmail.com
Subject: Do you ever want to meet?

Polaris,

I don't want this to end. And if you know me at all, you'll know I don't lie to myself.

There are enough unanswered questions in my life. I refuse to add one more.

So here goes.

I feel something in our emails. Maybe this makes me foolish or reckless, but I need to know—am I imagining it? Am I just a lonely woman reading too much into words that are nothing more than a kindness?

Excuse me while I throw up,
Alexis

P.S. Regardless of your answer, thank you. You don't know how much your words mean to me. The world is a lonely place without someone who truly understands you. And I'm thankful because I have that person in you.

P.P.S. If this feeling isn't all in my head, would you be open to meeting in person?

"Ugh, Lexy. He was asking if you wanted to continue emailing him and you pretty much asked him out. You're such an idiot!" I mutter under my breath.

Just then, I hear steady footsteps coming my direction, but I can't see who it is, since the low-hanging tree branches hide the view from me.

Before I can brush the branches aside and look, a pair of black boots appear in my vision.

Followed by dark jeans, a navy sweater hiding muscles I know are strong because I've felt them up close and personal before.

Five o'clock shadow, a sharp jawline.

The most addictive scent of leather and amber.

Ethan stands a few feet away, his feet coming to an abrupt halt, his startling eyes flaring.

"Nova," he whispers. "You're here."

CHAPTER 42

"Nova?" A muscle tics in his jaw, his hands curling into fists. His eyes darken and his throat works—like he's struggling to get words out.

"*Ethan*, why are you here? And why do you keep calling me that?"

My question jolts him, and he shakes his head like he's coming out of a trance.

"*Alexis*, why are you here today?" His voice sounds unused.

I narrow my eyes at him imitating me.

"This is my haven." I smile and motion to the quiet courtyard.

"Really now. Your haven. And here I am thinking this is *my* haven."

We have the same haven? A smile twitches my lips and I see a mischievous glimmer in his eyes.

"I like the gardens here. It's peaceful. I visit from time to time," he murmurs.

"Want to join me?" I point to my lunch set up. "I brought extra food. I was planning to park out here for a few hours to get some assignments done, but I'm happy to share."

I unpack the food containers from my bag.

Sliced ham and cheese cubes, fig jam and crackers, some sandwiches I picked up from the deli by my apartment—the crusts cut off, of course—and a bottle of water along with my iced tea.

When he doesn't answer, I glance up, finding his nostrils flaring, his intense eyes riveted on me.

"Do I have something on my face?" I brush my hair, untangling a few strands from my hummingbird earrings. "Why are you staring at me like that?"

Ethan stays silent. Almost as still as the gargoyles perched on the rooftops of the building.

I beckon him over. "Come on, live a little. Join my picnic. It's a perfect day for one, don't you think?"

His fingers twitch. I roll my eyes, reach up, and grab his hand.

Sparks alight when our hands touch and heat charges through me. Ignoring the wild pounding of my heart, I pull him down beside me and hand him a sandwich and the bottle of water.

I want to understand the mystery that is Ethan Anderson.

I want to know what he's hiding behind those soulful eyes.

I want to know why my body comes alive in his presence.

And as fates would have it, he's here in my haven, and I won't waste the opportunity.

"You never answered me. Why do you call me Nova?" I munch on a cucumber sandwich.

"It's short for supernova." He stares at the food I handed him, a lingering wistfulness rolling off his frame. "A supernova is a beautiful cosmic event—bright and colorful, more energy than the sun."

"And you're saying I'm like a supernova?"

His lips curve up slightly. My heart flutters and I bite back a grin.

He really should smile more.

The ice monster is beautiful when he smiles.

"Well, I can't look away whenever you're in the room."

I gasp and quickly gulp down a few sips of tea. But it doesn't calm the butterflies in my stomach, the way every atom inside me seems to be aware of his presence. How I can feel his body heat even though there's at least six inches between us.

How can I feel this way about him *and* Polaris, the god of war and the soothing poet?

"Do you come here a lot?"

"Sometimes. It's a special place for me." He doesn't offer more.

"I came across it a while back after I had lunch with Dayton. You remember him, right? You guys met at the hospital."

Ethan stiffens and nods.

"When I walked past this place, it was like coming home. I don't know how to explain it." I lean on my elbows and stare at the sky. "Maybe I discovered this place before the accident. I don't know, but either way, I'm lucky to have found it."

"Some things are worth remembering. And some things you'll never forget." He sighs and lies down next to me.

He said something similar during the interview at his apartment. I wonder what he's never forgotten.

Silence settles over us.

This should be strange. Me and Ethan—someone with walls more fortified than Fort Knox, the icy Deliminator—lying side by side next to me on the ground, enjoying a peaceful picnic on a perfect day.

It should feel awkward. My mind should race with questions to ask him to fill in these pauses in conversation.

But instead, there's a surety in my heart—the ache I usually feel isn't there.

I'm safe. Dark waters, screaming visions, splitting headaches. None of that matters because he'll take care of me.

I know it in my gut.

"Tell me your dream." I turn toward him, finding him already staring at me.

His eyes warm a smidgen. "What do you want to know?"

"Did you come screaming into this world wanting to be a CFO? Is the Deliminator a human or a robot?"

Ethan chuckles and shakes his head. "I can never predict what'll come out of your mouth."

I toss a napkin at him. "Hey! Quit dodging."

"Fine, to answer your question, *no*, I'm not a freak who thinks crunching numbers is my calling. Actually," his fingers fiddle with the cuff of the dress shirt under his sweater, and I realize he's once again wearing those cuff links, "I used to want to write. Travel the world, sit outside cafes and people watch. Then take out my notebook and jot down my observations."

"Really? You're creative?" I lean in closer, eager to learn more about him. His body is relaxed and there's a lightness I rarely see. "Stories? Poetry? Scriptwriting? What's your poison?"

"Poetry."

I arch my brow. A lock of brown hair falls over his face—this is one of those rare moments when he's not all put together, and I like it. "Hm. I can see that. You're a man of few words. So, of course you'd like to write the least amount of words too. Why make things easy for people to understand, right?"

Ethan barks out a laugh and I grin, my heart throwing itself against my rib cage.

He smiled! A wide, dimple baring smile. And *I* brought that to his face.

"No, Lexy. I like poetry because it's magic with words."

Magic. I inch closer. *This is magic.*

"The least amount of words to tell the most riveting story. Capturing emotions in its essence. That's magic, don't you think?" he rasps.

It's seduction. His voice. I can listen to it all day.

My mouth dries and I wet my lips. Those ever-changing eyes of his snare on the movement. His pupils dilate.

Heat shoots between my legs and I'm reminded of how we fit together that night at Mystique—hot and cold, fire and ice—how his raspy voice and talented fingers brought me to orgasm with the slightest touch.

My lips part and I look away, feeling out of sorts.

Ignoring the butterflies fluttering in my stomach, I sit up, grab my satchel, and pull out my notebook and a pen.

Flopping on my stomach this time, I kick my feet up and read the prompt.

Love, in Seven Lines:
Describe love without using the words "love," "heart," or "forever." Use exactly seven lines or sentences.

Frowning, I stare at the blank lines underneath it. How can I describe love in only seven lines? I think about my parents' volatile relationship—the intense highs and devastating lows, the fights, the kisses. I get seasick standing in their presence.

How can I describe *that* in seven sentences?

Have I ever been in love before?

My heart flutters. *Is that a yes?*

I groan—damn missing memories.

"Why do you look like someone is making you do math all day?"

"Not everyone is a genius with numbers, Mr. Deliminator." I shove him gently, and he slowly sits up. "My assignment. I'm stumped, but it's due next week. You love poetry, right? Maybe you can give me some ideas." I hand over my notebook and sit in front of him.

Ethan rolls his lips inward as he reads the prompt. He swallows, and when he speaks, his voice is hoarse. "Don't focus on the limitations. Seven lines is plenty when it's used wisely." His eyes snap to mine, and he holds out his hand.

I give him the pen and watch as he uncaps it. His gaze roves over my face—a soulful caress. Then he closes his eyes.

"Imagine it's the end of the world, and an asteroid is barreling toward you. You only have seconds left with the person you love. What do you want them to know?"

His lips curve in a bittersweet smile.

My lungs seize, riveted by the intensity on his face.

His eyelids flutter open, revealing a melancholic wistfulness, and he writes.

Moments later, he hands me the notebook and rasps, his voice thick with emotions, "It's been a long time. Go easy on me."

A scent of lavender lingers.
An imprint time will not erase.
Pain and distance cannot sever.
Her laughter, her light—a path I chase.
Once in a lifetime, a sure-fired arrow.
Even through agony, loneliness, and sorrow.
No regrets, only gratitude—the lavender, always, *woven into*
my soul.

I grip the pen tightly, the words blurring in front of me.

My hands are shaking.

Why is it so hard to breathe?

I read his heartfelt poem again, and two droplets of water smear the page. Glancing up, I don't see rain.

It's then I realize...those are tears.

My tears.

"Nova," he whispers, and cradles my face.

"I don't know why I'm crying." I wipe my tears away, but they won't stop falling. "What's wrong with me? Is this a side effect of the meds too? I swear, I feel like I'm losing it."

"Shh..." He crushes me to him. "Don't cry, Lexy. Please don't cry. Don't cry for me."

He smooths his hand over my back as I tighten my arms around him, wanting to feel his heartbeat next to mine.

I want the pain to go away. My pain. His pain.

Suddenly, everything is too much. Too intense. The rightness of me in his arms. The shredding of my heart inside me. The onslaught of grief coming from nowhere.

I need space.

Pulling back, I barely notice the alarm on his face. I quickly pack up my things, shoving everything in my bag—the notebook and the pen, my cell phone.

In my haste, I knock over the box Liam left me and the contents spill on the ground. Instead of putting them back inside the box, I toss the contents into my satchel.

"This. You forgot this." He hands me a pen from the box, but this time, the cap has fallen off, revealing a flash drive.

I don't have time to wonder about it when I grab it from him and jam it in with the rest of my things.

My breathing comes out in harried pants, and I stand, remembering to address the silent man behind me. "I'm sorry. I suddenly remember I have an appointment. Thanks for your help with the poem. It's beautiful. You really are a poet. This picnic has been wonderful. Stay longer—keep the food and the blanket. I'll see you back in the office on Monday."

Without waiting for a response, my pulse a cacophony in my ears, I scurry away.

Why am I feeling this way? Is this what a heart attack is like? Why—

Heavy footsteps pound behind me, and a second later, a firm hand grips my wrist and spins me around.

And I'm in his arms.

Ethan crushes me against him, like he wants to meld our bodies together.

I can't breathe.

And yet, it's like I'm breathing for the first time after I came out of my coma.

"Ethan—"

"Just let me hold you. P-Please. Just for a minute." His voice is thick.

I halfheartedly pull away, my mind and body split between wanting to stay in his embrace forever or to run screaming in the other direction because of how it makes me feel.

Safe. Loved. On fire.

"Please, Nova. Please. O-One minute." The words rush out of him in a choked exhale and the pain from moments ago spears into my chest again. His towering frame trembles against mine.

Closing my eyes, I melt into his hug.

Hug is too little of a word to describe this.

"Ethan," I whisper, needing to know the answer to a question that has haunted me since I woke up in the hospital, disoriented, and find myself in the tight embrace of a man who looked like he had lost, then found his world. "We knew each other before, didn't we? Those four years I've forgotten. You were there, weren't you?"

That's the only explanation that makes sense—why my soul seems to recognize him.

He stills.

The wind ruffles my hair and scrapes across my face.

"Are you staying in the medical trial?"

Yes. No. Yes. I don't know.

Taking my silence as an answer, he pulls away, the tormented expression on his face ripping the breath from my lungs.

He lifts his finger, like he has many times before, and I wait for the inevitable moment when he freezes mid-gesture.

But this time, he doesn't.

His fingertip skims the bridge of my nose, light as a feather, and warmth unfurls through me in quiet, shivering waves.

He whispers, "Let's leave it up to fate then."

CHAPTER 43

PRESENT: NINE YEARS AFTER THE ACCIDENT—THIRTY-THREE YEARS OLD

I SNEAK A GLANCE at the time on my computer.

Five o'clock p.m.

If I hurry this up, I can see the tail end of her presentation.

"Ethan. Hey, Ethan, you listening?"

I snap my attention to Liam, who is in my office with Trey to discuss the updates on the embezzlement situation.

"This is what I've got so far. The motherfucker hid his tracks well. Small sums less than ten thousand dollars, rotating payouts to legitimate looking vendors. If your auditors didn't randomly sample, you would've never noticed it." Liam turns his laptop around and shows us his findings. I've hired him to trace the funds off the books.

I don't want a press field day until I have the fucker behind bars.

"Shit. Over ten years, huh?" Trey murmurs, standing behind me.

"Office equipment, uniforms, housekeeping supply companies—they all look legit."

"Whoever did this is good. They know we won't flag these common transactions," I muse, scrolling through the rows and rows of orderly transfers from three of our operating accounts over the years.

Liam nods. "I get you aren't fans of your auditors, but they did a good job. The only red flag was the account numbers having consecutive sequences, like they were opened or created at the same time. Took me on a wild goose chase because the money bounced around so many times, even I got dizzy."

"So, are we stuck?" I push the laptop back toward him.

He grins and spits out the toothpick he's chewing on. I sigh. If he wasn't so good at his hacking job, I would've kicked him out of the room. "Well, you're looking at the best of the best. Nothing's too hard for me."

"So you got something?" Trey raps the table.

I glance at him, finding his gaze pinned on Liam, a muscle twitching in his jaw.

"I don't blame you, you know," I murmur. He's my mentor and friend. I know how he works, how much he cares about the company. "Bad people will do bad things. You can't catch them all."

Trey exhales, his fingers white-knuckled against my desk. "It shouldn't have happened."

"You guys can play the pity party later." Liam's fingers fly over his keyboard. "As I was saying, if you hired anyone else, the trail would've been dead months ago, but since you got me, I can bring the dead back to life."

Rolling my eyes, I wait for his big reveal.

Sure enough, it comes seconds later. "Cayman Islands. BoC Equitable Investment Fund. This is where your money went. They have twenty thousand firewalls I'm still trying to breach. Once I do, I'll find more info."

BoC? Bank of Columbia? The Vaughns' company?

Liam catches my eye and shakes his head. There's something else he isn't saying right now.

Clearing my throat, I murmur, "Good job. Keep digging."

The ping on my phone reminds me of Alexis's presentation wrapping up in fifteen minutes. I stand and the men follow suit.

"I'll finish up some things in my office then." Trey rakes his fingers through his hair, his shoulders slumped as he walks out the door. He's taking this situation very hard.

Liam and I stride toward the conference room where Alexis and her team are presenting the marketing budget to Maxwell and Ryland.

"What else do you know?" I keep my voice low.

"It's strange. Most fraudulent schemes are short term, a few years max. It's too hard to keep up the pretenses. But this is over a decade. Something doesn't sit right with me."

"BoC. Is that Bank of Columbia?"

Liam frowns. "That's how the bank labels their funds. But it wouldn't be us. There's no way Charles would stand for this. Something is fucking off about this whole thing. Until I find out more, the fewer people know about this, the better."

I nod and heave out a deep breath.

Damn bastards, whoever they are.

My bad mood soon disappears, however, when I hear the familiar lilting voice of my Nova from the opened conference room door. I smile and stroll to the back corner of the room.

"Based on our research, we believe the most cost effective use of funds will be to invest in infrastructure upgrades, rebranding The Strata to a younger, more on trend name, and establishing a membership rewards system," Alexis's hands fly as she speaks, her face animated while she describes the final project plan she presented last week to me.

After that picnic at Ravenswood.

Even though she has forgotten us, deep inside her mind, she still remembers her perfect picnic at the private courtyard, the one experience she was saving for when she had a full-time job.

With the person she loved.

I know I'm supposed to put the past behind me. I'm supposed to win her over again. But how can I forget all those beautiful memories—every kiss, every touch, every dream?

It's a different loss I'm grappling with.

The Alexis in front of me is driven, resilient, and alluring. The past her was whimsical, impulsive, and endearing. I love both versions of her, but in forgetting the past, I'm doing the one thing I swore I'd never do.

Letting the old Alexis die.

My heart twists behind my rib cage.

"This membership program will foster consumer loyalty and we can funnel these customers into our higher-end hotels once they age out of the target market."

She tucks her silky hair behind her ear, flashing the hummingbird earrings I gave her all those years ago. My fingers snag on my cuff link. We're both wearing pieces of each other, only she doesn't know.

"And that concludes our presentation. Questions?"

The audience erupts into applause and a flush creeps up her neck. Her eyes sweep around the room and I hold my breath, wondering if she'll see me all the way in the back.

She does.

Our gazes connect and her eyes widen before her lips curve up in the same brilliant smile I remember.

The air rushes out of my lungs.

Always radiant, my beautiful Nova.

Happily, she gathers her things and beelines toward us. Something has shifted between us since our picnic.

She let me hold her in the courtyard—a real embrace. Not one fueled by passion in a dark club, but one filled with emotion.

It was the first time in almost a decade that she held me back.

And now, she's no longer guarded the way she usually is around me.

"How was it, guys?" Her scent of lavender reaches my nose and I inhale.

Liam reaches for her hair. "Looking good, Fire—"

"Don't you dare, Liam. Don't you mess up my hairdo." She bats his arm away, her lips twitching.

"I like the idea of the membership program," Maxwell murmurs, walking up to us. "The rebranding I'll need more info on. Put some time on my calendar for next week." His Majesty, as we call him, saunters off.

"That's a compliment from Maxwell."

Suddenly, Alexis freezes, and Liam's brow flies up.

I frown and look down, finding her hand in mine. It feels as natural as breathing.

Shit.

Quickly letting go, I flex my fingers, still feeling the tingles from that brief touch. "Good job, Alexis," I rasp.

The flush on her face deepens.

"Is there something I should know about?" Liam narrows his eyes.

"W-What? I did a good job. Scared I'll no longer be the black sheep of the family, Liam?" She bites her lip and heat flows straight to my groin.

Liam huffs. "Please. You were never the black sheep. I was."

I shake my head, needing to stop the bickering before they brawl in front of me. "What are you guys doing after work?"

"I'm meeting a contact after this." Liam checks his watch. "Shit. I'm late. Got to go. You going to the Christmas Ball in a few weeks?"

"Of course. It's the first time we're hosting it outside of The Orchid." The Christmas Ball at The Orchid is considered *the* event of the year—who's who in the old money or powerful circles mingle under the guise of celebrating the holidays. But it's really where a lot of deals and secret handshakes happen. This year, to mix things up, according to Jack Szeto, our Entertainment Director, instead of hosting it in the ballroom, the event will happen on a luxury cruise.

"Well, I'll see you there then." He bolts out the door, leaving Alexis and me behind as the rest of the conference room empties.

Alexis shifts on her feet, her bottom lip once again under attack by her teeth.

Chuckling, I gently tug it loose and her breath hitches. "What has your lip done to you? You're going to chew it off."

Her face turns impossibly red. "You can't help it, huh?"

"What?"

"Taking care of people."

I smirk. "Only certain people."

She ducks her head and kicks the ground. Her phone buzzes and she quickly swipes it open, her eyes widening in obvious excitement, but seconds later, her shoulders slump. She looks disappointed.

"Everything okay?"

"Huh?" She glances up, then clears her throat. "Oh. I thought it was an email from a...friend. But I think I was overthinking it."

A friend.

She meant Polaris. Guilt punches me at the obvious sadness in her eyes.

I haven't responded to her last email.

I don't know how to without revealing my identity. How will she react when she finds out she's been pouring her heart out, revealing secrets I'm sure she hasn't told her closest friends, to me? Someone she was wary of until recently?

What will she do when she finds out the person I talk about in my emails is her?

She eyes the door. "Um. I have to go. I need to head off to practice."

"Practice?"

She grimaces. "Swimming. It's all in my head, honestly. I swim just fine in the kiddie pool. My instructor says my strokes are solid, and my form is great. But the moment I step into the big pool, I freeze. I think it has something to do with what happened to me."

My chest tightens, thinking about that horrid night. She doesn't remember the details, but it must've been traumatizing, submerged in the dark waters, unable to escape, knowing she was going to die.

All because you didn't teach her how to swim, Ethan.

Guilt seizes me, a vice around my neck.

"I'll teach you," I blurt out.

Her mouth drops open. "What?"

"Let me go with you. I've been swimming all my life. Let me teach you."

Ten years too late, but please let me teach you how to swim now, Nova.

"B-But, it's Tuesday. Don't you need to eat dinner? It's past five. And you don't swim in the afternoons unless it's Wednesday."

A small thrill sweeps through me. She remembers my routine.

"Screw it. Swimming is a lifesaving skill. You want to learn. I'm good at it. Let me teach you." Desperation grips me. I seize her hand, and those sky-blue eyes flicker—first to our hands, then to my face, then back again.

"Okay." She breathes out. "I might disappoint you, but...okay."

You'll never disappoint me, Nova.

I'll teach you how to swim if it's the last thing I do.

CHAPTER 44

I CAN DO THIS. I can do this. I can do this.

The smell of chlorine hits my nose. My palms sweat. The hairs stand on the back of my neck.

I want to throw up.

Huffing out quick breaths, I snap the rubber band on my wrist. I sneak one more look at my phone, hoping Polaris's email will pop up.

He always has the perfect words of encouragement.

A weight presses into my chest, the ache behind my rib cage making an appearance. Did I scare him off? It's been weeks. Why isn't he responding? Did he forget about me?

He's only a pen pal, Lexy. Just because you feel something doesn't mean he does.

I shouldn't feel sad. I've never met him after all.

Shaking myself, I stuff my phone inside the locker and slam it shut. Time to focus on the task at hand.

Swimming.

I can do this. I'm Alexis Vaughn and I'm stronger than my fears. I don't need anyone to encourage me because I'm motivated all on my own.

Blowing out one last breath, I step through the door separating the changing room and the Olympic-sized swimming pool inside The Orchid.

Then my lungs stop working altogether. My eyes malfunction too.

Because there's a hot merman in the water.

Sleek muscles flash, then disappear, the water rippling from his movements. Those powerful arms resurface and slice through the air, the motion full of strength and precision.

The perfect butterfly stroke.

Suddenly, my skin is too hot and I tug my black bikini top, trying to loosen it up.

Ethan's not lying. He *can* swim.

His movements halt when he reaches the end of the pool, and in one quick motion, he hoists himself up, bracing his forearms on the edge.

"Coming in?" He swipes his hair back.

My mouth dries. It's like watching a cologne commercial in slow motion. The water droplets glide across swaths of golden skin, trickling down his corded neck to those defined pecs and rippling abs.

Six-pack. No, eight-pack.

High school boys did *not* look like this.

I gulp.

"Cat got your tongue?" He unleashes a wry grin, his dimples flashing.

My heart stutters, then goosebumps form on my forearms.

Cat got your tongue? The question echoes in my mind.

He said this at Mystique. But the breathlessness inside me, his grin, his question...it's all distinctly familiar, and not because of that night at the club.

Textbooks scattered on the ground.

My laptop strewn on the pavement.

Blistering cold. Lots of snow.

A hand stuffing my things back into my bag.

"Lexy?"

I shake myself out of my trance, finding Ethan's concerned gaze on me. Was that another memory?

"Sorry. Trying to work up the guts to do this." I walk to the edge of the pool.

"You got this. I have faith in you," he murmurs and cocks his head toward the other end, where the ladder is. "Want to ease in slowly or just go for it?"

I peer into the water. The nausea comes roaring back.

It looks deep. Really deep. Deeper than the pool back at my apartment.

"Ten feet," he murmurs, clearly knowing what I'm thinking. "We can start in the shallow end if you like."

Dragging my gaze up to his, I stare into his eyes. They are steady on me. Constant. Reassuring.

I've lost eight years of my life in a coma, plus four years of memories.

I don't want to waste any more time.

"No. Let's go for it." My words echo against the walls. It's then I realize there's no one here except the two of us. "Is it always this empty?"

"I closed it off. Perks of being an Anderson. I figured you wouldn't want an audience."

I swallow, my stomach flipping. *He's thought of everything.*

"Come on then. I'm right here." He wades back a few feet, giving me room to get in.

I can do this. I'm going to swim, dammit.

Before I can talk myself out of it, I turn around and carefully lower myself into the pool, clinging to the edge for dear life.

"Sh-shit." My teeth clatter.

Strong arms wrap around me, caging me to the side, then his broad chest presses against my back. "I'm right here. I'm not going anywhere. You're safe."

I'm safe.

Blowing out a deep breath, then another, my rioting pulse slowly calms.

I'm safe with him.

After a minute, I turn around to face him, my hands still gripping the edge behind me.

"I can do this, Ethan. I *will* do this." I say it more to myself than to him.

A flash of admiration appears in his eyes. "I believe you, Nova. I have faith in you."

Nova.

I like the nickname.

"Hold on to me. I'll just swim us out a little bit, okay?"

Nodding, I throw my arms around his neck and shriek when my body sinks.

"I got you. You're safe. I got you." He grips me tightly as I hug him like a koala to a tree.

Slowly, my muscles relax, and we wade to the middle of the pool. My feet can't touch the bottom. If I let go of him and don't swim, I'll drown.

But somehow, the panic doesn't rear its ugly head.

Because he's here. He'll take care of me and protect me.

"Ready for more?" He smiles softly, his wet hair falling over his eye.

Unbidden, I brush it back and his nostrils flare. "Let's do this."

We spend the next fifteen minutes floating. He slowly eases me away from him—my hands sliding down to his shoulders, his biceps, then his forearms. Eventually, only our fingers are touching, and there's a wide gap between us.

"Look at you treading water. Doing just fine on your own. I'm barely holding you."

His encouragement spurs me on, and I take a deep breath. "I want to try swimming on my own."

Ethan scans my face, a muscle twitching in his jaw. "You sure?"

I nod. "I want to try it."

"You know the strokes, Lexy. You can swim. Just remember that. This is just the same as the kiddie pool. I'm here and *nothing* will happen to you. Whenever you're ready, let go of my hand and swim to the edge."

My pulse clamors in my ears, and I blow out another breath.

One.

Two.

Three.

I let go.

My body plummets. The water swallows me whole.

"I don't know what you're talking about!"

"Stop lying. Why did you have to be so nosy? You have a death wish, don't you?"

There's so much rain. I can barely see in front of me, the water cloaking the windshield, the wipers completely useless.

"Give it to me. I know you have it."

"No!"

Bright lights blind me. Headlights in my rearview mirror. I swerve but the car spins out of control and free falls into inky darkness.

I scream.

Water rushes up my nose, my arms flailing.

I'm going to die. I'm going to drown. I'm going to—

Strong arms band around my back, and the next thing I know, my head is out of the water.

"I got you. You're safe. You're okay. I got you."

Ethan.

Coughing, the water still burning my lungs, I cling to him—his warmth, the frantic beat of his heart, the quick puffs of air hitting my back.

"I got you, Nova. I won't let anything happen to you. I'll protect you with my life."

My pulse rings in my ear, the room swirling around me, and it isn't until a few seconds later when I fully register his words.

I'll protect you with my life.

"Ethan?" I pull back slightly, my fingers digging into his shoulders.

He dips his forehead against mine and vows, "I'll die before I let anything happen to you."

A gasp tumbles out of me. The fervency in his voice. There's no doubt. No hesitation.

He means it.

I lean back and look at him. His pulse batters against his temple. A desperate fire incinerates those stormy eyes.

Those familiar eyes.

What happened between us in the past?

"Ethan." The rest of my body finally flickers to life.

Every inch of me is plastered against him. My softness against his hardness. My agility against his strength. My core clenches and my nipples bead into hard points.

Suddenly, the water feels too warm.

He draws in a sharp inhale, his pupils slowly dilating. His gaze trails over me—my eyes, lips, breasts, then dips lower. The tension thickens, and he swallows hard before locking his eyes back to mine.

Just like before, he skates his index finger down my nose and a sharp current sizzles through me.

He's telling me something in that gesture, and this time, I'm learning the language.

"Someone once told me perseverance and effort are what it takes to succeed in life. And effort counts twice." His voice is husky. "I have faith in you, Alexis."

I stare at him, hypnotized by the reverence in his words.

"Shall we try again? You can swim. I know it."

Right. Swim lessons. That's why I'm here.

He's chased away my terror.

I nod.

Despite the failure just now, the strange flashbacks confirming something sinister happened to me the night of the accident, I'm not afraid.

Because Ethan is here. He'll protect me with his life.

This time, when he lets go, a new confidence surges through me, my body finally cooperating with my mind.

And I swim, on my own, for the very first time.

CHAPTER 45

"Don't feel like partying inside?"

Dayton strides up beside me, a champagne flute in his hand. Somewhere inside the ballroom on the Delfina, a luxury cruise owned by Fleur, a string quartet plays a melancholic rendition of "Have Yourself a Merry Little Christmas."

"No. It's too noisy."

I stare at the gloomy darkness of the Hudson, listening to the waves slapping against the hull. It's an unusually warm winter, no snow in sight, but there's still a chill in the air. The night stretches endlessly, the city skyline blazing in the distance, but a fine mist rises from the water.

I shiver.

The peaceful waters are deceptive.

I, of all people, know how deadly it is. How it almost became my grave.

"You're different now. The Lexy I knew would be in there partying it up with the best of them." He motions to the double doors separating the deck and the ballroom where The Orchid's famous Christmas Ball is in full swing.

"I suppose we all change, even if I was asleep most of the time."

I used to be sad about how different things were—the people, the relationships, my temperament.

But in the recent months, I've accepted this new version of myself.

I'm happy. My feet are finally steady on the ground. Even if I have a permanent limp and many unanswered questions.

"Change is often forced upon us," he mutters.

A crack in his voice draws my attention. His jaw clenches as he stares into the waters.

"Is everything okay, Dayton? You seem stressed."

His troubled expression clears, and he shakes his head. "It's fine. Just problems at work. Remember back in high school, I always wanted to make it? But now that I'm here, I realize things were much simpler back then."

He gives me his signature grin and nods toward the river, his fingers tapping the railing. "I'm honestly surprised you came tonight. I thought you'd want to avoid it, since it's on a cruise in..."

The place where I almost lost my life. I don't need him to finish the sentence to know what he's referring to.

A strange unease wraps itself around my lungs, and I grip the railing tightly. "Can't live my life in fear. And you know what? I'm slowly getting over it. Some memories are coming back too."

The tapping stops. "Really? That's amazing. Can you make sense of anything yet?"

"I-I don't think my car accident was an accident." I've never voiced my concern aloud until now, but it's been bothering me, the strange snippets I hear, the images.

The bloodcurdling terror.

"Shit." Dayton's nostrils flare and brows pinch. "That must be scary. Are you sure?"

I shake my head. "Maybe? It's like getting a few puzzle pieces at a time, and I don't know how they fit together yet. Maybe when I have them all, the picture will be something unexpected. I wish there's a way to find the Good Samaritan who saved me. Maybe he or she knows something."

My fingers twitch, my mind going through the flashes of that night.

I heard screaming in a loud place. Moaning—but they didn't sound like pleasurable noises, more like torture.

My lungs burning as I ran. But where?

Then the images of me driving, the pouring rain making it impossible to see what's in front of me.

A phone call, but the voice is blurry—I couldn't make out who that person was. But he or she sounded angry.

What happened that night?

A dull throb begins at the base of my neck—another one of those damn headaches.

Suddenly, Dayton clasps his hand over mine and gently tugs it off the railing.

"You look like you were going to break it." He chuckles. "You're brave, Lexy. Maybe you've changed, but those guts of yours sure haven't. It's amazing."

I stare at his thumb circling my wrist. Slowly, he lifts my fingers and blows on them, like he's trying to warm me up.

But instead of warmth sweeping through me, the pain in my head only intensifies.

My lungs constrict.

"Lexy... May I take you on a date?" He kisses the back of my hand.

My eyes fly up to his and just as I open my mouth to respond—

"A sweet reunion, huh?"

I quickly snatch my hand away and turn around.

Ethan stands next to the ballroom doors, looking irresistibly handsome in his tux. Even from the distance, I sense anger and hurt pulsing off him. He fists his hands at his sides and his eyes blaze into mine.

"Ethan, I—"

"I thought things changed," he rasps, his eyes turning into a glacial glare, reminding me of the ice monster who visited me in the hospital. "It's all in my head, apparently."

"We were just chatting. Nothing's happening." I step toward him but suddenly stop myself. Why am I explaining myself to him? We aren't anything. Sure, we've had a few special moments, but that's it.

"I wasn't aware Lexy answered to you." Dayton steps closer to me.

I tilt my chin up. "I answer to no one but myself."

Ethan scoffs and shakes his head. "No, she doesn't answer to me and she can damn well take care of herself." Then, as if catching himself, he straightens and blows out a sharp breath. "I have a party to host. Excuse me."

He spins around and disappears inside the ballroom.

I start to follow, but Dayton tugs my arm.

"Lexy, is something going on between you and—"

"I'm sorry, Dayton." My words come out in a rush. "I-I don't feel this way about you. You're a good friend. I have to go."

Before he responds, I run back inside, trying to find the infuriating man who occupies my mind and awakens my body.

Chandelier light sears my eyes the moment I step through the doors, the heat from the fireplaces pressing against my skin. Laughter and clinking of glasses, rustling of bejeweled gowns—everything blurs together as bodies move across the dance floor.

My eyes skate over the throng, trying to find a tall, lonely silhouette.

Ethan's an introvert. He'll be seeking a quiet corner somewhere.

Just then, a clang in the far corner catches my attention. Rex stumbles, and a champagne flute shatters on the floor. He flushes and wavers on his feet like he has had one too many drinks. A few ladies rush up to hold on to him and he unleashes a smile I'll bet anything is fake.

I frown. What's going on with him?

"There you are!" Taylor rushes up, her black ball gown sweeping behind her. "I've been looking all over for you."

"And she's dragging me along with her." Olivia grins and shakes her head.

I focus on the girls. "I just took a breather outside. Do you guys notice anything off with Rex?" I motion to the playboy and his gaggle of women. He has one arm slung around a brunette's shoulder and another arm curled around a blonde's waist.

"No clue. Probably the usual Rex shenanigans." Taylor shrugs.

I turn to Olivia, finding her gaze riveted on the man, her lips rolling inward. "Olivia? You okay? What do you think?"

She blinks and intakes a sharp breath. "W-What? Oh, I think something is going on with Rex. But then I don't know him that well, so I shouldn't assume."

"A gut feeling or a professional opinion?" Taylor asks, straightening up and glancing at her brother again.

"Both. I've seen this behavior before. Charm. Forced smiles. I just—" She shakes her head and faces us, a strained smile on her face. "Ignore me. Anyway, Taylor and I were looking for you, Lexy."

"Way to bury the lead, Olivia." Taylor snorts and jabs her friend's side. "This lady here keeps complaining she's the only single person at the party and I want to hand her off to you and—"

"Hey! I didn't say that. Lana's around somewhere too. I just don't see her. And as happy as I am for you, Tay, I don't need to see you and Charles undressing each other with your eyes."

"I'm happy. Well adjusted, as you doctors like to say, you should be thrilled—" Taylor frowns. "Lexy, is everything okay? You look...off."

I force out a grin, my eyes resuming the search for her brother. "Fine. I'm okay. Um, have you seen Ethan?"

Taylor cocks her brow.

Hastily, I add, "Just something about the project at work. He asked me for some stats earlier and I have them now."

"On Christmas." She narrows her eyes. "Bullshit."

"Have you seen him or not?" I huff out a frustrated breath.

"Not telling you until you explain why you look like you're ready to strangle me over a simple question."

That's it. Now I do.

"I think I saw him headed toward the library," Olivia supplies, pointing toward the back of the ship.

"Olivia, traitor! She was going to crack and tell us why she and Ethan are acting weird these days."

"You can satisfy your need for gossip later." Olivia steps closer to me. "Go find him. Give him those...*stats*." She winks.

"You're the best." I give her a hug and throw out a mocking glare at Taylor, who's struggling to keep a straight face. "Not done with you, Tay Tay."

I take a step when suddenly, blistering agony stabs my head again, and I squeeze my eyes shut.

"You aren't supposed to be here, young lady."

My heart jolts up my throat and I back away. What did I just see?

Ripped clothes. Terror on their faces. Thrusting and grunting.

I want to throw up.

More screams.

"You okay?" Taylor asks.

Focusing on my breathing, I ride out the throbbing pain before opening my eyes, finding the girls frowning at me with concern.

I nod and dole out a shaky smile. "I'll tell you more later, but...I think my memories are coming back, Tay. Something happened that night. I—I only have bits and pieces."

Her face turns ashen, and she sways on her feet.

Olivia clutches her arm. "Whoa. Easy."

"Is everything okay?" Grace rushes up and grabs her sister's other arm.

I look at my best friend, finding her eyes hollow and haunted.

"You're remembering it?" she whispers.

Alarm rings through me. My hold-no-prisoners, badass girlfriend. I've never seen her look so terrified before. "Tay, what aren't you telling me?"

Grace says, "I think Tay is just feeling sick. She was complaining about the shrimp cocktail, right?" She darts a frantic look at Olivia.

"Right. That she was," Olivia murmurs.

The color slowly returns to Taylor's face, and she lets out a nervous laugh. "You'd think The Orchid has better food." She turns around and calls out, "Belle! Over here."

Belle, Maxwell's wife, and Millie, Ryland's girlfriend, glide over, twin smiles on their faces.

"Tell your men they need better chefs for this party," Taylor grumbles. Her voice is light, but there's sweat beading on her forehead.

Belle's eyes sharpen. "What did we miss?"

"Tay has a stomachache from the shrimp cocktail, and Lexy is remembering the night of the accident." Grace strains a smile.

Millie's breath hitches and the girls exchange a worrisome glance. Something is terribly wrong.

"Go find Ethan. We'll take care of Tay and her digestive problems." Olivia nudges me.

"You guys are acting weird."

"Even if we are, we can't tell you anything. Medical trial, right? So, go. Find your man." She shoos me away.

Unsettled, I cut through the crowd and head toward the library. My mind swirls with questions and theories and dread knots in my stomach.

Ping.

Eager for a distraction, I whip out my phone from the hidden pocket of my forest-green gown and see a notification.

A new email from Polaris.

He didn't forget me.

My breath catches and I quickly stop to read his note.

To: <u>A.Vaughn@gmail.com</u>
From:<u> Polaris@LOH.manhattanmemorial.org</u>
Subject: RE: Do you ever want to meet?

Lexy,

I'm sorry for not responding.
It's not you. It's me.
What would you do if you loved someone desperately, but they didn't love you back?
What if you weren't who they thought you were all along?

What if these emails meant more to you than they ever did to them?

Would you feel betrayed?

Would I lose you again?

Yours,

Polaris

P.S. To answer your question—I *do* want to meet you. More than anything. But I can't.

Maybe you'd call me a coward. Maybe you'd say, *"Be brave, Polaris. Don't wait to live, because the clock keeps ticking."*

And you'd be right.

But it's not you. It's me. And I'm sorry.

My lungs tighten, squeezing until I'm no longer breathing. I reread his words, understanding nothing, and yet grasping everything he isn't saying.

He doesn't want to meet, but he desperately wants to meet.

I reread it for the third time when suddenly, my eyes sharpen on his words.

In particular, one small line tacked at the very end.

Maybe you'd say, *"Be brave, Polaris. Don't wait to live, because the clock keeps ticking."*

My heart stops.

It can't be.

But there's no other explanation. I remember every single email I've sent him and I've *never* included this motto in my messages before.

There's only one man I've mentioned this to in the past.

The man who looked like I gutted him when I woke up from my coma and asked him who he was.

The man whose eyes flashed with hurt and betrayal when he saw Dayton kissing my hand earlier.

Ethan.

CHAPTER 46

Quickening my steps, I brush past guests strolling down the quiet hallway. My heart restarts, its rhythm frantic, joining the desperate yearning in my gut.

I need to find Ethan to tell him he misunderstood what he saw on the deck.

I need to ask him why he's Polaris and why he's never revealed his identity.

I need to know if the woman from his emails, the person he loved, who broke his heart...if that person was me.

My breathing is in loud, rapid pants, and I lift my silk gown and rush to the end of the corridor where the library is.

Moments later, I stand in front of the large oak door, my fingers twitching, my pulse throbbing. Slowly, I turn the knob and step inside.

The door clicks shut behind me.

It's dark and quiet, except for the crackle of the fireplace.

The distinct scent of weathered pages and worn leather fills the air.

Moonlight streams in from the wall of windows ahead, casting a silvery glow over the endless rows of overflowing bookshelves. A small seating area rests atop a dark rug.

For a moment, I don't see him—my gaze fixed on the intimate room, half-veiled in shadows.

But then, I *feel* him.

A quiet presence. Unyielding. Impossible to ignore.

Ethan stands in the corner, looking out the windows at the dark waters outside. He has one hand braced on the glass, his forehead knocking softly against the pane, like he's trying to wake himself up. His muscles bunch, straining against the confines of his tuxedo.

He looks so lonely. Haunted. Worn down by pain.

A lump swells in my throat and my nose burns. The spot on my chest aches. With a shaky hand, I take out my phone and swipe it open. I pull up Polaris's email and type a reply.

To: <u>Polaris@LOH.manhattanmemorial.org</u>
From: <u>A.Vaughn@gmail.com</u>
Subject: RE: RE: Do you ever want to meet?

I don't accept that answer.
And I know who you are...Ethan.

I hit send and hold my breath.

A second later, his phone pings.

He takes it out and looks at the screen. A sharp inhale. He straightens to his full height.

It's him. Polaris is Ethan.

I should be angry. Furious at this breach of trust. But...I can't.

I can't bring myself to be mad at him. If anything, *everything* suddenly makes sense—why both men evoke such powerful reactions in me.

They are the same person all along.

Ethan has been with me every step of the way, even when I was cold with him after I woke up. The deep connection between us transcends the time we've spent together this past year. And when I'm in his arms—I feel safe, treasured.

Loved.

"I have faith in you... I'll protect you with my life."

His words at the swimming pool echo through me.

And before I can stop myself, a gasp tumbles from my lips.

Ethan's head snaps toward me, his eyes wide with shock.

"Nova," he rasps.

I stumble toward him, my right leg not quite working. My vision blurs from tears—grief I don't understand but somehow know intimately in my heart.

I love this man. I was already falling for him with every moment we'd shared since I awakened to this unfamiliar world. But now, I realize...perhaps I've loved him all along.

And from his glittering dark gaze, the way his arms are twitching at his sides like he's physically restraining himself from rushing toward me, I *know* feels the same way.

Ethan Anderson, Polaris, they're one and the same, and they both love me.

Desperately.

This is what's missing in my heart. This big gaping hole nothing can fill.

"It was you all along, wasn't it?" I stumble to a stop a foot away from him. The harsh moonbeam casts his features in stark contrast.

He swallows.

"You're the man I'm looking for, aren't you? The person I've forgotten but holds the missing pieces of my heart. You were in front of me all along."

I wish I remembered us, our past in those missing four years—those precious memories that formed the inexplicable connection I have with this man.

Wetness glints in his stormy eyes and his nostrils flare.

My fingers tremble as I reach up and caress his face. A sharp hiss escapes his lips before he snatches my hand and turns his head, pressing a searing kiss onto my palm.

"And I pushed you away for so long." Tears slide down my cheeks, but I don't care.

"How come you aren't mad at me?" I shove him in frustration. "I hurt you! I never understood why my heart ached or my head throbbed whenever I saw you. I thought it was fear, that my body was trying to tell me something, but it was the opposite all along, wasn't it?"

I shove him again, my mind overloaded with emotions.

Tears spill over, tracing silent paths down his cheeks, and the sight cleaves me in half. He hasn't spoken a word, but his pain crashes into me, raw and unrelenting.

My fists flail, landing half-heartedly against him. He catches them, pressing them against his chest—keeping me from hurting myself, from hurting him any longer.

"It was the opposite, wasn't it? Tell me, Ethan. My mind forgot, but my heart...my heart remembers. It was love all along, wasn't it? That's why it hurts so much to have lost it."

Sobs rack my body.

I don't deserve him. His kindness. His silent support. His love.

He's solved my problems—the internship, my fear of swimming, the loneliness of having no one to talk to—all without asking for recognition.

All without asking for me to love him in return.

My heart recognizes him, even if my mind has forgotten our story—what must've been a beautiful, heartbreaking story. Because what else can explain his devotion to me?

I gasp—*has he waited all these years for me? That's impossible. No one can do that.*

"I don't deserve you, Ethan." I shake my head. "I-I wish I could remember us. Our memories. I'm so sor—"

He yanks me to him and smothers my next words with his lips.

I'm finally home.

His mouth swallows my cries, and I kiss him back with everything I have.

We're a mess of tears and passion, grief, love, and desperation. He grips the nape of my neck and angles me to the side to deepen our kiss.

Harder. Conquering. Healing.

Moaning, I claw at his tux jacket and in a flash, he chucks it off. He groans and crushes me tighter against him, binding me almost to the point of pain, but I'm already lightheaded.

Drunk on him.

Ethan's tongue sweeps into my mouth, tasting me, savoring me, drinking me in like he's parched and dying of thirst. Fire burns down my body, prickling my nipples into tight buds, settling between my legs.

"Never," he rasps when we break apart for air. "*Never* apologize to me. You have *nothing* to be sorry for, you hear me? None of this is your fault. Fate stole a decade from us. I don't hate you. I'm not angry at you."

He caresses my face, the intensity in his eyes matching my rioting heartbeats. "I *love* you. I love you, I love you, I love you, I love you. I've waited," he chokes up, "w-waited almost a decade to tell you these words again, Nova. And now, I finally get to say them."

A ragged exhale escapes his throat, and he unleashes a devastating smile—one of pain and happiness. His eyes glisten with moisture again. "So don't you *dare* apologize to me. Don't you fucking dare. Because I love you so fucking much, and now I can finally tell you again."

I cry and throw myself at him, wrapping my arms around his neck, my legs curled around his waist.

I kiss and suck any part of him I can reach—his eyes, his lips, his rugged jawline.

He returns the favor, and our kiss quickly spirals out of control, the inferno overtaking us in a flash. Ethan carries me somewhere. I'm dizzy with lust, love, and everything in between, and before I know it, my back hits a bookshelf and darkness encloses us.

I might not remember if I've ever had sex before, but being with him like this feels as natural as breathing, like I've done this many times before and my body remembers.

My nails dig into his neck before I yank off his bow tie, then his shirt, and he makes work at removing my dress at a breakneck speed.

I can't get enough. Can't get close enough. Too many clothes. Too much distance.

"P-Please, Ethan. I need you. I-I need—"

I scream when he bites the pulse point on my neck.

"What do you need, Nova?" a deep guttural growl, and my pussy weeps, soaking my thong in a matter of seconds.

He sucks his way down my neck, laving my collarbone before he yanks off my strapless bra as well, baring my breasts to the night air.

"Fuck me," he grunts. He sucks a nipple in and tugs. Then he bites down.

I scream, the sharp pleasure shooting straight to my clit. I gyrate my pussy over his groin, his hard cock digging out of his pants.

"Shit!" His breath falters and I feel him throb and grow between my legs.

Moving faster, I rub my heat over his thick length, needing more friction, more pressure, more everything.

Dropping my head back, I hear the sounds of books toppling off the shelves. Then, the rough sound of the zipper and the rustling of fabric as his pants disappear between us. Followed by a heady burn when he rips off my thong.

"Yes...Ethan, oh my God, yes, just like that!" I moan when his bare cock glides over my folds.

There's a desperate need for him to fill me like this is a sensation I've been missing for a long time.

I'm so wet. I should be embarrassed, but apparently that only turns him on more.

"I can't go slow today, Nova." He slides his hand between us and rubs my swollen clit.

My legs shake as I barrel head first into what will be an earth-shattering orgasm.

"I...I need to be inside you. I can't last... It's been almost ten years." He grunts, and his tip notches at my opening.

My eyes snap open as his words finally register. "T-Ten years? You haven't—" *He hasn't been with anyone for a decade?*

His eyes are lightning. Thunder. Tornadoes. Breathtaking storm. "How could I? I'm taken. My heart and body belong only to one woman."

His answer sends me into a tailspin. *I've done this before with him.* The thought echoes in the back of my mind—a surety I'd bet anything on.

I claw his bare back and clamp my legs tightly against him, urging him on. "Fuck me, Ethan. I need you inside me. Bare. I'm on the pill."

There's no need to tell him I'm clear. He already knows. And from his revelation, I know he's the same.

He roars and surges in, his hard cock spearing me, but there isn't any pain. Instead, white-hot pleasure shoots into my veins as he pistons inside me. I feel so full, so complete.

This is not tender kisses and slow lovemaking.

This is a hard, rough fucking. A claiming.

The bookshelf groans under our assault as Ethan pummels me relentlessly.

The sounds of skin slapping against skin echo in the room, followed by the rumbling of more books falling to the ground as he hammers harder, his movements desperate.

It's insanity. It's heaven. It's everything I need.

"You're so fucking tight, Nova. You've been waiting like a good girl, haven't you?"

"Yes. Yes. Yes!" I bite his shoulder and he jerks inside me.

"A fucking biter too, my Nova. I've missed this." *Thrust. Thrust. Thrust.* "I've missed this so much."

He hoists me higher against him and spreads out my legs, holding me up by my ass.

My tits bounce as he ruts into me, his eyes glazed, mad with passion. He stares at my nipples saluting him, then at my lips, then my eyes.

My eyes roll back as a sharp current of pleasure surges from deep inside me, from a spot his cock is now hitting with every hard thrust, every gyration.

I shake against the shelf, my hands grabbing the ledge, sweeping more books to the floor.

My teeth chatter as sparks gather between my legs.

Tighter. Tighter. Even tighter.

"Come for me, Lexy. Bathe my cock with your cum. Let the world know who you belong to."

His words push me off the edge, and I explode.

"Ethan!" A lustful cry tears out of me and I tremble uncontrollably in his grip.

"Yes, yes, yes. Fuck, you're strangling me so good. Yes!" He roars his release, and I feel the hot spurts of his cum shooting deep inside me.

It's unending, like he's saved all his pleasure for me.

Lurid sounds of wetness echo with our loud breathing as he continues thrusting, not letting up, and soon, a new storm gathers where we're joined.

Within seconds, he has me on the edge again. He flicks my swollen nub and wetness spurts out of me as blinding pleasure obliterates my senses.

Our cum drips out, no doubt making a mess, but that only spurs him on.

"I can't get enough. Never enough," he rasps.

He slams his lips on mine as he carries us to the floor. Then, he hoists my legs over his shoulders, bending me like I'm a rag doll and slams back inside, this time getting deeper than before.

I bite his lip and he returns the favor, his hands reaching between us to grab my tits, his fingers pinching my nipples.

"Another one." He quickens his rhythm to jackhammering.

"I-I can't," I moan, but my body doesn't get the memo.

My pussy accepts his invasion and my mind is in a state of bliss as he pounds me like getting me off is the last thing he'll ever do.

"Yes, you can, Nova. I'm hungry. *Ravenous.* I haven't eaten in a decade. I haven't felt your pussy sucking the cum out of me, killing me and giving me life at the same time. You're going to give me another one, and this time, I want your scream to *deafen my ears.*"

He pins my legs down so they're by my ears, his cock growing impossibly thicker and longer. He's so deep inside me. I can feel him everywhere.

More wetness sluices out of me.

He pounds me harder, every thrust hitting a sensitive spot with the precision of a marksman.

My moans and cries are uninhibited, and my vision blackens. I'm once again perched at the edge of nirvana.

"Oh my God, I-I'm going to come!" I cry, my body locking, then spasming.

"Come, Nova. Who do you belong to? Scream it to the world." I feel his thumb breach my ass and that added sensation rips reality away from me.

"Yours. Ethan, I'm yours!" My answer echoes in the library. Pleasure shoots through my veins, rendering me speechless.

"Fuck yes. And I'm yours." A deep growl rumbles from his throat and he topples over the edge, his hot cum streaming out of his throbbing dick in never ending pulses, his hips moving, gyrating in a softening rhythm, riding out the intense aftershocks.

Sometime later—it could be a few minutes or an hour, I can't be sure—he slides out of me and lowers my legs.

Our cum drips out of me, and he growls his satisfaction when he pushes it back inside. "I want all of it inside you. Every drop."

My pussy flutters at the possession and obsession in his voice.

Sweat glistens our bodies as we lie on the carpeted floor, his larger frame spooning mine.

He presses a soft kiss on the sensitive spot where my jaw meets my neck and I shiver. My mind is mush and I sink into his embrace. His fingers twine with mine before resting on my stomach.

"I love you, Ethan. So, so much. My heart remembers you."

He clutches me tighter, and just when I think he won't reply, I hear his fervent response.

"Not as much as I love you. *Never* as much as I love you."

CHAPTER 47

I CAN'T STOP SMILING.

She loves me. Perhaps my Nova doesn't remember our past, but she loves me.

"Ethan! Stop grinning. You're drawing attention to us." Lexy nudges me as I curl her tighter against my side and lead her out of the library, down the hallway toward the elevators.

A loud laugh rips from my chest.

"Ethan!"

"What? I can't be happy? Because I'm so damn happy right now, I want to shout it from the rooftops."

"Yes, you can be happy during this walk of shame we're on, but *the Deliminator never smiles!*"

I pull us to a stop under a lone flickering sconce. A few folks whisper among themselves as they walk past us, and from their widening eyes and pointed fingers, rumors will swirl soon.

"Do you want me to hide this?" I murmur, my chest pinching as I drag up our interlinked hands.

"No! Of course not. I-I'm just...I mean, look at me. Anyone can take one look at me and know what we've been up to." She buries her face in my chest.

A rush of love infuses me as I pull her back to look at her. Her eyes—the same brilliant blue I love—are bright and sizzling with life, her lips are swollen, and love bites and scratches decorate her fair skin.

She looks well and truly fucked.

My cock twitches and I haul her flushed against me.

"Ethan!" Those beautiful eyes glaze over when I spin her around and grind her against the wall. She no doubt feels my sizable erection digging into her stomach. "Again, already?"

"I'm insatiable for you, Nova. I don't know how I've survived all these years. Fuck, I've waited and waited for this moment." My voice thickens. "I want to kiss you, make love to you, write you all the damn poetry in the world."

Her eyes cloud with tears.

"Ethan," she whispers, caressing my cheek, and I lean into her touch.

I've missed it so much. Her touch. I've been sick. Lovesick. Deprived for too long.

"You two, seriously. Get a room." Someone clears his throat.

Narrowing my eyes, I whip my head toward the intruder, ready to tear into him for interrupting this sweet moment between my Nova and me.

Rex stands there, his bow tie hanging around his neck, his hair tousled like he might have just gotten some action of his own. But his eyes are hollow, if not haunted. Is something brewing under the surface with him?

He grins and waggles his brows. "About damn time."

"Fuck off. I'm busy."

"Well then, I guess you're too busy for this." He dangles a gold key in front of him and unleashes his classic shit-eating grin. "Presidential suite. A lovely king-sized bed, double shower heads, a hot tub big enough to host an orgy, fireplace already stoked and roaring, room service set up on the table. Lasagna and rib eye with your fucking Pintzer and her iced tea."

I blink. He waves the key in front of my face.

"Ethan? Hello? Are you overcome with love and gratitude for your favorite brother? Or do you not want this lovely honeymoon set up? I can give it to—"

I snatch the key from him and Alexis giggles.

"How did you know that we—" A lump suddenly forms in my throat as I watch those carefree eyes of my least serious brother sharpen.

"Boned? Got your head out of your ass finally? Well, the two of you disappeared and I'm like, thank God. You were obvious, Ethan—a ticking time bomb waiting to explode. All those arrangements? Having Lana call you at Mystique? The intervention at the gentlemen's club?" He turns to Alexis and smiles. "And who did you think insisted you start on the campaign with him first?" He points to me.

"Y-You've been in on it all along?" Her eyes are the size of dinner plates.

"Nah, more like facilitating the longest slow burn in history. Giving it the much needed kick in the ass." Rex winks, then sobers. "I'm happy for you two. So damn happy."

An unfamiliar warmth hits me in the chest. All my life, I've felt like an outsider in my family. It's gotten better over the years, but I've always been jealous of the connection Maxwell and Ryland have with each other, or the camaraderie Rex has with Lana. I've always felt like the odd man out. The silent observer.

But it turns out, maybe they were right. Maybe my doubts were unfounded.

My family loves me, just as I am. I only need to open my mind and my heart to let them in.

Rex squeezes my shoulder and pulls me in for a hug. "Proud of you, dude. You're the best Anderson out of us all. Your loyalty and persistence. I'm floored. Now go get your happy ending with your woman." He slaps my back and pulls away.

But before he fully disentangles himself, I grip his arm. "Thank you, Rex. You fucker, I...I'm so glad to call you my brother."

He doles out a lazy wink. "I know. I know. I'm the best. Now go before Liam catches you. Good God, he's going to rip your head off. And I *can't* wait to see it." He laughs and shakes his head as he strides back to the ballroom.

Grinning, I tug Alexis with me to the elevator, my heart feeling a ton lighter.

Minutes later, we're in the presidential suite and before the door fully shuts, I have Alexis pinned against the wall.

She moans, her breathy sounds sending my blood to my groin. I press kiss upon kiss on her forehead, her cheeks, her lips, then trailing my mouth down her neck, tasting her unique blend of lavender and sweetness.

"Ethan, this is madness," she whimpers when I bite the enticing divot of her collarbone, my fingers making a work of her gown and bra and dropping them on the floor.

"Our love is fucking madness." I lick her rosy nipple. "I wouldn't have it any other way."

I hoist her up and carry her to the main bedroom before dropping her on the bed.

She's a seductress—her fiery hair fanned across the white bedding, her heavy tits shaking with each breath she takes. The way she looks at me, her pupils dilated, like I hold her universe in my hands.

A lost girl with a guy trying to prove himself—a love story that began in a hidden library. Maybe it has to end there, but it'll be fine.

Because we'll just write another one.

She might not remember the most beautiful years of my life, but I'm going to create the best years for us in the future.

That will have to be okay.

Ignoring the ache in my chest, I shed my jacket and shirt. Her lips part and her tongue dips out as I step out of my pants and underwear before gripping my thick cock.

"You've been warned," I growl. "I intend to *work* you hard, so every time you walk and feel the ache between your legs, you'll remember who put it there. I have a decade's worth of pent up energy and I'm going to use it all. Every. Single. Drop."

She swallows, her legs parting, revealing her glistening slit.

I crawl above her. "Look at that tight little pussy. It's pulsing for me already." I bite her earlobe and she shrieks, then I lave it with my tongue.

I do the same to her neck, then the tops of her swollen breasts. Sucking, nibbling, tasting, licking, making my little Nova writhe below me, desperate for release.

"I love my marks on you."

My cock twitches when I admire my handiwork—every mark is my signature.

Mine. This woman is mine.

Pre-cum drips out of me, making a mess on her stomach, but I don't care. I'm a bottomless well of lust and love right now.

Grabbing her tits, I roll her nipples and flick at the hardened tips. Then I press them together and bury my face in her swells, taking both buds into my mouth at the same time.

"Ethan," she moans, her back arching as I suck her sweet tits, my hips gyrating, dragging my dick against her body, marking her with my pre-cum.

I'm so fucking hard, I can burst.

Moving down, I kiss her stomach before parting her legs and pinning it to the bed.

"Look at you lying there, your fucking tits heaving, your rosy nipples pointing at me, begging me to suck them. Fuck, you make me so hard." I tug my dick, watching as more liquid drips down the length.

"But there's one place I want to taste—because I've been salivating for it."

I blow on her wet slit and she shudders. "This pretty little pink pussy." Groaning, I lick it from top to bottom and she screams, thrashing on the bed.

What a beautiful sound. I want to hear that every morning, every night as I invent a thousand and one ways to make her cry as she comes around me.

"Too sensitive, oh shit." She tries to wiggle away, but I pin her down.

"No way, my little hummingbird. You're going to let me feast." I dive in and suckle her swollen clit, nipping, licking, swirling it, then dragging my tongue to her sopping entrance, tasting her nectar—honey, lavender, an addictive sweetness making me drunk.

"So fucking delicious. I could drink this all day." I tease more wetness out of her before lapping it up.

"Yes, please, oh fuck, please, yes," she chants, gripping my hair and pulling it to the point of pain.

I insert a finger inside her and grunt as she sucks me in, gripping me like it's my cock.

"So tight, Nova. Your pussy needs me. You're going to drive me out of my mind."

A burning heat ignites at the base of my spine and licks its way up my body, my balls heavy and drawing up, ready to detonate.

The wet sounds of me finger fucking her as I suck on her clit make my ears ring. She claws at me, her legs trembling, locking around my neck.

I feel lightheaded. If I die right now, I'll be the happiest man on earth.

"Come, Nova." I fuck her harder with my fingers. Two this time.

Her mouth parts in a soundless scream, her fingers white knuckled around the bedsheets.

"That's it, fuck my face. Harder. Don't let me breathe. Drench me, baby." I bite her swollen nub.

"I'm coming, Ethan!" She detonates—her juices flooding out of her, wetting my face as she shakes on the bed like she's electrocuted by pleasure.

"Fucking squirter, shit." I lap all of it up, savoring her taste, groaning as I rut my cock against the bedsheets, seconds away from bursting.

Before she comes down from her high, I swipe my face, slicking back my hair, wet with her essence, and flip her on her stomach.

Tugging her ass up, I give the round swells a hard slap, watching the creamy skin redden in fascination.

"More, Nova?" Leaning down, I bite her ear and she wiggles that delectable ass over my cock. "My beautiful, dirty girl. Fuck, I've waited for you."

I slap those luscious curves again and she cries, "Yes!"

Damn, she reddens so well.

"Yes, Ethan. I need you inside me," she slurs, her face pressed against the sheets.

I can't think. I can't speak. My mind is a haze of love and pleasure, my body riding on the highest of highs.

Fisting her hair, I pull back and bare her throat, licking the tears streaking down her face before capturing her lips in mine.

With one deep stroke, I slam in and swallow her screams with my mouth.

My hips start up a maddening rhythm as I drive into her from the back.

It's insanity—blissful insanity.

I break our kiss to drag in mouthfuls of air, my cock tunneling in and out of her in a staccato rhythm.

"So good." I throw my head back and grip her hips tightly, my mind blissfully blank. "So fucking good. Never enough."

She lets out a keening wail, a flush spreading from her ass cheeks to the rest of her body.

I want—no, need—to keep pinkening her skin like this. Every day. She'll wear the flush as a badge of honor.

She's mine.

My cock thickens, the pressure seizing up inside me, my balls heavy and retracting. The sharp pleasure shoots up my shaft, and I'm seconds away from having the biggest fucking orgasm of my life.

"You're mine, Nova. Mine, you hear me?" The smacking sounds are loud in the room, eclipsing the roar of the pulse in my ears.

"Yours, always." She shakes again, incoherent sounds blubbering out of her mouth.

"I'm going to come. Mark you up from the inside, Nova. So much you'll feel me dripping out of you whenever you walk."

I slap her ass and she claws the bed, a raw cry tearing from her throat.

Her pussy throbs and clenches around my shaft as wetness shoots out of her. She hurls off the cliff, and that does it.

"I love you," I gasp.

My vision whitens, and my world obliterates. I fall into an alternate state of being, the pleasure coursing through my veins as I unload unending streams of cum inside her.

Much later, when she's tucked against my chest, a sweet smile on her face, my heart is whole for the first time in a decade. Despite Dreamer not remembering her Keeper, my Lexy fell in love with me again.

Completely spent, utterly at peace, I let myself believe something I've never thought possible.

This time, I can keep my Nova.

This time, I can protect her. Cherish her. Love her until the end of time.

But as I sink into sleep, a worrisome thread slithers inside me, and a last thought—to fate, to whatever higher power's out there—whispers across my mind.

Please don't take my happiness away this time. Please.

CHAPTER 48

"So why did you volunteer to be a pen pal with Letters of Hope?" Alexis stretches on the bed, her hair a messy halo, her eyes heavy-lidded after she woke up in my apartment.

She looks so goddamn beautiful.

We spent the last week between Christmas and New Year's holed up in my place doing nothing other than watching movies (*The Notebook* twice, *The Sound of Music*, where she sang along, completely off-key), reading poetry (Dickinson and Keats), helping her make her bucket list of traveling destinations (scaling Mt. Everest, take pictures with penguins in Antarctica), and trying out new recipes found online (lasagna made from scratch and according to her, the best turkey club in the world).

Two small oven fires and barely edible food later, we'd then call for takeout.

To some people, maybe it's boring—no jet setting to the Caribbean or dining at the best restaurants of the world.

But to me, it's the best week ever.

I smile as I button my dress shirt and loop a tie around my neck.

She climbs off the bed and traipses toward me, wearing only my white dress shirt and revealing an expanse of smooth thighs.

My dick twitches.

Damn. It's getting ridiculous.

"Let me help you." She grins and works my tie in practiced moves, fashioning it into a Windsor knot. "Liam is helpless with this stuff. I used to do it for him all the time."

My heartbeat kicks up at the mention of Liam. I'm telling him about Lexy and me and he's going to have to deal with it, whether he likes it or not.

She pats the tie and admires her handiwork. "Did I ever tell you how much I love the color blue on you?"

A sharp inhale lodges in my throat. She asked me the same question all those years ago.

I graze my finger over the bridge of her nose—my love in a gesture—and watch her cheeks pinken.

"Perhaps someday, you'll find out why I love the color blue," I murmur.

"And you'll tell me about the cuff links too?" Pursing her lips, she traces her finger on the black floral surface, and I'm tempted to slide open the latch to show her the hummingbird underneath.

But something holds me back.

I want to show her when I can tell her everything.

"Once you're out of your medical trial, I'll tell you our story. All of it. No more secrets."

"It must be so lonely, being the only one who remembers," she whispers, her eyes tearing up.

An ache forms in my chest, but I push it away. My Nova, the past or current versions of her, has the same beautiful heart.

I kiss her palm. "I'm not lonely anymore because you're here."

Alexis doles out a sweet smile and cocks her head to the side. "Right. We'll make new memories. So...why are you a pen pal? You didn't answer me."

"I actually started the program. Anonymously, of course. Not every good deed our family does needs to be advertised. Takes away from the focus on the right things."

After shrugging on my dark gray suit jacket, I check my watch, noting it to be seven in the morning. It's funny how the routines I clung to just to get through life without her suddenly don't matter anymore. Because she's awake and here with me.

"As the years went by, and you were still in your coma, I needed to do something with my time outside of work. Donating money to medical research wasn't enough. I wanted to be part of something directly meaningful to patients. Then I got to thinking, *when* you woke up, what would you need? How would it feel to have the world change while you were asleep?"

My voice thickens, and I cup her face. "I thought it'd be rough. It's hard enough to navigate this world when you're healthy, but it's ten times harder when you're sick. In the beginning, the program was small—occasional letters and gifts to patients. But later on, I asked Olivia—"

"Olivia?" Her brow raises at my mention of her friend.

"Yes, your Olivia. With her being a psychiatrist, she probably didn't tell you this because she wasn't allowed to, but she helped Maxwell with his anxiety. A few of us reached out for her services or referrals from time to time. Anyway, I asked her if a long-term mentorship or pen pal program could be beneficial for patients recovering from extended stays at the hospital."

I grab my phone from the dresser. "One thing led to another, and Letters of Hope became what it is today. There are over a hundred volunteer pen pals now and other hospitals have joined the program. I enjoy writing to patients, being a listening ear. It feels like I'm doing something for you. And when I heard you submitted an application, well I—"

"Elbowed your way into being my pen pal? You sneaky, underhanded Deliminator."

I bop her nose. "I'm normally a boy scout, I swear."

"Boy scout?" Alexis walks her fingers up my chest, lighting up tingles along the way. "Someone didn't seem very scout like the last few nights."

Growling, I haul her against me, letting her feel my not so innocent hard on. "Haven't you heard? Never judge a book by its cover. And," I bend down and lick the whorl of her ear; she shivers, "it's *always* the quiet ones. We're freaks in the sheets."

"You're insatiable." She giggles and my phone pings.

"Fuck." I groan and swipe to the barrage of messages waiting for me in the chat group my siblings started with our close friends.

"The Deliminator is in deep shit." Alexis snickers. Every year they rename the group to someone they want to haze, and apparently, it's my turn this year.

"Sometimes, it's good *not* to have a big family," I mutter.

Rex

> I tried. I really did. Don't kill me, Ethan.

Lana

> You should see me snorting.

Rex

> I don't need to see you do anything. You're sitting next to me and spat your water all over my jacket. Disgusting.

Charles

> Rex, remind me not to ask you for help. If your "trying" means spilling the beans in the first five minutes after Liam cornered you, I don't want to know what happens when you *don't* try.

Taylor

> Hell hath no fury than a best friend scorned. I hope you have copies of all your critical documents safely stored offline, Ethan.

Grace

> I'm so happy for you guys! True love wins!

Steven

> Just like those books you read. I love you, sweetheart.

Taylor

> Save me from this nauseating newlywed shit.

Lana

> I'm screenshotting this and showing it to you once you and Charles walk down the aisle.

Ryland

> Give Ethan a break. Once he resurfaces from his...*activities*, he'll probably be confused as hell.

Steven

> Agree with Ryland. TL, DR just for you: Liam found out. Although, I'm surprised it took him this long. You think you two mysteriously getting food poisoning at the same time is going to fly?

Maxwell

> God, I hate to admit it, but Elias is right. Anderson men are idiots when it comes to women.

Elias

> I'll say I told you so, but that'll be terribly cliche.

Rex

> What the *hell*, dude. You aren't in this group chat.

Maxwell

> I'm not surprised. Heck, I've always wondered how he got his info.

Ryland

> Long story short, Ethan, I hope you have some good excuses, because Liam is on a warpath.

"Oh crap. Is this why he wants to meet this morning?" Alexis frowns at my phone.

I swipe to my earlier texts that I actually answered.

Liam

> We need to talk in person. Eight a.m. The Menagerie.

Ethan

> Everything okay?

Liam

> It all depends. Just show up.

When I received his messages, I thought he had updates about the embezzlement case he wanted to discuss in person, since Liam thought the culprit might be someone well connected to our family.

"Probably. He's being cryptic on purpose." I roll out my neck muscles.

"What are you going to tell him?"

"The truth." Returning my gaze to Alexis, who's snapping her rubber band on her wrist, I murmur, "I'm desperately in love with his little sister and I'll cherish her until the end of time."

The snapping stops, and she gives me a watery smile. "Won't this mess up your friendship? I'm sure there's some bro code about this, right?"

"There is." She doesn't remember I've told her about my vow to Liam before. "But it doesn't matter, because you're the most important person in my life, you hear me? You're unforgettable and one of a kind. He'll just have to live with it."

Her eyes mist and I pull her into my arms before kissing her forehead, my lungs drawing in the calming scent of lavender.

— • —

Liam twirls a butter knife in his hand.

One rotation. Two rotations. Three rotations.

A tap on the table. Readjusting the grip. The twirling begins again.

Unease slithers its way up my body, but I maintain a straight face as I stare at my best friend.

Or maybe former best friend at this rate.

A lock of dirty blond hair covers his right eye, his legs sprawled, one arm draping behind his chair. The calm posture is deceptive. I might be overthinking this, but I think he's purposely dressed in a black short-sleeve T-shirt to show off his sleeves of menacing tattoos.

He holds my gaze, his fingers fiddling with the knife.

Rotations. Tap. Readjustment. Rotations.

If you were to ask me this morning if I thought a butter knife was capable of bodily harm, I would've scoffed and thought you were insane.

Now, I'm not so sure.

I tug my cuff link, unwilling to be the first to flinch or blink.

"So... You and Firefly," he rasps.

I nod. "We're together."

No use beating around the bush. I was supposed to have this conversation ten years ago.

"I distinctly remember someone vowed to me he wouldn't touch my sister." His lips twitch into a half snarl. "That our friendship was *too important*."

"We were kids then. You thought I was breaking hearts and had commitment issues. Things are different now. You should know that. I haven't dated anyone in forever."

"Hence the commitment issues. My concern still stands. She's been through enough. She doesn't need more shit from a non-communicative, brooding asshole."

"I was waiting for Lexy, damn it! If waiting for a decade and living like a monk aren't signs of commitment, then I don't know what is."

He jams the butter knife into the table, and I flinch.

Scratch my previous thought. Butter knives are definitely capable of inflicting permanent damage.

"So you're admitting this started *before* her accident then? After I specifically asked you multiple times and you swore to me and gave me your fucking word, you motherfucker."

My skin heats as guilt swirls in my gut. "I don't regret anything with Lexy, but I do regret keeping it from you for so long. When she got into her accident, I didn't see the point in telling you then."

"How long?"

"What?"

"How long were you involved with her back then?"

I swallow, my heart thundering in my chest. This one's going to hurt. He's definitely going to kill me. "Two years."

"Two *fucking* years? Ethan Delaney, whatever other middle names you have, Anderson, you messed with my sister for *two* fucking years and didn't have the *decency* to tell me about it? Really?"

"I could give you more excuses, but they're all bullshit. This one's on me."

He leans in and fists my tie, tugging me up from my seat. "If I tell you I don't buy this committed man in love act you got going on, if I tell you to break it off with her, what would you do?"

Grabbing his shirt, I snarl in his ear, "I'll tell you to go fuck yourself."

I let go and shove him back into his seat.

A tensed silence suffocates the private room inside The Menagerie, a lounge on the lower floors of The Orchid. I'm so glad we're meeting early and no one's here to witness the inevitable bloodshed.

No one can take my Nova away from me again.

Suddenly, Liam laughs, the abrupt noise shocking me. He slams his hand on the table and bends over, his body trembling.

The bastard.

"You should've seen the look on your face." He slaps his knee and wipes his eyes—the asshole has tears from laughing too hard. "Fuck man, you thought I was going to kill you, didn't you?"

"Fucking shit," I mutter and yank my tie loose, dragging in a deep inhale.

"You deserved it. You so fucking deserved it. I'm not a dictator, Ethan. You're my best guy. I want you to be happy. I love Firefly and I want her to be happy. If the two of you being together will make you both happy, then hallelujah."

Then the smile slips off his face and his nostrils flare, the icy glare back in his eyes. "However...if you break her heart, *your* heart will have a hole in it, just like this table." He yanks out the butter knife and tosses it onto his plate, revealing the damage he inflicted.

It doesn't faze me. "I'll hurt myself before I hurt her."

That's a vow.

He holds my gaze for a moment, then nods. Then he crosses his arms behind his head and lets out a relaxed sigh, like he didn't threaten me a few seconds ago.

"I've waited a decade to give you that spiel, so now that we've got that out of the way, I want to give you an update on your embezzlement case—"

"Hold on. Hold on a fucking second." I raise my hand. "What do you mean, you've waited a decade?"

Liam arches his brow and tsks under his breath. "You really think you guys snuck around without me noticing? Really? You think your lovesick smile when you scribbled in your precious notebook wasn't obvious? You think my sister bringing your favorite foods to *my* birthday party wasn't a big fucking clue?"

He shakes his head. "And then you had your one eighty degree personality change after Firefly's accident. Do you think I'm motherfucking blind?"

"You asshole. You let me believe—"

"You deserved it. You kept me in the dark and I returned the favor."

Blowing out a breath, I shift in my seat. My lips twitch as I try not to smile. It feels so good to have everything out in the open. No more hiding. No more sneaking around.

"Fine. You got your revenge. Moving on. So, what do you have for the case?"

"Don't say I didn't warn you." Liam straightens, pulls out a small piece of paper from his jeans pocket, and slides it over the table. I turn it around.

I snap my eyes up, flames singeing my chest. Gnashing my teeth together, I crumble the paper in my fist.

"You sure?"

"A hundred percent. That's the hedge fund behind BoC Equitable Investments. They moved the money already, but I tagged them before they shifted things around."

"But why? These aren't huge amounts. Sure, millions over a decade, but barely makes a dent. This makes no sense."

Liam drums his fingers on the table. "No clue. I don't think we have the full picture yet, so don't tell anyone."

I grit my teeth, thinking about the asshole I'm going to murder the second I walk out of the building.

"Don't you dare, Ethan. I see those wheels turning. I'm sure there's more to it. Don't do anything yet. Stay put."

"I need to protect her. Would you do nothing if you were me?"

"You think I don't care about my own sister? She's not involved—she isn't in trouble. If she were, I'd kill the bastard myself. Give me more time. Do I have your permission to get outside help?"

"Do you trust the person?"

"With my life," he replies without batting an eye.

"Do it."

"Burn the paper before you leave. Leave no evidence behind." He gets up, then throws on his leather jacket. "Remember, don't hurt my sister, or best friend or not, I'll hurt you."

Liam strides away, leaving me at the table, my mind whirring from the revelation.

Slowly, I unfurl my hand and smooth out the scrap of paper.

Ten digits. An account number.

And a name.

Dayton Sean Holden, Holden Investments.

CHAPTER 49

WITH A CLICK OF a button, I shut the automated blinds in my office, swathing the room in darkness. I rub my temples and review the evidence in the embezzlement case so far.

Transfers to shell companies resembling our vendors.

Wire amounts under the ten thousand dollar Federal Currency Transaction Reporting limit.

Pattern of embezzlement over ten years.

Dayton's hedge fund behind the Cayman Islands' account.

When I met Dayton in the hospital after Alexis woke up, I did a full workup on him. Holden Investments has been linked to a few shady deals with questionable businessmen in the past. In the past decade, Dayton had a meteoric rise in the financial world—growing his family's hedge fund from a boutique firm to a sizable company quickly becoming a power player in the industry.

This rate of growth is almost unheard of. Someone has to be pulling the strings behind it.

I'd also reviewed the past entries in Alexis's leather journal I kept at my place—paying attention to references on Dayton. I knew she didn't trust him before they broke up. She felt like he was hiding something from her. She had that strange suspicious "dream" where she thought she overheard something about leverage.

Of course, the current her doesn't remember any of this—she only remembers her sweet high school boyfriend, who's now a good friend and, as she recently learned, a man who wants her back. She told me the other day that Dayton had texted her after the cruise, but she hadn't responded because she didn't want to encourage his affections.

My urge to kill him for kissing her hand on the cruise—and for these text messages—notwithstanding, is that all this is? Dayton showing up time and time again because he likes her?

Or is it something more?

Is he befriending her because of some ulterior motive? Access to Fleur?

Unease churns inside me.

I'm missing something. I'm tempted to hire a bodyguard for Alexis, but she won't agree. After all, the Dayton she knows has done nothing to her.

I've promised her no more secrets and I don't want to worry her about my suspicions.

Before knowing Dayton was involved, I was fine with taking my time with the investigation—crossing the T's, dotting the I's. I knew I'd make the bastard pay me back tenfold once I caught him.

But now that Dayton is part of this and he's linked to Alexis, I can't help but be afraid. What if there's something more sinister going on?

I need to get to the bottom of this as fast as I can.

My phone rings, and I pick up. "Anderson speaking."

"I heard you're dealing with a snake. Thought I'd offer my exterminator services before you called me, since this all follows the trend of Andersons needing my help." The familiar gravelly voice chuckles.

"Elias, I'd ask you how you knew about this, but then I think I'd rather not know."

"This one's easy. Liam called me."

I sit up in my chair. "You're the person he trusts with his life?"

What on earth has my best friend been involved in? I wasn't aware he was that close with the king of the underworld, who even the mafia, mob, and bratva respect in the city.

"Are you surprised?" A clicking sound. That damn lighter again.

"I swear, someday, I'm going to steal that annoying lighter from you and chuck it into the ocean."

The clicking stops. "And you'll be a dead man."

"Tell me why you don't smoke but carry that damn thing everywhere."

"Maybe," the clicking resumes, "maybe one day, if I need your help, you can get the story out of me. We're more alike than you know."

I furrow my brows. I can never get a straight answer out of this man. "Why did Liam think you can help? This is a financial crime. I don't need someone killed."

"The walls have ears, Ethan. He couldn't tell you everything he suspected when you met at The Menagerie because it was too public, but he saw a few flags in the account at The Caymans. There was a second shell company with transactions moving in and out of that account. It's no simple embezzlement scheme you're investigating."

"What did you guys find?"

"The Association." My heart drops. *Fuck.* If they're involved, then things just got a lot more dangerous. "It's the same account that paid for Ian Vaughn's legal fees back then. And I have a vested interest in all things The Association."

"You've got to be shitting me."

I think back to what happened with the Vaughn siblings' uncle, renowned ballet choreographer, who is spending his life behind bars in a maximum security prison because of what he did to Taylor when she was sixteen. He claimed he was forced by the infamous international criminal organization made up of billionaires and powerful people, an association purported to control governments, politicians, and businesses.

Alexis still doesn't know her precious Uncle Ian is very much alive. The only reason I kept it from her is because of the damn medical trial, since this revelation happened right before her accident. Her brothers wanted to spare her the pain of learning the only father figure she had was actually the scum of the earth.

"I wish I was. That's why I called. We need to find the snake before it bites you," Elias murmurs. "I owe that to your family. You Andersons have honor and I respect all of you, and that's a rarity given what I know about the elite."

Our family came from a line of dukes in the British aristocracy before our ancestors moved to the States in the eighteen hundreds. Our motto, "valor and virtue, with honor, we stand," is drilled into every Anderson offspring since before we could talk.

We've kept our hands clean and stayed away from The Association despite multiple covert attempts over the years to loop us into their fold.

We don't associate with criminals.

Other than Elias, who's been nothing but steadfast toward us.

I clear my throat, uncertain how to respond to this rare display of emotion from my friend. "I'd thank you, but I'm sure that isn't why you called. You have something up your sleeves."

"I'd offer a more violent and expeditious way of finding out what's going on, but since I know you, and torturing Dayton isn't on the table, I took the liberty of setting up another shell company."

"For?"

"Bait. Dayton embezzles because he needs money for whatever reason. Flag one of the fake vendors he's using—nothing suspicious—just a routine audit or something like that, so he'll be forced to use another vendor. Then offer the one I set up. When he bites, we'll be there to follow the money and find out who he's sending the cash to."

I mull over his idea. It's definitely more legitimate than Elias gutting the bastard, which I secretly want, but am sure my siblings and Alexis won't appreciate. "Let's say your idea works. How do we get the fake shell company info to him?"

"If you were Rex, I'd say get drunk and let it slip at a club in his presence, but since you always have a stick up your ass and you're also dating his ex-girlfriend, it's probably best for you not to be involved. He'll be suspicious right away. Do you have anyone you trust with the investigation?"

"Yes." There's only one person I trust with this info.

"Get that person to leak the info then."

"I can do that."

"Good. The company details are in your email. I'll work with Liam to find out more. Keep me posted, we'll talk so—"

"Elias." I grip my phone. "Is Lexy in danger? Should I be worried?" Silence fills the line.

"I'd keep your girlfriend from meeting her ex for now. But nothing suggests this is anything more than a financial motive."

Blowing out a breath, I stand. "I can't let anything happen to her."

"Understood. Let me figure out a few things and we'll chat. You know how to reach me if anything changes." He ends the call.

Fucking shit.

I hit the button to open the blinds and the harsh daylight streaming from the windows sears my eyes.

The financial loss doesn't matter. Turning down another attempt from The Association doesn't worry me—it won't be the first time we've done it.

Lexy getting hurt? Unthinkable.

I need to catch the bastard and keep him away for good.

Determined, I stroll out the door and make my way to Trey's office.

Laughter filters out of his opened door—he's joking with a few managers and staff—well loved, as always.

I bite back a smile, thinking how he took in the nobody Delaney back then, and got me to where I am today.

"Trey, do you have a sec?" I knock on his door.

He snaps his head up, the smile on his face disappearing when he takes in my expression. "Of course."

"Sir," a manager mumbles as he squeezes past me along with his teammates and quickly closes the door behind them.

"Seriously, Ethan. Learn to smile more. You attract more bees with honey than vinegar."

"I smile. What are you talking about?"

Trey cocks his brow. "To your girlfriend, maybe. And yes, I heard. Heck, everyone knows the Deliminator, the impenetrable ice monster, is disgustingly in love with the Vaughn princess."

My lips twitch, thinking back to how I spent the week with Nova.

"Ugh. Your smile is sickening."

"Just because you're divorced doesn't mean all women are awful."

He snorts. "Anyway, what's up? You had that serious look on your face."

Sitting down, I pull up the email on my phone and show it to him.

Trey frowns. "What am I looking at?"

"Greenwich Housekeeping Services is our newest approved vendor for The Strata. They are subsidiaries of the existing Greenwich Housekeeping LLC we currently use and have great relationships with. That's the official front, anyway."

I explain Elias's plan, without mentioning the man, of course, and watch Trey's eyes widen, the gears obviously shifting into place.

"That might work. It's brilliant. Remind me not to piss you off," he murmurs. "So, I take it you want me to 'share' this info with Dayton? I don't know the guy though."

"I thought about it. This weekend, there's a reopening of Trésor at The Orchid."

"The strip club?" His eyes light up and I roll my eyes.

Until Nova, I never understood this basc desire of men being ruled by their dicks, but from what I know, I'm an odd duck.

"The exotic dance club. It's classy. Anyway, Lana has extended invitations to a few folks, so I'll have her send one to him. There's no way he'll miss it. He's a social climber." I stand and head toward the door. "And didn't you say you always wanted to visit The Orchid? Well, here's your chance."

CHAPTER 50

"LEXV8962...EXCLAMATION MARK," I MUTTER under my breath as I type my hundredth guess into my laptop. I have a few minutes to spare before Ethan comes by to pick me up for the Trésor reopening at The Orchid.

Access denied.

"Dammit. Question mark?" I try again.

Access denied.

"What the hell, Lexy? What's the damn password?" I grumble as I stare at the flash drive USB pen that tumbled out of the box of things from my old room when I had the picnic at Ravenswood.

Something about this drive bothers me, but I can't pinpoint the reason. It's a gut feeling—maybe the answers I've been looking for are locked away in there. I wonder if the USB drive holds the memories of Ethan and me—the memories of us I'm desperately searching for.

I sigh and pull out the notebook I brought to Ravenswood that day.

The one where Ethan wrote that beautiful poem when I asked him about the assignment.

The poem has to be about me, right? Lavender is my scent.

My heart would flutter every time I reread his poignant words. But then, a weight would settle on top of it.

Guilt? Grief? I don't know. Maybe a combination of everything.

Ethan would smirk when I asked him, but the amusement didn't show up in his expressive eyes.

While we've only gotten together recently and I'm still learning—or re-learning—the quirks and personality of the quiet Anderson, I know it pains him I've forgotten our past. It guts him he can't tell me anything.

And it hurts me to see him sad.

The spot above my rib cage aches again.

I wish I could remember—I wish I could understand the depth of his feelings for me. There have to be beautiful memories stashed away, moments that are irreplaceable. It isn't fair—for me, our love story is just beginning, but for him, I have a feeling it's already ingrained in his soul.

It's okay. We can always make new memories.

But it's imbalanced. How he feels for me versus what I feel for him. Sure, I love him, but how could my feelings ever match his? He's spent nearly a decade loving me, holding onto memories I don't have. How do I catch up to that?

It's not right.

It's devastating.

Maybe someday I'll be worthy of his devotion.

Exhaling, I stare at the error message on the screen. I fight the urge to tug at my hair because I don't want to ruin my perfectly curled waves before Ethan sees me tonight.

I could get into my other hard drives from my high school days. I laughed at the photos of Summer and Lil' Tay. Then there was my first ballet performance at The Met Opera, Homecoming Dance with Dayton—we wore identical crowns and sashes—Broadbent's King and Queen.

There was a rare family photo at Grandma's place in the Hamptons. My parents lounged on the lawn, quietly chatting with each other. Liam in his grunge phase, a devious grin tipping his lips as he curled his arm around my neck. Charles looked every inch the heir of the Vaughn dynasty in his polo shirt and khakis as he stood next to our proud grandmother. Uncle Ian beamed, his eyes crinkling with laughter.

I miss those days. I miss Grandma and Uncle Ian.

My eyes prickle and I shake myself. Olivia told me mourning a loved one could be an endless cycle, but the hurt would fade in time—these random memories would eventually bring both smiles and tears.

Clearing my throat, I close the error message on the screen. My usual passwords don't work.

There have to be answers in this flash drive from those missing four years. Maybe something in there will trigger my memories. Maybe it's only wishful thinking.

It looks like I might need to ask Liam to hack into it.

But are there things I don't want him to see in there—naked pics or spicy videos? And is this technically breaking the rules of the medical trial?

Someone knocks.

I'll think about it later.

Grinning, I traipse to the door and look through the peephole. Sure enough, my broody boyfriend is standing on the other side, looking completely delicious in his dark navy suit and crisp white shirt, no tie to be seen, his hair tousled with the slightest waves.

He's holding a bouquet of lavender.

"Ethan!" I throw open the door and watch his eyes flare, his corded throat rippling.

"Nova," he rasps. "Fuck me."

He scans me from top to bottom, then back up again, lingering on my cleavage and the nipples currently prickling under his intense stare.

When his eyes meet mine again, I can barely see his pupils.

"You're trying to kill me, aren't you?"

Heat suffuses me. It's my first outing to the Rose floors, something I'm excited for, especially after I've rediscovered my sexual appetite with Ethan. I want to dress to impress in this red silk halter mini dress with a deep-V neckline and my hair carefully curled in waves. "Like what you see?"

"Too much—I want to lock you up and throw away the key so no one can see you looking like this." His eyes flash—the same possessive streak I've seen before sends my pulse racing.

Slowly, I bite my fire-engine red lip and he snares on the motion. Ethan growls and pushes me against the doorframe, one hand braced above me, the other grazing my waist.

"I want to kiss and mark up every inch of your creamy curves, because they're mine," he growls, and my pussy flutters.

"Ethan," I moan, arching back and he presses his lips—a wisp of a kiss—on my neck before grinding his hips against my stomach, letting me feel every pulsating inch of him through his dress pants. Then he backs away.

"That's the appetizer, Nova," he murmurs, his lips tipping into a slow, seductive smile, and my clit swells.

"Not fair. You can't rile me up like this before we leave."

He hands me the flowers. "You're cheating with that outfit, and I don't play fair. Lavender for my favorite girl."

I beam, take a whiff of my favorite scent, and set it on the entrance table before locking the door behind me.

When I turn toward him, I find him staring at me again, but this time, his eyes are shadowed, their intensity changing flavor.

"What's wrong? Is something worrying you?"

An exhale escapes him, and he links his fingers with mine. "I have a big favor to ask you."

My brows furrow.

"You know that embezzlement case I'm working on?"

I nod, vaguely remembering him telling me about it a while back.

"We're close to figuring out who's behind it. And right now, unfortunately, your...friend, Dayton, may be involved."

"Dayton? But why? He's doing well with his company. He doesn't need money."

"We don't have all the answers yet, but he'll be at the event tonight. Some of my folks will chat with him to see what he knows. If he comes and talks to you, can you keep your conversation to a minimum? And don't go anywhere with him...at least until I clear him?"

What? "But Ethan, it's *Dayton*, the captain of the football team. The guy who stuck around and befriended me after I woke up. Are you sure?"

A muscle tics in his jaw. "I need you to trust me on this. Maybe I'm paranoid. But I need you to stay safe...I don't know what I'd do if you got hurt again. Can you do this...for me? Once I sort this out, I'll let you know. Please."

Unease swirls inside me as I look into his eyes. I think about Dayton kissing my hand on the cruise and how he wanted more. Maybe it won't hurt to stay away, just to set boundaries.

"Fine. But you need to tell me when you find out if he's part of this."

He nods, his frame relaxing. "Will do. And one more thing, just for my peace of mind, will you share your location with me on your phone? I'm probably paranoid, but I need to know you're safe."

A weight settles on my chest as I take him in—the muscle ticcing on his forehead, the urgency in his voice. I have a feeling he's not telling me the full extent of everything.

I take out my phone and hand it to him. "Sure. But you better share your location with me too. Quid pro quo."

Ethan smirks and taps a few buttons before handing my phone back. "I have no secrets from you. Stalk me, track me." He leans in and whispers in my ear, "It turns me on."

My core pulses and I give him a gentle shove. "Ethan!"

Chuckling, he holds my hand and leads me toward the elevator. "Ready for a night of debauchery, my little hummingbird?"

"Ready for anything with you."

CHAPTER 51

My mouth drops open as I gape at my surroundings. Deep reds, golds, and blacks, ambient and neon lighting—Trésor is the epitome of luxury, sensuality, and futuristic sophistication.

At the heart of the club is a large center stage, flanked by smaller floating stages, where girls in glittery burlesque wear are dancing to sultry music. This place is classy—somewhere I can imagine hors d'oeuvres and champagne being served instead of dollar bills stuffed into thongs.

Instead of traditional seating, there are two levels of circular pods surrounding the room. Each pod is private yet features glass walls that can turn opaque at a press of a button. I imagine they'll come in handy for private lap dances and other activities.

"Nova, are you okay by yourself right here for a few minutes? I need to talk to Trey over at the bar." Ethan motions to the coworker I met when he was coaching me on financial ratios in his office.

"Sure. I see my friends. Do your thing."

"I'll be back before the show starts." He scrapes his finger on my nose, and my heart flutters. Giving me a wink, Ethan saunters off.

I head toward Grace and Taylor, who are next to the refreshments table.

"Camille! You're working today?" Grace squeals and darts toward a stunning blond in a black-sequined leotard.

"Oui. Can't pass up on opening night. The tips will flow."

The girls giggle as I gape at them and Taylor saunters up to me.

"Grace did a stint here a few years ago."

"What? Grace was a stripper?" My eyes bug out.

"The term is exotic dancer. And it's complicated. She didn't completely strip or do lap dances. She was more of a burlesque dancer."

"And Steven let her?" I eye the tall, commanding Steven Kingsley standing next to some guys, smiling at his wife.

"Pssh. He doesn't get to *let* her do anything. She's the boss of her own life. Long story, but we got saddled with massive debt and if we couldn't come up with quick money, things would've gotten ugly. Steven didn't know about our issues back then. It caused a lot of drama, to say the least." Taylor sighs. "My sister took one for the team."

"Wow. I don't know what to say. You girls are tough cookies."

"You need to be to survive the underbelly of The Bronx. Things are better here on the Rose floors than at other shady places. Elias keeps a tight leash on things. No funny business. The workers get the final say in what they want, or don't want, to provide."

"I heard my name."

A tall, imposing man himself materializes next to us from thin air. I jolt.

"Holy crap, Elias! You need a cowbell or something." Taylor slaps her hand over her chest.

Oh, so this is the infamous Elias. I'd heard about him before but have never met him until now.

"I don't think a cowbell will go well with my outfit," he murmurs, a barely there smile tilting his lips.

I eye the mobster, taking in the dark hair and piercing green eyes, the masculine features that almost look aristocratic if it weren't for the long scar spanning his cheek. He's wearing a tailored black suit, no tie to be seen, and a green handkerchief tucked in his jacket pocket. A gold chain peeks from his vest and, as if he knows I'm curious, he pulls out an intricate gold and silver lighter.

He flicks it on and off.

"What were you guys saying about me?" He stares at the flickering flame.

"Girl gossip. Don't tell me you're interested in that now," Taylor deadpans.

"It's good to broaden my horizons. In my experience, women often overhear things or have unique insights into issues. I value your thoughts."

This is the weirdest conversation I've been part of.

"Tay was mentioning how you have a tight rein on the Rose floors." I cock my head, trying to figure out if his lighter flicking has a pattern. Morse code? His moods?

He smirks. Stuffing the lighter back into his vest, he turns to me. "Too many people take advantage of sex workers—male or female." His jaw works and he swallows. "The Andersons know I won't stand for that."

Elias stares at me—the unnerving intensity in his eyes reminding me of Ethan. "I may be many things, but I have a special hatred for crimes against women. Sex sells and will happen whether you like it or not. But taking advantage of the hard workers here—not on my watch."

A chill runs through my body from the dangerous rasp of his voice. This is a man I don't want to cross.

"Charles is waving me over. I gotta go." Taylor flashes me a peace sign and darts off, leaving me with the enigmatic man.

"I want to ask you." He steps to my side, his voice a low murmur. "Have you seen anything strange these days?"

Frowning, I glance toward the bar, searching for Ethan, because he'll know what I should or shouldn't say, but I don't see him. I only notice Dayton chatting with Trey.

"Ethan stepped outside with Maxwell," Elias says.

I glance sharply at him, finding him smirking.

"Reading facial expressions comes handy in my job."

I scoff. "Scaring everyone in a five mile radius?" I slap my hand over my mouth. *Why can't I keep my mouth shut?*

Elias barks out a laugh. "I get it now."

Huh? What does he get because I'm not sure what's going on? "What do you mean?"

"Ethan loves you. You're the light he needs. I've always wondered about the woman who held his heart for all these years. He'd deny it, saying there was no one. But I knew he was lying."

There's a strange solemnness in his voice, and I glance at him.

He's wearing a pained smile on his face. "Ethan's a good friend. Sometimes, when I look at him, it almost seems like I'm looking in the mirror. I want him to be happy."

Elias's words are nonsensical, like he doesn't believe he himself can be happy. It's rather sad.

"Anyway, I'm helping him with his investigation. Ethan's concerned about your safety because of the case he's working on. I thought I'd talk to you—get your perspective. Like I said, I believe in women's intuition."

I scrutinize the man. I believe in gut feelings, and perhaps it's the small sliver of vulnerability he's just shown me or how Ethan, my siblings, and my friends all seem to trust him, but I decide to take a leap of faith.

"Is this about Dayton?"

"Yes. I'm helping Ethan run things down and I want to do my due diligence."

My fingers twitch at my sides. "Everything's been normal. Dayton texted a few times to check in after the cruise, but I've brushed him off. Nothing strange."

"Hm. Interesting. Have you had any more visions or memories?"

I shake my head, the unease winding around my gut in tighter and tighter circles. What is this random line of questioning?

"You know something, don't you?"

"Not definitive. Just a hunch. The evidence tells me one thing, but it makes little sense."

He steps into my vision, a lock of dark hair draping over his forehead, and hands me a thick business card. "Here's my info. Call me if anything comes up. Anytime. I'm glad things are okay for you."

Without waiting for my response, he slips away, soon blending with the dark shadows in the club. Frowning, I eye the simple black card with gold lettering.

Elias Kent and his phone number.

"What's that?" Ethan asks, and I jump.

"Dammit, you and Elias should be twins. You guys walk with no sound."

"Elias?"

"He asked if I felt safe and if I remembered anything. It was strange. Then he gave me his card and said to call him if anything came up." I show him the card before slipping it inside my clutch.

"I swear I don't know what goes on in that guy's head," Ethan murmurs, staring at Dayton and Trey in the distance. "But I'm glad he's looking out for you. Elias has helped our family a few times. He may be dangerous, but he's good to us."

Suddenly, Dayton and Trey laugh before they clink their glasses together. Then Trey looks up and catches Ethan's eyes. I see him dip his head in a brief nod before striding off.

Ethan relaxes and tugs me flushed against him.

The lighting dims in the club, and I gasp at the sudden display of twinkling lights on the walls and around the stage.

"They're constellations." Ethan presses his lips against my ear. "People pay for out of the box experiences at The Orchid."

Three spotlight turn on, illuminating the center stage and the surrounding floating stages. The music changes into a new sultry beat.

The opening burlesque show is starting.

Ethan takes my hand and pulls me inside the closest circular pod.

He winks. "I reserved a pod for us. Ready for your first Rose floor experience?"

CHAPTER 52

ETHAN CLOSES THE GLASS door behind us, but the speakers still pipe in the music. His eyes glow with dark intentions as he takes a seat on the sofa, his legs sprawled. Ethan's eyes scan my body from top to bottom, his lips parting. A throbbing pulse batters against his temple.

My body heats under his perusal.

The ice monster is once again burning hot.

"Come." A raspy command.

Wetting my lips, I walk to him and he tugs me on his lap so my backside is plastered against his front. He runs his fingers lightly up and down my arms. My body heats, the earlier unease from the strange conversation with Elias dissipating.

Ethan chuckles, clearly knowing what his caresses do to me. He presses an open-mouthed kiss on my neck and I whimper.

Suddenly, my silk dress seems too abrasive. My body shifts, primed to move, to feed the fire slowly burning me alive.

Three scantily clad women wearing jewel-studded lingerie stride onto the stage as the music kicks up a notch. Their bodies twine against the poles, seductive, hypnotizing. A couple—a brunette dressed in a gauzy black dress and a bare-chested blond man appear on the center stage and the man takes a seat.

Then, the brunette slowly brushes her fingers across the man's chest before she sinuously slips out of her dress, revealing her perfectly proportioned body, the private areas covered with glittery pasties with tassels.

My breathing quickens as blood pools in my core. I didn't know I had a latent exhibitionist or voyeuristic streak inside me, and I wonder if Ethan knew this about me—if this was part of the us I've forgotten.

I shift my legs on his lap, needing more friction as need builds up inside me. While the glass is frosted on the sides of our pod, lending to privacy, the main windowpane is clear.

Anyone can see us if they're staring from the right angle.

A warm breath coasts up my neck. "Are the Rose floors living up to your expectations, Nova?"

Ethan suckles my pulse point right under my jaw, then laves the spot with his tongue.

I moan, closing my eyes, letting my head drop back against his hard chest.

"So fucking hot," he growls.

"Y-Yes, those girls are beautiful." I let out a shaky exhale as his hands travel up my legs, sliding over my dress, grazing the sides of my breasts before landing on my shoulders.

"I couldn't care less about them. I have the most beautiful girl on my lap." Slowly he tugs off the straps, and the silk dress pools at my waist. He sucks in a rough inhale.

"No bra, my naughty girl," he rasps, his hands closing over each swell, eliciting a whimper from me.

The girl on the stage begins a sexy lap dance on the guy, her hips moving over his groin in an expert rhythm, her fingers playing with the tassels over her nipples.

Ethan plucks my nipples, slowly gyrating his hips below me, his hard erection digging between my ass cheeks.

"We're in public," I moan, but I don't stop him.

I fight to keep my eyes open, to watch the couple on the stage simulating sex.

The man has his pants chucked off and is wearing the thinnest underwear. He's giving it to the girl, thrusting at her from behind.

I can't even tell if they're acting or not.

Another whimper slips out of me, my clit throbbing. I widen my legs, letting the outline of Ethan's cock graze my wet pussy, and he groans.

He slides his fingers under my dress and plays with my black lace panties. "Soaked. You're dripping, Nova. This turns you on, doesn't it? My innocent girl isn't really innocent, is she?"

He bites my earlobe, and I let out a loud whimper. "My hummingbird is secretly a slut for me, isn't she?"

"Yes." I move my hips faster, needing his fingers to slide under my underwear and play with my clit.

"Who do you belong to?" He clearly reads my mind and in one quick snap, my panties fall to the floor.

"Ethan, please." I move my core over his still finger. He withdraws and I whine.

"Whose pussy is this? Who can hear you moan and whimper? Who gets to taste your sweetness and feel you gushing around his cock?"

His words send me into a tailspin and with trembling legs, I turn around and straddle him, nearly coming at the glazed passion in his eyes, the way his muscles are clenching, like he's one restraint away from letting go and tearing into me.

I want to drive Ethan over the edge. I want to see the brooding, quiet man who holds a million secrets inside him come undone in front of my eyes.

An idea sparks in my mind.

As I hear the music crescendo, the couples' passionate sounds streaming from the speakers, I scan the neighboring pods, noting how riveted on the performance attendees are.

My heart rioting, my skin hot to the touch, I climb off his lap. Ethan's eyes widen in curiosity, a ghost of a smile on his face.

Biting my lip, I roll my hips to the beat of the music—my dance background taking over—and grab my tits, rolling and pulling at my nipples.

"Ethan," I moan, wetness seeping out of me, "I'm so horny for you."

"Shit," he grunts and shifts in this seat. "You're a siren. Fuck."

The sound of a zipper fills the air, and he takes out his throbbing dick, his eyes heavy-lidded as he tugs it to my movements. A drop of pre-cum glistens, then slides down the turgid length, and my mouth waters.

Abandoning my dance moves, I kneel at his feet and curl my hands around his velvety length. "You're so big. So hard. I can't wait to get you inside me."

I dip my tongue out, tasting his addictive saltiness. He fists his hands at his sides and hisses.

"Oh *fuck*, that's so good. Take it in. Every inch. Swallow my cock like a good girl."

Following his instructions, I slip his tip inside my mouth, laving my tongue over his slit.

He grunts and slaps his hands on the sofa as I try to take all his inches inside me, my throat protesting when he hits the back of my mouth.

Ethan's panting breaths are loud in the air, and my mind is buzzing with lust and love. Slowly, he fists my hair and the added pain makes me wetter between my legs.

After taking a deep breath to relax my gag reflex, I swallow him. His cock lodges deep inside my throat.

"Fuck!" he roars.

My eyes water, his reaction fanning the flames inside me, and I bob harder and faster.

"You're doing well. Shit. Taking it all. Deep throating me. You want my cum, Nova? Is this why you are sucking me into oblivion?" He bangs his free hand on the sofa again and bares his neck, the tendon flexing and rippling.

So hot and sexy. My breasts swell and wetness drips down my thighs. Seeing him teetering on the edge gives me the highest of highs.

His hips buck harder, faster, and just as I think he's going to unload himself, he yanks me off him, grips my waist like I weigh nothing, and hoists me over his lap.

Then, without warning, he spears his cock into my pussy in one rough stroke.

I scream, my head flipping back, my fingers digging into his knees behind me as he bounces me on top of him.

"Look at you, bouncing on my cock, your tight pussy welcoming me home," he grunts, his fingers working his buttons until he yanks open his shirt, baring his hard chest, already glistening with sweat.

"Ethan, Ethan, Ethan," I chant.

He slams into me repeatedly from below, each thrust filling me up almost to the point of pain, the burn only adding to the burgeoning pleasure.

"If anyone were to look over here, they'd see you riding me, your tits bouncing, your hungry little pussy swallowing my dick. They would see how badly you want to come. How cock hungry you are," he rasps.

"Oh, shit." His lewd words are direct caresses to my clit. His cock hits a sensitive spot deep inside, and the beginnings of an earthquake gather inside me.

"You're getting tighter, Nova. Are you trying not to come?" He pants into my ears. "Too bad, I'm going to fuck you so hard, you'll have no choice but to squirt all over me."

"Oh my God, yes...y-yes..." My mouth drops open, and I'm barely holding on, unable to move as pleasure blinds my vision.

"You look so sexy like this. On edge, your cunt strangling me." He grips my waist and starts pounding me from below. "Don't fight it. You want to come because there's a very naughty girl hiding inside you. Let it out, baby. Show the world what a slut you are for me."

He slams into me at breakneck speed, and every muscle inside me tightens, the knot of pleasure a white-hot supernova, shrinking, shrinking, distilling into its most intense state.

"Come, Nova." He pinches my clit, and I explode.

"Ethan," I scream.

My body shudders as pleasure overtakes me. Wetness streams out of me and my vision goes black, every nerve ending overloaded. My ears ring as I grip his thighs, hanging on for dear life.

He ruts into me—once, twice, three times—before slamming his lips on mine, swallowing our sounds of release.

His cock pulses, and he growls my name, unloading his cum inside me, each spurt extending my orgasm.

I'm one with him—not knowing where I begin and where he ends. Judging from the way his mouth feasts on mine, the way he bands me to him, the harsh thundering of his heartbeats pressing against my chest, I know he feels the same way.

"I love you, Lexy. So fucking much," he whispers between fevered kisses. "I don't know what I'd do if you didn't wake up."

As my body slowly comes down from the high, the music inside the club finally reaching my ears again, I brush the damp hair clinging to his forehead.

"I love you too, Ethan. I...I'm sorry I don't remember our story. I'm so sorry." I gaze into his stormy eyes, a spasm of pain centering on my chest.

The earlier lust and intensity are replaced with the soulfulness I associate with him. I can spend a lifetime trying to swim in his thoughts and never reach the bottom of it all.

"As long as you're safe and healthy," he murmurs, his voice thick, "that's all that matters to me. That's all that matters."

CHAPTER 53

I STARE AT THE text message.

Elias

> He took the bait. Two thousand dollars hit the dummy account. Liam's working on a trace.

I quickly type a reply.

Ethan

> He's careful—starting small. Keep me posted.

Working my jaw, I grip my phone, my mind swirling with questions.

Something's been bothering me, and I know Elias feels the same way.

Why does Dayton want Fleur money? The sums are insignificant to his net worth now. What is the whole point of this embezzlement?

What are we missing?

Frustration is a bitter taste on my tongue as I pace in front of my office windows. Dark clouds cloak the city as buildings come alive with glowing lights.

Knock. Knock.

"Come in."

I smell the familiar hint of lavender before I turn around.

Breathing in deeply, I relax my muscles. "Lexy. Still here?"

"I thought I'd wait for you." She smiles, her thick hair arranged in a loose braid today, her curvy figure molding to the tan dress she has on.

I pull her in for a brief kiss, mindful of the nosy eyes outside my office. Even though our relationship is out in the open, there's no need to flaunt it. Lexy wouldn't want that.

"Dealing with the auditors again—going to put in more hours tonight. Don't wait for me."

Her brows furrow. "You look extra stressed. Why don't I stay and keep you company? I'll read a book or work on my online assignments."

"I'll get nothing done if you're here. It'll be a distraction." I brush my finger on her nose and her cheeks pinken. "Need I remind you what happened at The Orchid last weekend?"

She flushes, no doubt thinking about our passionate, semi-public sex inside Trésor.

I may have hauled her back home right after the performance, the caveman inside me refusing to let any other red-blooded male see my Lexy with her post-orgasmic glow.

"Fine. But are we still on tomorrow?"

"You and me enjoying a quiet morning at Ravenswood, then heading back to the apartment for another cooking adventure?" I wink. "Can't wait."

Alexis grins and presses a soft kiss on my cheek. "Fine. Good luck with your CFO stuff then. I'll go back to my apartment and be a *good girl* tonight."

She throws me a saucy wink and walks toward the door. My blood heats as I watch her sashay away from me.

But suddenly, a chill sweeps inside me.

"Did you call a car?" Goosebumps prickle my forearms. I glance at the darkened skies outside.

Unease. Similar to how I felt on the stormy night that changed our lives.

"Yes, the driver's on his way. You and my brothers are colluding, aren't you? No one wants me to drive, I swear." She tsks and wags her finger.

The pressure in my chest eases slightly. "Good. We're just worried."

"I know, but you guys have to let go sometime. Love you. Don't work too hard." She blows me a kiss and walks out of my office.

Olivia mentioned I might have PTSD. She brought it up yesterday during our call to discuss the expansion of Letters of Hope.

"Lexy's doing well, Ethan. Aside from her memory and her limp, she's fine. More than fine. Tay's right. Her best friend is resilient," Olivia comments. I hear a rustling noise on her line, followed by the keyboard tapping sounds.

"I know."

"I sense a but."

I'm not one to pour out my thoughts—it makes me uneasy. But seeing how much she's helped Maxwell with his anxiety, I try anyway. "I can't get rid of this feeling that something bad will happen. That I'm too happy, and the last time I felt this way, my life got ripped away from me."

The typing stops.

"Have you considered talking to someone, Ethan? Not me if you feel uncomfortable. This isn't a professional intake or diagnosis, but you've been through a very traumatic experience—almost losing someone you love and being stuck in a limbo state for so long. It can be PTSD. You don't need to feel this way forever."

Exhaling, I stride back to my desk. Distraction. Routines. Things to refocus my mind and to distract myself from the storm cloud swirling in my gut.

I spend the next hour tuning out my worries, working through emails, proposals, budget reviews, and audit requests.

As I'm jotting down my questions on a project forecast, my phone buzzes.

An unknown number.

"Hello? Anderson speaking."

Silence fills the line. The unease I shoved away comes roaring back.

Glancing at my phone, I notice the call is still connected. Normally, I'd assume this was a spam call and would hang up, but something stops me.

"Hello? Who's this?" The hairs rise on the back of my neck.

Finally, I hear a ragged breath. "Ethan, this is Dayton. Dayton Holden."

Every atom inside me stills, focused on the voice coming across the line.

"To what do I owe the pleasure?"

"Let's drop the bullshit. You're looking into me and I know it."

"I don't know what you're talking about."

"Greenwich Housekeeping Services. Really, you think I'm stupid?"

Quickly, I hit the record button on my phone in case the asshole says something incriminating.

"I'd ask you how you knew about our housekeeping vendors, but I suspect you'll enlighten me."

"You saw the two grand move. I'd tell you there's more to this than you know, but if you don't believe me, then I guess we have nothing to talk about."

Drumming my fingers on the table, my mind races as the silence stretches on. The asshole didn't specifically admit to anything, but it's safe to say the jig is up. He knows we've caught him red-handed, and now he wants to trade something for leniency.

"What do you want, then? I'm a busy man."

"I'm sure you have questions. Why is Fleur targeted? Why the small amounts? I have your answers, but I'm not doing this over the phone. Meet me on the Delfina in fifteen minutes. No cops. No wires. Nothing shady or else I'm gone."

The Delfina is still parked in the Hudson as the crew finishes maintenance after the Christmas Ball.

"You're insane if you think I'm meeting you at all."

He scoffs. "Not insane. I just happen to have something—or *someone*—you care about."

My stomach plunges, the ground suddenly unsteady beneath me. "What. Did. You. Say?"

"Got your attention, didn't I?" I can almost hear the sinister smile in his voice. "If you care about Lexy, you'll show up. Alone."

"You motherfucker," I rasp and force myself to calm down, to not give away my panic. "What makes you think I care about her enough to show up?" My pulse thunders in my ears, my hand gripping my phone in a vise. *Lexy. Fuck, if he has her, I'll—*

Dayton snorts. "Drop the act. Your behavior at the ball told me everything. I don't have her right now. But like I said, there's more to this than you know. Aren't you curious how she ended up in the Hudson all those years ago? A car accident but no witnesses or photos from traffic cams?"

My breathing grows thready. The cops ruled it as an accident—a rainy day and an inexperienced driver. Charles and Liam believed it. I was too overwhelmed with grief to question it. But now...my tightly leashed control snaps.

"You piece of shit! If you harm one hair on her head, I'll find you no matter where you go. I'll tear you apart, limb by limb until you lose your voice from screaming. I'll—"

"Save your breath. You want answers? You want Lexy safe? There are people out there who won't hesitate to hurt her again. Meet me on the Delfina and I'll explain everything. No time to waste, Anderson."

Shit. Fucking shit. I tug my hair and pace in front of my desk. I won't survive if anything happens to Lexy. My heart throbs behind my rib cage, as if reminding me of the pain I endured when she was asleep—the torture that was worse than death.

I can't let anything happen to her.

"How do I know you don't have something up your sleeve?" Every atom inside me screams, *this is a trap.*

"You don't. But you and I want what's best for Lexy. If you want to keep her safe, you'll show up."

He hangs up and ice fills my veins.

My mind sweeps to the woman I love—the brilliant hair, the mischievous smirk, the life and energy finally shining in her eyes. Eight long excruciating years, not knowing if she'd ever wake up, stubbornly holding on when everyone around her, her brothers included, spoke about her in past tense, as if she were already gone.

I'll die before anything happens to you.

My vow to her at the swimming pool.

Nothing will happen to Nova. Not if I can help it.

Quickly, I send a text. Then I grab my car keys and rush out the door.

Twenty minutes later, I arrive at the pier, a frigid gust burrowing deep into my bones as I walk toward the dark cruise ship.

I'm late, but the damn bastard should know it's impossible to get anywhere in New York City within fifteen minutes during rush hour.

It's unusually quiet tonight, not a single soul loitering about, which in and of itself is an eerie sight in one of the busiest cities in the world. It may have something to do with the police activity a block away—a ten-car pileup, which cordoned off most of the surrounding streets.

Even so, my sixth sense is waving red flags.

The dry air singes my lungs—it's now the end of January, and there has been no snowfall in the city, another harbinger to doom if I were to believe in that stuff the way Lexy does.

Harbinger or not, I'll protect Nova with everything I have.

Huffing out a breath, I swing my legs over the railing, landing on the boat with a quiet thud.

I curse myself for not keeping a gun in my car and I pray to God this doesn't end in me coming out in a body bag.

Because I still want my lifetime with Nova.

Swinging by the kitchen, I grab a knife before I slip back out onto the deck, finally spotting a faint glow coming from a suite ahead.

I creep toward the light, my heart racing, my breathing thin.

Find him, get answers, get out, that's my pl—

"You're late."

Before I can turn around, pain explodes in my temple, and I briefly register the warm trickle of blood as the ground rushes up to greet me.

Darkness swallows me whole.

CHAPTER 54

"LVDANCES53SLASH," I MUTTER AND hit enter. A beep sounds from my laptop.

Access denied.

"Dammit!"

Our driver safely deposited me in front of my apartment an hour ago. At first, I had my night planned out—a bubble bath with my favorite lavender bath salts, spending quality time with a new stack of romance novels that arrived this morning. And maybe some sexting with Ethan, which is probably a bad idea considering he's busy with his work and needs to focus.

So, scratch the sexting.

But ever since half an hour ago, my heart has been racing and something's churning in my gut, like I ate a bad piece of cheese or am on the verge of getting sick.

Then, the flashes of memories started up out of the blue. This time, I didn't even have a headache to warn me about them.

A desperation burns inside me—to keep busy, to do something useful that may help me get my memories back. With the way I'm feeling, I'm leaning toward walking away from the medical trial in favor of knowing the past—whether it be from photos or family and friends telling me what they remember.

And that's how I spent the last hour trying to get into the flash drive again. One last attempt before I ask Liam to help. Something in my gut tells me I'll have the answers there.

But none of my passwords work.

My mind drifts to those horrifying visions again, and my hands tremble.

"They're in the past," I mutter. "The past can't hurt you."

"Stop it," someone moans.

Acid rushes up my throat as I creep toward the cracked open door, the thumping beats of the music sounding far away.

Screams. More screams.

I look down and see my silver heels.

Slapping sounds. Crying. Thumping—but that may be my pulse in my ears.

Water. Lots of water rushing in from the closed windows and doors.

Me screaming, pain exploding over my body. My leg is trapped.

I can't get out.

It's so dark—I can't see.

Then the images change.

Hummingbird window. Dreariness outside.

It's freezing, but I'm happy.

"Stop daydreaming, Nova. Don't you have work to do?"

Ethan.

I turn around, finding him staring at me, a boyish grin on his face. His hair is disheveled. He looks so lighthearted and happy.

"You're no fun," I grumble, turning back to my laptop. "Why are you even here?"

"I'm the keeper of your dreams. Your north star."

My breath stalls in my throat and my eyes tear up as I relive this precious scrap of memory. The only piece of the past Ethan—the past us—I remember. This smallest flash tells me the precious memories I've lost are still buried inside me.

"Keeper of my dreams," I whisper. What a beautiful sentiment.

But then I startle, goosebumps pebbling my forearms from a sudden awareness.

Can it be?

My fingers shake, and I click on the USB drive folder again, the password prompt popping up on the screen.

"Keeperofdreams," I murmur and hit enter.

No beeping.

"Yes!" I pump my fist in the air, elation sweeping through me as the explorer screen opens, showing the contents of the mysterious drive.

"Photos, assignments, journals," I mumble, scrolling through the many folders I have in there. But then I stop when I come across one particular folder.

Dayton's Important Stuff.

I frown. Why would he have important items with me? I must've accidentally backed up his folders in the past.

After clicking it open, my eyes widen when I take in all the PDFs and screenshots. I click on a few of them and gasp. There are bank statements, wire transfer receipts, and financial records of accounts in the Cayman Islands.

My muscles seize, and I think back to Ethan and Elias's warnings about their investigation.

"No," I whisper, inspecting the documents, "Fleur Entertainment Holdings Operations Account." One of the originating bank accounts' sender's information is Ethan's company. "But why?"

These items are over a decade old. What was he involved in?

I click on a jpeg file. My heart stops when I flag the words, "The Association."

I remember reading about it, the suspected shadowy organization that allegedly murdered a high-profile businessman.

Then I read the text messages in the folder.

My heart stops. I slap my hands on my desk, accidentally jolting the laptop, and the flash drive topples to the floor.

"Shit." Quickly, I squat down and pick it up. How did I not know about this? Did I never open this folder in the past?

Something in my gut tells me this is the first time I've seen this information.

"Shit. Shit. Shit." I need to talk to Ethan and Elias. I need to tell them what I've found.

Without looking above me, I get up.

And accidentally slam my head on the hard edge of my desk.

Pain explodes across my skull. I drop to the floor, the sharp pain robbing me of my breath.

The past drags me under again.

The music thumps loudly. Muted conversations and clinking of glasses filter through the walls. The hallway is dark, like someone purposely turned off the lights.

I should turn around. A sixth sense tells me I'm not supposed to be here.

But my body refuses to listen. My feet inch forward of their own accord.

I need to find Tay Tay. The party is over. Everyone from the ballet studio went home, and we've had our fun.

There's still school tomorrow.

I should turn around and leave. I'm obviously lost.

Then I hear it. Screams. Gut-wrenching screams. The sounds of fabric ripping, skin slapping against skin.

My blood curdles and my breath freezes in my lungs.

Before I know it, I'm standing in front of the door at the end of the corridor. The cries are louder and whatever's going on inside the room is utter terror.

It's something that'll change everything as I know it.

Holding my breath, I peek through the gap, and what I see has me slapping my palm over my mouth.

Men over women—multiple women, all drunk or incapacitated.

An orgy—an unwanted orgy.

My feet inch backward. I need to get out. I need to call the cops.

They can't see me.

But then, something stops me.

Thick raven hair, slender willowy limbs, the beautiful dress I lent her earlier that night.

No!

I bolt forward, not caring about my safety. I need to rip the man off her. Shit, he's tucking himself back into his pants. The deed is done.

It's too late.

Then I see the blond hair. The familiar frame. The profile I recognize. No. No. No.

My mind spins, frantic, I blink, hoping I'm actually asleep and in the throes of a nightmare.

But no, he's still there.

I need to stop him… I need to stop him.

I need to put him away. Another man steps into my vision. He's murmuring something, a slimy smirk on his face.

Uncle Ian grunts, his face flushed. He responds in rapid French…calling the guy Archambeau. Something about The Association.

Evidence. I need evidence.

Hands trembling, I take out my phone, swipe to my camera app, and click record.

Then I hear thundering footsteps coming from my right.

My mind blanks, my head still throbbing, and the next thing I know, I find myself curled up on the floor of my apartment, my fingers knotted in my hair, tears soaking my face.

Tay.

Tay.

Oh my fucking shit. Tay.

I draw in quick breaths—one right after the other—but my lungs don't seem to be intaking enough oxygen.

I can't breathe.

This can't be real. These can't be memories, can they? It can't be.

Then I think about Taylor's face in the hospital whenever I brought up the past. My gut feeling that she's been through something dark but doesn't want to tell me. The way the blood rushed from her face at the Christmas Ball when I told her I was remembering things from my accident.

Is this what she's been hiding?

The fragments of my memories collide with each other in my mind—the threatening phone call, what I witnessed—and a sudden wave of nausea threatens to purge my stomach of whatever I ate earlier today.

My accident wasn't an accident. I suspected that from the brief flash of memories, but there was always an element of uncertainty. Why would anyone want to hurt me?

Now I know. I saw something I shouldn't have seen.

I was supposed to die in the car crash.

My fingers shake. I quickly scramble back up and grab my phone from my desk to pull out my contacts.

Tay. I need to talk to Tay.

I need to find out what happened. Screw the medical trial.

I. Need. To. Know. Now.

But before I press dial, an incoming call flashes on the screen, a number I don't recognize.

"H-Hello?"

"Alexis, are you with Ethan?"

I recognize the gravelly voice—dark, mysterious, a thread of danger in them.

"Elias." His name comes out in a shout. "I-I think I remember what h-happened."

"I need you to calm down right now and explain in the clearest and quickest way possible."

"I have a flash drive." I grab my hair, pulling it. "I didn't remember the password until now. And I opened it. There's all this evidence against Dayton and The Association. I don't know why he's involved. Then I bumped my head, and I remembered what happened to Taylor...and Uncle Ian, and I...I—"

"The Association? Fuck!" The sound of glass shattering comes across the line.

"Elias?"

"I need you to listen very carefully. I'm not in the city right now, but Ethan sent me a message saying he's meeting with Dayton for information. But if what you saw on your flash drive is legitimate and The Association is involved, then Ethan's in danger. Do you have any idea where he might be? The last location I have of him is at his office. But his phone is off."

My pulse riots, my lungs feeling like they'll give up on me at any second. Where would he be? Why does Dayton want to meet him?

Think, Lexy. You know Ethan better than anyone. You know this. Think.

Suddenly, I remember something.

I put Elias on speaker and swipe to the track my phone app.

Polaris. Last seen ten minutes ago. A singular blue dot.

"H-He's at the pier." I snap my head up. "I know where he's at. The Delfina. It's still docked there."

"Alexis, I'll call my guys. Whatever you do, stay put and don't—"

I hang up.

Ethan's with Dayton. He might be in danger. Dayton knows me...he cares about me. I might be able to talk some sense into him.

I need to find Ethan. I need to save him. I can't let him get hurt.

Standing up quickly, I grab my keys and rush out the door.

CHAPTER 55

DREAD COILS INSIDE ME as I slip onto The Delfina. A hazy fog rolls over the river, the Statue of Liberty distant and spectral in the mist.

Like a ghost watching over us.

Get a grip, Lexy. Ethan needs you.

I called Charles on the way over and, as expected, he went ballistic when he found out I was heading here by myself.

I'm sure he's on his way with reinforcements, along with whoever Elias is sending.

But I can't wait.

Deep in my gut, I *know* Ethan needs me. That only I can get us all out of this mess.

I'm the key to everything.

The sharp, briny scent of the Hudson floats to my nose and I hold my breath as I tiptoe on the deck toward the singular room with the lights on.

Pepper spray. Check.

Panic button. Check.

It's only Dayton. He won't hurt me. I know he won't.

I hear voices as the suite door comes into view. Someone groans.

"You don't need to do this." A strained exhale. "We can work something out."

Ethan. But he sounds like he's in pain.

"Shut up. Let me think!" More muffling sounds. "One mistake. One damn mistake and I'm stuck in this fucking mess," Dayton mutters.

My pulse clatters inside my ears.

Ethan knows nothing. I do. And I have the evidence. Dayton doesn't need to hurt him. I need to calm him down. Dayton will listen to me, I know it.

Determined, I take a deep breath and stride into the room. "Dayton, whatever you're thinking, don't do this."

The two men swivel their attention to me. Dayton pulls his hair, his eyes wild with disbelief.

Ethan is tied up on the floor, blood seeping from his temple. Upon seeing me, he strains against the binds around his wrists and ankles. His mouth is now gagged, but I hear him yelling my name.

Automatically, I take a step toward him, but then I remember why I'm here. I need to talk some sense into Dayton. I remember the charming guy who whisked me down the halls at Broadbent, cheering me up whenever my parents made me upset. The guy with dreams of becoming something great when he grows up.

I can get through to him.

"Dayton, don't do this. I don't know why you stole from Fleur. But it's not worth it. Don't throw your future away." I look at Ethan, who's still struggling unsuccessfully with his binds. "We'll forget about this, okay? None of this happened. We can all walk away."

Fifteen minutes. The average response time of the NYPD. I remember reading this somewhere. I just need to hold on for another five to ten minutes and the cops will be here.

"Lexy," Dayton buries his face in his hands. "You remember that fund I started in college? I only wanted to make it successful. I invested everything into it—it was my ticket to make a name for myself. When he reached out to me, saying he could fill in the gaps of my initial losses, that I could pay him back with the profits later on, I didn't hesitate."

"What? Who?" I reach inside my bag to grab the pepper spray.

Dayton doesn't have a weapon. Maybe I can incapacitate him if talking doesn't work.

Dayton ignores my question and continues rambling. "I didn't even think about why he'd want me to help him, but you know what? When I asked, he said it was because I had access to you and Charles—that your family's Bank of Columbia was also on their target list. I thought it was just introductions he needed. I didn't know he'd—"

"Who on earth are you talking about? Who's 'he'?" The answer is at the tip of my tongue. The Association. Bank of Columbia. My family. Ethan's family.

"Me."

Another man steps out from the en suite bathroom and my mouth drops.

The light blond hair. Lips usually tilted into an easygoing smile. A face I've seen time and time again walking down the halls of Fleur.

Trey Spencer, Ethan's VP of Finance, the guy *everyone* likes at Fleur.

"Trey? What? Wh-Why? Aren't you Ethan's friend? His mentor?" I grip the pepper spray and step backward.

His jaw works, his normally jovial face austere and angry. "Take your hand out of your purse, Alexis. I won't ask twice."

Slowly, he unbuttons his jacket and pulls out a gun from his holster.

A deadly click echoes in the air.

He's disengaged the safety.

Ethan throws himself across the floor in front of me, his hands and legs still bound. "Lexy, go!" he mumbles through his gag.

My eyes burn. He's still trying to save me.

He spent a decade waiting for me, a decade loving me when he could've moved on.

I won't abandon him now.

Slowly, I raise my hands in the air. "Trey, we can talk through this."

"I wish you didn't wake up," Trey mutters, hurling a hateful glare at me. "Ethan was investigating—I knew that, I was part of it, but he wasn't desperate like a man possessed until he found the link to Dayton. And you know why?"

At my silence, he continues, "He *needed* to protect you. The Andersons don't care about the millions they've lost. It's loose change to them. But *you*," he spits out the word in disdain, "you're precious to him. Irreplaceable. At the thought of you being in danger, Ethan pulled all the stops, even enlisting the help of *the* Elias Kent. And who the hell wants Elias's wrath?"

Trey barks out a deranged laugh and shakes his head. "Even The Association is wary of Elias. The man holds too many secrets. Time's running out. There are only so many ways someone can embezzle from a company. Elias has already started poking around in the HR files. It's only a matter of time before this useless prick," he jabs his thumb at Dayton, "will crack and give me up."

"But *why*?"

Buy us time. A few more minutes. Rescue is coming.

I try to convey those thoughts to Ethan with my gaze, but the man I love shakes his head vehemently, his eyes darting to the door, pleading at me to leave.

Trey's hand trembles, the barrel of his gun wavering. My breathing is thready as my attention rivets on the weapon that may very well end our lives tonight.

"The Association has invited The Andersons and your family to join them for years. *Years.* But you all resisted. Your grandmother, Charles, and the great Linus Anderson and his impeccable children have too much honor and pride to join the ranks of other powerful businessmen and politicians in the plan to reshape the world as we know it. *No one* defies The Association."

He leans down and pistol whips Ethan's jaw and I shriek, watching the blood oozing from his lips.

"They got to me when I stole the first ten thousand to shut my ex up during our divorce. She was threatening to air out some dirty secrets I had." Trey shakes his head.

"I was supposed to help them with one transfer, but I was too naïve. Like the idiot over there who unfortunately caught my attention with his up and coming mutual fund, promising returns that were un-heard of. Too damn good to be true." Trey glares at Dayton. "I dug around and found his connection to you and Charles. I told The Association I could get them in the door with your family—that I'd do them a favor in exchange for them destroying the evidence they had on me."

Trey snarls. "But there's no such thing as one favor for The Association. Once you're in, you can't get out...unless you're in a body bag. Ever since then, I was at their mercy—moving funds, doing whatever they asked me to do. A pathetic lackey."

Ethan grunts in the background, and I know he's trying to escape. I step in front of him, blocking Trey's view.

Trey adjusts his grip on the gun, his face mottled as he reflects on the past. I can't believe this is the same guy we all joked with in the office. The guy who took my dinner order in Ethan's office.

"For the last ten years, I was instructed to dirty Fleur up for them. Infiltrate. Destroy it from within. If I said no, all the evidence of the embezzlement—among other illegal things—would be aired out. It'd be life behind bars. But you know what? If I couldn't escape, I might as well get rich doing bad shit, right? The end goal is to leave Fleur—and your family's bank—with no choice but to join us."

He towers over me, his eyes maniacal. "Do you know those funds we siphoned off Fleur's accounts were used to traffic women? All in the name of the precious Vaughn's Bank of Columbia Equitable Investment Fund? There's a paper trail miles long implicating Fleur and BoC in this shit?"

Ethan stills behind me, and despite his disadvantaged position on the ground, I feel the wrath wafting off him. Without a doubt, if he were unbound, he'd kill Trey.

Trey tsks. "Ethan, I wish things ended differently. I enjoyed working with you. But you stuck your nose where you didn't belong. And it appears," he glances at me, "the woman you love has the same problem as you."

He cocks his head to the side and steps closer to me. "Why didn't you die the first time?"

"T-The first time?"

"Still don't get it? Your little party in the Hudson ten years ago… Who did you think gave you that send-off? Knowing you couldn't swim?"

My mind swirls, trying to process his words. My car plummeting into the Hudson wasn't an accident, that much I already figured out, but then his comment about me not being able to swim.

I whip my head toward Dayton, who hangs his head, not looking at me.

"You fucking shit!" I yell at him. "You knew I couldn't swim. It was you who ran me off the road that day, wasn't it?"

"Goddamn it, Lexy. You saw too much! You saw what happened at the hotel lounge—you saw Archambeau, one of their top enforcers. You saw what the guys were doing to the girls. You interrupted an initiation for The Association just because you saw your uncle joining their ranks. You recorded it. You think you would've gotten away?"

"They were assaulting them!" I scream, thinking back to my memories.

Taylor was assaulted. Violated. By none other than Uncle Ian, the man I'd looked up to all my life. The man I thought died tragically while I was in a coma.

The person no one in my family would mention every time I asked about him.

It all makes sense now.

Everyone knows. The father figure I had, my father's brother, was a monster. Just like the people in this shady organization called The Association.

"Trey got orders to get rid of you. But he didn't want to get his hands dirty. He would've turned me over to the cops if I didn't follow his instructions. I had to get rid of you."

"You bastard!"

Dayton crumbles, his eyes glistening. "I-I'm sorry, Lexy. God-damn it, I'm so sorry. I really liked you. You were in the wrong place at the wrong time, and now you're in love with the wrong person. But in the end, I couldn't go through with it...I couldn't kill you."

Trey scoffs.

What? My attention bounces from the two men—one with a crazed gleam in his eyes, the other looking like he's seconds from collapsing onto the floor from guilt.

"The useless idiot fished you out of the water. Couldn't hack it." Trey snarls in derision.

"*You're* the Good Samaritan?" *What the fuck?* That's why he didn't stick around for the ambulance. That's why no one could find this mysterious savior.

"All because of one terrible choice I made in college. And now I'm stuck in this shit forever," Dayton mutters, rocking on his feet.

A thought occurs to me. "Is this why you wormed your way back into my life? To see if I remembered anything? What were you going to do if I remembered it all? Kill me?"

Dayton doesn't answer, but his silence is a response by itself.

Suddenly, Trey claps, the sound drawing our attention back to him. "Story time's over. Chop chop." He drags Ethan up and shoves him out the door, his gun still pointed at me. "No funny business, Anderson, or she dies."

Ethan's face pales, the dark blood still dripping from the gash on his temple. He staggers out, following Trey's directions.

"Come on, Alexis. You too," Trey commands.

A minute later, he has us crowded against the cold railing sep-arating The Delfina and the icy depths of the Hudson River. The waves crash against the ship, the sounds harsh and violent, and a sudden wind kicks up.

Ethan shoves himself in front of me, still intent on protecting me with his life. I shiver and inhale his reassuring scent of leather and amber.

I can't let our story end this way. But what can I do? Where are the damn cops?

"Aw. How sweet. Gallant to the very end." Trey lets out a deranged laugh. "I'm sorry it had to end this way."

He cocks his gun and points it at Ethan's head. *No!*

"I-I have evidence! A hard drive!" The words burst out of me, adrenaline fueling my bravery.

Trey freezes, a hard glint in his eyes. "What?"

"I-If we die, the contents of that drive will be released into the world. If you let us live, I'll burn the evidence." My heart quakes inside my rib cage.

"I don't believe you."

Stiffening, I jut my chin out, my fingers grazing Ethan's hands tied behind his back. He clutches me and squeezes, as if letting me know he'll protect me. I squeeze him back, telling him this time I'll protect him.

"Try me," I whisper to the madman in front of us.

Trey's eyes rove over us, his lips pursed. I hold my breath, hoping he'll cave.

But then he straightens, his finger steady on the trigger. "Well, I guess we'll just have to take the risk, won't we?"

He swivels the gun toward me and fires, a loud boom echoing in the night.

Before I can react, I hear a loud roar followed by a grunt, then Ethan drops to the ground.

"No!" I scream, watching crimson blood seep out through his white dress shirt.

He threw himself in front of a bullet for me.

Ethan gurgles, more blood dripping from his mouth. I crouch and clutch him in my arms.

"Ethan!" I tug out his gag.

His breathing is harsh, the color fading fast from his face. "Trey... Sh-she doesn't know anything. She's bluffing. Your secret dies with me. Let her go."

"The downfall of Anderson men. Their women," Trey murmurs, and I hear the telltale click of the gun again.

With strength I don't know I possess, I hoist Ethan up and spin toward the inky waters of my almost-grave.

I hurl us over the railing as the second shot rings out.

Icy water swallows me as I clutch the man I love, the currents dragging us under into the dark depths.

Swim, Lexy. Swim.

CHAPTER 56

"Sir, you should stay for one more night. You aren't ready to be discharged yet." The nurse hurries behind me as I yank off the IV and put on my clothes.

My breath comes out in a hiss, the pain ricocheting from the bullet wound in my abdomen—a through and through that somehow missed all my vital organs. Other than significant blood loss requiring transfusion yesterday and prophylactic antibiotics, I'm weak, but fine.

"I'm not staying here. Tell the doctor to send the discharge papers to Fleur."

I can't stay here.

I can't bear the smell of antiseptic agents, the annoying barrage of beeping noises from the machines, the way everyone tiptoes on the tiled floors because they're afraid of disturbing the patients resting in nearby rooms.

It reminds me too much of the eight long years of waiting at Alexis's bedside, hoping she'll wake up.

The nurse scurries away, no doubt shaking her head in exasperation, and I march toward my destination, which quickly comes into view.

There she is, my sleeping beauty.

My heart clenches when I step into yet another sterile room, but this time, my Nova lies on the bed, her eyes closed, her copper locks fanned out on her pillow. Logically, I know she's fine—she's asleep, not in a coma.

But my mind doesn't compute, my emotions and panic sending me into a tailspin.

Olivia and Taylor rise from their chairs. Charles gives me a nod from the window, his brows furrowed.

Liam and Lana hurry over.

"Ethan! Why are you up and walking around?" Lana fawns over me, her eyes shining with concern.

Liam squeezes my arm. "She's fine. The doctors just gave her some IV fluids and said she passed out from exhaustion. Nothing to worry about, man."

I shake my head.

I can't answer them. I can't even bring myself to look at him and Charles.

Their sister almost lost her life because of me.

Against all odds, she saved us last night in the Hudson. She held onto me, a dead weight because I'd already passed out from blood loss and somehow found herself a buoy and swam to the nearby Chelsea pier in waters so cold, even a healthy person would've had difficulties navigating it.

I was told Elias's men found us first, and she collapsed in front of them. The cops came minutes later with her brothers.

They said her lips were turning blue and her skin was just a shade above white.

Exhaustion. Overexertion. Near drowning.

Trey and Dayton were caught as they tried to escape the Delfina. Wisely, they're keeping their mouths shut about The Association, because snitches in the past have ended up dead behind bars. But between the findings from my investigation and the proof Alexis says she has, the duo will be locked up for a long time.

But the victory is hollow.

"Come on, let's give them some privacy." Lana presses a kiss on my cheek, then beckons the others out of the room. "I love you, Ethan. I'm so glad you guys are okay."

"She's fine," Taylor murmurs as she passes by me.

"I'm here if you need to chat. Don't overthink this." That's Olivia, using her psychiatrist's voice. She knows the guilt eating me up inside.

"Those fucking bastards," Charles seethes, his lips snarling.

"Elias and I will handle The Association." Liam's voice is thick as he grips my shoulder. "Thank you for taking one for her." He looks at my bandaged abs.

"I'd do it all over again." *Without hesitation.*

Liam's eyes glisten and he pulls me in for a hug before filtering out of the room with the others.

Blowing out a heavy exhale, I walk to her bedside and sit down.

Quietly, I take her hand in mine and close my eyes.

The same sterile smell burns my nostrils.

The same *beep...beep...beep* of the machines echoes in the room.

The same chill of the AC brushes against our skin.

My hands shake and cold sweat beads on my forehead. I feel sick to my stomach.

"I can't do this, Nova," I whisper, my voice raw. "I almost lost you ten years ago, and it tore me apart. I spent *years* blaming myself because I didn't go to you that day. Because I didn't teach you how to swim."

Pressing a kiss on the back of her hand, I continue, "And now, a decade later, I got you back. It's a m-miracle." My heart twists in my chest. "Even though you don't remember us. I got a second chance with you. But then, this happened, and I almost lost you again. You risked your life for me... You shouldn't have done that."

Guilt presses heavily on my lungs and I strain my next inhale. "If you died by saving me, how could I go on living?"

The Anderson men aren't lucky in love.

The phrase reverberates in my mind.

My heart ripped open all those years ago, the wound nearly terminal when she was in a coma. When she woke up, she painstakingly mended me, and for a few months, I thought I might recover. I may have a scar, or I might need a pacemaker for the rest of my life, but I'll have a lifetime with her.

But now, seeing her once again sleeping in a hospital bed, this time because of me—a serrated knife severs the old wound wide open, and fear strangles my heart, squeezing the blood from it.

I'm too damaged.

Olivia's right. Perhaps I do have PTSD.

"I'll love you forever, Nova," I whisper and stand. Reaching inside my jacket, I pull out a note I wrote earlier and set it on her nightstand. "I need time... I need to fix me. I'm so, so sorry."

Alexis

I must've slept like the dead.

That's the first thought in my head as I blink my eyes open, wincing at the cold daylight streaming in from the windows.

Then I feel it—the pain in my muscles—no doubt from overexertion. Fighting the current and swimming with an unconscious man in my arms will do that to you. I was lucky to come across a detached buoy. Otherwise, I don't know how I could've held onto Ethan and still made it to safety.

But you did it, Lexy. You saved him. You got over your fear! I bite back a smile. *I kicked ass.*

"You're awake." Taylor hovers over me, her forehead pinched with concern. Behind her, I see Millie, Belle, and Olivia.

"How are you feeling? Does anything hurt?" Millie asks, her blue eyes roving over me.

"I'm fine. Sleeping really helped. I've never been so tired." Slowly, I sit up and wince as pain sizzles up my right leg. Dammit. More physical therapy in the future.

"Maxwell and the boys were here earlier, but I sent them home. Even your high school friend, Sandra, dropped by." She motions to the small bouquet on my nightstand, a small card tucked within.

Get well soon. The Lexy I knew back at Broadbent was a badass—and she still is today.

Sandra

A bittersweet smile tilts my lips. Oddly, seeing her flowers by my hospital bed feels like closure. The world moved on while I was in a coma—we've both changed and so has our friendship.

But that's okay. Because I love what I have now.

"I should call them and let them know you're awake." Belle wraps me in her arms. "I agree with Sandra. You're a badass, just like Tay." She looks at my best friend, who's still fussing over my blankets.

The goth ballerina has the warmest heart.

"How's Ethan?" I sit up, wanting to check on him.

I saw him after they sewed him up and told me he was okay. He was resting when I headed back into my room, exhausted to my bones.

The girls exchange a glance, and Olivia gives me a strained smile. "I think he needs some time to process everything. This was a lot for him, especially with what happened back then when you were..."

Her voice trails off, but I know what she's going to say.

Coma. When I was in a coma.

He must blame himself. He must be worried sick about me.

My heart clenches as I relive the horrible moments of the man I love throwing himself between a bullet and me.

I'll die before I let anything happen to you.

His fervent vow.

I almost lost him.

"I want to see him." I need to hold him, to kiss him, to feel his strong arms around me.

"He discharged himself a few hours ago. He left you a note." Olivia motions to the folded paper on my nightstand.

Unease seeps inside me as I unfold his note.

My Dearest Nova,

When you slipped into a coma a decade ago, teetering on the edge of the living and the dead, my soul died.

I'd never felt such excruciating pain before—a cocktail of regret, guilt, sadness, and loss so deep, so unfathomable, I questioned my will to live.

But I told myself I had to, because you needed me. Because I needed to give you strength, so one day you'd wake up and find me at your side.

Then one month became two, then three, then it became one year, two years, and more. My heart hardened.

I became bitter, a cold shell of my former self.

But I needed to stay strong for you. Because you were still sleeping.

I told myself I'd pay any price to have you wake up and look at me with those beautiful blue eyes of yours. Even if the price was your memories.

And you did wake up. A miracle, and against all odds, you fell in love with me again.

While I grieved losing the past Alexis, all the beautiful memories only I remembered, I celebrated the fact I get to love the present Alexis—beautiful, enthralling, as intoxicating as ever—and I could create more memories with you.

Maybe eventually, my heart wouldn't be riddled with pain. I wouldn't feel those scars.

But then, this happened.

You almost died saving me. I almost lost you again.

The thought suffocates me. The idea of you, your vibrancy and spark, your zest for life being snuffed out.

It terrifies me to the core.

And I realize how messed up I am. How fear has me tightly in its grasp. Unrelenting.

Lexy, I've loved you for over a decade, but for you, you've only loved me for a few months.

I can't help but wonder, don't you deserve someone without all these scars, fears, and wounds? Don't you deserve someone to love you without being afraid?

I don't know what I'm trying to say, but I need to get my thoughts out. I know this is the fear talking.

I guess I'm telling you this—I need time. Time to process everything. I need to fix myself, to be a man worthy of your love.

Love,
Ethan

I promptly burst into tears. I can't believe him. Even after everything we've gone through, doesn't he know we're better as a team? That he doesn't have to navigate this alone? "Stupid, stupid man. He can fix himself with me next to him."

Taylor sits on my bed and pulls me into a hug. "Men *are* stupid. If it weren't for the fact we need them to reproduce, they would've gone extinct years ago."

"He'll come to his senses," Olivia murmurs. "He loves you too much. He went through hell in the last decade. The accident took a lot out of him. Give him grace, Lexy. He's not thinking straight."

The other girls nod.

"I know. I don't blame him. Heck, if I were him, I wouldn't be thinking clearly either," I mumble into Taylor's shoulder.

Olivia's words echo inside me. The things we've gone through the last decade.

The accident. The memories. *What happened to Taylor.*

I gasp, pulling away, and stare at the familiar gray eyes of my best friend.

"Girls, can I talk to Taylor alone, please?"

Belle opens her mouth, but Millie grabs her wrist and shakes her head. Olivia stands and pats me on my back. "We'll be outside if you need us."

The girls leave the room.

"Is everything okay, Lexy?" Taylor asks, sitting on the edge of my bed.

I take her in—my best friend—how she sits straight, her shoulders back and eyes fierce.

The strength in them. Despite the darkness she went through.

Taking a deep breath, I push out the next words. "I remember what happened, Tay." I swallow. "What happened to you."

She intakes a sharp inhale, her hand flying to her lips. Her throat ripples as she clearly tries to compose herself, but a wet sheen appears in her eyes. "You do?"

I nod. "Uncle Ian violated you, didn't he? Because of The Association?"

Her lips tremble as she looks away, the tears pooling in her eyes. She nods.

I crumble and sob. "I'm sorry I couldn't save you that night. I was too late. I tried to get evidence to put him away, but they got to me. They got to me before I could get you justice. I'm so sorry I wasn't here with you."

"You're silly!" Taylor throws herself at me, her voice thick. I feel wetness on my shoulders and I know she's crying, just like I am. "You tried. And maybe you don't remember...but you stashed a copy of your video at the ballet academy. That was how we put him away. It wasn't your fault. It wasn't my fault."

"He's not dead, is he? That's why no one talks about him."

"He's rotting in jail."

"I...I don't understand how he could do this. Tay Tay, I'm so sor—"

"You can't stop greed, Lexy. Ian wanted power only The Association could give, but joining the organization had a price. A crime of their choosing. He had a choice, and he chose to be a violent criminal. You and I are victims of shitty circumstances, but guess what?"

She pulls back, and despite the tears streaking down her face, a fierce glint shines from her eyes. "We're fighters. You and me. Badasses. Our pasts can't take us down."

Warmth rushes through me, a lump thick in my throat. I nod, in awe of her strength, her resilience.

"Focus on yourself, okay? I've worked through it. I see a therapist. Don't you dare feel guilty because none of this is your fault."

Nodding, I swipe away my tears. My memories aren't all back yet, and I'm sure someday I can piece together all the missing pieces, but something significant finally slides into place.

After a few moments of silence, she asks, "So, what are you going to do about Ethan?"

I stare out the window.

"I'll give us both time to process everything, then we need to have a chat."

CHAPTER 57

"YOU'RE HOLDING ON REMARKABLY well, Ethan. You should be proud of yourself." Sheila Moore, LMFT, the therapist Olivia recommended to me, smiles, and sets down her notebook.

"It doesn't feel that way."

"Has anyone ever said you're too hard on yourself?"

I snort. "Too many times."

"I thought so." She sits back in her leather chair and perches her reading glasses on top of her brown hair. "What do you want? If you never experienced these events, what would you want to do?"

My breath hitches. It's a no-brainer. "Be with Lexy. Love her. Grow old with her. Do her bucket list with her. Add more items to her list."

The images spin in my mind—a beautiful slideshow tugging at my heart.

"Does she love you back?"

"Of course she does. Even if she doesn't remember our past. She...she risked her life for me. You don't do that for someone you don't care about." I grip my cuff link then slide out the cover, revealing the painting of the bird that'll forever remind me of her.

"What would you do if your places were switched, if you were the one who lost your memories, but you fell in love with her again? And one day, she was in danger and you jumped in, no questions asked, to save her, but it triggered her fears. What would you say to her?"

I trace the wings on the hummingbird; her smile all those years ago appearing behind my eyelids. She was so excited to find a pair of cuff links that matched the earrings I gave her.

"I'd remind her of her motto, 'don't wait to live because the clock keeps ticking.'" I smile, thinking about the hope in her eyes whenever she said the phrase in the past.

She's so inspiring.

Taking a deep breath, I continue, "I'd tell her not to let her fears hold her back from her happy ending. To take it one day at a time and I'll be with her every step of the way—good days, bad days."

The words ring true. Because if our roles were switched, I'd want a lifetime with her, even if the lifetime included fights or tears, moments where she'd pull away or be angry at me. Because for every one of those moments, there'd be ten more that were happy and hopeful. Ten more moments filled with so much love, we'd forget what we went through, and the past would feel like a faint echo, something that strengthened us.

Because we survived.

"It isn't easy, having PTSD. You just encountered an intense, triggering event. It makes sense to be afraid. In fact, I'd be worried if you didn't. But think about what you just told me. How easy that answer came to you if your positions were reversed."

Sheila leans forward, her eyes intent on mine. "You're taking the first step to reclaim your future by facing your past. It's the hardest step. And you just told me, with remarkable clarity, what the objective you, not muddled with fear or anxiety, would do."

A lump forms in my throat as I mull over her words.

She's right. I think deep down, when I sought her out, I knew the path forward.

I needed to face my problems so I could enjoy the future with Alexis.

The grandfather clock chimes—my hour is up. I stand and Sheila follows suit.

Sheila smiles, her gaze compassionate. "Be proud of yourself for taking this step, for seeing clarity even when your emotions want to take over the reins."

"Thank you, Sheila." I shake her hand.

We make an appointment for next week, because I suspect my therapy sessions are long overdue, and it'll take some time for me to work through everything.

But for now, I feel more in control. The fear gripping me when I saw her asleep in the hospital recedes into the background.

I miss her, my Nova.

Half an hour later, the smell of worn old books greets me as I step inside Ravenswood Library, a rush of nostalgia soon to follow. I make my way up the spiral staircase to The Wing of Eternal Dreams.

I paid a small fortune to rename the rare text archival floor after our journey—a lonely keeper who fell in love with a whimsical dreamer in the halls of love stories.

Walking to the hummingbird window, I think back to my beautiful years with Alexis.

Literary scavenger hunts I looked forward to weekly.

Her lips hiking up in a smile as she read my poetry.

Learning I was capable of love after all...that my heart was waiting for her.

Cooking in my apartment, flour dusting her nose and hair.

Curling up with her on the sofa, watching movies and listening to the rain.

My fingers graze the red belly of the stained glass bird and gaze at the courtyard below. The skies are dreary, clouds hanging low.

Will today bring the first snow of the year?

She's always loved the first snowfall.

I wonder what she's doing now.

She had a courier deliver a letter the afternoon I checked out of the hospital, a response to the note I left her on her nightstand.

Ethan,

I understand. I'll give you time. But I won't give up and neither should you.

Always yours,
Lexy

I asked the courier to wait while I scribbled a response to her.

My Nova,

Thank you for your love. And your patience.
I will get there, I promise you.

Ethan

My breath fogs up the window as I admire the barren branches of the beech tree swaying to the wind.

Then, as if I willed it, glittering white flecks descend from the sky.

The first snowfall of the new year.

CHAPTER 58

"The arrests sent shockwaves through the financial industry. Dayton Holden and Trey Spencer have pled guilty to multiple counts of racketeering, blackmail, embezzlement, and attempted murder—among other charges. Legal analysts predict they'll spend the rest of their lives behind bars. The pair claimed full responsibility for the crimes, though rumors persist about The Association's involvement—"

I turn off the TV, not wanting to see Dayton and Trey's faces ever again. They look haggard, their eyes haunted. My guess? They're afraid for their lives—when you're caught, you become a loose end for The Association.

I don't give a crap about them anymore. They don't deserve another second of my thoughts.

Blowing out a breath, I walk over to the windows and stare at the dreary skies when the doorbell rings. Despite missing Ethan, I'm glad he's taking the time to work on himself.

He needs to heal—I can't imagine how traumatizing it is to almost lose the person you love twice. He's waited for me for almost a decade. This time, I'll be the one waiting—in whatever capacity he needs me—because I love him and I know he loves me.

We'll come out of this stronger.

The doorbell rings again.

"Coming!" *Who is it? Is it Ethan?*

My pulse quickens and I hurry to the door and yank it open, only to deflate when I see the person on the other side isn't him but is his sister.

"Wow, you look so disappointed to see me." Lana smirks, her expression reminding me so much of him. She's elegant as always in a brown wool dress and a beret, and she's holding a large paper bag.

I smack my forehead and give her a hug. "I'm an idiot. I was hoping Ethan came to his senses, but I'm glad to see you. What brings you here? Is he okay?"

"He's fine, don't worry." She steps inside my apartment and looks around. "I'm doing a welfare check. Good—the blinds are open, no pigsty. You look like you're coping well."

"It's a speed bump. I don't like it, but I'll survive."

Lana nods and turns toward me, her thick braid swinging from the movement. "I stopped by his place this morning to check in on him—making sure his fridge is stocked, he's eating, and whatnot. I came across something I thought you should have."

She hands me the paper bag.

"What is it?" I pull out a large leather book and frown. This looks really familiar.

Then it occurs to me.

This is the book Ethan has in his arms in every one of the artsy photos decorating his apartment and his office.

"He'll probably kill me when he finds out it's missing. But I'm thinking if I were you, given what happened, I'd probably quit the medical trial in favor of learning about my past."

My fingers tremble and my pulse riots inside me as I carry the book to the living room and sit down.

I trace the faded gold lettering on the cover.

Letters to the Universe

The hairs prickle on my forearms. The answers I've been waiting for. Call it a gut feeling, but I know they lie within these pages.

"Thank you, Lana," I whisper, unable to tear my gaze away from the scuff marks on the cover.

"Don't mention it. I'll leave you to it. I'm a phone call away if you need me," she murmurs.

A whiff of her rose perfume hits my nose, and I hear her quiet footsteps and the soft click of the door shutting behind her.

My hands fist on top of the book, my heart drumming a rapid beat.

Before what happened on the Delfina, I'd already decided to drop out of the medical trial. I don't want to let the past hang over me and prevent me from living the future I deserve.

I want to know my love story with Ethan even if I might never remember.

Open it.

The urge grips me—a gut feeling so strong, I have to listen to it.

Taking a deep breath, I slowly flip open the cover and read.

To the Keeper of My Secrets,

Yes. That's you, the nosy person reading my journal.

A gasp slips out of me, my eyes absorbing the entries a lost girl on the cusp of womanhood wrote to her mysterious pen pal.

A familiar headache forms at the base of my neck, and I know it'll hurt—whatever I'm going to remember next.

But I can't stop reading. I can't flip through the pages fast enough.

These are letters between me and Ethan. I recognize his masculine scrawl.

P.S. Not that this helps, but I don't think you're easily forgettable. You know the saying, "A picture speaks a thousand words?" I actually have an opposite belief—words illuminate the soul. I haven't met you in person, but based on your words, your zest for life, I know you're the type of person who leaves an impression. You're unforgettable, remember that. And I'll always remember you. Don't be too hard on yourself.

My eyes tear up as I trace his words. *You're unforgettable, remember that. And I'll always remember you.*

How true they are.

"Oh Ethan," I choke out, watching our love story unfold in front of me.

I hope you find genuine love, even if you don't believe in it. Perhaps I haven't experienced the heart-wrenching twist of loving someone. But I've seen it. My parents, as flighty as they are, truly love each other. But their love is volatile—a tsunami drowning everyone in the vicinity.

I want what they have, minus the wreckage. I hope to find it someday and I wish for the same for you.

Your confidant,
Dreamer and Believer

P.S. Clue: *Another name for this journal.* I know, I'm lazy with this one, but ballet practice and school have been kicking my ass, so I haven't had time to come up with something cleverer.

Suddenly, a knife of white-hot pain drives through my skull.

It's blistering. It isn't just pain this time—it's an explosion.

I cry out and bury my face in my hands as the headache bursts from behind my forehead, rippling out like a bomb just went off.

Then the images come. Vivid. Sharp. A slide show.

The missing pieces, the memories of us I've been searching for.

Me huffing down the steps of Ravenswood Library to the DVD room, freedom in my veins after I broke up with Dayton. I wanted a glimpse of my keeper, even if that broke the rules.

The beautiful man—the god of war—smiling at me that first day outside the library after he picked up the things I dropped on the ground.

Me describing the perfect picnic at the hidden courtyard to be shared with the man I love—Ethan—once I graduated from college and got a job.

A picnic I inadvertently had years later, not knowing how hard it must've been for him to live out this beautiful future we planned together, but I'd become a stranger.

A violent storm and a blackout. The elation I felt when I saw him walking up to me. His words, *"I knew you'd be beautiful,"* before he kissed me like his life depended on it.

Our passionate sex, his tutoring sessions, the way he grinned when we jotted down the first seven items of my Twenty by Forty list.

My hummingbird earrings and his vintage cuff links.

The gentle graze of his finger on the bridge of my nose—his love in a single gesture.

His favorite color, blue, because it reminded him of my eyes.

"Marry me," his words to me when he crouched over me, shielding me from the violent hail during the first snowstorm of the year.

I teased him, saying he didn't have a ring, that I wouldn't answer him until our date for the ghost pepper curry challenge.

The what-if game, me asking what he'd do if a rock struck me and I lost my memories. His fervent response that day at the library.

"If a rock smacked you on the head and you lost your memories, I'd do everything in my power to make you remember. Even if that meant recreating our love story, reminding you with every touch, every word. Because there'd be no way I'd let you slip away. No way."

I sob into my hands.

He did everything. He never gave up on me.

Every single moment since I've woken up from the coma carries a different meaning.

The memories continue to slam in—relentless—an avalanche finally tearing down the mountain after one too many snowstorms.

I shake in my seat, my fingers clutching my head.

And I remember.

Each and every moment. Those four missing years.

The dreamer and his keeper.

How could I've forgotten?

Eventually, the pain subsides, but the chasm in my heart splits wide open and tears continue pouring down my face.

Those four missing years—the ones I've long associated with pain—held memories my mind tried to protect me from. Moments too painful to relive. But hidden among these memories were priceless, beautiful moments I'd give anything to keep forever.

I spend the next minutes reading our journal. Pages and pages of love letters, pressed flowers, inside jokes.

I laugh and cry as the words trigger more precious flashbacks.

My mind makes the connections now. The photos in his apartment and home—all from places on our bucket list. The little trinkets I found stashed away in the hospital nightstand when I woke up—the gold coin, the sea glass, the ghost pepper curry spices, every item a souvenir from the bucket list challenges.

His way of doing the list for me, of keeping hope alive, of keeping our love alive.

His vow to teach me how to swim, because he was supposed to in the past.

Oh Ethan, did you take on that guilt too? Did you think if you'd taught me back then, perhaps I wouldn't have nearly drowned?

I know he did. My Ethan carries the weight of the world on his shoulders. He must've been gutted and riddled with guilt.

His poetry.

Did he regret it? Loving me? Waiting for me for almost a decade only to lose me when I don't remember him?

Then I remember the poem he wrote for me in the courtyard when I asked him for help with my assignment. Love in seven lines.

A scent of lavender lingers.

An imprint time will not erase.

Pain and distance cannot sever.
Her laughter, her light—a path I chase.
Once in a lifetime, a sure-fired arrow.
Even through agony, loneliness, and sorrow.
No regrets, only gratitude—the lavender, always, *woven into* my soul.

Sobs rack me as the full meaning finally hits me. The depth of his love, the steadfastness, the fact he only holds gratitude despite the years of pain he endured.

"Ethan, oh my God, Ethan." I stand, needing to find him, to tell him I remember.

I remember everything.

A sheet of paper flutters to the floor and I pick it up. The ink is newer and I see water marks dotting the page.

His tears. His grief.

Tibet

Memories dance behind my eyelids as I go to sleep,
Visions of you, soaring high in my dreams.
Ribbons of fire twirling in the wind,
Your lavender scent lingers, a longing I cannot rescind.
Hearts, once aflame, now smolder in smoke,
Our love, bittersweet, broken as fate's cruel stroke.
The world spins on, blissfully unaware,
My life, forever changed, hollow as the air.
My Nova, my star, bright in the sky,
Farewell, my hummingbird, my darling butterfly.

He must've written this right before I woke up. Liam told me Ethan was on a plane when I woke up and he dropped everything to rush to the hospital.

Only for me to reject him—because my mind hurt too much, because I didn't remember him.

I need to find him.

I don't care if he needs more time to heal. I don't care if he pushes me away.

He fought for me all these years.

This time, I'm fighting for him.

CHAPTER 59

SNOWFLAKES DUST MY HAIR and clothes—the small crystals glinting off daylight.

A smile curves on my lips as I tilt up my head under the weeping beech tree in the courtyard, admiring the first snow of the year descending from the sky.

She'd love this.

The first snowfall represents new beginnings. Her favorite time of the year.

Putting my hand out, I watch the delicate flakes land, then melt in my palm, the world slowly becoming a white winter wonderland around me.

I'm going to find her after this—to apologize for running away in the hospital, for allowing my panic to drive my actions.

Fate has given me a third chance with her. I can't waste it.

Inhaling the frigid air, I close my eyes and listen to the sounds of nature—the branches swaying; the birds singing their songs.

Then I hear it.

Soft footsteps, the lightest breathing.

My favorite scent—lavender—floating to my nose.

"Ethan?"

The dulcet voice, which to this day, doesn't fail to rouse a heat inside my body. Slowly, I turn around, finding her, my love, my Nova, standing there, looking like an angel descended from the heavens.

She's clad in an ivory puffer coat, dark jeans and boots, her fiery tresses draping over her shoulders. Her cheeks and nose are pink as she stares at me with those brilliant, sky-blue eyes.

"Lexy," I murmur, watching as she stops a foot away from me.

"How could I've forgotten?" she whispers, her eyes glistening with tears.

My heart stutters. *What is she saying?*

"You're wrong." Her gaze roves over my face, her lips tipping in a watery smile. "My love for you isn't only for a few months… It's for a decade too."

She rests her hand on my cheek, and my breath hitches. I feel her touch in my heart. "You're the keeper of my dreams. My north star."

My breath freezes, her words reverberating in the slither of air between us.

Keeper of her dreams. North star.

"Nova, wh-what are you saying? Are you saying you—"

A teardrop slides down her smooth cheek and she nods. "I remember, Ethan. My heart has always remembered you, but now, I remember *us*. I remember it all. Our journal, our literary riddles, our texts. I remember my keeper and Delaney, the man who'd have a beautiful picnic here in this courtyard with me because I loved him. I remember planning out our future, starting with the ghost pepper challenge."

My muscles seize, a burning sensation forming rapidly behind my nose and eyes. I snatch her hand in mine, my fingers trembling, shaking at what she's telling me.

"Ethan," she sobs, "you must've been so lonely all these years." Alexis shakes her head, her face crumbling as I press my lips to her icy fingers, a multitude of thoughts throwing themselves around my mind.

I can't think. I can't process.

I'm afraid to hope.

"How could I've forgotten you? How could I?" She bites her lip as more tears wet her cheeks.

Her grief and guilt wreck me. I don't want her to feel this way. It isn't her fault.

"Shhhh," I whisper.

She throws herself into my arms, and I bury my face in her lavender-scented hair.

I'm finally home.

"It's not your fault, Lexy." My voice is raw. "You're a fighter—against all odds, you came back to me. You clawed your way back from death's door and gave us a second chance. And for that, I'm forever grateful. So damn grateful."

"P-Polaris." She shakes in my arms and I hold her tighter against me. I don't want to let go ever again. "That's the name for the north star. You've given me all these clues all along—teaching me finance, just like before, your emails, your poems, your photos, I-I've been blind to them!"

I shush her, not wanting her to beat herself up anymore. "Do you blame me, Lexy? Maybe if I'd taught you how to swim back then, if I insisted on coming to you that day, we wouldn't have lost all this time."

She shakes her head vehemently. "Stop it. If you aren't angry at me for losing my memories, why would I blame you for something you couldn't control?"

Alexis cradles my face, her voice urgent. "You listen to me, Ethan Anderson. You *did* save me. You taught me how to swim. Without you, we both would've drowned in the Hudson. I'm not mad at you. Not a single bit!"

A weight lifts from my chest. "You once asked me why I always stood to the side in the photos, and I never answered you. But I want to tell you now."

Drawing back, I wipe her tears from her cheeks. "Because you stood next to me as I completed each bucket list item. You were there in my heart, on my mind. Every item I did was me hoping to send good karma into the universe, because I knew you believed in it."

Her breath hitches and moisture gathers in her eyes again.

"Don't cry, Lexy. Everything I did was out of love. I was hoping you'd feel the love and hope I had for you. That I held on to the belief one day you'd come back to me. That I never forgot you."

My voice is raw. "Because you're unforgettable."

She hiccups and hooks her arms around my neck before slamming her lips on mine. Our kiss is desperate, fire and ice, a winter storm brewing for a decade. My nerves come alive, a warmth spreading from my heart to the rest of my body.

There's no room for fear, doubts, or anxieties.

There's only room for our love and the certainty that we're the readers of each other's books, that we're the happily ever after poets and writers pen in the novels housed in the beautiful building next to us.

I taste her tears and swallow her moans, and she does the same with me. Our lips and tongues tangle, my hands gripping her tightly, molding her to me.

She remembers. She remembers everything.

"I love you, Ethan. I-I fell in love with you twice—all those years ago, and again after I lost my memories. I love you so much." Alexis gasps when we break apart for air. Her lips are swollen and plump, and my heart skips a beat.

"Not as much as I love you." I press another kiss on those pouty lips.

I brush her hair away from her face, watching a new flush bloom on her cheeks.

There's still something I need to do.

Slowly, I drop to my knees and pull out the ring box from my jacket pocket. I had it with me because I knew I wanted to give it to her tonight, if she'd still have me—fears, scars, and all.

Her eyes widen and her hand flies to her mouth.

"Lexy, my Nova, my darling hummingbird and dreamer." My voice is rusty with emotions as I utter the words I was afraid I wouldn't get to say again. "I've loved you since you barreled into me on the doorsteps of this building, and I've fallen deeper and deeper in love with you with every letter you've written and every moment we've shared. Because of you, I realize I'm capable of love. Because of you, I'm the luckiest man on earth."

Raking in a shaky breath, I continue, "I've loved you for a decade and will love you for all the years to come. I can't imagine life without you. Will you take me as I am—scars and all? I can't promise you I'll never be afraid, that I won't be overprotective or overbearing, but I'll work on it, with you by my side, if you'll have me."

I open the lid of the box and reach for her hand. A lump forms in my throat. "My supernova, will you marry me?"

A ragged sob escapes her lips and she nods. Vehemently. "Yes! Yes, I'll marry you. I'll marry you a thousand times."

My heart bursts with light, elation rushing through my veins.

My hands tremble as I slip the ring onto her finger. She falls into my arms, pressing unending kisses on my lips.

"I've waited a long time to hear your answer, Lexy." I close my eyes, clutching her tightly. "A very, very long time."

"I love you. I love you. I love you, Ethan." She kisses me over and over again.

We finally pull apart and look at each other—our faces a mess of tears and clumps of snow sticking to our hair.

I lift my finger and graze it down the bridge of her nose, and I smile.

"Not as much as I love you, Lexy. *Never* as much as I love you."

Epilogue

Six Months Later: Ten Years After the Accident—Thirty Years Old

"And now, you may kiss the bride," the officiant exclaims, and steps to the side. The small crowd of our family and closest friends cheers and claps in the background.

True to our personalities, we wanted something small. No press. No pomp and circumstances. Just him and me and our loved ones in the hidden courtyard at Ravenswood, with the lush green leaves of the weeping beech tree swinging to the summer breeze.

I like to think the tree is weeping with joy today.

Ethan stares at me, a small grin tipping his lips, a lock of hair grazing his eyebrow. Butterflies flap their wings inside me and I fight the urge to rip off the small veil I have on and throw myself at him.

His startling eyes skate over my simple white sheath dress and linger on my lips—the ruby red, the only pop of color I have on today. He slowly lifts my veil and drapes it over my head.

"Hello, Mrs. Anderson," he murmurs, his raspy voice sending shivers down my spine.

"You better kiss me soon, Mr. Anderson, or I won't be responsible for my actions."

He throws his head back and barks out a loud laugh.

"Nova, you make me so happy," he murmurs and clasps his hand around my nape, his other arm sliding around my waist and yanking me to him in one smooth, powerful motion.

My secret alpha. The possessive streak inside him.

All my erogenous regions light up.

It's always the quiet ones.

Ethan crushes his lips over mine and pulls me under a sea of pleasure with his drugging kiss. He tastes like whiskey, smooth and masculine. I can't get enough.

Gripping his hair tightly, I kiss him back—sucking, licking, taking in his tongue as he invades my mouth.

The cheers and catcalls fade into the background and my body lights on fire, needing more.

It's not enough. It's never enough with him.

Abruptly, he pulls us apart, his face flushed, hair disheveled. His eyes glaze over with passion and our chests lift and fall from our panting breaths.

Ethan's throat ripples, a pulse thudding against his temple, and he rakes his finger down my nose, before dipping the tip into my mouth.

His eyes darken and pupils dilate when I suck it in, just the tip, and give it a quick lick, knowing we're in front of our family and friends.

A growl rumbles from his chest.

"My wife," he rasps, and I blow him a kiss.

"My husband." I add a wink as well.

We smile at each other.

"Go get a room, you guys!" someone yells and everyone laughs. I think that's Rex, but I don't really care.

Ethan pulls me against him, and we face the crowd. Maxwell, Belle, and their little boy are clapping in the front row. Ethan nods at his oldest brother. Linus, Ethan's dad, is next to his eldest son, and smiles proudly at us. Ryland grins, his arm curled around Millie. She wipes her teary eyes, her new engagement ring glinting under the sunlight. The professor has finally proposed to his student. Steven and Grace catcall from their spots in the second row. Elias slinks around in the background, smirking. Liam is busy recording with his phone.

We stroll down the aisle to a rainfall of flower petals.

"Can't believe you cut in line, bestie!" Taylor cups her mouth and yells, her brows wagging. Charles shakes his head in amusement and presses a kiss on her hair. "You completely skipped the long engagement step of the process."

"It's been over ten years, Tay! I should've been first in line!" I stick out my tongue and everyone laughs.

"Looks like it's just you and me, Lana," Rex mutters.

He winks at us as we pass by them, but the usual lightness and levity are missing in his eyes. In fact, there's a weariness to them, a tension he can't hide.

I think back to a conversation I had with Ethan a week ago. He's noticed the same worrying signs in Rex: the self-destructive partying, the circles under his eyes, which tell us he isn't sleeping, the way he hides behind fake smiles and larger-than-life jokes.

After we're back from our honeymoon, we're staging an intervention.

And I'll drag Olivia with me—she's a brilliant doctor and has helped Maxwell and the other Andersons. She'll know how to handle and treat Rex. I just know it.

Rex grumbles, "Loveless and single. Maybe the curse of the Andersons now falls on us."

"Speak for yourself." Lana shoves her brother. "I'm a winner—whether I have someone or not. And we also have Olivia." She points to our friend, who's sitting in the far corner and waving at me.

I wave back and she blows us a kiss.

Rex stares at Olivia, his jaw clenching. "Not all of us are meant to have love."

Olivia's eyes dart toward Lana and before she quickly looks away, her face flushing. *Interesting.* Is that just doctorly concern...or something more?

Ethan dips his head and whispers in my ear, "Let's ditch our reception."

"What?"

"I have something planned. A car is already waiting outside."

Gaping at him, I look at the crowd behind us. "B-But, the food, the venue, our family—"

"They'll be here when we come back. I've secured us a rare meeting and a private tour of the Drak Yerpa Monastery and the monks there. Then we can go to the Jokhang Temple to tie the cloth." His throat ripples. "Tibet. The first bucket list item we're completing together."

Ethan presses a kiss on the back of my hand. Electricity courses through me from the point of contact. "I got the confirmation last night—this was the only time they had for the private tour. Maxwell will handle everything here if you want to go, but we need to leave now."

He quickly adds, "I'm the luckiest man either way and happy whatever we decide to do. Because you're by my side."

Warmth flows through me and I smile. Dinner and dancing I can do at any time, but a once in a lifetime trip to Tibet? "Well, you know what I say, 'Don't wait to live...'"

"Because the clock keeps ticking," he finishes, and we grin at each other. "And just to let you know...you are married by thirty. You were never behind."

"How can I be behind when I'm with you?" Of course he remembers everything I've said in the past.

He cocks his head toward the exit. "So, are we ditching our own wedding reception?"

Excitement flows through me and I nod.

He chuckles. "I love you so damn much, Mrs. Anderson."

I shriek when he suddenly lifts me up and throws me over his shoulder.

My ice monster. My caveman. My Ethan.

Raucous laughter sounds behind us.

"You go, Ethan! Go get your woman!" Rex yells, followed by more cackling.

"We aren't objects. You don't get to 'get' us. No wonder you're single," Lana says, followed by a loud *whack* sound.

"Ow! Violence is never the answer," Rex complains.

"Violence is *always* the answer." Elias scoffs.

My skin heats as Ethan all but tosses me into the backseat of the limo. The driver closes the door and my husband advances on me, his hands quickly working off his bow tie, the earlier teasing glint in his eyes morphing into a ravenous intensity.

"Just because we're skipping the reception doesn't mean I can't have dessert first," he murmurs, shrugging off his jacket.

I gulp and clench my thighs together, arousal quickly firing inside me.

Ethan hits a button and the privacy screen rolls up.

"Strip, wife. Fuck, I can't believe I get to call you that and we're finally doing our bucket list together." He tosses his dress shirt on the floor, and his rippling muscles make my mouth water.

"Keep looking at me like that. I'm going to make you scream so hard, your voice will become hoarse. Take off that dress, Nova. Let me see those beautiful tits. I think it's time we make some new marks on you."

My nipples harden on command. I can't think when he looks like he's going to swallow me whole.

I pant, my fingers moving to the zipper on the back of my dress.

But then a random thought barrels into my mind.

"B-But Ethan, we only had seven things on the bucket list...this is the last item."

He pins me to the leather seat, his face hovering inches above mine. His lips curve into a devastating smile, dimples showing, and he murmurs, "We'll add more items to your list. Every day is an adventure as long as I'm with you. I love you."

Then he kisses me and shows me how much he loves me.

Thank you for reading WHEN HEARTS REMEMBER. Hope you've enjoyed Ethan and Alexis's story as much as I did writing it.

Bonus Epilogues: Want to go on the honeymoon with Ethan and Alexis? Will they finally hang the flag at Jokhang Temple? Will there be more spicy times? Sign up for my newsletter to get **THREE EXTRA BONUS CHAPTERS**. Just click on the "When Hearts Remember Bonus Epilogues" link on the website: https://www.victorialum.com/bonus

Read Rex's Story Next: Do you know Rex and Olivia's story is next? Fall for the final Anderson brother in this dark, forbidden, doctor patient romance where healing hurts and love could cost everything. Read WHEN HEARTS UNRAVEL here: https://geni.us/whenheartsunravel

Please Review: Please consider leaving a review on the retailer website and Goodreads https://www.goodreads.com/book/show/223504649-when-hearts-remember. Your reviews will really help this author out and will allow more readers to find this book.

THANK YOU

As I WRITE THIS note, I'm preparing to begin the final book in *The Orchid* series. (I know, I will miss the Andersons too. But don't worry, they will show up in my other books.)

This is the ninth book I've written in my two-year author journey, and along the way, there have been stories that were incredibly hard to write (looking at you, Charles and Taylor) and others that flowed the moment my fingers touched the keys.

Ethan and Alexis's romance is the latter.

Every time Ethan appeared in Charles and Taylor's story, my heart broke for him. I wanted to give him his happily ever after right then and there. I wanted to showcase the power of love—not the kind that's about grand gestures or beautiful declarations, but the kind built on quiet, unwavering action. Ethan is a man of a few words, but everything he does for Alexis, how he waits for her year after year, showcases true love. The sacrifice. The devotion. The choice to continue loving the other person day after day, even when the circumstances feel impossible. Their story might not be as dark as some of my others, but it's one of the most heartrending I've ever written.

And side note, if you were wondering why there are actual poems in their story, it's because of you, my readers. I've been told I have a poetic way of describing things, so I thought, why not try my hand at poetry? I loved the experience—capturing emotions in just a few lines. I hope you enjoyed the poems as much as I did writing them.

As always, thank you to everyone who has supported me, in no particular order:

My family: I love you to the moon and back, until the end of time.

My editors: Theresa Leigh and Amy Briggs, thank you for your guidance as always.

Proofreader: Thank you to Virginia Tesi Carey for your eagle eye and catching all those pesky errors.

My PA: Thank you to Nikki Johnson keeping me sane.

Cover designer: To the awesome LK Farlow of Y'All That Graphic, thank you for your wonderful covers.

Beta readers: Malia, Jenn, Jess, Denny, Erica, and Erin, thank you so much for insightful feedback. Ethan and Alexis's story is much more beautiful because of you.

My ilLUMinati girls, ARC Team, and Street Team: I love you all so, so much! Thank you for being the best cheerleaders an author can ask for.

Fellow authors: So many authors have helped me on this journey—it is impossible to name everyone, but I appreciate each and every one of you.

PR Firms: Thank you to The Author Agency for your promotional efforts and helping me get the word out!

My Fellow Readers: Without you, there would be no me. Thank you for being here, for all your messages, and for loving my stories.

Xoxo,

Victoria

Also by Victoria Lum

CATCH UP ON VICTORIA's backlist! Don't miss these swoony, romantic stories with all the sizzling spice and angst. All stories are standalones and can be read out of order.

LA Hearts:

The Sweetest Agony (James and Jess)

The Coldest Passion (Parker and Liz)

The Harshest Hope (Adrian and Emily)

The Brightest Spark (Jack and Sarah)

The Orchid:

When Hearts Ignite (Steven and Grace)

When Hearts Collide (Ryland and Millie)

When Hearts Surrender (Maxwell and Belle)

When Hearts Awaken (Charles and Taylor)

When Hearts Remember (Ethan and Alexis)

When Hearts Unravel (Rex and Olivia)

About the Author

Victoria Lum writes angsty, emotional romances that dive deep into the complexities of love and the human heart. She's the author of *The Orchid* and *LA Hearts* series, which follow characters through love's twists and turns, secrets, and second chances. A true romantic at heart, Victoria loves crafting stories that resonate with readers who crave a mix of passion, tension, and genuine connection. When she's not writing, you can find her curled up with a caramel latte and a good book or spending time with her family in sunny California.

Keep in touch!
Sign up for her newsletter below:
Newsletter
Follow Victoria on social media:
Victoria Lum's Luminaries Facebook Group
Facebook Page
Instagram
Tiktok
Bookbub
Amazon
Goodreads
Scan the QR code below for all the links!